WHO CAN SAVE US NOW?

**Brand–New Superheroes
and Their Amazing (Short) Stories**

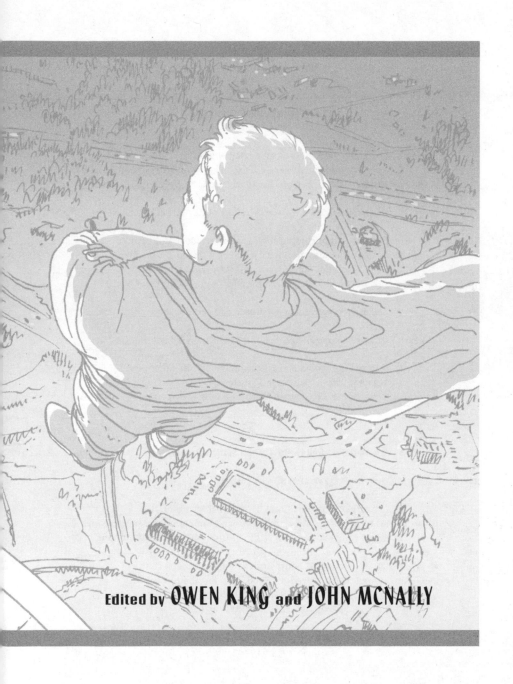

Edited by OWEN KING and JOHN MCNALLY

FREE PRESS

New York   Toronto   London   Sydney

FREE PRESS
A Division of Simon & Schuster, Inc.
1230 Avenue of the Americas
New York, NY 10020

This Free Press trade paperback edition July 2008

FREE PRESS and colophon are trademarks of Simon & Schuster, Inc.

For information about special discounts for bulk purchases, please contact Simon & Schuster Special Sales at 1-800-456-6798 or business@simonandschuster.com.

Designed by Kyoko Watanabe

Manufactured in the United States of America

10 9 8 7 6 5 4 3 2 1

Library of Congress Cataloging-in-Publication Data
Who can save us now? : brand-new superheros and their amazing (short) stories / edited by Owen King and John McNally; illustrations by Chris Burnham.
p. cm.
1. Heroes—Fiction. 2. Short stories, American—21st century.
I. King, Owen. II. McNally, John, 1965– III. Burnham, Chris, 1977–
PS659.2.W48 2008
813'.0108352—dc22   2008007896

ISBN-13: 978-1-4165-6644-1
ISBN-10: 1-4165-6644-9

*Dedicated to the selfless, high-flying hero-editors of all those
journals and magazines that help keep America safe for short fiction*

CONTENTS

CONTENTS

THE BEAST WITHIN

A SHADOWY FIGURE

CONTENTS

BEHIND THE MASK

CONTENTS

SUPER ORDINARY

INTRODUCTION

In 1938 a gawky, bespectacled man walked through a door, and when it opened again, a benevolent giant in red and blue tights emerged, gave a wink, and lifted right off the pages of ACTION COMICS #1 and into the sky. As the years have gone by, countless other champions have joined this remarkable gentleman in the firmament of the popular imagination, and created a mythology for the twenty-first century.

However, in the sixty years since Jerry Siegel and Joe Shuster created Superman, our collective story has grown a good deal more complex. The black-and-white conflict of World War II is a speck in the rearview mirror, and the road ahead is a smashed causeway north of Baghdad. Racial and sexual politics have been radically transformed. Technology has made our planet miraculously and terrifyingly small. It's more apparent than ever that the worst of the bad guys don't wear spandex and live in underground ice palaces in Antarctica, but can generally be found in three-piece suits at the head of gleaming boardroom conference tables.

The raccoon-eyed purse-snatchers of the Golden Age comic books are the least of our problems. We have suicide bombers, dwindling oil reserves, global warming, and an international community in complete disrepair. Not even the biggest and broadest bulletproof chest could stop all these out-of-control locomotives.

To put it bluntly, Superman just wasn't built for times like these. The antidote? You're holding it in your hands!

Within these pages, you'll find twenty-two brand-new stories about men and women whose amazing abilities reflect and address our strange and confusing new conditions. These superheroes are different from the Technicolor do-gooders you remember from the rack at the drugstore. These heroes are conflicted, frustrated, freaked out, and desperate; they're brave and afraid and not sure; they're a little nuts. In other words, you're going to recognize these people—they're a lot like us.

And the supervillains? We've got them, too. And maybe they're even more familiar, those carnival glass reflections of our murkiest compulsions.

Who Can Save Us Now? introduces a plethora of origin stories (How does a girl with bad luck come to shape the events around her? How did a band of Quick Stop drones become an unlikely team of super-heroes?); stories of heroes whose powers derive from nature's most peculiar creatures (A flock of flying orphans, anyone?); stories of the sinister draw that unbelievable power has on all-too-believable men and women (Why is it that this little town never had any trouble until that band of superheroes showed up? What becomes of a man whose soul has been lit on fire?); and stories in which the extraordinary is used to help the ordinary and protect the innocent (What awesome power is capable of manipulating televangelists into assisting those truly in need? What vast strength empowers the hero of this city's dis-regarded streets, the defender of its disregarded people?).

You'll meet the Big Guy, the Rememberer, the Meerkat, Mr. Big Deal, the Silverfish, Bad Karma Girl, Ghetto Man, and, yes, even Bob Brown. You'll see submarine monstrosities, fiery conclusions, reporters searching for answers, and neighborhood taverns destroyed. Whether your own origin story includes an obsession for comic books and a pen-chant for the darker worlds of graphic novelists like Frank Miller and Alan Moore, or a love for superhero-inspired literary fare like *The Fortress of Solitude* and *The Adventures of Kavalier and Clay*, we promise that within these pages you'll find stories that suspend your disbelief without insulting your intelligence.

How are we going to stay alive in this world of trouble?

Read on!

Can anyone save us now?

We repeat: Read on!

What use is all this fancy in the face of so much real darkness?

If we're honest, we have to concede that it's probably no use at all. The sky is falling. And yet if we're courageous enough to see things as they aren't—to believe that a flying man can catch a flaming satellite before it destroys the city—then maybe we can summon enough heart to see things as they could be. This is just a book, a few hours' diversion, but we believe in heroes, and we need them now, like never before.

. . . And look! There's one now—

THE MOST UNLIKELY
BEGINNINGS

You remember the day he first swooped into our lives, the sky bathed bright orange with zeta-rays. You remember that stray satellite crashing toward San Angelo, and what emergency shelter you were fighting the mob to get to.

I myself, oblivious to personal safety, was snooping around the power plant, looking for the scoop on flawed disaster fail-safes. That's when the Klaxon sounded. Blast doors slammed, wrenching me off my footing, leaving me to grasp and dangle from an inverted railing. On page 46 of *Flight of Justice,* his so-called memoir, he says he heard my screams from miles away.

Let me assure you, I did *not* scream, at least not till much later. I was too busy clutching steaming grillwork, a radioactive roar below me, my wrists about to give. I *never* scream when these things happen to me.

Instead I muttered my last ritual gutter curses at all villains, sports editors, and ex-boyfriends. It was then that he barreled through the blast doors like a heat-seeking missile.

You want to know. What he said to me that first time he saved me, when he whipped up from below and hugged me against his chest. You want to know what he uttered into my ear, my arms looped around the thick sinews of his neck, the scruff on his cheek scratchy against my own.

He said, "Great legs," his voice husky in a roar of wind.

Where did he take me, you ask? Where does one fly with a woman when there's a satellite hurling toward a city of millions of other potential casualties?

To the top of a radio dish. You know the one, right off the 59 Freeway? There I was, plucked from danger only to be plopped hundreds of feet off the ground, my boots standing on bird droppings and graffiti.

"You saved my life," I said.

He shrugged. "That's what a hero does. Saves the girl."

He was wearing spandex. Another gal's head would be reeling, but I had assessed the situation. I didn't bother asking him who the hell he was, since the ridiculous costume gave him away. Some kind of vigilante, a superhero wannabe. Except that this one, admittedly, could fly.

"Lots of gals out there to save," I said. "A city full, in fact."

"Not with legs like yours." He winked. Then he made to go.

"Wait," I said. "Why are you leaving me here?"

"So if you need me, I can hear you," he said. He cupped his hands and waggled his middle finger, miming a radio dish. "It magnifies the sound of a scream."

"Where are you going?" I asked.

"The big guy has someone else to save."

Don't believe him when he writes about this making me "jealous." After all, it was a time of disaster. Why should I begrudge the saving of some orphans? The Governor maybe? But when he told me who, it's true I was horrified.

"Mr. T-bone," he said. At first I thought this was the name of some other superhero, maybe a washed-up mentor of sorts. Until he said, "I've got some money riding on him—you know, in case the track survives."

"You're flying off to save a dog?" I asked. Why wasn't this would-be superhero doing something to save the entire city?

"So you can fly," I said. "How about incredible speed and strength?"

"Sure, the big guy's quick. Strong. And there's some other talents, too," he said. Wagged his eyebrows, I swear.

"Are we maybe aware that this city is in a state of crisis?" I said. "That thousands of people are about to become satellite stew?"

"The big guy knows that." He looked wounded, like I'd insulted his intelligence, but I could tell it wasn't the first thought to have crossed his mind.

"It *has* occurred to you to try and do something to save San Angelo, hasn't it?" I asked.

5

"As a matter of fact, the big guy was just thinking he would try and, you know, do something about that," he said.

I don't know what in my sharp-honed instincts made me put it this way, but somehow I knew to stand firm on the slope of the radio dish, fold my arms across my chest, and announce: "A *real* hero would be flying off right now, to stop that satellite and save the world."

"How exactly would he do that?" he asked me.

"Maybe he'd fly up to the satellite," I said.

"Yeah?"

"Divert its trajectory, so it misses the city?"

He nodded. Then suddenly he was gone, as were my panties, whisked away in a blur of red, white, and blue.

This, I'll admit, was the first hook in my would-be hard-boiled heart.

———

Later that night, as I tried to write about the man in tights who'd saved the city, I couldn't concentrate. Safe in the busy newsroom, it suddenly flooded over me with radioactive heat that his crushing embrace had saved my life. I opened up a new file on my computer that I named "Mystery Man" and started typing. I approached my new article from the human angle, what it felt like to have gravity's pull against my legs, my chest bound to his, breast to pectoral, by one thick, muscled arm in the small of my back. "Girl Reporter Saved by Caped Mystery Man" ran on the front page right below the news that the city had been spared when he fly-balled the satellite into the drink.

I took the long way home from work that night, pacing the streets in my black boots and trench coat. Steam bellowed up from underneath the sidewalk grillwork, as the rest of you slept dreamless, new-lease-on-life sleep. I scanned the sky but there was no one, nothing but the skewered cityscape, and the tension of expectation. The moon above me, the stars hidden by an orange night sky, offered me nothing in the search for my scoop.

In retrospect, this night was the last night of my innocence, when I still believed I sought nothing more than the truth, with the scrappy swagger of someone who's always picked herself up after a fall. I was a gritty girl reporter after all, ready to investigate what was underneath his electric blue tights.

It turned out there was a lot.

You want to know, don't you? You've read his memoir, gawked at the photos of him in his spandex suit, and you think you suspect the truth. Well, I'm here to set it straight, to clear the smog. All his talk about Justice and Honor is based on lies and fantasies, and we'll start with this simple fact.

There was more than a schoolgirl crush between us.

It was 4:30 A.M. when he came to my basement apartment, and don't think he knocked on my window. I was dreaming of falling, down a dark and empty elevator shaft, and in my sleep my hands slapped the mattress in reflex. It woke me. My eyes flicked open and there he was, illuminated by my screensaver. He was crouched across the room, watching. I leaned over to my bedside table, whipped out my derringer, and aimed.

He may have been looking through my negligée, but he couldn't see into my mind. This is what I was thinking. Finally, a *man*. Simple and sweet, minus the neuroses of your average stockbroker-by-day, beatnik-by-night, with commitment issues?

I decided to commence with the research. "Ditch the getup," I said.

He stood, and stripped. I could hear my computer humming. The screensaver changed scenes, from the black of one astronomical constellation to the black of another. The shadows shifted on his muscles. I put my derringer aside.

You want to know what I saw, in the early morning light, what was bulging out of him. But I'm not here to titillate. This isn't superhero porn masquerading as confession. This was an act charged with desperate groping, a search for someone to hold on to in a world of sudden disaster and random salvation.

Suffice it to say, the earth moved. Literally.

Afterward he drummed on my belly, and I finally asked him the question that I hadn't asked him before. "Who are you?"

"Just a big guy who knows how to fly," he said.

"And how exactly do you do that?" I asked.

"Like this . . ." He patted on my pubic bone softly like a drumroll and then snapped his fingers. "It's all in the hips."

"How exactly do you navigate?" I asked, fishing for more technical information. "Airplanes have instruments. Radios. Ground control."

"Ah," he said. "See, the big guy uses the stars."

"Where do you come from?" I asked. "We all have stories. Skeletons. People and committees who've screwed us over. What brings you to the bedroom of an investigative reporter, on a cold night like this?"

"You think it's cold in here? The big guy can take care of that," he said. He then attempted to employ what I later would pinpoint as one of his typical techniques, the use of heat vision for distraction and stimulation.

"You want something," I said.

"Heroes don't *want* things," he said, his voice rising a pitch.

"That's right. A hero," I said. "Right."

"What, you don't think the big guy's a hero?" he asked.

"Too simple. I don't buy it. We're all more than an idea. Heroes are myths."

"But you're going to write about the big guy like he's a hero, right?"

"Ah, the truth comes out," I said.

He sat up in my bed. "Remember your article on the Wrestling World Confederation," he said, suddenly gushing. "You nailed it. You got it all figured out, all that stuff about good versus evil and what people want in a hero. You know, color schemes? That's how the big guy decided on his suit, from your article. Red, white, and blue. You know. Patriotic."

My God, I contributed to that ridiculous costume of his? "I'm glad someone reads what I write," I said.

"Okay, the big guy admits it," he said. "He wants you to help him out."

"Help you with what?" I asked.

"Give him a good name to go by. A couple of one-liners to drop with the bad guys and press. Maybe some props."

"Props?" I asked.

"You could come up with a whole background," he said. "Maybe a tragedy or something, that people will really go for."

"My job is to write the truth."

"Oh yeah? What will the little girl write about this?" he asked. Drumroll. He held the covers up to remind me. Wagged his eyebrows, I swear.

I had to admit it. He had me. He cackled a cartoon-villain evil laugh and then flip-pinned me to the bed.

"You. Are going to help. The big guy," he said, his full weight pressing me down into rumpled, sweaty sheets.

"No one tells me what to do."

"You'll help, because he's got something you want. The old rackaracka-diggadig."

In case I'd forgotten what that might be, we screwed again. And then he rolled over and the biggest scoop of the decade fell sound asleep, my arm crooked under the tendons of his neck.

In the morning glare he wasn't as pretty. He slept with his mouth open, air fluctuating through his trachea. I could see his blackheads. He even had one of those bilevel haircuts, short on top, long in the back. He doesn't mention in his memoir leaving my toilet seat up.

But see, that's what got to me. He was real. This perfect image he presents of himself, his *Flight of Justice* "superhero" act that the rest of you believe, was never what I fell for. Each belch and fart, the scratching of his balls, slouched and slack in his sleep, made him real.

Not to mention standing at my refrigerator, drinking my carrot juice out of the carton. That's when he flashed me a smile and said, "The big guy needs to borrow your car."

"My car? Why?"

"Errands," he said, leaning on the open fridge door.

"Why would you need my car when you can fly?" I asked.

"It's Sunday. The big guy doesn't fly on Sundays." He put the carton back.

"Why?" I asked.

"It's part of the code."

"Right," I said. "Heroes need codes."

"But I'm willing to change codes when you help me come up with, you know, a better one."

"Real heroes close refrigerator doors," I said.

"The car?" he asked.

"What do I get in return?" I asked.

He gave me a look, like *Isn't it obvious?*

"I mean I have questions," I said. "I'd like answers. You're the biggest scoop in the city this morning."

"I'll get the car back to you by sundown." He finally shut the fridge and I heard its suck of relief.

So I let him drive off in my Tempo, still wearing the ridiculous cape and spandex.

My skills as an investigator are honed and varied, and like many in my profession, I'm not above using my intimacy with a source to get to the scoop. The boys at the lab peeled his print off my pelvic bone. Then we did a swab test. Neither his fingerprints nor his semen sample had a match. I came up as empty as that bottle of carrot juice he left in my fridge.

Lending him the car proved to be more telling. Here was the tally of evidence: My dials were moved to AM talk radio. There was the smell of drugstore perfume in my car and evidence of a chili dog in crumpled microwave paper. A couple of crunched beer cans. Used race-track stubs. One long strand of blond hair. And the old Tempo ran better than it had in years.

This is what he was really like. Can't you see how in a moment of weakness any self-respecting investigative reporter with an Honorable Mention for the Pulitzer Prize could feel compelled to forsake her ethics and give him a makeover?

The fact is, he needed guidance.

Rank injustices flourished while he made the world safe for movie stars. The racetracks became the safest places in town. As for crimes against blondes? Unheard of, on his watch. And think about the little pranks of his early days, how he left an opium boss on top of the media building, forty stories up, bound and naked with a beeping car alarm taped to his backside? His early good deeds were as tasteless as his clothes.

And then there was the fact that each time he did something headline-spinning, he came to my basement apartment.

Each time I reported it straight. Just the facts. "Caped Mystery Man Leaves Crime Boss Dangling, City Hanging." Skipping the part that came after of course. "Girl Reporter Gets Good Banging" would have been a beeping car alarm on my reputation, and I wanted to be more than just runner-up for the Pulitzer. I still thought my exposés made a *difference*.

It's true he got me out of a few "scrapes." Though a glamorous profession, mine is also a dangerous one. Once I ducked into an oil mogul's private jet in order to research his shady dealings with freeway expansion lobbyists, and was thrown out. Of the plane. While it was in midair.

But I reiterate, though I may have plummeted through the air, sputtering curses at old landlords and stepfathers on my way to what I thought would be a certain smashing death, I never "erupted into shrieks and screams for help." Contrary to what he claims, only once did I scream for him. The radio dish incident would come much later, though.

So yes, he would save me. And then he'd round up the "bad guys" who "did his little girl wrong." And yes, as my own search for the scoop started to affect the news, I became fond of the power that gave me to *change the world,* every reporter's secret dream.

It was with my influence that he started to tackle more noble endeavors. Remember how he wiped out the child prostitution rings around the military bases? How he was there to protect ethnic minorities from municipal crackdowns? The drought, alleviated with iceberg transports? (Whose idea, you might ask?) I even pointed out to him that brunettes and redheads deserved as much protection as blondes. Can't you see how easy it was to compromise myself? I no longer merely reported the news. I helped make it.

But don't think my attraction to him was some power trip. It wasn't just about influencing world events. And it wasn't just about doing it with a guy who can fly. Maybe, just a little bit, I was falling for him.

One night, I said to him, "I want to fuck in a sweaty boxing gym." There's nothing like the smell of iron and decades of stale male sweat to make a gal wet for a pounding. So he took me to Silverado's Gym after hours, in one of the warehouses down by the docks. We broke into the weight room. I stripped and lay myself out on the blue vinyl mat. I could see my reflection in the mirrored wall, amidst rows of barbells and weight machines. I was pliant and powerful.

"All right, stud. Ditch the suit."

He started to tug at his boots.

"First the cape," I said.

He stripped it off and flung it away. It wrapped itself around a weight bench.

"Now the shirt," I said. Grinning, he ducked his neck and yanked off his shirt and tossed it aside. Even in dim light the bulge in his tights was off the goddamn charts.

"Now the boots." He kicked them off, and one flew up into the warehouse rafters, the other landing with a thud, white patent leather on top of a metal water fountain.

"Now the tights."

And there he was.

Don't misunderstand. Don't think I'm some exhibitionist superhero sex groupie telling all, providing erotic anecdotes for pulp pleasures. All of this is just to say that when we were done and we were lying on sweaty vinyl, and he had said his customary, "You sent the big guy into the upper ionosphere," the discussion shifted back to what he really wanted from me.

"You hate the suit, don't you?" he asked.

"Didn't they have it in black?" I stared at the exposed metal pipes of the warehouse gym ceiling, my arm limp under his neck. "Something more . . . urban?"

"But black's so . . . evil. People associate black with bad guys," he said.

I casually mentioned the name of another well-known hero whose trademark cape is black.

"Shit. That outclasses the big guy, doesn't it." He fell silent.

I turned my head to look at him, his profile, thick-jawed and heavy-browed. He was thinking, eyelids fluttering. He was so thuggishly adorable when he was thinking. Suddenly the feeling of his crushing embrace flooded over me, as if he was somehow saving me, just by lying in my arms. I wondered if love was a sudden disaster, or a random salvation, if it was a stray satellite about to explode or a safety net, arms that clasp you before you fall. I couldn't help myself, I pulled closer to him and kissed him gently on the scruff of his cheek.

He looked at me and said, "That black cape business? That guy must have a whole PR team. No one could think up all those props on his own."

"Shhh," I said. My ethics were fleeing. When you have knowledge, taste, talent, insight, how can you withhold from someone you're starting to fall for?

"This costume's ridiculous, isn't it?" he asked.

"Maybe a little," I said.

"Is it the cape?" he asked. "Whenever we do the old foofoo-doofoo, you always make the big guy take the cape off first."

"Capes *are* corny," I said.

"See? This is why the big guy needs you," he said. "It's a stupid costume, isn't it?" His brow puckered as he looked at his carefully constructed identity, red, white, and blue strewn across barbells.

"Hypothetically speaking," I said. "If I had certain abilities, like I could fly, and I wanted people to think I was a hero . . ."

He looked at me, plaintively. "Yeah?"

I talked, softly, rolling his slouched balls in my hand. He closed his eyes, relaxing. "I'd change the world," I said.

"Like what?" he asked.

"I'd help the weak."

"Mmm. That's good," he said, his voice a murmur.

"I'd save the oppressed."

"Save the oppressed . . ."

"My mantra would be justice. It appeals to our desire for things to be fair, no matter how much experience tells us that's not how the food chain works."

"Justice." His eyes flipped open and he snapped his fingers. "Yeah. That's it. Everyone falls for that." (See chapters 2, 3, 5, 17, 19, and 20 of his memoir for references to the dogma he came to form on "Justice.")

"But there's more," I said. "I'd be noble."

"Like, what do you mean?"

"No practical jokes or tasteless humor."

"Oh no?"

"I'd be above mere human cravings. I'd especially stay away from blondes."

He turned his head to look at me. "You're kidding me. These other hero guys aren't wholesome. They always get the girl."

"Oh sure, I'd have a *certain someone* I'd reveal myself to."

"Okay," he said. He propped himself up on one elbow to look at me in the dim light.

"Also, a hero can't have weaknesses. No cheap beer."

"Right, no cheap beer."

"Gambling."

"Right, no gambling," he said. "Not even the dogs?"

"What kind of hero owes money to a bookie?"

"Oh."

Once I got going, I was on a roll. "I wouldn't belong to any specific religious denomination, but I would represent the morality of religion without ever mentioning a favorite god or prophet," I said. "I'd be classically handsome. But not threateningly so. Which means I would *not* have a bilevel haircut. This is the kind of hero people will believe in, the kind who can change the world."

"Wow. That's the kind of hero the big guy is."

"But," I said. "What if people want an explanation about why I can do the things I do?"

"How would you explain the things you do?" he asked.

"How *would* I explain the things you do?" I eyed him.

He smiled, innocent, a wide-eyed "How should I know?" look on his face. "Power of prayer?"

I said, "Maybe I'm a scientific experiment gone awry." I looked for a flicker, that I'd stumbled on the truth.

Suddenly, he gassed the gym, rubbery flatulence adding to the general manly smell of the room. "The big guy apologizes for that."

I chose to ignore this obvious stalling technique, no matter how cute it was. "Genetic tinkering, maybe? Biomechanics? Maybe it's all in the suit," I said. "Magnets. Microchips. Or, maybe you're an alien," I said.

He looked at me with wide-eyed respect. "Wow. Yeah, maybe."

"Raised among us, perhaps?"

He cocked his head. "Okay, I'm liking it," he said.

Suddenly I was pissed. I wasn't his spin doctor. "I'm getting nowhere," I said. "There's nothing in this for me."

"What do you mean?" he asked.

"You come here and give me nothing, reveal nothing about yourself, and then expect me to put my career on the line."

"You're acting like you don't need the big guy, and you do," he said. "Maybe the big guy's an alien, raised among you, and he doesn't want to reveal the truth, okay? Because he doesn't know if the little girl could take it."

"Do you know what two people who are intimate together do? They reveal themselves. They share their pains and disappointments and personal histories. But it looks like a good fucking is all I'm going to get," I said.

He stood, chiseled flesh in dim light. "You know, it's Thursday night. The big guy has people to save on Thursday nights. He thinks he hears a blonde screaming right now, as a matter of fact." He walked to where his cape was wound around a weight bench, pulled it off, and wrapped it around himself, with wounded dignity.

"Don't you dare leave me down here at the docks in the middle of the night," I said, standing up, naked in a warehouse gym.

"Don't fall down the stairs," he said. "Since the big guy gives you 'nothing,' he won't be around to catch you."

"*I do not fall down stairs,*" I said, but I was calling out to an empty room.

And there went your Mister Noble, your defender of Justice and women, a gust of cold whipping by my naked flesh. I stood there alone, looking for a fire escape with nothing but my trench coat and black boots to walk home in.

So here's the truth, about him as well as myself: I'm not proud to say it, but I am partially responsible for the biggest media-image scam in American history. I helped to create the lie. It wasn't long after that he started to give press statements, cheesy lines about Justice you're all so familiar with, and make references to his alien birth. It was the beginning of his mythic status.

I should add here that I had nothing to do with the name you all now know him by. He came up with that one himself, as you can tell by the sheer arrogance and cheesiness of the moniker.

Weeks later, in the parking garage at work, he came to me. He was wearing his new and improved costume, hiding behind a huge concrete piling when I came out of the elevator. He followed me to my car. There was something silly about him walking through a parking garage in that getup. I ignored him, though the other commuters in the parking garage couldn't help but stare.

He followed me, ducking his head under the low cement ceiling. I opened my car door and he was a step behind, sliding into the passenger seat. There, parked in my Tempo, as drivers in cars sharked by, straining to watch, he announced, "We are now willing to give you that interview."

"What, all that stuff about being an alien?"

"It's true, we came from another planet. It's true we were raised among you, only to grow up and fight Justice, wait, fight *for* Justice."

"Who do you think you're fooling?" I asked. "You think I don't recognize this stuff? I'm not after fictions I made up myself. I'm after the truth. And if you can't offer me that, then at least I deserve a good banging."

"We can't do that," he said.

"On a battleship," I said. "In the tropics. I want to screw under the stars with hundreds of sailors sleeping down below."

"We don't do that kind of thing. Okay?" he said, as if offended to his core. He pointed at me. "That's not what we're about. We're about Justice."

Suddenly I realized the enormity of what I'd done. I snapped on the interior light in my car and stared at him.

"Where's the big guy?" I asked.

"We're here, we're here. But, you know. No dog races. No girls."

I stared at him, suddenly realizing the bilevel haircut was gone, as was his easy charm. He sat awkwardly in the car, not knowing what to do with his eyes, which normally should be looking through my clothes, or his hands, which normally should be creeping under my trench coat, into my lingerie. He crossed his arms, fists tucked into his armpits. Then he gave me a quick sideways glance, the light dim in his eyes.

"We decided to give you the interview first, if you want it."

Suddenly, I had one of those flashes of insight, where everything seems interconnected, like when you're staring at the stars over the city, and you suddenly realize you can see the outline of a bear, or a huntress. I'd helped him create a sham of an identity, and I knew what torment follows, the fist-shaking need to prove you *are* the person you've created.

I wanted to run my hand along his smooth-shaven cheek, but didn't. "You can't live this lie." It was only after I spoke that I realized it came out as a whisper.

"Fine. There's others who want to interview us." And then he was gone. Suddenly I was alone in the car, the engine beeping at me, the passenger door hanging ajar.

My one consolation is that I refused to interview him. People with far less talent and credentials than I had the dubious honor of cashing in on the scoop. The Pulitzer that year would go to someone else.

In a way it was over. He no longer came to my bed, and he no longer consulted me on which fascist coups he needed to interfere with, on which smuggling blockade to dismantle. He had "Justice" to guide him.

But by far the worst indignity was that he continued to save me.

Case in point: the incident at the border where I posed as a patrol officer, trying to infiltrate a casino-girl smuggling ring, and was tossed off a cliff. I remember standing on the edge of an ancient rockface, still wearing a beige border patrol uniform, my ankles and wrists bound with duct tape, my captors smoking cigarettes behind me, my derringer tucked uselessly inside my pants. The nighttime sky was smoky with the Milky Way. I struggled against the duct tape, trying not to reel from the immensity of the drop before me, of the sky above me, dripping with falling stars.

My captors pushed me off.

As I fell down that sheer cliff, I'll tell you who I cursed. *Him.* For being able to change the world, for being able to fly, and for still eluding me.

You think I wanted him to save me? You think I wanted to feel the breath-pounding security of his thick embrace? When you're defying the forces of the universe, shaking your fist, daring the ground to meet you head-on, you think you want someone to hold your hand? Proving, with a clutching forearm in your back, that you're powerless? Well, here was my reminder, saving my life, yet again.

He flew me to my basement apartment. When he set me down it triggered the motion detector lights. "Here we go," he said.

There in the glare I realized he was getting the act down better. He was more sure of himself, and now with his forearms folded across his chest he no longer looked like someone trying to keep his hands from wandering. He looked strong, confident about his identity.

I bent down, tugging at my bound ankles. "I didn't ask you to save me," I said.

"If we didn't save you, you'd be dead," he said.

"You think I don't know that?" I stood up, losing my balance, stumbling on knotted duct tape.

He looked at me, shrugged, took a step backward, then flew away into the dark, leaving me alone, standing in a yellow circle of motion detector light. Still trailing duct tape on the bottom of my boot, I stepped down into the empty street, so that I could watch him go, until he merged with the black night sky, and all I could see was the stars. I knew these constellations well, from my screensaver, and as he disappeared I suddenly saw them for what they really are. Nothing more than a random conglomeration of chemical gases spaced throughout a black vacuum. We're the ones who connect the dots and decide, this grouping is a bear, that one is a huntress, those three together are a damsel in distress.

That night, while lying alone in bed, listening to the sound of my screensaver clicking from one astronomical chart to another, I saw the truth like a vision. Despite that one near miss at the Pulitzer, my own powers are merely mundane, a gut-churning stew of talent, conviction, insight, and ego that couldn't change a made-up mind, let alone the world. Alone in bed I lamented, what I could have done with his strength! I knew exactly which crimes I'd solve, which social movements I'd back, which death squads I'd dismantle, which dictators I'd have a little ionospheric chat with, which bedrooms I'd haunt. I wrenched the sheets in my fists, hot angry tears in my eyes, as I declared to the dark that if I was the one who could fly I would never *ever* wear blue spandex.

Then *Flight of Justice* hit the bookstores. Oh, I'm no different than the rest of you. I, too, have his memoir sitting on my bedside table, next to my derringer and vibrator. And I admit, the day I read his book is the day I went back to the radio tower on the 59 Freeway and screamed for him.

Gripping steel bars, I climbed, one foot over the other, thin wrists reaching for steel, weighed down only by his book in my shoulder bag, and all of the lies he'd told. Below me was concrete city sprawl. When I reached the top I flung a leg onto the welcome steel surface of the dish and hurled myself into it. I wore my black boots. My trench coat. Lip liner, I'll admit.

There I stood, a tiny feeble figure in a glaringly white two-story rounded structure, with its huge metal transmitter pointed at the sky. My heart pounding, breathing in beige air, I screamed, yes, screamed, on waves of sound, for him to come—screams of the ground swirling and buckling under me, screams from my nightmares, of falling, screams of helplessness.

And then he came, that familiar blue blur, suddenly standing across from me.

"What are you doing up here?" he asked, arms crossed at his broad chest, his eyes belying nothing.

"Why did you write these lies?" I asked. I pulled out his book, knocked on its cover.

"We wrote the Truth."

"I never said I was in love with you. I never screamed for you to save me."

"Maybe we can hear things on a different frequency, that other people can't hear. Like dolphins can. And bats."

"I've got a byline, bucko, a reputation as a hard hitter. You make it look like I had a schoolgirl crush on you."

"Wouldn't it compromise a journalist's *integrity* to have more than a crush on a hero?"

"You didn't tell the truth about us." I tried to calm myself. "Think back," I said, trying to sound rational. "Remember our sweaty nights? Remember your raw, shattering need and the slouched aftermath?"

He stood across from me, arms folded at his chest. "We don't do that kind of thing. We don't even sweat."

"Remember how it was?" I said. "You were my satellite ride, my explosion at dawn. You were elusive and mysterious, and riddled with ambition."

The sun came out from behind a cloud, and in the afternoon light his face was sharp angles and shadows, and the bright spandex of his suit seemed to shimmer, like it was made of brushed metal instead of polyester. "All this? It isn't about ambition," he said. "It's about Justice."

"Don't you want to reveal yourself to me? Share with me your deepest secret? Right now, right here is your chance. Don't you want to tell me the truth?" I admit, my voice had risen to an agitated pitch. My gut was flooded with the memory of his deep pores, his fingers drumming me, and suddenly my head was spinning. I teetered, there on the edge of the radio dish, grasping onto his arms, a desperate groping, a search for someone to hold on to in a world of sudden disaster and random salvation.

"Maybe someone's got her own lies she needs to look at," he said. Slowly, raising his eyebrows.

Far below us freeway traffic hummed by and suddenly I knew my ending as well as any TV evangelist. One day, I will fall from the sky and no one will catch me. I will fall and curse every event in my life that I could not control, every eviction and betrayal, every secret kept and prize awarded to someone else. Legs kicking, arms swinging, I will fall to my death, knowing that my yearning to fly is doomed. When all is over, my claim to want the Truth is exposed for what it really is, a kind of denial that what I really want is to defy gravity, fate, the universe, and my own unremarkable, helpless place in it.

I steadied myself and looked down at the freeway and power lines and knew better than to let myself fall. I looked at him. "I admit it, okay? I remember when the big guy pried open the blast doors to the nuclear core of my heart. Does the big guy remember that?"

His eyes cast about, darting over the cityscape horizon, looking for something to fixate on. Finally he shrugged and said, "That's the thing about Truth and Justice."

I stood across from him in the radar dish, folded my arms at my own chest, and said to him, "You can put me down now."

He picked me up, gently, and flew me down to my Tempo. He kissed me on the cheek, smoothed my hair, then flew away. I watched him go. And then I stood amidst freeway fumes, cars whipping past me, and stared down at the asphalt and gravel. My legs felt strong, my ankles sturdy, anchored on the ground. I knew, right then, where I belonged.

He showed me the truth about myself, as he flew off to fight for Justice and change the world. In return, I'm telling you the truth about him, revealing what I know.

He is less and more than a myth.

As for me, you'll want to know my diagnosis. Superhero envy, textbook case. Every gal knows, never fall for someone who can leave the earth, who can fly, who isn't bound to the laws of physics you're bound to. All of my investigative abilities have led to this little revelation. I didn't just fall for him, I wanted to *be* him, and under those moon blue nights he was the one who could fly, streak away, leaving me on cold cement.

Sure, I still stare up at the nighttime sky above San Angelo, but I no longer look for him. Sometimes when I see a conglomeration of stars that seem to have no shape of their own, I borrow a couple, imagine them as my own constellation, one I call "Girl Reporter." If you connect the dots you'll see the outline of an unflinching heroine, the kind of gal who can accept the truth, the fact that she can fall. It stretches across the sky and can be used to navigate the city streets, by those whose black boots are stuck to planet Earth.

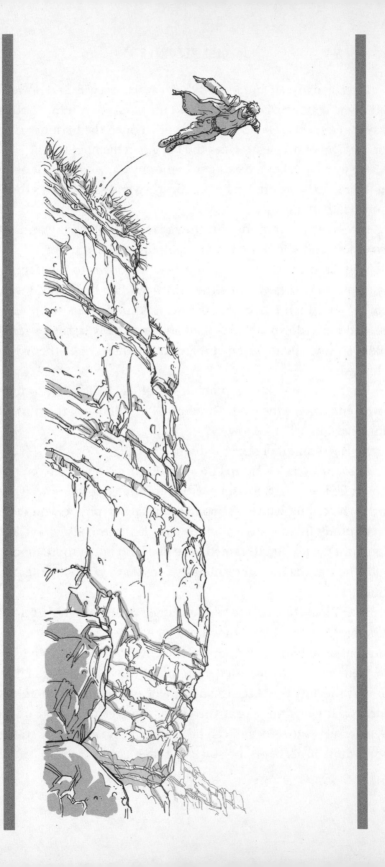

Graham Joyce

THE OVERSOUL

It was the burning summer of 1976 and the water in the quarry pool was lower than ever I could remember on the day something came out of it and climbed inside me. When I think about it (which is frequently, since you don't easily forget a thing like that) I reckon it might have had something to do with the presence of blue-green algae in the water. Of course that could have been a coincidence. Though anything could be a coincidence really. When you think about it.

I'd read something in the local newspaper about the presence of blue-green algae in the slate quarry pool. Stuff about it poisoning your dog. Well, I didn't have a dog and didn't want one. There's got to be more to life than throwing a stick for some dog.

The pool was a hole in the ground left behind after a century of quarrying industrial slate. The quarry hadn't been worked for seventy years and had filled up with rainwater. It was just somewhere I went when I wanted to get away from the war on the home front. Somewhere to sit in peace.

"Why hasn't he got a job yet?" My Dad, a retired confectionary salesman, sat on his sweet arse all day and referred to me in the third person, even when we were in the same room. "Why does he wear these black clothes all the time? Is he going to be an undertaker?" This was one of his funnies, though his favorite was: "Why has he got that expression on his face?"

Mum might defend me a little. "What expression?"

"There, he's doing it now. Looks like a bulldog chewing a wasp."

When he started like this I'd just sigh and get my coat. "Goin' out."

"Where's he going?"

"Ask him yourself."

But he wouldn't ask. He hadn't asked me a direct question in two years.

When I went out it was usually up to the slate quarry to stare into the water. Sometimes Shadrack would come along, and Shadrack had the tootle. Shadrack had tousled red hair and freckles and was too tall by about six inches. He worked as a grill chef at the Motorway Service Station, and he had a contact who came by every Tuesday afternoon. Together we would sit on the mounds of cracked, brittle blue-gray slate smoking the tootle and gazing into the pool. Some days the sky would be exactly the same color as the blue-gray slate we sat on. And on some days, both the sky *and* the water would be the same as the blue-gray slate. Earth, water, sky. The blue-gray of heaven.

"Fuck this," said Shadrack one day.

"What?"

"This is pants."

"What?"

"I mean this, man. This." Shadrack waved a hand through the air to indicate everything there was to behold, weigh, contemplate, and forget at that very moment. "Sitting here like this. All we ever do is sit here and stare at the water."

"What are you saying? Like, you've got a girlfriend or something?" I knew Shadrack hadn't got a girlfriend. He looked like a lanky version of that kid who used to be on the cover of *MAD* magazine. Whatsisname.

"I'm going to London," said Shadrack.

"Who is?"

"Me. Going to join a rock band, man."

"Who, *you*?"

"Yeh me. Don't look so fucking surprised."

"Well. It's just that your guitar playing is—and how can I put this delicately to a friend—not so hot."

"I'll improve."

We both stared at the water for a while. "Also," Shadrack continued, "I've been reading Nitch, man."

"Fuck's that?"

"However you say it. Anyway, Nitch says you are what you do. Right. So all we do is come and stare into this fucking puddle. And Nitch says you should struggle to find your superman inside yourself."

"Superman?"

"Yeh, superman, man. So I've had it. I'm off to London. I quit my job at the service station."

"You did?"

"Yup. Told 'em where to shove it."

"This Nitch guy. He tell you how to get a gig in London? How to pay the bills?"

"You lecturing me, Frank? You sponge off your cranky folks and you're lecturing me about paying my way?" Shadrack scrambled to his feet and looked out across the pond to the line of spruce and fir trees and spreading oaks on the other side of the water. "Anyway, I came to say good-bye."

"What, you're leaving today?"

"Yep. Getting a bus to the smoke in two hours."

"Bit sudden, isn't it?"

"Come and wave me off if you like, man."

To be truthful, I was hurt. We'd known each for years, through school. Got roughed up by the same playground bullies. Failed with the same girls. Screwed up our exams together. We'd been sitting here smoking tootle for almost two years now. I didn't respond to his invitation to wave him good-bye.

"Please yourself. Anyway, brought you a going-away present." He handed me a little transparent plastic sachet.

I took the sachet and inspected its contents.

"I'm finished with that stuff. Forever." Shadrack held out a large bony hand for me. "Well, see ya."

I just looked back into the water. "See ya."

"No handshake, Frank? No hug?"

"You been watching too many movies."

"Have it your way. I'll drop you a postcard."

———

Shadrack left and I kept my eyes on the water. I hadn't realized how much I needed Shadrack. I was eighteen and washed up before I'd even started out, and the only person I had to talk to in the world had just buggered off to London. I sat on the broken shards of slate gazing down into the water for a couple of hours and that's when something came out of the pool and climbed right into me.

I don't know what it was but I saw it take shape out of the brown algae-flecked mud at the edge of the pool. Saw it move in a rolling motion right up to me. Felt it gently but firmly thrust its way inside me, through my chest. It made me push out a little puff of air, a tiny cough.

That's it. It was in me. Easy as that.

Whatever it was, it didn't hurt to have it inside me. It was slightly uncomfortable at first but then it slipped into the background until I only remembered it at odd moments. Like having braces on your teeth, you could feel its shape slowly molding to you. It was as if it had just taken up residence and gone to sleep and it never seemed to actually do anything.

If Shadrack had been around I would certainly have told him. But now he was in London going *yeh yeh yeh man* so I couldn't. I didn't have anyone to tell. I went home and said nothing.

Dad looked up from the TV set. There was nothing on the TV. I mean the power was off, but he sat in his customary position with one leg stretched in front of him, toe pointing at the screen, watching the TV even when it was switched off. "What's the matter with him now?" Dad said to Mum. "He looks like he's found a pound and lost a fiver."

"Have you, Frank? Have you found a pound and lost a fiver?" she asked me.

"No."

"No he hasn't," she said.

Dad tugged at an earlobe and went back to scrutinizing the empty screen.

When I went to bed that night a funny thing happened. It was just as I was dropping off to sleep. I mean I think I was gone, drifting, and then a voice said something right in my ear. It said, *Do it.* Just that. I leaped up in bed. I flicked the light on to see if there was anyone in the room.

There was no one. But I had dreams that night. Flying dreams. I was flying through the air, yes, and I was wearing a cape like . . . Yeh, a cape.

————

After a few days a postcard arrived from Shadrack. He made out he was having a great time. Said he'd found a place to live in a squat with some other musicians. Said he'd met a girl called Muffin. Right. Told me I should join him. He also said he'd been reading more Nietzsche. I hadn't got a clue what he was talking about. Nietzsche: sounds like a dust sneeze. When we sat by the quarry pool he used to bang on about this guy called Nitch and maybe that was the same person. I never used to listen to him anyway and here he was on my postcard saying he preferred the word *oversoul* to the word *superman* and he was finding his oversoul. What a way to sign off a postcard.

I prefer the word *twat* to the word *pillock*.

"What's that he's reading now?" Dad.

"Looks like a postcard." Mum.

"Who's going to send *him* a postcard?"

"Perhaps it's from a friend. Is it from Shaddy, Frank?"

"I'm going out."

I went back up to the quarry pool and took my bag of tootle. I was annoyed to find a mother and her two kids picnicking near my usual spot, so I scrambled up the steep incline and squeezed through the fence to go to the other side of the quarry pool. It's a prohibited area because the quarry has a thirty-foot sheer drop into the water, but Shaddy and I always used to go there to get a bit of peace if there were other people around. It's always overgrown with ferns so you could spy on the people who came by on the other side and they wouldn't know you were there.

I found a shady spot and rolled myself a smoke. I was seriously thinking about Shadrack's offer to go and join him in London. Live in a squat. I'm tone deaf but maybe I could bang a tambourine. Trouble is I'd lived in a squat before and I only lasted three days. There was no heating, no plumbing, and never any food. Hell with that.

I could spy on the mum and her two kids at the water's edge on the other side of the pool. They were probably about fifty yards away from me, but way, way below. One of the kids, a little girl, was only just able to walk. The other kid was a boy of about four. He was playing with a stick near the edge of the water. It wasn't dangerous because the water was so shallow; at least it was where the kid was playing. The center of the pool was shockingly deep, though, and cold, too. One time a couple of scuba divers went down and planted a few ceramic garden gnomes on the bedrock. Then one of them came up too fast, got the bends, and almost died. I mean it's that deep.

It wasn't the depth that concerned me. It was the blue-green algae. I wondered if the mum had heard about it. No one had heard about it much back then. All the nutrients from the runaway were making it spore like crazy. Anyway, it seemed to me that if it was bad juju for your dog it was bad juju for your sprog, too. After a moment the mother called the kid back from the water, so I could stop whittling about it.

I watched them for a while. The mother sat with her back against a tree and her pretty knees tucked under her chin. I could see up her skirt a little way. Not that I was trying to look. I mean I didn't have my eyes glued to her legs to see the action, but I could see the cotton of her knickers. Maybe if I wasn't so far away I might have been able to see wispy pubic hair poking under the elastic of her knickers, but I wasn't looking that hard. Actually her face was more interesting.

She had brown hair with blond streaks. I like that. But she looked a little strained. Tired. Maybe it's tiring looking after little kids all day. I wondered where the kids' father was. If I had a beautiful wife and two lovely kids like that, I wouldn't let them go to the quarry pool on their own. I'd want to protect them all the time. Play with your kids, man, give her a break. I certainly wouldn't want her to come out and have people spying on her and looking up her skirt.

I watched her. Not much happened. She put her hand on her belly and held it there for a while. Then she crossed her arms and kind of slapped them together two or three times, quite hard. I felt she wasn't a happy person. From time to time the kids would approach her with a leaf or a snail or something they'd found at the water's edge.

Eventually I got bored. I wanted to go, but I'd have to walk past them. I squeezed back through the fence and made my way down the incline. When I drew near to the mum and her kids I avoided all eye contact. She was still sitting under the tree. I planned to just walk straight past them but I must have glanced over, because she smiled at me. Well, kind of smiled. It was more like she just made her mouth go wide for a second.

I didn't want to smile back but I didn't want to ignore her either, so I said, "There's blue-green algae in the pond."

"What?" She used the flat of her hand to shield her eyes to look at me, like you would if you were looking into strong sunlight. But the sun was behind her. "What's that?"

"In the pool. Blue-green algae. It's, like, dangerous. For the kids."

"Blue-green algae? Is that a problem?"

I felt pretty stupid. Maybe the thing I'd read in the paper was a load of old bollocks. "I think it can be." I was just making it up now.

"Really?" She looked alarmed, glancing about at her kids. "Are you sure?"

"Well, it depends," I said.

"Kids, come away from the water, will you?"

"I think it depends on the weather."

She gathered her children to her. "I hadn't realized."

"No." I was gazing stupidly at her. Blinking. The truth was I was mesmerized by how pretty and how tired she looked at the same time. Her eyes were blue-gray, exactly the color of the slate underfoot.

"Nice coat," she said. "But aren't you a little hot in it?"

"No. It's a trench coat."

"I can see that. It's like having a long cape."

Every time she said something I felt more and more stupid. I felt confused. Her voice seemed to have the power to make my mind swim and this in turn made me answer with something idiotic. "I got it at the Army and Navy Stores."

"Really?"

"Yes, on Silver Street."

She shook her head quizzically.

"You know Silver Street? Just off Mount Street?"

She shook her head again.

"You know the little street behind the cathedral?"

"Yes, I think so."

"Well, you go up there, to the top of the street, and it's on the left. There's a little alley that leads in to a group of shops. It's directly opposite a café. Army and Navy Stores."

"Right."

It was obvious she hadn't got a clue what I was talking about. Her kids were looking at me oddly. "Anyway, I have to go."

"Okay. Bye."

"Bye."

I walked away pretty quickly, crunching broken slate under my boots. As soon as I got out of sight I walked up to a birch tree and smacked my forehead hard against its trunk. Why the fuck was I telling her where to get a trench coat from the Army and Navy Stores on Silver Street? Why? I am such a dildo! I smacked my head again on the silvery trunk. Dildo! Again: Mong! Again: Dork! Again: Pillock!

I hate myself.

Truly.

I dreamed about her. The thing that had come out of the pond and had climbed inside me was annoying me in the dream by sitting next to her at a polished, candlelit dinner table, holding her hand, making her laugh. When I complained, the thing looked at me pointedly and got back inside me.

––––––––

She was there the next day. I'd been up on the ledge over an hour before she arrived, all the time hoping that she would come. Got myself into position so I could watch her when she did. I had some plastic binoculars that were almost useless, but at least they had a bit of magnification. I could look at her face. She had smile lines around the corners of her eyes. Her hair was kind of tangled. She didn't seem to mind her kids playing by the water, even with what I'd told her about the blue-green algae.

She sat against the tree again. For a moment she closed her eyes and I thought she might go to sleep. It made me anxious about her kids. I don't know why, but I felt protective toward them. But when one tripped and howled she was instantly up and attentive. Maybe she was doing that thing of sleeping with one eye open. I'm sure she was a good mother.

When she sat down again she smoothed her short skirt with the flat of her hand. With the aid of the binoculars I could see she didn't have a wedding ring. I was watching her hand when I saw it slip under her skirt for a moment, as she adjusted the elastic on her knickers before wriggling her bottom on the broken slate to get a better seat.

Speaking as a guy, that sort of thing can drive you mad.

I didn't just look at her legs all afternoon. I kept an eye on the kids, too, making sure they didn't get too close to any algae. They were sailing little stick boats at the edge of the water and I could see clumps of the stuff about fifteen yards in. I thought if it drifted in somehow I would nip down and prevent them from getting it on their hands.

After a while she got to her feet and gathered up her tartan picnic blanket and some of the kids' playthings. I dashed for the fence, squeezed through, and hurried down the embankment in time to skirt the pool before she left. I was a little out of breath.

"Hello again," she said. "What brings you here every day?"

I felt my cheeks flaming. "I read up about it. In the library. Blue-green kryptonite spores in warm weather. It's not like it would be fatal. But it might cause skin rashes or diarrhea or things like that if they got it on their hands and then put their fingers in their mouths."

"What's kryptonite?"

"Eh?" My knees turned to fluid. I mean I felt my body sagging.

"You said blue-green kryptonite."

"No, I said blue-green *algae*. I looked it up at the library."

"Well, you said kryptonite."

"I'm sure I said *algae*."

"Well, okay." She made her mouth go wide. Again not long enough to be called a smile. She put an arm round her youngest kid.

"I better be going," I said. "Things to do."

"Okay. Bye."

I dragged myself off to the woods. My muscles behaved like slush. It was ridiculous. I had to lean against a tree to get my strength back. Every time I went near her I felt weak.

————

When I got home there was a package awaiting me. It was from Shadrack in London. Things hadn't worked out with Muffin but he'd found another girl called Storm. He'd moved out of the squat and in with Storm. He said all that hippie-shit music we used to listen to was out and there was a new scene. He'd formed a band with Storm and a junkie drummer and they were getting pub gigs. He said he was a punk. I wondered what had happened to the oversoul if he was a punk. *Come and join us,* his letter said, *all you need is three chords and you're a rock star; anyone can do it.*

Also in the package was a little leather pouch that he said was for keeping the tootle. It clipped neatly to my belt. It gave me the idea of hanging the plastic binoculars on my belt, so that neither of the things could be seen under my coat. A hidden utility belt.

Dad: "Who's sending him packages?"

Mum: "Must be Shaddy in London. Is it Shaddy, Frank? Is it from Shaddy?"

I nodded.

Dad: "What's in the package?"

Mum: "Ask him yourself."

Dad: "I'm not asking the little bugger."

Me: "I was adopted, wasn't I? Go on, admit it. I was adopted. Just say it." I meant it. I knew that either I was from outer space or they were.

They ignored me and went back to watching the blank TV. Suddenly I felt bad about that adoption crack. The sunshine through the window struck the blank TV screen in a certain way and I noticed for the first time how dusty the blank screen was. I felt compelled to do something for them, so I went to the kitchen and found a soft cloth and a can of spray polish. I went back into the lounge and proceeded to clean all the dust from the TV screen. They sat watching me as I gave it a good polish. "That's better," I said.

———

Later, I wrote a letter to Shadrack. More of a note. *Sounds great,* I said. *Would come and join you but I've met someone here.*

That night I had another dream. I was in a swimming pool—no, it was more like the edge of the ocean on one side and a swimming pool on the other side—with the lady I'd been watching for the last few days. We were holding hands and laughing. Then the thing that had come out of the lake climbed out of me and sat on my shoulders with its legs round my neck. But she couldn't see it. Then the thing reached round and manipulated my jaw and made me say, *Can I have a lock of your pubic hair?* She looked pretty shocked. I was angry with the thing that had made me say this and it crept back inside me without a word.

———

She wasn't at the pool the next day. Nor was she there for the next three days. The only person I saw was a creepy old guy in a long coat. Okay, having a long coat didn't make him creepy. Heck, I've got a long coat. I'm just saying he seemed out of place, that's all.

Anyway, on the following Monday she turned up again. She wore a blue cotton summer dress that showed off her legs. Her children had brought little sailboats to float at the edge of the water. I supposed it was okay. I could see scummy patches of blue-green algae in the water but it didn't seem close enough in to be a threat.

The kids soon got bored with their boats and turned to finding pond life and other things kids find more interesting. It was the middle of the day and the sun got too hot. She sat there with her back against her favorite tree, stunned by the heat. Something about the way her head was angled against the trunk of the tree suggested to me that she'd fallen asleep. I didn't think that was good: not when you're responsible for a couple of lovely kids.

I spent some time watching her through my binoculars. I also kept an eye on her kids. I felt protective and anyway she probably needed the sleep. I was pretty certain she was snoozing. Her body twisted slightly and as it did so her dress rode up her legs, exposing the tops of her thighs and the white cotton of her knickers. I wished I had a more powerful pair of binoculars.

But as I squinted through the weak lenses I saw a little waving movement behind her. I immediately trained the binoculars on the woods to see what it was. I had to refocus slightly, but there, in the trees, a man was watching her. It was that old guy in the long coat. I don't know how long he'd been there but he was crouched behind a bush and moving his hand vigorously in front of his groin. I couldn't believe it. He was pulling himself off.

I scrambled to my feet, squinting harder through the cheap binoculars. I thought about making a noise to let him know I could see him. Or maybe I should throw a stone. I didn't know what to do and I was in an ecstasy of indecision when I heard a plop.

It was the youngest of her children. The little girl. I could see what had happened. Her stick boat had drifted out and she'd waded in to get it. The beach of the pool shelved rapidly and she'd fallen over and was foundering. I knew there was also deep mud and I could see that the kid couldn't get out. She was drowning.

I looked at the sleeping mother, and the man in the woods, still pulling himself off. It would take me some minutes to squeeze through the fence and make my way down to the edge of the pool. The delay might be fatal. I stood on the edge of the quarry face. The drop to the cold dark water swooped thirty feet down. I felt a bubbling like hot tar inside my chest. Then the thing that had come out of the mud that day just climbed out of me and looked at me like it was angry. It grabbed me by the throat. *Just do it!* it commanded. *Just do it!*

I gazed down at the water below, and I stepped off the slate ledge. My coat filled with air, like a cape, billowing behind me as I fell. I seemed to hang in the air forever. At last I hit the water with an angry slap.

I expected to bob up to the surface immediately, but the heavy wool of my army greatcoat sucked in the water and became leaden. I went down. I couldn't kick my way out. It was too heavy. I had to try to get the coat off me underwater. The water was freezing cold and I couldn't seem to shrug myself out of the sodden coat. It was like trying to pull off my own skin. My lungs were already cracking. Although it was murky underwater I distinctly saw the thing—the mud thing—tugging at my sleeve, trying to free me of my coat. At last I peeled a single arm free. Then I peeled off the other arm. When I was finally out of the coat both it and the mud thing sank away from me. I kicked hard and when I made it to the surface of the water my head exploded with the bright sunlight, like lime, like acid, like a sudden attack of migraine. I tried to take a huge mouthful of air and instead gulped back a lungful of water and glittering blue-green algae.

Fighting my way to the edge of the pool, I could see the kid still foundering in helpless silence. The water shallowed suddenly and I dragged myself through the mud toward her. I scooped her up in my arms but she somehow pulled me back down and I rolled with my face in the mud. I got to my feet and hauled her out of the mud. She came out with a sucking sound, as if the pool had already started to digest her and didn't want to give her up.

By now the woman was on her feet and shouting. I carried her little girl over to her, where she gathered the kid in her arms. Mum's pretty summer dress got covered in mud from her bawling kid.

"Oh my god oh my god!" was all she could think of saying.

I wiped sludge from my eyes and looked for the man in the woods, but he'd scarpered. I was covered in black ooze. I must have looked like a creature from the depths of the pond.

Her eldest was shouting and tugging on her sleeve. "From up there! He came from up there!"

She shielded her eyes and looked at the quarry top. "You did? You jumped?"

"She was drowning. It was the quickest way down."

"Who are you? Who exactly are you?"

I said, "I'm just here to . . . help people."

"To help people?"

"I've got to go." I felt ridiculous, dripping with water, oozing with mud, no doubt with a sprig of blue-green algae stuck between my teeth. The thought of what I'd swallowed was making me feel weak. Or maybe it was her again. "I'm going to London," I said.

"London?"

"I'm joining a rock band. Going to help more people. Bye."

She shook her head in disbelief, squeezing her little girl tighter.

My shoes squelched as I walked away from them. I knew they were all staring after me.

"From up there," I heard her boy shout. "He flew down from up there. He did. He did."

Elizabeth Crane

NATE PINCKNEY-ALDERSON, SUPERHERO

Ask Nate Pinckney-Alderson, age six, what he wants to be when he grows up, and he will say, *I want to be a superhero.* Ask him which one, like his parents did, *Batman, Spider-Man, Wolverine, Cyclops?* and Nate Pinckney-Alderson will say, *Bob Brown,* and if you look at him like *Bob Who?* Nate will say again, *Bob Brown,* with yet another dramatic and exasperated sigh, *the superhero who saved the kid from the bus.* Nate P-A's parents, remembering the man from a recent local news story, consider explaining the difference between a hero and a superhero, but quickly realize that it's a pretty good kid who wants to model himself after a real person he admires.

In fact, Nate P-A has, since birth, had the ability to dream of actual crimes before they happen, but since there's no way for him to know this right now (he knows only that he wakes up screaming on an almost-nightly basis), there's also no way for him to put this super-power to good use.

Turning now to this Bob Brown, to say that he is an average guy is to flatter him. It's true, you'd be unlikely to notice him on the street— Bob Brown has a wardrobe of polo shirts primarily in unnatural-seem-ing shades of blue, and rotates a couple of pairs of poly-blend chinos; he's also been wearing the same style of Rockports, which he's been special ordering from an outlet store, since 1989, and although he has the good sense not to style his balding hair into a comb-over, he's got a lone, slight, unfortunate puff of it in the center of his forehead that there's really no good solution for.

The thing about Bob Brown and why he's not average is that he's not very nice. He's not the kind of guy who turns into a murderer and then when they interview the neighbors they're all like *I'm shocked, I never would have guessed*. He's the kind of guy who when he turns into a murderer and they interview his neighbors they all have stories about how he always puts his trash bins in front of their garage door (and then defends his actions by shrugging and saying *Sorry,* in such a way that it is very clear that he is the opposite of sorry) or always plays loud world music (and then defends his actions by saying he's bringing culture to the neighborhood) or always letting his lawn grow in, to the point where it would more appropriately be referred to as a "field" except for the fact that it's lawn-sized (and then defends his actions however he pleases at the moment—it's *fuel-efficient*, it's *natural*, this is my *aesthetic*). Mr. Brown's not-niceness comes in a lot of always. Even his friends have alwayses, and also some nevers (always sends sarcastic text messages, never returns calls, and some always/ never combos, always says he'll come to your party/help you move/ give you a ride, but then never shows up), to the point where it's hard to believe he has any friends at all (he has one from grade school, one from high school, and one from work, and none of them are very nice either—they bond a lot over shared grievances relating to what's wrong with everyone besides them), or a wife, who has her complaints as well (always uses the word *stupid* to describe her actions, never tries very hard to please her sexually once he's been pleased himself).

So when Bob Brown one day is waiting at the bus stop at Western and Belmont for his bus home from work (Bob teaches physics at Lane Tech—he's not a bad teacher at all, but he's perpetually cranky, and is frequently ridiculed behind his back or in notes passed in class), and a kid wearing those pants down around his butt to where he has to hold on to them while he's running or even just walking, except this time he is running, bumps hard into this other kid, a much littler kid, pushing him into the street in front of the oncoming bus, Bob does what you assume most people would do (or maybe not, since no one else does right then), which is to run out after the boy and push him out of the way. Via the grateful parents of the little kid and the amazed onlookers, the media quickly latch on to this story as the uplifting one they use at the end of the broadcast to try to make everyone forget the rest of the show, and for a brief time Bob Brown is celebrated as a hero.

Shifting our attention back again to Nate, of late he has been endeavoring to save lives to the best of his ability. Unfortunately, still completely unaware of his superpower, Nate has begun to assemble outfits that fall less than authentically into the style of Bob Brown, insofar as the hues of blue are more muted, his chinos are 100 percent cotton, and also he has taken the liberty of adding a cape that his mother fashioned for him from a remnant of blue velvet and some gold fringe trim patched onto the back to read BB. Regardless of the authenticity of the overall look and the fact that he is endlessly teased on the playground, Nate feels empowered by this garb and has been keeping his eyes open lately for crimes in progress or babies in jeopardy, but the reality of his life in first grade is such that it just doesn't come up that much. Hypervigilant now, though, Nate begins pushing kids away from anything he remotely perceives as harm—a lowering teeter-totter, a pair of snow boots propelled by a fast-moving swing— the unfortunate upshot of all this pushing being that it is recognized by others as pushing, and not the intended saving that Nate has in mind, in spite of his explanations. Counterexplanations are subsequently offered by teachers and parents to Nate about "appropriate" behavior, the need for respecting boundaries, and various other phrases he doesn't understand. In spite of this, Nate is undeterred in his mission, although he is for sure beginning to feel misunderstood and decides to take his superheroing to the streets.

Here in the streets Nate does not fare much better. For one thing, he is never outside the company of one or both of his parents. He is, remember, age six. If this doesn't immediately seem problematic in terms of crime prevention, try to picture the Incredible Hulk walking down the street holding hands with his mommy. It would be a hindrance, to say the least, not to mention embarrassing. Nate P-A tries to distance himself as best he can, though, and on one occasion throws himself on top of a Rottweiler that from his vantage point appears ready to bite a small child in a stroller, only to discover too late that the Rottweiler was in fact trying to lick the child's ice cream cone, resulting in an accidental paw punch to Nate's eye, three horrified parents, and, worse, the final retirement of the cape. Nate, depressed, takes to reading comic books in his room and napping a lot, which means he is dreaming even more, which is when a glimmer of his superpower begins to add up in his head. One afternoon Nate dreams that a certain classmate is bombarded with eggs on the playground—arguably not so much a crime as a major bummer for the classmate. Nevertheless, the next day, this event takes place on the playground at Nate's school, more or less exactly as he dreamed it. Nate, now forbidden to act on his impulse to save, remembers the dream but doesn't quite connect the dots until there are several more dream/reality occurrences, at which time Nate tells his parents what's been going on, at which time he is signed up for psychotherapy. Months later, when the Pinckney-Aldersons ask their son what he wants to be for Halloween, Nate, who has silently vowed to be a superhero when he grows up, in spite of his counselor's suggestions that his dreams are coincidental, says he wants to go as Bob Brown. His parents agree, *As long as there's no saving.* Nate raises the possibility of cutting the front of his hair to achieve the perfect Bob Brown look, which is summarily rejected, but they do make a trip to Wigs 'n Plus on Milwaukee for a wig that Nate trims very carefully in order to create just the right puff in front.

Halloween night, Bob Brown, fifteen minutes long ticked out, is at home in Albany Park with his wife—she is dressed as a Desperate Housewife (the perfect but tense redheaded one, although she briefly considered being the slutty blond one before she decided she couldn't pull it off) and Bob is wearing a Karl Rove mask, and they are handing out caramel apples, and they're not poisoned or anything, but they were on special at Aldi four weeks ago, which is to say that these apples are not at all fresh, that they are very possibly rotten, a fact Bob is completely aware of and unconcerned about. (*They're perfectly good,* Bob will say. *Apples don't go bad.*) The truth is, if all these kids got from Bob Brown was a piece of bad fruit, the worst thing likely to happen would be that they'd go home and throw up, whereas they now face the combined possibilities of vomiting and having to deal with Bob's crummy attitude and insults, and maybe even an accompanying lecture on health for any kid who dared to complain. Additionally, Bob seems to have appointed himself costume critic, as though he perceives a need for this job, as though Halloween would be more effective, as a holiday, or at least more pleasing to his *aesthetic*, which he seems to care a lot about, if the costumes were uniformly well considered and executed. Only very rarely does Bob declare a costume successful (and when he does, he actually uses that word, *successful,* he'll say to a kid, *Okay, now that getup is successful,* it should be observed, always implying that the costume of someone else present is not successful, and, not unimportantly, it seems like a kid would rather hear something like *Awesome costume* than the more dry *Successful,* or, as is more often the case, anyway, *Weak, Failure,* and *What the hell are you supposed to be?).* Even more unfortunate is the fact that over the course of the evening Bob will proclaim four costumes to be *Offensive to my sensibilities,* three times to girls under the age of eight in various princess-type attire, once to a boy dressed as Captain America, and twice in the presence of his speechless wife. Most of the time Bob conveniently chooses to make these comments to children who do not seem to be accompanied by adults. Conceptual costumes elude Bob altogether, and several artier kids dressed as things like "joy" or "office politics" or "the morning sky" leave in tears.

Of course, there are more than a few questions about Nate P-A's costume. Several people guess that he's a Munchkin. Others guess from the colors and the cape that he's a Best Buy salesman, which would be a good guess if any kid would ever go out for Halloween dressed as a Best Buy salesman in a cape. (*It says BB on the back,* says a snarky fourteen-year-old in a black trench coat who either isn't in costume or is dressed like one of the Columbine killers. *Aren't you a little old for this?* says Mrs. Pinckney-Alderson, in a fakey-sweet tone, to which the trench coat kid says *Aren't you a little old?).* Eventually, Nate's mom loses count of how many times during the night her son tells people he's *Bob Brown, the superhero,* and she seems grateful that Nate does not seem frustrated by the experience. Bob Brown himself does not recognize Nate's homage, although Bob's wife does, even though she's now slightly tipsy from the cognac she started sipping straight out of the bottle after Bob's first few insults of the night. Mrs. Brown giggles and bends down to whisper in Nate's ear that she thinks his costume is very authentic, which of course makes his night even though he simultaneously receives a *That looks nothing like Superman!* from his adult counterpart. Nate P-A is about to explain to Bob Brown, in a creepy mask that Nate doesn't recognize either, that he is not in fact Superman, but before he has a chance to finish, his mother, eager to avoid any further abuse from the man in the Karl Rove mask, drags her son off to the next house.

Over the course of the night, very few people get it really, even after Nate's repeated explanations, but most try to pretend they do, and he stands out, in his little middle-aged-man outfit, among the ghosts, goblins, Teletubbies, and SpongeBobs (a Bob Nate is decidedly uninterested in), yet he seems neither to know nor to care. Nate seems very focused on explaining to anyone who will listen that he is dressed as a man who saves a baby.

So never mind that the man who saved the baby has just snatched a caramel apple back from the hand of a crying four-year-old dressed as Dora the Explorer whom he deems to be less than grateful, or that he appears to take delight in insulting preschool-age ballerinas. To Nate, Bob Brown is a superhero. Someday, Nate will be, too.

Cary Holladay

THE HORSES ARE LOOSE

At last, it's New Year's Eve: Summer Godbolt has been waiting. At dusk, kids will get to run down Main Street in Orange, Virginia, on bubble wrap, and ten-year-old Summer is determined to be among them. Now it's late on a balmy afternoon, with the light draining away into evening. If Summer's going to make it to town for the bubble wrap run, she has to get her mother fed and herself, too, and keep her mother from dawdling, yet here they sit on the front steps of their little rental house out in the country, watching the sun burn down.

Summer's mother is as much in love with the bubble wrap run as Summer is.

"I want to do it, too. If I did run, somebody would try to stop me," Summer's mother says. "Anybody else could get away with it," she says, "any other grown-up, but not me."

"It's all right, Mama," Summer says, patting her mother's hand.

"It's not all right," her mother says.

This is typical of her mother—the desperation, the negativity. Summer realizes that her mother, Twyla Godbolt, is far gone in depression—unpredictable, given to tears and silences, spending hours on these steps, staring at the grass. She has been this way for much of Summer's life, but she's getting worse, and Summer can't stand it anymore, so she has decided to use her secret weapon.

She, Summer Godbolt, has known all her life that she possesses one burst of extraordinary strength to use as she wishes. She was born with this knowledge; she has never told anyone about it. She has decided to use it to save her mother. This will require gaining the attention of the most prominent citizen in Orange County, an elderly widow by the name of Abigail Paylor, who owns a grand estate of a thousand acres, including the house that Summer and her mother rent. Abigail Paylor raises race horses. She once lay down in front of bulldozers to prevent the creation of a new housing development. That was on TV. The name Abigail Paylor lives in Summer's brain as a fork of lightning.

Summer knows that Abigail Paylor will be at the end of the bubble wrap run to hand out apples to all the children. There are no rules in this event. It's not a race. Kids will get to pop as many bubbles as they want. Summer plans to zip down the bubble wrap so quickly, so showily—popping more bubbles, faster, than anybody else—that she will command Abigail Paylor's notice. Her next step will be to convince the old lady to save her mother. Just why this has to happen on New Year's Eve, at a bubble wrap run, Summer can't say. After all, Summer and her mother live on Paylor land. Summer could ring Abigail's doorbell and attempt to speak to the old lady, but she doesn't believe that would work. Abigail Paylor is practically a celebrity, and Summer is a ten-year-old tenant. Yet Summer knows that kids and old folks share a love of pageantry. Abigail Paylor will be awestruck by the performance Summer will give, so charmed that she will heed whatever Summer has to say, and that will be: "Adopt my mother."

Now Summer says, "We can get bubble wrap of our own, Mama, and spread it out right here." She gestures toward the weedy yard.

"It wouldn't be the same," her mother says.

"Well, I'll fix supper," Summer says, trying to keep her voice cheerful, "and then we've got to hurry, Mama."

Summer hugs her mother—why does the hug feel like *good-bye*?—goes inside to the kitchen, and opens a can of chili with beans. She feels as if she has already raised a family, an anxious little family of herself and her mother, the beseeching woman in a bathrobe of forgotten pink. She doubts her mother will ever get married again. The men her mother brings home are too tired to love her: truck drivers, farmhands, roofers; there is little hope in most of them, only the bone-deep weariness of work.

Summer stirs the chili until it steams, aware that her mother is still out on the front steps, and that the light is a shade rustier than it was a few minutes ago.

"Mama!" she calls. "Supper's ready," and in response, her mother sighs.

———

Just last week, something happened that convinced Summer her plan will work. Summer and her mother were wandering near a fenced pasture where two old Thoroughbreds lived, when a voice called out. It was Abigail Paylor, empress of the realm, saying, "Dorothea!"

Abigail Paylor drew closer and said to Summer's mother, "For a moment there, I thought you were my daughter, Dorothea. Oh, wishful thinking! My daughter has just died."

Summer's mother said, "I'm so sorry to hear that." She pointed vaguely in the direction of their house. "I'm Twyla Godbolt. We rent from you."

Abigail Paylor said, "I know who you are," and turned and left them, the name Twyla Godbolt of so little consequence, it might have been a sneeze.

Summer knows that Twyla Godbolt scarcely exists for Abigail Paylor except as a tenant, a remnant of a lease; there was once a Randy Godbolt, husband of Twyla, father of Summer, who decamped when Summer was four. Somehow, Summer's mother has paid the rent all these years, earning money as a waitress or daycare worker, going on welfare when she has to. Twyla Godbolt avoids asking Abigail Paylor to do anything in the way of upkeep. Twyla's boyfriends and Summer take care of things. On the first of each month, Summer scurries to Abigail Paylor's front door and slides the rent money beneath it. She never sees anybody there, but she imagines a maid picking up the money and delivering it to Abigail Paylor on a tray.

After the talk about Dorothea, Summer and her mother watched the old lady go. Then there came a sound close by, a gentle whinny.

"Look, the horses are loose!" Summer's mother cried.

It was true. Somehow they had gotten out, with no human assistance. Had they jumped? The gate was open; perhaps with their long heads they had jogged the latch askew.

Summer's mother, who was scared of horses, sat down on the grass and clutched her knees. The horses paused, as if they hadn't decided what to do next. They were old, but they were strong; they shook their manes in luxurious freedom. They could gallop east toward Fredericks-burg and tangle the traffic on Route 20. They could tear out to the west, where the Blue Ridge Mountains cut a high purple silhouette in the sky.

Summer moved toward them. The horses pricked up their ears and trotted away with a beautiful plunging motion. Summer called, "Wait! Please wait for me."

They looked at each other and stopped right there. She caught up with them. She had petted them so many times. It was no different to stroke their noses now, except they could take off and there'd be no stopping them, and Abigail Paylor would blame the Godbolts and kick them out of their house. The huge old Thoroughbreds showed their teeth. They could stomp Summer into the ground. Yet to her amaze-ment, they allowed her to lead them back into the field.

Was that power or just luck?

That very next day, Summer looked in the paper and saw a death notice for Dorothea Paylor, Dorothea who lived in Florida and was a socialite, the paper said, who grew up on the Paylor farm. There was a picture of Dorothea Paylor in girlhood, her face a fist of sunlight and tension. Yes, there was a resemblance between Dorothea Paylor and Twyla Godbolt, Summer thought, in the haunted planes of their cheeks. Summer read agony in Dorothea's face, and she concluded that Dorothea died from being sad, from being herself, although maybe liv-ing in Florida and being a socialite had something to do with it, too.

Abigail Paylor has people who tend the horses, mow the grass, and accompany her at a stately pace when she goes out riding. She has a chauffeur. Presumably, housekeepers clean the mansion and gardeners clip the hedges and deadhead the roses. Abigail Paylor has all those people, but she does not have a daughter anymore. Summer has heard of grown-ups being adopted by even older grown-ups. Obviously, in this case, that is the solution: adoption or some sort of permanent employment for her mother, as a sort of paid pet, rewarded just for being herself. Summer will find some way to stay close to her mother, watching over her but no longer taking care of her. It would be such a relief to have somebody else taking care of Twyla Godbolt.

———

Summer knows that the burst of power that will come to her when she needs it, power like the sting of a honeybee, will be available only once before she dies. So it's New Year's Eve, and six miles away from the stove where Summer spoons chili into two bowls, grown-ups are unrolling bales of bubble wrap down Main Street. Dozens of kids are massing at the corner, primed to run, and Summer's hands are shaking because it's getting so late. Her mother pushes through the screen door and heads to the bedroom where Summer has laid out slacks and a sweater, to make it easy for her to get dressed. Summer pockets her mother's car keys so they can't be misplaced in these last crucial moments. She sets the bowls on the table, with glasses of water and a box of crackers. Too nervous to eat, she washes out the pan.

There's a pickup truck pulling up in the yard. Summer's stomach knots: A visitor is the worst thing that could happen. Stepping outside, she finds a man climbing out of the truck, stretching his arms. It's Fernando, the man she likes best of all her mother's boyfriends, and his son, Luis, who pops out and runs around the yard.

Summer walks to meet them, saying, "Mama and I have to go out."

Fernando favors Summer with a broad, sunny grin. He says, "She'll be glad to see me."

"We have to go!" Summer's voice screeches so high that Luis stops in his tracks like a puppy hearing a whistle. She says, "We're going to the bubble wrap run, and she hasn't eaten yet, and it's getting late," and she is afraid she'll cry, that this is the wreck of all her plans.

Still Fernando doesn't seem to understand. He approaches the house saying, "Twyla, oh, Twyla."

Summer plants herself in front of him. "Please," she says, an idea coming to her, "can you drive me? Luis can go, too."

Luis pipes up, "Yes! Papa, can we go?"

Fernando seems to be considering this.

"Mama!" Summer yells into the house. "Are you ready?" No answer. Summer races inside and into the bedroom. There is her mother lying down in the bed.

Her mother says, "I'm too tired. We'll have to stay home."

"But you wanted to go. You've been talking about it all day," Summer begs.

"I've changed my mind. You don't need to go to that silly thing."

"Fernando is here," Summer says. "He'll drive all of us."

Her mother smiles. "Tell him to come on in."

"No," Summer says. "I have to go," and the words feel like a rehearsal of words she will say over and over. "You come, too."

A yawn. A pulling up of covers to chin.

She herself will never do this to another person, Summer decides, this languid refusal, this dopiness. Anger explodes from her: "Damn it, Mama, don't be this way."

Her mother's eyes fly open. "Well, sweetie, how on earth could that bubble wrap business matter so much? And don't talk that way to me, don't say damn."

Summer whirls out of the room, calling to Fernando, "She's not coming. Let's go." If Fernando resists, Summer will drive her mother's car and figure out driving as she goes.

"Okay," Fernando says, and chills of relief chase up and down Summer's spine.

They pile into the truck, all on the front seat, with Luis mashed between Summer and Fernando, but that's fine. They're moving. The truck's lights sweep the yard. Summer prays her mother won't appear in the doorway, distracting Fernando. But the doorway is dark, and Summer has the eerie feeling that she dreamed the woman in that dim room.

Spanish music floats from the radio, and Fernando sings along.

"Your mother is a beautiful lady," he says.

Summer registers the dip and bump of the truck as they turn off Abigail Paylor's land onto the road. The inside of the truck smells warmly of tacos. She dares to relax a little bit. She knows her power is good. Benevolent. God's very mind has spoken to her mind; God will work through bubble wrap and Summer's strong legs.

She has been practicing running and jumping in the yard. The playground at school would have been better, but she no longer goes to school. Her mother overslept and didn't drive her, and there is no bus service this far out of town, so when fifth grade started, she and her mother went by the school and picked up books and lesson plans. Summer reads the books and grades the tests, writing compliments to herself.

"What grade are you in?" she asks Luis.

"First," he says. "I never see you at school. Do you go?"

"I'm absent a lot."

Oh, Summer misses school, even the bad things—lockdowns, bomb threats, closings due to staph infection, when only the janitors are there, scrubbing germs off desks and sinks.

Near town, they find a traffic jam, which means three cars in front of them. Startled, Summer groans, because ahead of those cars are many more. Their truck creeps along. Fernando eases down a side street and finds a parking space, and he and Summer and Luis slide out onto the narrow sidewalk. Summer's heart jumps like a scared animal's, and she clenches her fists.

Luis reaches for her hand. "Are you okay?" he says.

She has never been so glad for a hand to hold. "I'm okay," she says.

People stream toward the corner where the race will begin. Summer has on jeans and a sequined T-shirt that her mother gave her for Christmas, but no jacket, thinking it would slow her down, and now she's cold. Goose bumps tingle along her skin. Fernando calls out to somebody he knows, and Summer and Luis lose him to the crowd. The streetlamps are hung with tinfoil wreaths. Electric candles glow in store windows, and a huge banner, stretched high across the street, declares *Happy New Year* in red script.

It's dark now, the whole town in the edge of shadow as if the sun has set close by, perhaps behind the Bank of America Building, which is a hundred years old with squat columns that end in paws like a lion's. The sun lurks just beyond the bank, watching.

Now that the moment is close at hand, Summer could faint from fear. She has always believed that the power would make her feel grand. She has not expected this excruciating awareness of each passing second. She and Luis join the mass of noisy kids.

"Don't push," a woman warns, and Summer recognizes her third-grade teacher.

A man says, "There's plenty of bubbles for all y'all. Go for the sides, Makenzie!"

An alternate plan is voiced by the grown-ups: Maybe there should be more than one starting line, to give more kids a shot at fresh bubbles.

"Well," says the teacher, "they'll spread out on their own."

"A riot is more like it," somebody else says. "Worse pileup than a football team."

"They'll have fun," the teacher says. "Lordy, I could do with a little fun myself."

If there is a pileup, Summer will leap right over it. She suddenly knows that she won't run: She will fly. The realization makes her gasp. Her spine and her feet are behaving the way a bird's must, becoming flexible and hollow. Luis's hand slips out of hers.

"On your mark," somebody says.

The children freeze. The voice comes from a loudspeaker high above them, anchored on a rooftop: God's voice, though Summer recognizes the baritone of Mr. Sedgewick, the principal. His heart must be pounding, too, to hear his own voice so loud.

"Get set."

Chins forward, shoulders hunched, the children make arrows of their bodies.

"Go!"

Main Street erupts in a long wild dance. All around Summer, children leap and jackhammer, cartwheel and curtsey and jitterbug. She's in the middle of a million pans of popcorn popping. Yet time stretches out languidly, time is elastic. She steps delicately on a cluster of bubbles and presses with her sneakers until the bubbles snap. Then she ducks into an alley, raises her arms like a ballerina, and lifts off.

It's so easy. And it's glorious! This is what everybody yearns for.

High up and sailing forward, through air thin and icy with random snowflakes, she hears the popping far below. It sounds like laughter, pure crackling hilarity, and she realizes that she's hearing happiness. Many people will remember this night, and some will remember it for a long, long time.

But Summer has a mission. Her mother is a horse penned in a field, but her mother does not have a long clever nose with which to knock a latch loose. Her mother lies in her bed, back there in the rented house, her youth slipping away, a new year upon her before she has decided how she feels about the old one.

Too bad that the bubble wrap run is only three blocks long, a space Summer is covering in a matter of heartbeats. She swoops above the flat, humble roofs of thrift store, pizza parlor, and barber shop. There is the courthouse with its Confederate statue out front, the tip of the soldier's rifle a little gleam. Church steeples reach up to Summer, and down on the street, the crowd shifts like a puzzle, with dogs chasing around the edges. At a table covered in green foil that dazzles darkly in the streetlights, volunteers hand out ginger cookies and cider. Summer smells the spices. On the loudspeaker, God clears his throat—not the principal this time, but God himself, chuckling, "Go, go, go!" in a voice so gentle and low that Summer knows only she can hear it. She wishes she could preserve this night, this moment, where joy surges and crests and builds again, where as long as there are bubbles to pop, nothing bad can happen to anybody.

Yet it will end. Even if new bubble wrap were unrolled all the way to Richmond, the children's energy would eventually flag. They will tire, they will need to go home to bed. In the morning, grown-ups will gather torn plastic and lost treasures—toe ring, trampled iPod, twittering cell phone, tousled graphic novel.

Summer's eyes blur. She could cry for the people, for these children, for the busy muscles of their legs. She doesn't want to come down. She spies Abigail Paylor's bent shoulders, Abigail Paylor beside a stack of apple crates filled with red fruit, not the too-perfumy kinds sold at the grocery store, but tart local winesaps and McIntoshes, coaxed through central Virginia's long drought. Summer smells the apples and the sea-

soned wooden boxes that hold them. And flowers? Yes, she smells carnations, still chilled from a florist's refrigerator: Abigail Paylor wears a
corsage on her mink stole. A scent of mothballs rises from the stole,
and the oily musk of the long-ago living minks, wild ones that fished
in Virginia creeks. Abigail Paylor probably doesn't realize how old her
stole is, how native its creatures. Summer smells their leathery paw pads
and the last specks of clay caught in the claws that dangle from the
pelt, little clever feet that jerk when Abigail Paylor moves.

Can she afford to fly a little longer? She'll risk it.

She veers north, toward the lake, leaving the town behind. She flies
over woods and swamps. Roads spool out beneath her, dirt paths and
two-lane highways. There is the Harley dealership, its rows of motor-
cycles shining like teeth. Her nose twitches as she crosses the landfill,
a dark gash dotted with white appliances—dryers, stoves, refrigerators.
Here comes the water tower, so tall that its top catches a last pink ray
of sunset, for day has lasted a little longer here. A dozen vultures perch
in absolute stillness, holding out their wings like great black curtains,
gathering every bit of fading light and warmth. She sucks in her breath
from the beauty of it.

Why only one burst of power? Why can't she fly any time she
wants, or use her power in some other way, again and again? Faint
barking reaches her ears. She's above the animal shelter now. Her heart
reaches out to the cats and dogs; she feels the helplessness of their
numbers, their loneliness, and her love. She would like to find homes
for all of them, to stop people from ever hurting them. Maybe she can
do that, if she focuses her mind on the idea of *animals* and *stop*—but
no, there is only this one time of power. The knowing was part of her
earliest life. She remembers hearing her father and her mother argue
and thinking, I could use it now, but she didn't; she let her father take
the TV set and all of the breakfast cereal and leave the house, while she
sat in her mother's lap. There she was, four years old, deciding to save
her power for something more important than keeping Randy Godbolt
at home.

It hurts to remember.

The silver sweep of the lake unfurls beneath her. Its humid wintertime warmth rises up to buoy her. Does she dare to drop down and trail her feet in the water? She kicks off her shoes. Plop, plop, they go. Carefully, she buzzes the surface with her bare feet. Oh, it's lovely water she'd love to bathe in, warmer than she'd have imagined, but she launches back into the air, shaking water from her toes.

Does everybody have a chance to do this? Thunderstruck, she realizes she has never asked a single person if they, too, might have power. She has assumed that she alone can do this. Everybody in the world might be able to fly or do some other awesome thing, so that all the stories about characters in capes and boots are in fact ordinary stuff. At this very moment, Luis might be drilling into the ground somewhere to save trapped coal miners. Fernando could be feeding poor people at a giant picnic table. Her mother might be able to rise up from bed and sing and dance—that being the most un-Twylalike behavior Summer can imagine—so beautifully that everybody who saw her would sing and dance, too.

All Summer knows for sure is that suddenly, she no longer has the sky to herself.

A V of geese pulses at her side. A baleful eye catches hers, and in wonder, she reaches out to feel the primal slap of a beating wing. So often she has observed them traveling through the sky, has heard the muted calliope of their breathy honks. They're silent now, moving with startling speed.

Oh, but time is passing. She has been up too long. She should go back, but she doesn't. This is her time, and it's all her own. If she had endless power, she would use part of it to hear a train whistle any time she wanted to. The lonely music of a train is a wonderful thing, and she'd like to hear it right this second, and she considers finding some railroad tracks and following them until she catches up with a train, but no, she'd end up flying far, far away, and come down somewhere nobody knew her, late in the New Year, a stranger thin and hungry, and still her mother would not be any better off. So she has to finish what she started.

The geese wheel away in one direction, and Summer hurries back to town through gathering fog, fog that thickens so that she has to navigate by the tall, glowing clock tower of the bank, its bell-like chimes marking the hour. She smells Main Street before she sees it— the cigarette smoke from puffing teenagers and grown-ups, the kibbly breath of excited dogs, the Scotch-tape smell of the bubble wrap itself.

At last, the fog blows away, and Main Street stretches before her like a brilliant runway. A few children still jump. The popping has waned to a slow sizzle.

Another heartbeat more, and she will dive down and land, by her calculations, right in front of Abigail Paylor, not so close as to scare her, but near enough that Abigail will see her arrive, will know that she flew, and will hearken to Summer's request, *Save my mother.* Twyla Godbolt will make such a good daughter that Abigail Paylor will forget all about Dorothea. Twyla Godbolt's proper role is lady-in-waiting. She can plan luncheon menus and hang the mink stole out in the fresh air. Abigail Paylor will thank her stars that she found this kind companion.

But Summer doesn't want to stop flying. This is how the horses felt, free and out of the pasture, the mountains beckoning, but she has got to go back down. She bends her neck and torques her arms. Closer, closer she comes, not fifty feet above the heads of the celebrants, yet nobody looks up. A dust devil whirls dead leaves on the street beside Abigail Paylor and rises into a spinning updraft that flips Summer over. She's a bug on its back, waving her limbs. By the time she rights herself, she feels her flight power waning.

She gasps to realize how much the gust has cost her. She has accidentally traveled way up the street, to the dark end of a block where a gas station sits closed and sidewalks peter out into grass. She lands in somebody's front yard, with a hard somersault, and rolls to a stop. The yard belongs to a house with withered chrysanthemums in front. No lights are on. The people who live here must be at the party. The commotion of the bubble wrap is a distant hum.

Nobody saw her land. Nobody sees her as she picks herself up and runs toward the lights, swaying on legs that feel unfamiliar. Her shirt strains under her arms, and her jeans ride up above her ankles. She has grown inches and inches; she is almost a woman in her height. The sky stretched her out. Her bare feet scrape against the rough street.

Abigail Paylor is a silhouette mobbed by children, arms pinwheeling as she hands out apple after apple. Summer runs as fast as she can, shedding sequins, but to the old lady in mink and corsage, there is nothing special about panting, breathless Summer Godbolt.

When Abigail reaches toward her, Summer grabs her hand. "Save my mother!"

"What's that, honey?" The old lady's face in this flaring light is garish as a clown's.

Summer says, "You need my mother. She'll help you. She can be like Dorothea."

"You knew my daughter? My Dorothea? Oh, give me a hug," and Summer is enveloped in carnations and fur. Mink feet tickle Summer's cheeks as she tries to explain, but Abigail Paylor is saying, "Take all the apples you want, dear," and then the hug is over.

Summer plucks again at Abigail's sleeve. "Please," she says. "You've got to adopt her."

The old lady squints at her.

Summer bursts out, "Aren't you lonely? My mother can take Dorothea's place. I've thought it all out!"

If she had landed in time, her words would have been persuasive, irresistible. But Abigail Paylor frowns; her brow beetles. She could have Summer arrested. Abigail Paylor opens her mouth wide, wider, so that Summer sees all kinds of weird stuff inside, like bolts and hinges that must mean false teeth. A scream is coming, or a telling-off.

"Happy New Year!" Summer yells at her, and escapes at a dead run. She bumps into somebody. It's Fernando, with Luis beside him.

"We've been looking for you," Luis says.

"Are you ready to go home?" Fernando asks.

"I guess so," she says.

Luis says, "I took off my shoes, too." His sneakers dangle from his wrist.

Summer helps him put them on, then she holds out her arms. He jumps into them, and she cries into his hair. Her mother will never know what her life might have been like if that rogue gust of wind hadn't come along. Summer has got to get her mother to eat, get dressed, and go out into the world. She doesn't know how she'll do that, only that she will, now that she's almost grown. Already she sees that her plan was a child's scheme. It wouldn't make sense to anybody but a child. For the rest of her life, she will think of other ways she could have used her power, if she hadn't squandered it—to put out a deadly fire, prevent a car wreck, help a falling airplane land safely. Oh, and aren't frogs and honeybees in trouble, dying out from some mysterious thing? She could have saved them, and saved songbirds, too, whose woods are being cut down.

The rest of her life might be a cascade of if-onlys, every day a catalogue of what she could have done. She'll have to live with that.

Luis squirms out of her arms. Families regroup and trail away. A car pulls up beside Abigail Paylor. Her chauffeur springs out and opens the door. Abigail steps in, and off they go. Summer imagines Abigail will host a masked ball, with feasting and champagne. If there are fireworks at midnight, maybe Summer and her mother will be able to see them from their house.

Luis grabs the last apples from the crates, pushes them into Fernando's hands, and says, "Juggle, Pap!"

One by one, Fernando tosses the apples into the air. Faster, faster, higher, higher. Finally, down they come, for Summer, for Luis, for Fernando, and the last one, "for Mama," Summer says.

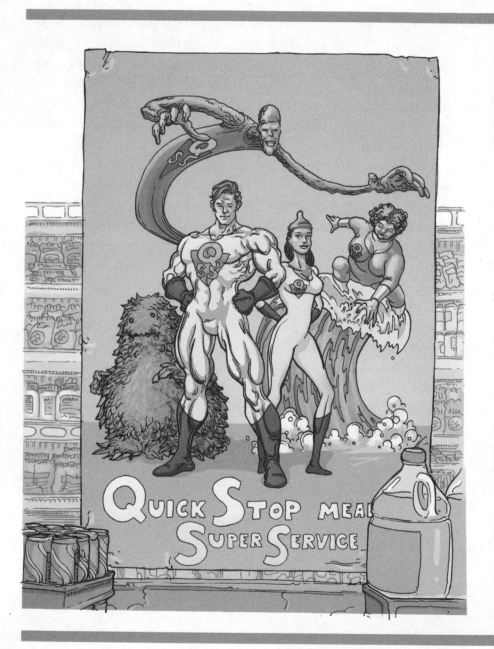

Sam Weller

THE QUICK STOP 5®

When it comes to the legends and lore of the superheroic, more often than not, most spandex-clad stalwarts fight crime in cities. Superman protects Metropolis. Batman looms over the nocturnal streets of Gotham. Spider-Man swings high above New York City. Of course, these larger-than-life characters are fictitious creations, sprung from the imaginative minds of Shuster, Siegel, Kane, and Lee. In the real world, heroes are far less archetypal, considerably less cut, and they often hail from the most everyday, most mundane of milieus.

They also have lucrative endorsement deals.

This is certainly the case with Earth's Most Unlikely Super Team®— The Quick Stop 5.

®

On the outskirts of Eden Prairie, Iowa, where rural Route 12 meets Interstate 80, is the Quick Stop convenience store and fill 'er up. As the advertising slogan states: "You can't miss the Quickie.®" At night, it can be seen from miles away, standing out there alone, surrounded by miles of stubbly farmland. An omnipresent dome of white, ambient light casts high into the starry sky from the array of halogen lamps, illuminating the vast fueling area with its sixteen pumps. The convenience store—part of a corporate chain—stands in the eastern corner of the property, a clean, gleaming rectangular building with floor-to-ceiling windows, covered with innumerable ads for cigarettes, gift cards, lottery tickets, sixty-four-ounce colas. Inside, more fluorescent lights shine, and it smells of deli meat, hot coffee, and citrus ammonia cleaner. The Quick Stop is a beacon of sorts, a promising respite for road-weary travelers. It also has one of the finest selections of adult magazines to be found anywhere in western Iowa.

But the Quickie's real draw is simple: It is the last chance for fuel for a good forty miles in either direction. For truck drivers, the gas station supplies a prototype blend of biodiesel—an affordable ethanol and petroleum mixture that burns clean and, as a result, is more ecofriendly than traditional gasoline. Make no mistake: Today's big-rig drivers—the ones doing the long hauls—feel good that the Quickie's newly unveiled blend of B5 biodiesel helps reduce America's dependency on foreign oil.

On an icy, gray December afternoon, an eighteen-wheel fuel tanker steered off the interstate and pulled into the Quickie. It was on this day that history was made, and the Quick Stop superteam was born.

The biodiesel delivery truck rolled in and, with a tremendous whoosh of air brakes, came to a halt. It was there to replenish the station's massive underground tanks. Inside the convenience store, a crew of five employees worked (the larger-than-usual staff was on duty as part of a quarterly inventory and cleanup, readying the store for another busy holiday season); a sixth employee, with nothing better to do on his day off, came in just to lurk.

Employee #1: Marty, the manager.

Thirty-two years old. Marty wore a red-and-blue visor with the bright yellow Quickie logo on it. His greasy, long brown hair hung down just below his shoulders. He had a thin, patchy goatee and a tattoo of Albert Einstein's famous theory of relativity, $E=mc^2$, on his left arm in black Old English lettering. Marty could have been a brilliant scientist. In fact, he was just a year away from receiving his Ph.D. in microbiology when he was expelled from the University of Western Iowa for selling marijuana on campus. What the powers-that-be at UWI did not know—fortunately for Marty because he would be in prison still—is that the quarter-ounce plastic Baggie that he was dealing was homegrown. *By him.* It was a perfect and monstrously potent, better-than-government-grade crop of weed; it was like some mutant peyote or a hopped-up hookah pipe concoction so strong it could've gotten King Kong stoned. Marty was certainly a gifted scientist, now relegated to convenience store/gas station management.

Employee #2: Kayla.

Sixteen years old and working her first job. A cute, if bratty, black-haired, gum-smacking, lip-glossed, eye-linered, MP3-wearing, cell-phone-texting teenager packed into a lithe five-foot frame.

Employee #3: Douglas.

A chubby twenty-two-year-old. Always wore a black and yellow Iowa Hawkeyes football jersey underneath his Quickie work shirt. Always had a bulge of chewing tobacco tucked into his bottom lip. Because of this, he was nicknamed Dip. Douglas was a walking ency-clopedia of heavy metal history. He loved to tell the story about the time Geezer Butler from Black Sabbath filled up at the Quickie; in fact, he told this story to whoever would listen.

Employee #4: Mama.

Fifty-one. No one knew her real name. Everyone at the Quickie just called her Mama because she was always saying, "I'm old enough to be your mama." Short, with wisps of gray weaved in her hair, she was maternal, often worrying about the crew.

Employee #5: Tim.

Twenty, rail thin, a mediocre mechanical engineering student at the local technical trade college. Since coming to work at the Quickie, Tim had developed a deep affinity for beef jerky.

Employee #6: McManus.

Twenty-eight. First name John. The Quickie crew called him by his last name for no apparent reason. McManus was a brilliant musician, painter, and poet, a Renaissance man of sorts. He also loved (with a capital L) smoking weed. His dealer was his boss, Marty. McManus was known to get high three, four times a day. At breakfast. On break at work. When he went home. When he went to bed. Sometimes if he woke up in the middle of the night, he would light up. Marty the manager knew he smoked on the clock and didn't care, as long as McManus did his work.

It was this unlikely group, on that fateful December day, who would soon become superheroes.

®

When the biofuel truck arrived at the Quickie, none of the employees paid it any mind. Gas stations get fuel deliveries. So Marty counted the cash in one of the two registers on the front counter while Kayla, smacking gum, organized and restocked a rack of condoms. Dip cleaned the coffeemaker island as he opened a packet of Super Chief® chewing tobacco for a fresh pinch; Mama, before wiping down the frozen Slushee® counter, throttled the machine to pour a wild mountain berry frozen drink for herself. Tim was simultaneously mopping the candy aisle and gnawing on a slender roll of Slim Jerky®. McManus was in the bathroom rolling a joint.

Marty, opening a bottle of vitamin water, looked out the window over a roll of scratch-off lottery tickets and watched the delivery driver connect a wide hose from the truck to a stainless-steel refueling port in the ground. When the driver turned the spigot on the truck, biodiesel fuel spurted out. The hose was threaded improperly into the port, and the pavement around the pumps flooded with the fuel—a murky, quivering brown liquid seemingly with a life of its own. Before the frantic truck driver could turn off the flow of biodiesel, a large pond of the substance spread quickly across nearly the entirety of the fueling area.

"He just spilled a shit-ton of gas," remarked Marty.

McManus emerged from the bathroom, lit joint in hand. The rest of the crew moved to the front of the store and looked out the windows at the scene by the fueling pumps.

"Should we do something?" asked Dip, spitting tobacco into a Styrofoam cup.

"Probably," said Marty. "Let's go."

All six Quick Stop employees didn't even drop what they were holding as they stepped outside.

"It's okay!" yelled the truck driver, waving to the crew. "I've got it under control. Sorry!"

The smell was overwhelming. A wave of fuel swirled up their nostrils, almost singeing the nose hairs. It was at once intoxicating and overbearing. All six members of the Quickie crew felt instantly light-headed.

McManus, with a look of gratification on his face, said, "Sniff that. You could get a major buzz."

It was then that Mama noticed that McManus still held the lit joint in his hand.

"Put that out. You could cause an explosion."

McManus put the joint to his lips and inhaled for one elongated last draw. He held the smoke in his lungs and then extinguished the glowing end of the reefer against the exterior wall of the food mart. Then he exhaled. He turned and closed his eyes and breathed in the strong stench of biodiesel through his nose. "That's some strong shit."

The others sniffed. Long and hard. Why not? They breathed in through their noses. Marty stood there in his red-and-blue-and-yellow Quickie visor, holding his bottle of vitamin water. Dip clutched his spit cup. Kayla held a packet of Excalibur® condoms. Mama had her wild mountain berry Slushee. Tim gnawed on a roll of beef jerky. They all stood there by the food mart and inhaled, and their minds swirled and it felt good and wonderful, as if nothing bad would ever happen again.

The truck driver had reattached the hose to the fuel port in the ground and was now safely replenishing the station's biodiesel tanks. He turned and looked at the Quick Stop crew standing there, inhaling. They were a band of misfits—a ragtag bunch dressed in primary-colored work uniforms.

"What the hell are you people doing?" the driver yelled.

But it was too late. The Quickie crew was completely, utterly high.

"Get back inside. Go back to work," the driver said and shook his head.

"He's right, let's get back to work now," said Marty. But he knew this was near impossible. He was high as a mountain. When he and his team managed to return inside, all the colors in the store seemed brighter. For a moment, the shop twirled before their eyes in a kaleido-scope dance—multiple images of doughnuts and paper towel rolls and biker magazines and bottled water spinning in a wild, uniform pattern, like some synchronized swim team of consumer products. Marty felt good. Not just good. Great. And he felt strong. Stronger than he had ever felt before. Like he could bench-press his Oldsmobile Cutlass.

By the end of the day, when the sun was setting over the expanse of western Iowa, their biodiesel buzz had worn off. The fuel delivery truck had long gone, the spill miraculously cleaned up, and the next shift of employees arrived. Marty and his crew punched out on the time clock, said good-bye to each other, and headed home.

Later, as Marty pulled into the dark parking lot behind his two-story apartment complex and turned off the ignition, something odd happened. He opened his car door and it ripped like tissue paper off the hinges, flying out of his hand and thirty feet across the lot, clang-ing loudly against an overflowing trash dumpster. Lights turned on in a few apartments.

"What the hell?" Marty muttered, stepping out of the car, con-fused. He looked at his hands and then at the open space where the car door had been. He turned and looked at the door lying on the ground thirty feet away. Bewildered, Marty stood there for a moment, and then he glanced down at his body. His chest, arms, legs—all of it—had bulked up. Then he knelt on the ground and did something that no one would believe. He put his hands under the running board of his gold Oldsmobile Cutlass and lifted it. Almost effortlessly, the car rose from the ground. All four wheels rose above the pea-gravel park-ing lot. With both hands, Marty hoisted the two-ton automobile into the air. Up to his chest. Up and over his head.

The following morning, while it was still dark and diamonds of snow flittered from the sky, Marty pulled into the Quickie and parked his car. He was surprised to see five cars there already. Mama was the only one scheduled to relieve the overnight crew. But Kayla's automobile was there, along with McManus's and Tim's and Dip's. Marty stepped out of his Olds. He could hear the hum of traffic on I-80 as he walked toward the food mart. When he entered the store, he saw his crew. There was a small pool of neon-blue Slushee on the floor at Mama's feet. Kayla's skin was shiny and appeared lubricated, and there was a growth on the top of her head—it looked like a little Baggie, rounded at the top, standing erect. Tim's face and hands and arms were a smoked, darkish leathery brown; he smelled like a butcher shop. Next to him was God knows what. Marty wasn't certain. It was amorphous, a wet, dark, leafy pile. It had big cartoonlike eyes, small arms and feet, and it stood about five feet tall. It looked like a glop of used chewing tobacco. Marty stared it for a moment. It reminded him of some freakish plant creature from a B horror movie. "Is that you, Dip?" Marty asked, finally.

"It is," the tobacco pile responded, its mouth opening. "Dude, you look like you've been pumping some serious iron."

Marty looked at his crew, who looked both worried and pissed.

Mama stepped forward. "Something weird happened to us."

McManus exhaled a tremendous cloud of reefer from his mouth and nostrils. Marty swore he could feel the effects of the secondhand smoke immediately.

"Like what?" Marty asked, suddenly feeling relaxed about the whole situation.

"Look at me," said Tim, scanning his leathery body. "I've turned into a freak."

"At least you look human," Dip said, waddling in place. "I'm supposed to go to the Ozzy Osbourne show tomorrow. What the hell am I gonna do?"

"*You* don't have a freaking reciprocal tip growing from the top of your head," said Kayla. "I'm a walking condom. My boyfriend is *not* going to like this."

"I have superhuman strength," said Marty.

The door to the convenience store opened and a man walked in talking on a cell phone. When he saw the group, his mouth dropped.

"What the hell?" he said, quickly retreating out the door.

"That response does not bode well for business at the Quickie," said Dip.

70

"I bet this has to do with that spill yesterday," Marty surmised. "Inhaling the fumes must have changed our physiologies."

"That truck driver who delivered it must inhale fumes every day," said Kayla. "Why hasn't it turned him into a sideshow freak?"

"I'm not sure," said Marty, calculating things in his mind. "I need time to think. There has to be a way to make us normal again."

"That would be good," said Tim. "And can we do it soon? 'Cause when I left my house this morning, a bunch of dogs came out of nowhere and tried to eat my leg."

Marty turned to Mama. "How have you changed?"

Mama held up one stout finger and a stream of icy blue liquid shot out from the tip. "It's ice mountain Slushee," she said. "If I think about it, I can shoot it from my hands, even the bottoms of my feet."

"Where else?" asked Dip.

"What about you, McManus?" asked Marty, ignoring Dip.

McManus exhaled and another potent cloud of herb floated from his lips and out of his nostrils. "I haven't smoked since yesterday, but I'm completely baked."

Marty was quiet for a moment. "What were you all holding yesterday when we sniffed that fuel?" he asked.

The crew was silent.

"I think we've inherited the characteristics of whatever it was we had in our hands," said Marty.

"But I don't want to be an Excaliber condom!" cried Kayla.

Suddenly, from the direction of I-80, came a tremendous sound of tires skidding across asphalt. It lasted for a few seconds and then there was the cacophony of wrenching steel, shattering glass, and, finally, a terrific crash that momentarily caused a temblor so seismic, the Quick Stop crew could feel it through the soles of their shoes.

All six employees ran out the door to investigate. The morning light was just breaking, causing the black night sky to lighten to a dark blue. A cloud of oily smoke rose from the interstate. An overturned eighteen-wheel truck was on fire at the bottom end of an overpass. Cars came over the rise in the road, and when the drivers saw the accident at the bottom, they swerved drastically to avoid hitting the debris scattered across multiple lanes. Three cars had careened off the inter-state into snowbanks. With a crash of metal, another car clipped the eighteen-wheeler and spun 180 degrees.

"Let's go!" said Marty, and the crew took off in the direction of the accident. Marty led the charge, running at a remarkable speed. Kayla ran, a spring to her step. Tim and McManus followed at a sprint. Mama ran behind, out of breath. Dip took up the rear, waddling almost in place.

The tractor trailer on I-80 continued to burn. More oncoming automobiles careened wildly around the scene, lurching left to right to left and skidding madly.

There was 150 yards of dirt-clod field between the Quick Stop and the freeway. Marty's legs were like an Olympian's as he raced to the scene. With each step, he ran faster and faster, his legs chugging like great pistons. As Kayla ran across the snow-covered field, she started bounding, each stride giving her more spring until she was bouncing ten feet with each step. McManus raced at an average pace, while Tim sprinted and, inexplicably, his limber, beef-jerky-colored legs began to stretch, longer and longer and longer, like a daddy longlegs spider. As Mama panted and ran, ice mountain blue Slushee began pouring from her feet at a terrific volume until suddenly she was lifted up on a great wave of the electric-blue ice beverage. Mama surfed to the freeway. It took Dip the longest; as he duckwalked toward I-80, he left a trail of brown tobacco juice on the ground in his wake.

The scene on the interstate was bedlam. The eighteen-wheel truck, belonging to All-Mart®, the national discount superstore (Eden Prairie had two super All-Marts, complete with grocery stores, automotive repair, and optical shops), had turned on its side. Broken glass and shards of metal littered the pavement, and fuel leaked from the truck. The double doors on the back of the truck's trailer had opened and hundreds of robotic teddy bears spilled out onto the road. The soft and fuzzy toys were everywhere. The impact of the accident had acti-vated many of them, causing their mechanical arms and legs to flail. A chorus of high-pitched, childlike robotic laughter emanated from the toys.

More oncoming traffic came down the overpass and swerved to avoid the crash scene and the debris field of teddy bears.

Mama rode a huge, cresting blue Slushee wave and landed on the top of the overpass, where she held her hands up in the air, frantically waving for oncoming motorists to stop.

Marty reached the cab of the overturned truck. The driver's side of the vehicle was facedown to the pavement. Marty crouched and peered in through the shattered windshield. The driver was inside, lacerations on his face, unconscious and still seat-belted in.

"It's gonna be okay, friend. We're here to help."

A local television news truck came up the overpass and pulled to the shoulder and parked. The driver and reporter stepped out.

"What happened?!" the reporter yelled to Mama. She was still waving her arms frantically for approaching traffic to stop.

"The All-Mart truck lost control and overturned!" said Mama.

The reporter turned to his driver. "Get the camera!"

Walking atop massive stilts of beef jerky, Tim reached the interstate. His arms quickly elongated into enormous lassos of brown, leathery jerky and he swung them high and wide into the wintry morning air.

"Holy Moses!" cried the reporter when he saw Tim's huge, lassoing arms of beef jerky twirling overhead. "Get this! Get this!" he yelled to the cameraman.

The light atop the video camera blinked on.

Tim's huge, twin beef jerky lassos landed on the interstate and he quickly began reeling in dozens and dozens of giggling, robotically twitching teddy bears so no more motorists would swerve to avoid them.

Kayla bounded onto the side of the road, followed shortly by McManus. Dip was still seventy-five yards from the scene, snailing along through the field. McManus looked at the multitude of stuffed toys littered across the interstate and his eyes widened. "That's the new Tickle Me Teddy®!"

"The what?" asked Kayla.

"Tickle Me Teddy. They've been sold out across the nation. It's *the* hottest Christmas gift this year. People are paying three times the retail value on the internet. They must have been delivering them to All-Mart!"

Tim's beef jerky lassos gathered the rest of the toys.

"Teddy likes to be tickled!" dozens of dolls repeated, in unison.

Meanwhile, having successfully stopped all oncoming traffic, Mama rose into the air once more and surfed a wave of blue Slushee down to the burning eighteen-wheeler. She held her hands up and thick jets of icy blue liquid poured out, quickly extinguishing the fire.

Marty inched his fingertips underneath the cab of the overturned truck. Slowly, and with terrific strain on his face, he hoisted the cab up into the air and righted it. He ripped the driver's-side door off and unbuckled the truck driver. The man was coming to. He would be all right.

The cameraman continued to film the entire unbelievable scene.

McManus raced over to one of the automobiles that had crashed into the snowbank on the side of the interstate. A woman behind the wheel of the car was crying hysterically.

"It's okay," McManus said. "It's okay." He opened the driver's-side door. "Are you hurt?"

The woman continued to sob. "You need to settle down," McManus said. "Everything will be fine." But the woman continued wailing. Moving closer to the woman's face, McManus inhaled deeply and then exhaled. A cloud of marijuana smoke gusted out into the hysterical woman's face. Within a few seconds, she stopped crying and relaxed, her tension eased.

Amid all the chaos and otherworldly feats, one last vehicle, doing fifty-five miles per hour, rounded the crest of the overpass. When the driver saw the scene at the bottom of the hill, his eyes widened and he hit the brakes. The car skidded violently toward the crash scene. Kayla was standing in the middle of the interstate, in the path of the oncoming car. Alarmed, she turned just as the automobile neared her. The driver jammed the brake pedal to the floor and slowed down, but the car still hit Kayla, straight on. It bounced off her, followed by a tremendous reverberating rubber sound—like a cartoon totem pole rattling in place. Kayla nonchalantly dusted off her pant legs.

The people in the various cars had stepped out of their vehicles and took in the fantastic spectacle. The television cameraman continued to film. The reporter looked on, incredulous.

And at that moment, Dip finally made it to the side of Interstate 80.

"What on earth is that?" asked the reporter.

®

In the hours that followed, all of Eden Prairie, and soon all of Iowa, and all of the country, was abuzz with news of Earth's Most Unlikely Heroes. The media quickly grabbed the story and dubbed the group "The Quick Stop 6." The video footage captured on I-80 by the local news team aired endlessly on television. In one day, the fantastic feats of the Quick Stop 6 had become YouTube's most requested clip of all time. Journalists from all over the world converged on western Iowa. It was bigger than the Super Bowl. Bigger than the O.J. trial.

Meanwhile, in a dark and monolithic skyscraper in Manhattan, Richard Chernei, the vice president of marketing for Quick Stop International, held a copy of the *New York Daily News* in his stubby little hands. The headline read: "SUPER! Iowa Super Heroes Save Lives and Christmas for Children."

Chernei picked up the phone on his desk, adjusted his four-hundred-dollar silk tie, gently moved his glasses up the bridge of his hawkish nose, and dialed a number on the telephone keypad. Someone on the other end of the line picked up.

"It's happened again," said Chernei. "Another group of employees has inhaled the precise amount of biodiesel."

Chernei stood at his desk in his dark office and listened to the voice on the other end of the telephone line. He looked out his forty-third-story office window at a luminous New York City.

"Agreed," said Chernei. "We don't want to run into the same problem we did last time. They'll be taken care of immediately. And if for some inexplicable reason that fails, we will resort to Plan B."

Chernei hung up the telephone and then dialed another number. He waited for a moment and then said, "Do whatever it takes to dispose of the problem."

®

Marty and the rest of the newly christened Quick Stop 6 were inundated with interview requests. They were hounded by the paparazzi. For the quiet group of underachievers—convenience store employees—it was all far too much. Far too much for everyone but Dip, who made the rounds on all the national morning news programs.

"Everyone wants to know how you gained your unique powers," they asked.

"I don't really know," Dip said.

"Well, what's it like being a walking glop of chewing tobacco?" they asked.

"It's going to take some getting used to," Dip said. "I can spit a hundred yards! But this isn't the only incredible thing to happen at the Quick Mart. I once met Geezer Butler, the bassist for Black Sabbath, when he came in to buy taquitos and an energy drink."

The rest of the Quick Stop 6 kept a low profile as they came to terms with their newfound abilities. After a few days off, Marty and the crew went back to work. They still had car payments, rent, utility bills—life went on. The media frenzy had died down. In fact, a new story was leading headlines (a popular Hollywood starlet escaped a rehab facility and led police on a high-speed chase on the L.A. freeway, and the entire episode was broadcast on live television). The swarm of journalists, with a new cause célèbre, stowed their tripods and cameras, coiled their microphone cables, and loaded up their vans. For the few who remained in Eden Prairie, there was little payoff. Besides Dip, the Quick Stop team declined to comment on their situation. They waited and hoped that Marty could do some scientific research to reverse the effects of the biofumes. Even though they had been lauded internationally as superheroes—even though they had saved hundreds of Tickle Me Teddys, just in time for Christmas, for the children of western Iowa—the team just wanted things to return to normal. So they tried to go about their lives.

One afternoon, when Marty, Mama, and Kayla were working, and Tim, McManus, and Dip were loitering and commiserating with their newly superempowered peers, the eighteen-wheel biodiesel delivery truck arrived at the station. It idled in and came to a halt. The driver stepped down from the cab.

"I'd like to go out and strangle that guy with my silicone grip," said Kayla, looking out the window.

"It wasn't his fault we turned into heroes," said Dip.

"You know, Dip," shot Kayla. "Why do you like this so much? You're all over the TV. You look like a freakin' turd! Doesn't that upset you!?"

"Not really," said Dip. "I'm somebody now. *We're* somebody. We're rock stars."

"Let's not turn on each other now," Mama chastised, shaking her finger at Kayla.

The door to the Quickie opened and the delivery driver walked in. He glanced down at Mama's feet, at the small pool of Slushee oozing from the soles of her shoes. Without saying a word, he walked over to her and knelt, putting the palm of his hand just over the blue liquid. With a sucking sound—like the tube vacuum a dentist inserts in a patient's mouth—the icy mess quickly absorbed into the driver's hand. The Quick Stop 6 looked on in wonder. The driver looked up at them, a thin smile on his face.

"You're not the only ones with powers," he said.

"Cool!" said Dip. "What abilities do you have?"

"I'm a wet/dry vac and I've come to clean you up." The driver held his hands up. McManus was closest. A loud vacuum sound emanated from the deliveryman. Thick clouds of marijuana smoke quickly billowed out of McManus, disappearing into the driver's palms. With the force of the suction, McManus stumbled toward the driver. His left shoulder suddenly began vanishing into the driver's left hand. He was being vacuumed in.

"Leave him alone!" Dip yelled, spitting a projectile tendril of brown tobacco juice that shot across the store and bull's-eye-slapped the truck driver's face. Momentarily blinded, the driver stumbled backward. This gave McManus enough time to compose himself and catch his breath. His chest filled with air and his cheeks puffed out and then he exhaled. A bank of pot smoke gusted forth, enveloping the driver. McManus continued to breathe out. Tim rushed over to assist, coming up behind the driver. Tim's arms elongated into ropes of beef jerky that coiled around the attacker's arms and chest, subduing him as McManus continued to blow weed into the man's face. After several seconds, the driver went limp, his head slumping. He passed out.

When he regained some awareness, they demanded that he explain himself. Who was he? Why the attack? What did he know about the biodiesel fumes? When did he get his powers? Did he know anything? But the driver was far too blazed to speak coherently.

"Can I get a bag of chips?" was all he could muster.

They kept asking him questions but got no answers. Giving up, Marty warned the man to leave and to never return or he would face the consequences. Outnumbered and still high, the fuel deliveryman readily complied. The Quick Stop 6 loaded the stoned driver into the cab of his truck. He started the engine and pulled away, hurriedly and jerkily, from the Quickie. The Quick Stop 6 stood in the fueling area and watched the eighteen-wheeler merge onto I-80.

"Is he safe to drive?" asked Mama. "He could barely talk."

McManus put his hand on Mama's shoulder. "He'll be fine. You ever hear of someone getting pulled over for 'driving while stoned'?"

®

The following morning, Marty scheduled the Quick Stop 6 crew to clean the convenience store; he wanted to convene the group for a meeting. Mama, Kayla, Dip, McManus, and Tim all arrived. They gathered near the front counter of the store.

"Before we get to work," Marty said, "I'd like to draw your blood and screen it. My old science professor at the university says he'll help me. But I have a question . . ."

"What is it, Marty?" Mama asked.

Marty sat on the front counter. "What do we want to do with these powers? We saved people the other day. We did some good. Maybe the media are right. Maybe we should become a team of superheroes. What do you think?"

Before the group could weigh Marty's suggestion, a black limousine glided into the Quickie and came to a stop. A short, stout, balding man with glasses stepped out. He was dressed in a suit and tie and cashmere overcoat. On his lapel, even through the window the crew could see that he wore a metal pin bearing the Quick Stop logo. The man entered the store.

"Good morning," he said.

"Hi," replied Marty. "Can we help you?"

"My friend, it's how I can help you—how I can help you all." The man reached into the interior pocket of his coat and withdrew a business card. He handed it to Marty. "Richard Chernei, Associate VP and Chief Marketing Officer for Quick Stop International."

"Cool," said Dip.

"Indeed. And we think you're cool, too. So cool I am here to make you an offer."

After the incident with the driver the day before, the Quickie crew was understandably skeptical. Kayla folded her arms across her chest.

"Look," continued Chernei, "I'm going to be frank with you folks, and I'd appreciate it if what I say stays here, in the Quickie. Quick Stop International is the largest provider of biodiesel fuel in Iowa and we have plans in the near future to expand throughout the Midwest. Our long-term goal is to export the fuel internationally. We could become the next Saudi Arabia. No more dependency on foreign oil. We'd get everything we need right here from Iowa farmers. And the B5 blend is unlike any in the world—it's cleaner, more efficient, and it's ours. We here at Quick Stop created it."

"What're you getting at?" asked Marty.

"Look," said Chernei. "We've been aware for some time that there's a problem with the B5 blend. An unfortunate side effect that is extremely rare but nevertheless worrisome."

"And that side effect is?" asked Kayla.

"You know better than anyone. From what my R and D team can ascertain, when B5 fumes are inhaled at just the right distance for a precise period of time, it can cause terrific and instantaneous transmutations."

"Like turning into a beef jerky stick man," said Tim.

"I'm afraid so," said Chernei. "I'm also afraid you people will go out and tell the world that you gained your, shall we say, *abilities* from inhaling B5. No sooner would you be on television than Congress would start holding hearings and B5 production would be halted. Immediately."

"You said you came to make an offer," said McManus.

"We're talking billions of dollars in biodiesel revenue here. We cannot afford six employees to expose the one flaw in our product."

"I'd call the condom tip on my head a major flaw," said Kayla.

"For you, it is," said Chernei. "For me, it's all part of doing business."

"Get to the point," said Marty.

"I'm a marketing man and you people are marketable. We'd like to offer you all a multimillion-dollar contract to represent Quick Stop. This is all contingent, of course, on continuing the superhero act. We will have costumes made with the Quick Stop logo on them. You will go out and save people. Do good deeds. In return, the company gets incredible, positive publicity."

"You said multimillion-dollar contract?'" asked Kayla.

"Indeed. And that's just the beginning. Along the way, we could strike endorsement deals with other companies—the beef jerky manufacturer, for example. The income possibilities are endless."

"What's the catch?" asked Marty.

"You can't say a word about how you got your powers. We cannot risk production of B5 biodiesel getting shut down. And one other thing," said Chernei, turning to McManus. "Unfortunately, you have to go."

"Go where?" asked McManus.

"You're not a part of the offer. You're unmarketable. Unless you want to move to California to represent medical marijuana. Seriously, I'll have enough trouble with the repellent tobacco guy. I pulled together a focus group yesterday, and we think he can at least connect to the NASCAR crowd. Philip Morris has expressed interest, too."

"Wait," said Marty, stepping forward. "McManus gets nothing out of this deal?"

"Not from us. There's nothing in it for Quick Stop International. He's a walking reefer. You can't sell that. He's illegal."

The Quick Stop crew looked at McManus. His head was hanging low. He was hurt.

"No deal," said Marty. "It's all for one and one for all. You know the saying."

"Do you understand the magnitude of my offer? Do you? Beyond the multimillions, the fancy houses, the fancy cars, the groupies, this is your chance to change the world. Think about it. As superheroes, you could save lives, fight crime, inspire millions. You would bring unprecedented goodwill and publicity to your corporate sponsor— Quick Mart. This would establish our product—our chain of stations, but, more important, the B5 biodiesel blend. This, my friends, would allow the great country of the United States of America to once and for all be free of its addiction to foreign oil. What does this mean? We don't need the Middle East! No more wars! It doesn't get any more Red, White, and Blue than that, folks. *You* would be the greatest of all American heroes."

The Quick Stop crew was thoughtful for a moment. McManus looked at all of them as they pondered Chernei's words.

"Did you say 'groupies'?" asked Dip.

Chernei nodded.

"Well . . . count me in."

"I'm in, too," said Tim.

"I'm so sorry, McManus," said Mama, glancing over at her friend. "I'd like to do it, too."

"All right, whatever, I guess I'm in," said Kayla.

McManus, even through his bud-induced stupor, was beginning to feel mildly angry. "But I thought we were a team? We do everything together. I even had a name for my superhero alter ego."

"What was it?" asked Marty.

"Secondhand High!" replied McManus.

Marty sighed. "McManus, I'm sorry. Don't hold it against us. We'll work something out—we'll give you a cut or something. Think about it. You're permanently stoned. You can't save the world. Besides, you know how much money you'll save every month? You never have to buy weed again."

Incredulous, McManus looked at all his friends, but they all turned away from him. The deal was done.

®

Super Bowl Sunday, with its national audience of 150 million viewers, is the single largest cash cow in the advertising business, and a thirty-second commercial spot during the game costs in excess of four million dollars. So, a month after signing contracts with the Quick Stop 5, Richard Chernei made arrangements for his company to be the sole sponsor of the Super Bowl halftime extravaganza. The world was abuzz. The heroes of the I-80 rescue would be officially unveiled.

The stadium was packed. Fans cheered, their shrieks of excitement growing louder and louder as fireworks exploded overhead and the stage erupted with music; a rap artist wearing dark sunglasses that reflected the stadium's flashing strobe lights pumped his arm in the air; a pop princess, her long blond hair cascading down her bare back, sang, danced, gyrated; a venerable, legendary blues guitarist ripped through a solo; the cheerleaders pranced and leaped and rustled pom-poms, up and down the stage, around the singers; Cirque de Olé, a renowned French-Mexican troupe of circus performers, floated about, twirling, spinning, waving colorful flags; a squadron of fighter jets screamed over the stadium; it was bold, it was bawdy, it was colorful and garish and exciting, and then the lights in the stadium dimmed. Spotlights played across the field.

"Ladies and gentlemen," a deep-voiced announcer said over the public address system. "Introducing . . . the World's Most Unlikely Super Team . . . the Quick Stop 5!!!"

"CAPTAIN QUICKIE!"

Marty, freshly coifed, in a skintight white latex costume with the Quick Stop logo in the middle of his chest and blue latex boots and gloves, ran, gazellelike, out onto the football field. In each of his hands he twirled a 325-pound football player.

"PROPHYLACTIC GIRL!"

82

Kayla bounded out, ten feet, twenty feet high in the air, in the same white latex suit, with the logo "QS5" on her chest, and stopped in front of the cheerleaders, who wheeled out a cannon covered in sequins; she ran directly up to it, and the cannon fired a lead shot, which bounced off the impenetrable heroine and puttered to the turf.

"SLUSHEE!"

Squeezed tightly into her latex costume, Mama surfed out on a curling wave of ice-blue liquid, while jets of the beverage shot from the palms of her hands.

"SLIM TIM!"

Like a great, elongated rope of beef jerky, Tim stretched out before the stadium crowd, and twisted and coiled his legs until he had propelled himself high, high into the air.

"DIP!"

No costume, just a wet, leafy glop of chewing tobacco, Dip waddled onto the field, and when he finally reached the end zone, he reared back, his whole body almost bent over, then lurched forward and hawked a huge sputter of brown tobacco juice that fired ten yards, twenty yards, thirty . . . forty, and kept going until it arced through the goalposts. The crowd roared.

®

At the Eden Prairie Cancer Hospice, McManus sighed and turned off the television. The image of Dip with his arms raised victoriously in the air on the thirteen-inch screen slowly shrank to the center of the desktop TV and then went dark. A nurse walked into the tiny, orderly office.

"It's time," she said.

McManus pushed his chair away from the desk and stood up. He walked down a long carpeted hallway to a room with a dozen patients, lying motionless in wheeled hospital beds, intravenous medication hanging in drip bags on steel posts at their sides. Taking in a long, slow breath, he held it in his lungs. Finally, he exhaled a cloud of marijuana smoke that billowed out, enveloping the room and its patients.

THE BEAST WITHIN

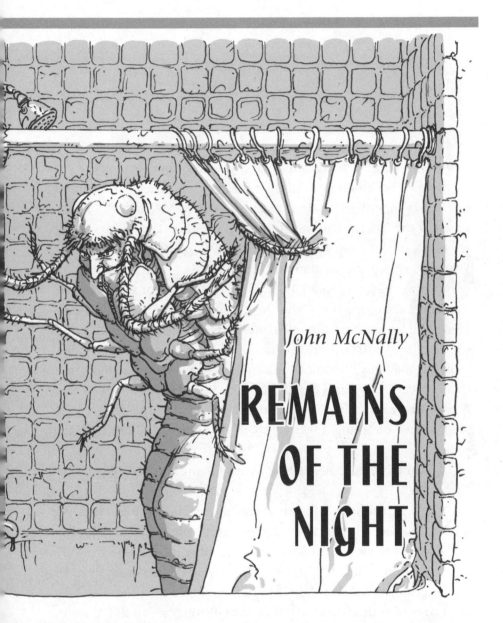

John McNally

REMAINS OF THE NIGHT

I'm his butler. You know him, of course: the Silverfish.

A *Sun-Times* columnist calls him the *creepy* superhero. He's not the first insect superhero, that's for sure, so why *creepy*? Is it the antennas? Is it the fact that he crawls instead of walks? Hard to say, but I'd wager it's the whole package—the way he looks, the way he moves. Women in peril are hesitant to accept his help. Men committing crimes have been said to soil their pants at the sight of a six-foot fish-like insect slithering down the street after them. He doesn't photograph well, either. No smile. No hands in the traditional sense. A little too bloblike. A little too bottle-shaped. "He looks more like the villain than the good guy," a famous talk show host has noted, and it's true, if only because his suit is too lifelike. I tried telling him this once, suggesting that maybe a skintight bodysuit with the *image* of a silverfish embroidered on it might be the way to go, but he wouldn't have any of it.

"I'm not a poseur," he replied. "When I'm the Silverfish, that's what I am."

I tried explaining to him that *real* silverfish, the small ones, are known to cause psychological distress, so just imagine what people think when they see a 250-pound one barreling toward them!

"Is that my problem?" he asked. "And what do you mean by *real*?" He wagged his head and glided out of the room.

I have seen the Silverfish out of costume only a handful of times. He's a normal-looking fellow, unassuming, even slight of build, but make no mistake, he's still the Silverfish. In costume or out, he eats glue, paper, sugar, hair, dandruff, and dirt—anything with starch in it, anything with polysaccharides. I'd walk into his library and see him with a book cracked open, licking the adhesive holding the pages together.

"Oh . . . uh . . . *sorry,*" he'd say, caught, embarrassed.

Unlike most butlers, who keep their houses impeccably clean, my job is to maintain a certain level of untidiness. Furthermore, the house is to remain humid year-round—ninety, ninety-five degrees most days. These are non-negotiable duties. It's not easy to live here. I'm always short of breath and kicking shit out of the way, but the pay and benefits are good, and though he can't offer a 401(k), he's set up a modest trust fund for me that activates at retirement age, so long as I remain with him until then. And for the past twenty years I've imagined myself staying until the bitter end, but lately I'm not so sure. On nights when the Silverfish is out doing what he does, I sometimes sneak away and meet up with other butlers and maids, usually at El Mar Bowl, where we can get ourselves a lane and enjoy pitchers of cheap beer for those few pilfered hours we have together.

And so here I am tonight at El Mar with Tommy and Oula. They both work for the enemy, but that's what most people don't get: just because you work for an asshole doesn't mean that you yourself are one. Take Tommy. He's Spiderhole Man's butler. Spiderhole Man is a notorious terrorist who lives in hand-dug holes in the ground, and it's Tommy's job to keep each place in order and stocked with necessities. But who in their right mind, other than someone in desperate need of employment, would spend his life living in one dirt hole after the other, keeping it stocked with fresh ice for refrigeration and diet cream soda (Spiderhole Man's favorite)?

And then there's Oula: she's maid to the Silverfish's archenemy, Earwig Man. Earwigs are predators to silverfish. In a perfect world, I should pledge my undying loyalty to my boss and keep my distance from Oula, but once you put aside the superheroes and the villains, you realize that the rest of the world exists in shades of gray, and that every day we must trudge through the murk that is our hearts and desires. The truth is that I'm in love with Oula and have been for years, though I have never told her. For all she knows, we are good friends, nothing more.

"Oula," I say, "your turn," and point to the bank of bowling balls.

She's distracted tonight, and I want to reach out and squeeze her arm, but I don't. I offer her my small smile of encouragement, my bowler's curt nod as she walks up onto the lane.

"Concentrate," I tell her as she blows her hands dry.

Oula has been with Earwig Man as long as I've been with the Silverfish: twenty years. Neither the Silverfish nor Earwig Man knows that we know each other, let alone go bowling together. I know things about Earwig Man that only Oula knows. For instance, how most of his underwear is over ten years old, and that he recycles. He's not all bad, she assures me, and I believe her. I told her the Silverfish once ate his own molted exoskeleton. "But isn't it just a costume?" she asked, and I had to tell her that I could say no more, that I wished I could, but that I'd said enough already. I couldn't tell her about the enormous silverfish farm in our basement, hundreds of thousands of the little buggers wiggling around down there, or about how Mary the seamstress miraculously patches up our hero's silvery blue costume using the real silverfishes' recently shed body scales. Mary's not as fast as she used to be, and the Silverfish and I both fear what will happen when arthritis finally gets the better of her. This is all the more reason for me not to bank on that trust fund. Mary is the key, really, to the Silverfish's success. No Mary; no Silverfish.

Oula throws the first ball, too straight down the middle, and though there is power in her throw, she is left with a seven-ten split.

"Ouch!" I say, and Oula shakes her head, already defeated. She waits glumly for the ball to pop out of the mechanical chute. She picks it up and, without taking the necessary time to consider strategy, runs gracelessly to the line and releases. The ball rockets into the gutter.

"Wow," I say. "The power!"

She walks past me and plops down in the hard plastic row of chairs, slumping down.

"What's Earwig doing tonight?" I ask.

"Oh, you know, being a pain in somebody's balls. What about the Silverfish?"

I shrug. "Same ol' same ol'," I say.

Tommy, standing to retrieve his ball, says, "Goody-two-shoes shit."

"That's it in a nutshell," I say.

"He ever get laid?" Tommy asks, then looks over at Oula and says, "Pardon my French. Just wondering if there are ever going to be any little Silverfish running around."

"It's not that easy," I say. "He leaves these—how shall I put this?—gossamer-covered sperm capsules around for a female to fertilize, but it's not like there are any female silverfish hanging around. It's pretty disgusting, actually."

Oula sits up in her seat, suddenly interested. "So he really *is* a silverfish?" she asks.

"Kind of," I say. I shrug. "Sort of." I realize I've said too much already. "It's complicated." I stand with the empty pitcher, ready to change the subject. "Is Bud Light okay?"

Later, after we stumble across the parking lot and say our good-byes, I get into my car—a fifteen-year-old Toyota Corolla stick shift. The car has over two hundred thousand miles on it, coughs thick blue-gray exhaust into the eyes of the drivers behind me, and shimmies when it goes over twenty-five, but I can't bring myself to ask for a company car. For all the press he gets, the Silverfish hasn't figured out yet how to cash in on his fame. He had a manager for a while, but the only endorsement offers that came in were from exterminators.

"Fuck that shit," the Silverfish said. "What do I look like—some kind of punch line?"

He was dressed as the Silverfish when he asked me, and his antennas were nervously tapping the ground.

"No," I said. "Of course not."

On my way home from the bowling alley, I'm followed by a cop for a good two miles before we go our separate ways. The last thing I need is to get pulled over for a DUI while the Silverfish is out making the world a better place to live. For all he knows, I'm home baking cookies for him or boiling rice. Sugars and starches: that's what keeps my boy sharp, that's what keeps him on edge.

I park on the street in the same spot where I was parked when he left home earlier tonight. At the front door, I ease my key inside the lock so as not to wake Mary, hoping to sneak in unnoticed, but when I open the door and step inside, I see that the Silverfish is waiting for me. He's sitting in the living room, the way my old man used to wait up for me in high school, ready to ground me for staying out after curfew.

"Where were *you*?" the Silverfish asks. He's holding the Mega Glue Stick in his hand, as though it's a bar of chocolate-dipped ice cream. Mary and I use the Mega Glue Stick to make congratulatory posters for the Silverfish, posters that say things like "Another Evil-Doer Down. Yay!" or, for his birthday, "300 Million Years Young!" The Mega Glue Stick is in the same receptacle as a stick of deodorant. The Silverfish, keeping his eyes on me, twists the dial until a good inch of glue appears, and then he raises it to his mouth and takes a bite. "What if the house caught fire?" he asks. "What if someone called?"

"We have voice mail," I say.

He says, "I wasn't out *playing* tonight, you know. I diverted a nuclear missile. I sidetracked a civil war. I removed a cat from a tree."

I know that only the last thing he says is true, so I ask, "What kind of cat?"

The Silverfish stops chewing his glue and stares at me. Then he resumes chewing.

"I'm not a prisoner here," I say. "I should be able to take a night off every now and then, and go bowling with my friends."

"Bowling!" he says and snorts. "You went *bowling*? With *who*?"

I leave the room. I head downstairs. Mary is still awake, darning the exoskeleton. I can hear the low-grade hiss from the thousands of real silverfish squirming over one another, searching for a morsel of sugar or a strand of hair to nibble on. I have all the respect in the world for Mary, but I sure as hell wouldn't want to be her. She has no goals of her own; she expresses no desires. To her, the Silverfish is our new messiah. She sees none of his faults. She questions nothing he does. Like that time a photograph of the Silverfish appeared on the front page of the *Trib*. He was in a seedy-ass motel in Cicero with a crack pipe stuck jauntily into his bug mouth. Behind him, slumped on the bed, sat a hooker wearing a faded denim miniskirt and a tube top. This was his Marion Barry moment, and it almost caused our little empire to come tumbling down, but when I tried commiserating with Mary about it, all she said was, "He has his reasons." Mary sees the Silverfish only in light of the bigger picture—the greater good he accomplishes— while the rest of us, well, we are all just little people. Our job is to serve.

I'll admit that whenever I think of Mary's blind faith, I end up feeling pretty damned petty for thinking ill of him. Every man has his demons, right? So what if a six-foot insect smokes the devil's dandruff with a skanky crack whore in a twenty-five-dollar cat-piss-smelling motel room? Given all the good he's done, was that really so bad? Who among us, at one time or another, hasn't stooped so low? But my guilt lasts for only a flash, a blip, and then the dark truth slow-burns inside me: The longer I'm with the Silverfish, the more I hate the bastard.

———

I wake up the next morning, the cobwebs of a hangover filling my mouth and throat. The extent of my pain is such that my head feels as though it's giving birth to another head. I can hear the tap-tap-tap of the Silverfish's old manual typewriter. He is upstairs working on his damned manifesto. If there's one thing I've learned over the years about manifestos, it's that things never end well for the person writing one. Until now, I had considered it his hobby, something he liked to chip away at in his spare time, but lately he's been spending every waking minute in his room, hammering out page after page with no apparent end in sight.

I make the mistake of saying something to Mary about it while I pour my coffee, but she just stares worshipfully up toward the ceiling and says, "I'm sure it will be his masterpiece!"

"Yeah-yeah," I say, yawning. I shift my weight from one leg to the other, stifling the pending explosion of gas from last night's microwaved burrito. I pour my coffee into a Styrofoam cup to go.

"I see you're hungover," Mary says, staring at me now. "Again." She turns away from me and says, "You're acting more and more like a homeless person."

I shrug, and a peep of gas leaks out. Since it sounds like the creaky hinge on a door, I turn and pretend to see who's coming. I don't tell her about the time the Silverfish drank an entire bottle of Mad Dog and then slithered across the Eisenhower Expressway underneath a speeding semi, nearly getting squashed and causing a pileup. Or the night, after polishing off a bottle of peach schnapps, he drunk-dialed his archenemy the Earwig to see if he wanted to go clubbing. Despite his reputation for unusually cruel methods of torture, the Earwig is notorious for his sobriety and politely declined.

I go upstairs. The curtains are pulled shut. They are *always* pulled shut. I open them just enough to look out with one eye. There's an exterminator's truck parked in our neighbor's driveway, and the man from Orkin is carrying inside two jugs of boric acid. "Oh, no," I say. Some of our silverfish from downstairs must have gotten out and made their way to the Johnson place. It's hard to catch and kill the little bastards, but boric acid and sugar will do the trick: sugar lures them; acid kills them. I shut the curtain.

As I walk past the Silverfish's room, the typing stops. "And where are *you* going?" the Silverfish asks from behind a closed door.

"Out," I say.

"Could you pick up a few more of those Mega Glue Sticks?" he asks. When I don't say anything, he adds, "Pretty please?"

"If the Dollar Store has any more," I say. "It's not high-quality glue, you know. I can get Elmer's when I do my next Target run."

"No, no," he says. "Mega Glue Stick, please."

I wait a second, thinking he wants to say something else, but then the typing resumes, and I leave the house. The house is just a 1950s ranch, a little bigger than most because of an addition built on in the seventies, but we're not talking a castle here by any means. It's no fortress. It's no stronghold. We have neighbors; we have a lawn that can be mowed with a push mower; we have a short driveway with a two-car garage. No one, in fact, knows who really lives here. They think it's just me and Mary.

Like I've said, the Silverfish isn't rich. He's not one of these trust-fund superheroes. His parents worked at the old 3M factory on Harlem Avenue. A psychologist would have a field day with that detail: parents who worked at a place that made adhesives, a child that grows up craving the very thing his parents once made . . . But it's all too convenient, this explanation. If you ask me, that's Monday-morning quarterbacking the Silverfish's life. He eats glue because silverfish eat glue. Sometimes things are simply as they seem.

Outside, Mr. Johnson calls to me from his lawn as the exterminator backs out of his drive.

"Do you have a silverfish problem?" he asks.

Do I, I'm tempted to say but shake my head instead. "Nope. I don't think so."

"Keep your eye out," he says. "I woke up this morning and found *thousands* of them in my basement."

"Will do," I say and then give him a tiny salute.

From a pay phone, I call Oula to see how she's feeling.

"I can't talk now," she says. "The Earwig might be listening." Then, in a near whisper: "Meet me at Duke's at noon."

Duke's is a local Italian beef sandwich shop, an unlikely place for Earwig Man or the Silverfish to appear. I tell her that I'll see her at noon, and then I give Tommy a jingle, but reception isn't good. He's down in a hole somewhere in Oak Park, waiting for Spiderhole Man to return from a car bombing.

"Can you hear me now?" he asks.

"Yeah-yeah. Can you hear *me*?" I ask.

"What? Say that again."

"I'll call you later," I say.

"You're breaking up," Tommy says, and I return the receiver to its cradle. There's no sense prolonging the misery of a bad connection.

At noon, I meet Oula at Duke's. I can tell she's been crying, but I wait until we order our beef sandwiches before I ask her what's wrong.

"I can't take it anymore," she says.

"What?" I ask.

"I love him so much, it's killing me."

"Who? *Earwig?*"

"No," she says. "The Silverfish."

"The Silverfish?" I say. "Really?" My breathing grows shallow. I pull out my inhaler, put it to my mouth, and knock back a blast of albuterol sulfate.

"I know, I know," she says. "It's not even realistic, is it?"

I shrug. "Anything's possible," I offer, though I'm not sure I really believe this.

Oula grabs hold of my arm and presses her face against it. She's weeping uncontrollably now, and everyone who's in line to order their food has turned to stare at us. I feel, for the first time since I was a teenager, empty, and I can't help shivering like the lovelorn fool that I am. *What now?* I wonder. *What now?*

———

I drive to Oak Park and find Tommy's hole in the ground. The hole's cover is a Styrofoam cooler lid with fake plastic flowers poking up out of it. There's no room on the lid to knock, so I just push on it until it falls into the hole.

"What the fuck?" I hear, and then, "Oh, hey, it's you."

"Want to get a drink?" I ask.

"Sure, sure," Tommy says, "just give me a hand out of here. Spiderhole Man took the ladder so I couldn't get out. I know he's a terrorist and all, but sometimes he's just a regular run-of-the-mill asshole to boot."

I offer Tommy my hand and hoist him out of the hole, and then we drive to Bar Louie. In a few short hours, we are annihilated.

"And another thing," I yell. "The Silverfish isn't that bright. No, really. I was reading his manifesto, and he doesn't know the difference between *its* possessive and *it's* as a contraction. Fucking *its* and *it's*. It's not that hard, my friend. It's not rocket science, that's for damned sure!"

Tommy slams the counter with his palm and says, "Where's his goddamned grammar handbook?"

"No shit," I say, and then I motion to the bartender for another round.

"Listen," Tommy says, his voice low. "You know all these stories about Spiderhole Man's car bombs? Well, I'm starting to think they're not all true." And then Tommy tells me how Spiderhole Man went off his meds while in the Iraq War, and how it was shortly after he was dishonorably discharged for shooting bottle rockets out his ass and accidentally burning down a few tents in his unit's bivouac that Spiderhole Man emerged in the States. "The timing," Tommy says, "is suspect, to say the least. I mean, yeah, sure, he blows shit up every now and then, but you want to know what I think? I think he isn't so much a terrorist as he is a compulsive liar with a trust fund."

"Get the fuck out of here," I say. "Get. The. Fuck. Out. Of. Here."

"No, really," he says. "Just a rich bastard who needs some Prozac. That's all."

I wag my head, but the motion of my swaying head messes with my equilibrium, and I almost fall off my barstool. "Whoa!" I say, grabbing onto Tommy, who, in turn, almost falls off *his* barstool.

"Time to go, li'l fella," he says.

We stumble back to my car, and after I drop him off at his hole, I drive home. I have to keep one eye closed most of the way so as not to see two sets of Harlem Avenues. I pull into the driveway, a bit too fast, and almost hit the garage, but I manage to stop with just enough room to slide a sheet of paper between bumper and garage door.

Inside, as I stumble past the Silverfish's room, the typewriter pauses, as if taking a breath from talking. "Did you get those Mega Glue Sticks I asked for?" he says.

"Shit," I say under my breath. Then, "I'm sorry, but they were out."

"Out?" he asks. "Are you sure?"

"I couldn't find them," I say.

"Did you look in school supplies?"

"Of course," I say.

"How about home repair?"

"I looked everywhere," I say. "I *scoured* the whole damned place, okay?"

"Don't get touchy," the Silverfish says. When I look down and see one of his antennas slipping under the door and starting to feel around for me, I back up. "Where are you?" he asks.

"Listen," I say. "I'm tired. I need a nap before my shift starts." As I walk away, the antenna retracts back under the door and into its room.

That night, I toss and turn, unable to fall into any kind of deep or meaningful sleep. I wake up at three in the morning. The Silverfish is already out for the night, saving the world and whatnot. I'm supposed to have been awake, keeping an eye on things, but my afternoon bout of drinking had gotten the better of me—that, and a dark depression over Oula's revelation. *Jesus,* I think.

I get out of bed. I put my flask of whiskey in my back pocket. I pick up my cell phone and walk upstairs, my feet pushing all the licked envelopes out of the way. The Silverfish, before going out, needs his fix. He's done this before. I've seen him do it, too—lifting the flap with arms that narrow like miniature pool cues, then swiping his mouth across the adhesive. Whenever he sees me paying the bills, he insists on licking the envelopes. We'll sit side by side—me writing checks, the Silverfish waiting impatiently.

"Can you go any faster?" he'll ask.

"Don't rush me," I'll say. "You'll make me put a check in the wrong damned envelope."

After each lick, the Silverfish lets out a barely audible orgasmic moan. His antennas vibrate for a moment, and then he sighs. One time I left the room to find some stamps, and when I came back, he was eating an envelope. Real silverfish don't have well-built mouth parts for chewing. What they do is sit on top of paper and gradually grind down the surface. If you pick up a book and find words missing from its pages, you know a silverfish has been there already, snacking. But the big guy, he uses some combination of his own human mouth with the silverfish's, giving him a variety of ways to ingest his daily nutrients.

I go into the Silverfish's office. His manifesto sits on the desk, a pile of drivel. My cell phone vibrates. It's Tommy.

"Dude," I say. "I'm so hungover."

There's silence. Then, "Spiderhole Man hasn't come home. I've got a bad feeling."

"Where are you?"

"I'm standing outside the hole," he says. "I couldn't breathe anymore."

"Any idea where he was going?"

Tommy says, "He said something about blowing up a CVS, but I just figured he was getting his Viagra refilled."

"Spiderhole Man uses Viagra?" I ask. This is news to me.

"You don't think this is serious, do you?" he says. "I don't know why I thought you would. I mean, you work for *him*."

"Yeah, well," I say, and I'm about to unload a few of my own problems, but Tommy hangs up.

I sit down at the Silverfish's desk and flip through the manifesto while Mary snores loudly in the room below. His new working title is *Everything I Learned I Learned in the Paleozoic Era: Notes from a Much-Maligned Insect.* I flip through chapters on subjects as diverse as the failures of the American penal system and the three years the Silverfish spent in college downstate shrooming his ass off. Near the bottom of the pile, in chapters he must have typed these past few days, I find a chapter titled "The Butler Did It." My hands shake as I remove this section from the rest of the manuscript.

In "The Butler Did It," I am described as one of his many charity cases, a man who, without the assistance of the Silverfish, would probably still be living in his parents' basement. I'm a sad sack, according to the text. But worse: I may not be stable anymore. Lately, he's been suspecting that I'm suffering from some kind of mental deterioration with possible psychotic episodes. "I would dismiss him," he writes, "but twenty years is a long time to be with someone without feeling some moral sense of obligation toward them. Even so," he continues, "he's under the delusion that I've set up a trust fund for him, and that, upon retirement age, he'll start collecting monthly checks. These delusions worry me, of course, but worse are those times, like right now, when I know he's standing outside my door listening in on me. What's he up to? What's he planning to do?"

I return the chapter to its proper place in the manifesto. My cell phone is blinking. It's the Silverfish.

"Hello?" I say. I take the flask from my back pocket, uncap it, and take a swig.

"Guess where I went tonight," he says.

"How should I know?"

The Silverfish says, "I went to the Dollar Store. They were closing, but a cleaning crew let me in."

"Of course they did," I say.

"And you know what I found in the aisle with all the school supplies?"

I say nothing. I know where this is going.

"No guesses?" he says. "Okay, I'll tell you. I found Mega Glue Sticks. A whole wall of them on hooks. Probably two hundred of them."

"Your point?" I ask. I take another swig from my flask, then cap it.

"No point," he says.

"Where are you now?"

"I'm waiting for someone," he says. True to his nature, when the Silverfish waits for an enemy, he stands in the bathtub or sits in a sink. Imagine, if you will, opening a door, turning on the light, and, bam, there he is: the Silverfish in your tub!

I shut my phone. A few seconds later, he calls again. The phone blinks for a good thirty seconds before stopping. He hates when I hang up on him. *Hates* it. I go outside and light a cigarette. I've been trying to quit, but I still carry a pack around with me in my shirt pocket—Marlboros—and tonight I need one. My hands are shaking.

"Jesus," I say, and I no sooner finish hissing the Lord's name in vain when I see them, a caravan of tiny silverfish making their way from my house to Mr. Johnson's. The moon is bright enough and my eyes have adjusted sufficiently for me to see that they're heading toward a metal cookie sheet near the Johnsons' downspout—but then I also see, just around the bend, the two jugs of boric acid and, on top of their picnic table, a pound of sugar. I snuff out my cigarette and tiptoe over to the Johnsons' yard. I tuck the sugar under my armpit and lift the two jugs of boric acid. Then I tiptoe away.

I make the short trek to the Stevenson Park over on Eighty-fifth and State Road. I squeeze myself inside the jungle gym and, walking in ever-widening circles, sprinkle all the sugar onto the ground. Following the same swirling motion, I empty only one jug of the white powder boric acid onto the sugar granules. Then I make the call.

"Yo," the Silverfish says. "Whazzup?"

I take a deep breath. I say, "I heard on the police scanner that there's a hostage situation at Stevenson Park."

"What time is it?" he asks.

"Four-twenty," I say.

"A.M. or P.M.?" he asks.

"A.M.!" I say. "Four-twenty in the A.M."

"Okay, okay," he says. "I've been sitting in a dark room all night. And I forgot to bring my watch." This is no surprise: The Silverfish's short-term memory is no better than his namesake's. On more than one occasion, after I have berated him for leaving his keys at home or forgetting to take along an umbrella on a cloudy day, he had replied, "I live in the moment!"—as if this were a strength and not a weakness.

"So?" I say. "Are you coming?"

"I guess," the Silverfish says. "Do you think I should?"

"It's a *hostage* situation," I say. "What do *you* think?"

"Hostages." He sighes. "All right then. I'll be right over."

I camp out on the park's outskirts—one jug still full of boric acid, one empty. So this is what it's come down to: I'm going to kill him. Tonight. The Silverfish will die. When he comes to the park and realizes that there is no hostage situation, he'll get a whiff of all that sugar, and then how can he resist? He'll glide between the jungle gym's bars, and while the lethal white powder starts tugging him through that murky space between life and death, I'll emerge with the full jug of acid and finish him off. After he's dead, I'll remove his suit and put it on for myself, and then I'll slither over to Oula's and whisk her off her feet. I'll wrap my antennas tightly around her and shimmy away with her. She'll get her wish; I'll get mine. And then, in a few days, when it becomes clear that the Silverfish's longtime butler has disappeared for good, I'll hire Tommy. It's a perfect plan, and I'm so happy with how the pieces are falling into place, I remove the flask from my back pocket and take a celebratory nip. I don't want to pound it, that's for sure, but the longer it takes for the Silverfish to arrive, the deeper my swigs become. I open my phone and call the Silverfish. No answer.

"Shit," I say. "Where the hell are you?"

"I'm right here," he says, and when I look up, there he is, wrapped around a thick tree branch and peering down at me. I drop the cell phone and knock over my flask.

"Oh, no," I say, but it is too late: The Silverfish falls from the tree and lands on top of me, his squishy legs holding me in a grip from which I cannot break. "Ease up," I yell, "you got me," but he squeezes harder. With my face pressed flush against his flaking underside, I can barely breathe. I fear he's going to snap my spine and paralyze me. As the world begins to pulsate and blur in front of me, I realize that I have no choice: I take a bite of his scaly flesh, and because I have nowhere to spit, I chew it quickly and swallow. Still, he doesn't loosen his grip. I take another bite, confirming my suspicions that the Silverfish, like every other insect on this planet, feels no pain whatsoever—nothing at all. With all the air squeezed out of me, I start blacking out. I honestly never thought it would come to this, a man being smashed by an insect, and yet here we are—my fate in the Silverfish's hands. "You win," I say before finally slipping under.

———

It's not bad here, I guess. I room with a guy who scratched his arms until they bled and then tried to hang himself with the cord to a heating pad, so now they belt him in each night for his own safety, not to mention the safety of others. Since I don't sleep well, I tell him stories about the Silverfish to lull him to sleep. I tell him the big stories, the ones about daring rescues he made or disasters he averted, not any of the small stuff, like how his favorite TV show is *Dog the Bounty Hunter* or how he likes to sing show tunes when he thinks no one's listening.

When Tommy finally comes to visit, we have to stay inside. I haven't yet earned outdoor privileges.

"What ever happened to Spiderhole Man?" I ask him. "Did he ever come back?"

"What?" Tommy asks. Then, "Oh-oh, yeah. *That.* Turns out I was just overreacting. He went to a movie. Some Iranian film playing at the Music Box."

"And Oula? Do you still see her?"

Tommy averts his eyes. He squints over my shoulder, as if reading a posted sign. "No, no," he says, but I can tell he's lying. I get the feeling she and the Silverfish have finally hooked up, a thought that makes my knees turn to jelly and my heart kick into overdrive, but I don't push him.

"You want to play chess?" I ask.

"I . . ." He pauses, thinking. "I better get back. Spiderhole Man has a little, you know, *project* to take care of today."

"Oh, okay," I say. "Sure. No problem. Will you come again?"

"You betcha," he says, standing. He pats my shoulder, but when I stand and move in to hug him, he takes a step back. "It's great to see you," he says. "You're looking good."

I want to ask him why he's treating me like the crazy one when it's him that lives in a hole. But I don't go there. "Good to see you, too," I say.

I sit alone at a table in the recreation room. This place is clean. And it has air-conditioning. No more sweltering heat. But lately I've started to miss the mess, and my body craves both heat and humidity.

"It's so *cold* in here," I complain, and an intern says, "It's seventy-five. It's the perfect temperature."

I shiver all day, and when I get into bed, I ask for more blankets. I feel changes taking place inside me, and my skin has become dry and brittle. I know what's happening to me. Even so, I don't tell anyone that I ate the flesh of the Silverfish. It's nobody's business, really.

Every morning at eight, after breakfast, I sit in a semicircle in Conference Room B with six of my fellow floormates, and we share stories about what was going on in our lives in the days just before we were forced to come here. Bill set his house on fire one afternoon for no reason he can remember other than that he was watching a TV show in which a house was on fire. Larry swallowed everything in his medicine cabinet, beginning with all the prescription drugs but working his way to the tropical-flavored Tums and giant bottle of expired ginkgo biloba tablets. Jimmy shot a flare gun through his neighbor's window and then watched the whole family come running outside, screaming. Jimmy still chuckles when he tells that part of his story, a pretty good sign that he's not ready to leave the facility any time soon.

When it's my turn, I tell them simply that I was butler to the Silverfish and that we'd had a falling-out.

"No big whoop," I say.

The therapist stares at me, but she doesn't press. She thinks I'll eventually come around and tell the whole story.

Every morning at eleven we work on our arts and crafts. Some days, we nail together prefab birdhouses. Other days, we paint coffee mugs and then send them off to get glazed. Today, we're making posters for patients in the oncology wing of the hospital. I have scissors, construction paper, and glitter to choose from. I have Sharpies, Crayolas, and little jars of tempera paint. But I don't have what I want, what I *need*.

I stand up and walk over to Tiffany, who is working on her own poster. Last month, from what I've been told, Tiffany got into her car and ran over every mailbox on her street, and then she drove as fast as she could into a power line tower, knocking it down and causing an entire city to lose its electricity for the day. Two boys playing basketball almost fried to death when the whipping live wires brushed against them.

Tiffany stares up at me now, her cold eyes speckled black and white in their centers, like a guppy's tail. "What," she says flatly.

"Mega Glue Stick, please," I say and point.

She gives me the once-over, her eyes taking in the whole of me, moving from head to toe and then back to head, like a scanner. She's cute, I think. Her hair, thick and brown, looks edible. When she grudgingly leans over for the glue, I lick my forefinger and gently touch a piece of dandruff stuck to the back of her blouse. The sight of it clinging to my finger causes my eyes to water; it makes saliva pool up inside my mouth. I wipe the white flake onto my pant leg and take the glue from her.

"Thank you," I say and walk back to my project.

I uncap the glue stick, spin the dial to adjust the size, and start smearing it all over the poster board. When no one is looking, I raise the Mega Glue Stick up to my mouth and take a bite. I start to take another bite when I notice Tiffany watching me from her end of the table. As though it were a phantom limb, I feel the antenna I don't yet have reach over and pat her on the head, letting her know that everything is all right, that with every passing day I'm feeling a little stronger, and that any day now I'll be slithering out of here under my own steam, disappearing into the dark and clammy night.

Will Clarke

THE PENTECOSTAL HOME

FOR FLYING CHILDREN

aby oil and iodine works way better than Crisco," Tamara Cooksey admonished her fellow cheerleaders. Then to prove her point, she hiked up her cheerleading skirt, pulled down the left side of her bright yellow bloomers, and revealed a stripe of fluorescent white skin on her otherwise mahogany hip. "See, look at that tan line."

Tamara Cooksey was Shreveport's version of Christie Brinkley. She was blond and famous. Tamara's double-decker smile and her savage tan were sure signs of hope for our hard-luck town. After all, she had sprung up from all the chaos and shame brought upon us in the seventies, just as pure and radiant as a lotus bloom growing from a pile of dung. She was one of the best things that Shreveport had going for it in an otherwise very grim time in our history.

Tamara Cooksey had dedicated her life to tanning and cheerleading. When she wasn't practicing her pom-pom routines, she was lying out, making sure that she was the darkest girl with the blondest hair in all of Shreveport.

You could always tell when she was sunbathing because there, high above the Cookseys' ranch-style house, would be a flock of circling buzzards. However, upon closer inspection, you'd see that those weren't buzzards at all; they were a flock of flying teenage boys—the abandoned sons of the Redbird. The boys would fly over Tamara Cooksey, as she lay there all greased up and glistening in her string bikini. They would shout stupid teenage-boy things like, "Look-see, look-see, it's sexy Tamara Cooksey!"

Some days the boys would hoot and holler. Other days, they'd just fly in circles, with one or two diving to take a closer look. Sometimes they would shout things that were profound if not a little odd, like, "The seed of God is within all of us!"

Other times, they'd shout profane and disturbing things, like, "Hey, Tamara Cooksey! Suck it!"

Some of the flying boys, the gentler ones, tried to shower Tamara with rose petals. They were crestfallen when the wind carried the flurry of velvet-red petals into the backyard of Tamara's neighbors instead of bathing her in their beauty.

One petal, however, did drift down to her, and it landed on her belly button. This made Tamara laugh. So the next day, in an effort to thrill Tamara Cooksey even more, the boys stole thousands of Hershey's kisses and poured them on her as she lay out. The silver kisses pelted her, bringing huge, red welts to her perfect tan skin. Tamara had to cover her head with her beach towel and run inside to escape the chocolate hailstorm.

Afraid that they might have hurt their earthbound crush, the boys never showered her with anything ever again. Instead, they settled on circling high above, as she lay there, glistening and sweating, in the midst of her father's tomato garden.

It was Mr. Cooksey's tomato plants that kept the Redbird brothers far away from Tamara. The flying boys knew that all Redbird children were deathly allergic to any plant in the nightshade family— tomatoes, bell peppers, eggplants, even potatoes. The mere fumes given off by the leaves and stalks of a nightshade could drop a Redbird child from the sky and kill him. So the boys flew high above Mr. Cooksey's tomato garden and rode the thermals as they spied on his sylphy daughter with stolen binoculars and deer rifle scopes. Like the rest of Shreveport, the Redbirds had to admire Tamara Cooksey from afar.

———

In 1984, Shreveport, Louisiana, was experiencing a woeful lack of economic growth, turbulent race relations, and a rash of flying teenagers. The airborne bastards were the offspring of the Redbird—a handsome alien half-breed who had once graced the cover of *Life* magazine for rescuing Chicago from the Stalinizer—a radioactive cosmonaut who could shoot lasers from his mouth.

Unfortunately, the Redbird didn't possess the necessary might to be a major-league superhero. In the world of superpowers, flight was pretty much table stakes. Who couldn't fly? Flying was just the delivery method, a mode of transportation for real superpowers like invincibility, colossal strength, or energy blasts. You couldn't very well *fly* a supervillain to death. Without invincibility and superstrength, how could you ever stop a nuclear missile? Sure, the Redbird looked pretty up there doing loopty-loops in the sky wearing those bright red tights, but other than marshaling Fourth of July parades, he really wasn't much use in America's fight against superevil. So the Redbird was relegated to working in the superhero farm leagues. He was banished from New York and assigned to Shreveport.

Our town welcomed the Redbird with more than open arms. Everyone loved the idea that we had our very own superhero to look after us. We didn't care if all he could do was fly. That was more than any of us could do.

In fact, the Redbird united our city with hope. We loved this alien half-breed with his magic red hair and his black mask, and this love we had for him overflowed from our hearts and spread to one another. Redbird mania transcended racial lines and mended our violent histories with one another. The Redbird allowed us to see the good in everyone— black, white, rich or poor. The Redbird's reign ushered in a golden age for Shreveport. We became a city known for our brotherly love and dreamlike prosperity.

However, as the years passed, it became apparent that the Redbird had moved to Shreveport for less-than-savory reasons. Turns out the Redbird came to our town not just for the easy work, but for our chronically bored housewives, our prodigal daughters, and our all-too-easily seduced Baptist Ladies Prayer Circle.

By the time we figured out that the Redbird was turning us all into pillars of salt, he up and flew away—leaving his lovers' hearts ragged, his redheaded babies abandoned, and our city unprotected.

———

The Pentecostal Home for Flying Children was founded by Pauline Pritchard, a barren Pentecostal woman with long gray hair that hung to her ankles when she took it down at night. One day while eating a dipped cone at the Dairy Queen, Pauline Pritchard heard a terrible mewling sound coming from the restaurant's dumpsters. So she walked over to the trash, still licking her ice cream, thinking it was perhaps the screams of feral cats mating, but the sounds were loud enough and human enough to press her concern.

When Pauline opened the dumpster lid, she dropped her ice cream cone and screamed. There among the greasy wrappers and the industrial-sized mayonnaise jars was a naked baby boy with red locks that danced and shone like the fire of the Pentecost.

The baby was crying just as loud as Pauline was now screaming. Then something happened that took Pauline's screams away: The wailing infant began to float like a soap bubble out of the trash bin, drifting into the air above Pauline's considerable mound of gray hair. Pauline quickly removed the pale brown cardigan that she had just bought at TG&Y.

Pauline jumped, jumped, jumped—swatting at the infant with her sweater before finally netting him out of the air. She then swaddled the child in the sweater and ran as fast as her ankle-length skirt would let her.

———

"The good Lord has answered my prayers just like He answered Sarah and Abraham's." Pauline pulled her makeshift blanket away from the baby's face to show her husband the redhead she had just found.

"We should call the police." Jeffery Pritchard put his finger into the baby's tender fist and shook it ever so gently. "Someone's probably missing this little fella."

"They left him in the dumpster, Jeffery."

"It's the right thing to do."

"Jesus gave him to me."

"All I'm saying is that you can't just up and take a baby."

"I didn't take him."

"Then what do you call it?

"I found him like Pharaoh's daughter found Moses in the basket."

If you had ever dared to ask Pauline Pritchard if she was submissive to her husband as it says to be in Ephesians, she would have been wildly indignant that you had even asked such a question.

"My husband is my master," Pauline would have said without a whiff of irony. And Jeffery would have agreed.

"I wear the pants around here!" he would have barked.

While Jeffery Pritchard may have worn the well-starched pants in that marriage, it was Pauline who brandished the fiery iron. In short, Jeffery Pritchard never called the police and Pauline named the boy Zaccheus.

One night when Pauline was washing Zaccheus in the kitchen sink, she was given a word of faith—a message straight from the Holy Ghost. Pauline hosed off the baby with the vegetable sprayer and ran into the garage where her husband Jeffery was repairing the lawnmower.

"The Lord! He spoke to me!" Pauline held the dripping baby to her chest.

"Calm down, woman. You'll drop the baby."

"He said we should open our home to all the Redbird's babies!"

"Well." Jeffery looked into the engine filter and shook it. "Then I guess we better get busy."

Being a man of exuberant faith, Jeffery Pritchard painted a sign and hung it on his front porch that very night. The sign alerted the brokenhearted harlots of Shreveport that the Pentecostal Home for Flying Children was now open for business and ready to receive their newborn sins.

From that point on, the Pritchards' doorbell rang at all hours of the night and day. Every time they unfastened the seven locks and seven bolts on their big blue front door, there stood a shorn-haired Baptist woman, a painted Methodist, a pants-wearing Presbyterian, a cleavage-baring Catholic, an ankle-flaunting Lutheran, a drunk Episcopalian, a teenage Pentecostal, a divorced Jewess, a lock-jawed Seventh-Day Adventist, a black-eyed Mormon—all holding crying babies or struggling toddlers in their arms.

Sister Pauline gathered up the flying babies from their mothers. Despite Pauline's warmth and grace, there was often very little said in the exchange. Sometimes the women would tell Pauline the child's name. Sometimes they would be weeping so hard that Pauline had to pry the child from the mother's arms, and then politely shut the door. Each handoff was painful both for the mother and for Pauline. Because now that Pauline's heart was full of babies, she could feel the sting of these women's tears as if they were her own.

Pauline's husband and master, Jeffery, had wanted to splash the weeping mothers with holy water and cleanse them with prayer, but Pauline broke with her code of wifely obedience.

"Don't you say a word to them, Jeffery."

"They brought it on themselves, fornicating and carrying on like that." He mixed a flask of holy water imported all the way from Galilee with a bucket of tap water.

"Maybe so. But that's between them and the Lord and their husbands."

"A little splash would do them good."

"Don't, Jeffery. I'm asking you, don't."

———

As the flying babies filled the Pritchard house, Pauline rejoiced in the squalling, the feeding, and the diapers. Her house was blessed with chubby redheaded babies everywhere just as the Lord had promised. As the Redbird babies grew, they learned how to walk and talk, and of course, fly. This made keeping them out of harm's way almost impossible, but somehow the Pritchards managed to do it.

Their biggest problem was when the children slept. The babies would float out of their beds while dreaming and sometimes fall to the floor in a start. Once a red-haired babe drifted out of an open second-story window, but luckily for him, he landed on the boughs of the Pritchards' magnolia tree, where Jeffery found him sleeping the next morning.

Flying babies were a much bigger problem to take care of than any of us would have ever imagined. And soon the babies were all over the place, bumping their noggins, busting their lips, knocking out their teeth, and breaking every little delicate thing that Pauline had ever loved. But Pauline Pritchard was a faithful and industrious woman who loved the Lord and those wayward children. She would sit in her rocker on the front porch of her enormous old home, speaking in tongues and crocheting for the babies. She would pour her prayers into pink and baby blue tethers that she fastened to the children's ankles and bedposts to keep them from floating away in the night. During the day Pauline would gather up the babies by their tethers and carry them around like a bunch of squirming balloons. It was a sight to behold, and eventually a now-famous photo of Pauline and her tethered babies made the cover of the *Shreveport Times*.

To remedy the bumps and bruises of the babies' midair collisions, Pauline had Jeffery staple-gun goosedown pillows to the ceilings of their house. She also used donated quilts as wallpaper and she glued down bushels of disregarded stuffed animals to cushion the floors. Pauline Pritchard amazed us with her maternal ingenuity, and there was a time there that we almost admired her for it.

The real mystery for most of us was how Pauline got all those flying babies potty trained. We can all remember a time when the Pentecostal Home reeked of piss and poo. The stains were everywhere: on the pillowed ceilings, the stuffed-animal floors, the padded walls, and the tattered yarn restraints. Bits of who-knows-what were forever caught in Pauline's hair, and the stains were eternally splattered all over Jeffery's coveralls. How Pauline and Jeffery Pritchard took care of all those crying, pooping, suckling, slobbering, flying babies was surely a miracle of God's own hand—at least that's what Pauline told everyone.

Apparently, she had made some kind of blood covenant with God, and that's why she was able to take care of all those flying babies like she did. It's also why she rechristened the children with biblical names of famous sinners like Cain, Bathsheba, and Lot. Pauline gave the children the most unwanted names in the Bible to forever remind them that they, too, had been born unwanted, and that the only way to make their lives right with God was by washing away the sins of their parents.

While it was disconcerting for most of us to call a three-year-old girl in pigtails Jezebel, and her adorable baby brother Onan, we did appreciate Pauline and Jeffery Pritchard's hard work. By taking in the Redbird bastards, the Pritchards allowed our families to heal. The Pentecostal Home for Flying Children offered many of us a certain kind of grace. So we all pulled together and everyone did what they could to help out. Some of us made cash donations to the cause, while others donated canned foods and clothes. It wasn't cheap keeping all those flying children clothed and fed. Eventually we had to resort to sending our own kids out to sell popcorn and candy bars door-to-door while our churches raised money with weekly bingo nights, cakewalks, and car washes. We did what we had to do to keep the lights on at the Home. We did it because we had to, because we had to keep our mistakes in a place where we could live with them.

———

From the moment that Pauline had wrapped Zaccheus Redbird in her sweater, he had clung very closely to her heart. Though Pauline would have denied it, everyone knew that this child was her favorite. She was often heard around town telling the boy that one day he "would bring the devil to his knees." Pauline Pritchard saw something special in Zaccheus, something that the other Redbirds didn't have, and that was why she named the boy for a redeemed tax collector instead of a whoremaster or a sodomite. It's also why she kept all his baby teeth in the jingle-jangledy lockets that she wore on her wrists despite her religion's strict rules against jewelry.

Now that Zaccheus, or Zac, as his classmates called him, had entered high school, he was living proof that Pentecostalism could redeem even the most wretched among us. Zac, though he was quite obviously the Redbird's son, refused to fly. Which to Pauline proved that Zac had somehow conquered his father's wicked ways.

Zac refused to indulge in any sort of pride that would put him above the rest of us or do anything that might seem cruel. Instead, he did as he was told: He sold Gideon Bibles in front of K&B Drugs to raise money for the Home, he took care of Sister Pauline when she lost her leg to the diabetes, he troubled over scripture and his schoolwork in equal measure. He wasn't just respectful of everyone he met, he was kind—effortlessly kind in the way that one would imagine that Jesus must have been to lepers and whores and the like. And because of this, we all thought that Zaccheus Redbird was the biggest weirdo we had ever met.

———

"Why don't you ever fly?"

"I don't want to talk about it."

"Your brothers landed on my roof today."

"I'm sorry. They shouldn't do that."

"Don't apologize. I think they're funny."

———

Why and how Tamara Cooksey fell so hard for Zaccheus Redbird was not public knowledge. Tamara for once in her life was keeping her mouth shut. Which was odd, because usually Tamara was a one-girl power station broadcasting Tamara Cooksey's ever-fascinating, always-scintillating life twenty-four hours a day.

Typically, Tamara Cooksey held court in the cafeteria, where she would report on the most intimate and minute details of her teenage life: the brutal frequency of her menstrual cramps, the adorable iced cookies that she made for the JV football team, her need to make herself throw up after her mother made her eat meat loaf, the kind of toilet paper she used to vandalize Lacey Monroe's house, the number of lipsticks she had filched from Selber's Department Store.

But when Tamara's friends asked her about Zac, she would only wink and say, "Nunya."

Eventually, her friends grew weary of this response, and they mounted a full-fledged interrogation with Tamara's best friend, Holly Peterson, leading the charge.

"Oh, come on, Tam. Don't be a whore. Tell us about you and Zac," Holly said one day in the locker room after a pep rally.

"I already told you. Nunya. Nunya business."

"What's the matter? Are you embarrassed to be dating one of those Pentecostal flying retards or something?"

"Embarrassed?"

"Yeah, embarrassed."

"Holly, I'm not the one stomping around out there with my big white thunder thighs and cellulite. So, no, I'm not embarrassed."

There are words that can never be taken back or forgiven. For Holly Ferguson, *thunder thighs* and *cellulite* were three of those words. From that day forward, she never spoke to Tamara Cooksey again.

So that left the rest of Shreveport to pry where we shouldn't be prying, to figure out how someone like Tamara Cooksey ended up with someone like Zaccheus Redbird. Ten thousand notes were passed back and forth in civics and algebra classes. Two hundred forty-two malicious theories were whispered by concerned mothers at PTA meetings. Seven hundred seventy-seven phone calls were placed by the cheerleaders alone. Zac and Tamara's secret romance became the impolite topic to broach at potluck suppers and church picnics all over town.

———

"I. Love. You."

"Shhh, my dad will hear you."

"I don't care."

"You'll care when he comes in here and shoots your pecker off."

———

The now-famous phrase "beat you like a redheaded stepchild" was actually coined in Shreveport. It referred, of course, to the Redbird children, and Jeffery and Pauline's tough-love efforts to set them on the straight and narrow. Jeffery never spared the rod to spoil the child. He'd take his belt off and whip their little hides as red as their hair if he had to. And not a day went by that Pauline Pritchard wasn't seen chasing one of the flying children down the street with a flyswatter, and when she finally caught the offending brat, she would beat the devil out of the child. Some hippies actually protested the Pritchards' public whippings of the flying children. The hippies made signs and picketed the Pentecostal Home. They sang folk songs and shouted, "Free the Baby Birds!" Nobody paid them much attention, though, so the hippies eventually took their free-loving, no-deodorant-wearing ways down to New Orleans.

Now history has proven that those hippies were bigger idiots than we initially thought. In fact, the Pritchards were perhaps not strict enough with their Redbird charges, as Jeffery Pritchard met a dubious end in June 1985 when he supposedly fell from the roof of the Pentecostal Home and broke his thick neck.

The Pritchards had dedicated their lives to putting the fear of God into those Redbird bastards, but foster parents can only do so much. Once most of the Redbirds reached their teenage years, their alien blood somehow trumped their strict upbringing—the lone exception being good-hearted Zaccheus.

The problem with most of the flying children was that you never knew what one of them would do. They were constantly pulling pranks. The boys' favorite stunt was to fly up behind people, grabbing their victims underneath the armpits and taking them fast and high into the sky. All the while their victims would be kicking and screaming, terrified that they would fall to their death. The Redbirds would then drop their victims into a swimming pool or a shallow lake. The little bastards laughed maniacally, as if this life-threatening attack was just one big joke. Many of their victims reported that their flying attackers smelled of Pabst Blue Ribbon and marijuana.

The Redbird girls were actually worse than their brothers. They had no shame. They would strip down naked and fly all over town, through grocery stores, church services, weddings, even funerals. With their long, red Pentecostal hair, they thought of themselves as flying Lady Godivas, but they were no better than common strippers and prostitutes to most of us.

The Redbird girls were notorious for floating in front of our teenage sons' windows, knocking at the glass and giggling. When the boys unlatched the windows to let them in, the Redbird girls would fly away. This kind of teasing was meant to drive our sons crazy, and it did. Oh, how it did.

It was during one of these stunts that Bobby Tyler discovered the full power of the nightshades. One night, Salome Redbird was hovering by his teenage son's window, pressing her breasts up against the glass, torturing his son like the devil's own succubus. Bobby grabbed the closest thing he could find to throw at the tramp. He grabbed a rotting tomato.

"Get!" He hummed the tomato at the girl, hitting her square in the chest. The tomato exploded into a fury of seeds and juice, killing the girl and crashing her into his wife's pink azaleas below.

Our town had run out of patience for those flying freaks, and now that Pauline had the diabetes and Jeffery was dead, something had to be done. Those scurrilous Redbirds were using the Pentecostal Home for Flying Children as a haven for their misdeeds and their liquor-sloshing parties. Meanwhile, crazy old Pauline Pritchard, with her one good leg, stayed locked away in her room, watching Oral Roberts and Pat Robertson, ignoring her duties to us and her promises to God.

It was finally time to rid our city of this scourge. So we planted gardens full of red, yellow, and green peppers. We grew tomatoes of every variety: Big Boys, Yellow Brandywines, Cherokee Purples—you name it. There were over fifty varieties of eggplants growing all over our fair city. Our ladyfolk kept tomato sandwiches in their purses, and we all kept handfuls of new potatoes in the glove compartments of our cars, just in case.

Eventually, the Redbirds got the message, and interestingly enough, none of them thought it was very funny to fly naked through the funerals for their own brothers and sisters. We, the mere mortals of Shreveport, had finally taught the Redbird bastards a lesson: Don't mess with good people.

———

"I wanna run away."

"Tamara."

"I'm serious."

"I can't."

"They're going to kill you.

"Trust me, they won't."

———

The Nightshade Retaliation Program was the city-sponsored initiative for "growing and throwing" nightshade vegetables at Redbird delinquents. State laws were even amended to clear any citizen of murder charges if they had to resort to throwing a nightshade in self-defense. This program was hugely successful. It only took five nightshade throwings for all the Redbirds to pick up and fly away from Shreveport—well, all except for one, Zaccheus, who was so kind and mannerly that most of us forgot that he even was a Redbird.

However, the terror that the Redbirds had raged over our town for all those years had obviously affected the tender minds of our own teenagers, and many of our kids had a hard time turning the other cheek here, which would explain why they had such a hard time with the last Redbird dating Captain Shreve's head cheerleader, no matter how nice he was or how much he refused to fly—which would also explain why our otherwise very Christian kids left eggplants and death threats in Zaccheus Redbird's locker.

———

On August 13, 1986, Zaccheus Redbird was with Tamara Cooksey, holding hands at the Circle K on Youree Drive. They were both drinking Icees and smiling when Holly "Thunder-thighs" Ferguson snuck up behind them.

Holly Ferguson held her breath and lobbed a Hazel Mae yellow tomato at Zaccheus Redbird's head. The golden fruit splattered against Zac's skull and ran down his neck in yellow gobs of seed and slime.

That's when the holy kindness of Zaccheus Redbird must have curdled into biblical vengeance. Because he exploded into hundreds of redbirds—cardinals, to be exact. Tamara screamed and covered her face, while Holly Ferguson dropped to the ground, scared that the birds would scratch out her eyes for what she had just done, but the screeching flock of cardinals flew past her. They flew high into the sky, multiplying with each flap of their wings until the flock was in the millions.

The skies turned red and our blood turned white. Millions upon millions of redbirds pecked and ravaged our tomatoes, peppers, and eggplants. They even pulled up our potato plants and flew away with them. It was like a plague of the Old Testament kind.

After tearing our gardens and yards apart, the waves of cardinals once again darkened our skies, but this time they blanketed our homes, our parks, and our cars in oceans of horrible splatters. By nightfall, they had nearly destroyed our town.

Now that there wasn't a single nightshade vegetable left in Shreveport, we waited under our beds with our guns loaded and our doors bolted. We waited for the Redbird Children to return and take their revenge on us. We waited for weeks, but they never came.

Some people say that they saw the cardinals swarm together that night and reform into Zaccheus Redbird, and it was a reborn Zaccheus who stole Tamara Cooksey from us. Others say that the cardinals landed on the Cookseys' front lawn, and when Tamara went outside to see them, to say good-bye to what was left of Zac, the birds tore her to pieces and flew away with her remains in their tiny yellow talons. Some people swear that Holly Ferguson, a half-eaten box of Ding-Dongs, and a piano wire were somehow involved in Tamara Cooksey's disappearance. Somewhere between the gossip, the legends, and the lies is the truth, but we won't go looking for it now. It flew away with the redbirds.

Owen King

THE MEERKAT

Washington, D.C. (Now)

After Wade Hanes had registered himself with the proper authorities, sworn an oath to use his powers for good and to protect the innocent, submitted to a battery of blood drawings, measurements, and intrusive questions, the Homeland Security official who was to act as his liaison, an elderly, choleric woman named Doris Krimsky, took him to a steak house called Shuster's on K Street. In her dark purple pantsuit and with her gray hair pulled back tight, Doris was diminutive and unremarkable, but something about her warned people on the street to give her a wide berth.

She reminded Wade of one of those rigid little antique chairs you see in roped-off Victorian tableaus. He thought if he touched her, either she'd clatter to the floor in a pile of tinder or an alarm would go off.

Two steps inside the restaurant, Doris rasped at the bartender for a gimlet, pronto. When the drink arrived at their leather-padded booth in the back room, she glared at the martini glass and opened her mouth wide enough to say *ahhhh*, revealing a cavern of gray, capped teeth, as well as a pale, filmy tongue. The liquor rose from the glass in a glimmering, arcing stream—hesitated—then lashed into her mouth, and hit the back of her throat with a gurgle.

The old woman rocked back and gave a moan of relief.

When she sat forward again Doris caught the expression on the other side of the table. "Don't worry. They know all about our kind here. You can order whatever you want. Friskies or whatever."

"I'm not a cat, I'm herpestid," said Wade, and immediately wished that he hadn't.

"That doesn't impress me," said Doris. She snapped her fingers for another gimlet. "And get Morris here some tuna!"

Over lunch she explained that the superhero business was a lot like newscasting. You worked your way up through bigger and bigger markets. "You pay your dues for a year or two in Cleveland, and then you move on to Tampa. After that, Chicago, and after that, if you're lucky, you could be called up to the Atom League and get national exposure."

"That doesn't concern me really. I like it in Cleveland. I mean, it's Cleveland—the river caught on fire once—but you know." Wade shrugged. "It's home."

"Well, the brass thinks there's a real niche for someone like you, someone who appeals strongly to the youth market. Good for the public trust. Kids love cats, you know."

Wade spent a couple of minutes using his fork to slide the block of tuna around on the plate.

When he risked a glance at Doris, he found she was watching him intently with her arms crossed, while before her, seemingly of their own accord, her fork and knife went about the business of carving up a slab of rare prime rib. (There was something undeniably collegial about the way the instruments labored together, the fork stabbing and holding, the knife sawing briskly, then turning over flat to press down on the meat so the other could withdraw. After, the two would linger in the air for a moment, as if admiring their work, before recommencing on the next cut.)

"So what's the problem?" Now the silverware stopped and gently lay down on the tablecloth. The old woman frowned at him. There was something sad in the set of her mouth.

They were alone in the back room. The light from the wall sconce spilled a dismal orange puddle across the table. Beneath the droll tinkling of the player piano in the corner, the blaring of horns could be heard from the street.

"I just wish it was something more, you know. Normal." Wade paused before adding by way of a clarification: "That I was something more normal."

The old woman shook her head. "You mean like me? You know what happens when I sleep? My dreams rearrange the pictures on the wall. It's goddamned creepy."

"Yeah, but meerkats—they're kind of—"

"—freaky?" finished Doris.

"Thank you," said Wade. "I might have used the word 'different.' As in, Meerkats are a 'different' species than human beings. As in, I am not exactly human anymore. Physically. Emotionally." He took his napkin from his lap and dropped it over his untouched tuna. "In every way."

"You're freaky."

"Okay."

"You're a freak. Just like me. You have to accept that. You know what my second husband said to me before he left? He said he couldn't live with a person who used their mind to wipe their ass."

Silence.

"What the hell are you talking about?" Wade asked.

"I'm talking about you and whoever it is that's giving you the long face. I'm talking about the love that dare not speak its name: relationships between individuals like us and regular folks. Paranormal beings work long hours. They're famous. Sometimes they have to travel to other planets, other dimensions, back in time. There are groupies. Regular folks can't appreciate the pressures. It's a big fat recipe for dysfunction. The sooner you accept that, the happier you're going to be."

Excusing himself, Wade retreated to the bathroom. He washed his face and took several deep breaths.

The thirty-year-old man in the mirror above the sink did not appear unusual or exceptional in any way: white, thin-cheeked, dark-eyed, and blond. The only change to his physiognomy was a pair of downy brown muttonchops that clashed with the fairer hair on top. They had sprouted virtually overnight and he had kept them. Wade actually sort of liked the chops; he thought they made him look like the bassist for a rock band. A production engineer by trade, Wade had never been all that outgoing. He was the man in the booth, behind the board, wearing the chunky headphones, watching all the action on a dozen monitors, safely shielded behind an inch of soundproof glass. But now Wade was on the other side, being pushed onto the stage, expected to perform. It was discomfiting.

Still, the person in the mirror looked to be—save for the whimsical facial hair—essentially the same as the one who had flown to Zimbabwe four months earlier.

"It isn't your fault, Wade," Heather had said to him the day before. "But it isn't mine either."

"Can't we try and roll with this for a little longer?" he had asked.

"*This?*" Heather laughed, and then she had snorted, once, twice, and started to weep. She looked so small in her puffy pink jacket, the one he had given her for Christmas the year before. Her chestnut hair was still damp from the shower. "There is no *this*. I'm a grown woman, Wade, and you—you're not *you* anymore. You're this thing now. And I'll always love you, but I can't be with—"

Heather looked away from him, down at the mitten she was squeezing in her hand. She brought the mitten to her face and blew her nose into it.

"—an animal," she finished in a soft voice. "I can't, Wade. I'm sorry."

Heather blew her nose on the mitten again. She stared at it. It was knitted, black with a pattern of silvery snowflakes. "Shit!" she screamed, and threw it in the trash.

After that Heather gave a last sob, and kissed him on the cheek, and left, carrying her suitcase with her mittened left hand, the bare right balled at her side.

Now, here he was, in Washington, with this old witch.

And he had a hell of a pair of sideburns.

Wade returned to the table.

"Look, I have two questions for you, and I need you to be honest."

The old woman grunted. Her empty martini glass rose from the table and floated away in the direction of the bar to be refilled.

"Doesn't anyone—in the business—have a traditional relationship?"

"Not that I know of," said Doris. "I'm sorry, kiddo. That's just the way it is. Maybe there's no good reason. Maybe they just never look at you the same way after they see you flying around in a codpiece on television."

The glass returned from the bar and dropped to the table with an abrupt thump, sprinkling the tablecloth with gin. Wade ran a hand thought his hair.

"Well?"

Wade glanced up.

"What's your other question?" asked Doris.

"Oh." He cleared his throat. "What do you mean you 'wipe your ass with your mind'?"

For the first time during the entire meal, Doris raised one of her arms. She made a circular motion with her index finger. "I don't use my hands to take the paper off the roll. Why would I?"

Why, indeed.

Outside, it was hailing. Doris and Wade paused under the trembling awning of Shuster's to say good-bye. A funereal line of black sedans with diplomatic plates idled at the corner stoplight while the hail pinged off roofs and trunks. The naked branches of the street trees rattled. A group of young aides raced down the sidewalk, smiling and laughing, their coats billowing and their ties streaming while the white pebbles bounced harmlessly off their broad shoulders.

"I hope they trip and break their noses," said Doris. "Goddamned showoffs."

She told him that his costume would be waiting for him at the Cleveland offices of the FBI.

Cleveland (Before)

Seven months earlier, before Heather invites Wade to come with her to Africa, his knowledge of meerkats is limited to the animated film The Lion King, *which features one of the adorable, furry scamperers in a supporting role, voiced by Nathan Lane. Working from this basis Wade assumes—not unreasonably—that since they are called meerkats, they are a type of cat. A very cute, very clever, very theatrical, and slightly effeminate type of cat.*

Heather Rudolph, his girlfriend of more than a year, is an associate director of the Cleveland Zoological Society (CZS). She rolls her eyes when Wade relates these observations.

THE MEERKAT

Meerkats are not cats, she explains, they are herpestids, or in the more common usage, a type of mongoose. "It's true that meerkats are damned cute and damned clever, but trust me, they're not the kind of cute and clever that you can teach to do tricks or cuddle with or keep as a pet.

"They live in the Kalahari Desert, one of the harshest, most varied environments in the world. Brutally cold at night, insanely hot during the day, predators everywhere, scant resources. That's what these animals deal with every day. And they dish it out, too. Meerkats are cold-blooded killers."

"Maybe," says Wade, "we should rename them 'fearkats.'"

Heather pinches Wade in a sensitive place. Wade swears. The production engineer and the zoologist are lying in bed. They are naked.

"I'm serious, Wade. I mean, we don't call their families 'families.' We call them 'mobs.' They eat scorpions. Nothing that eats a scorpion can be considered even remotely effeminate. Meerkats are badass." *She pauses before repeating for emphasis,* "Badass."

"Hey, you don't have to convince me. I'll see for myself."

"Really? You'll go?"

The CZS has awarded Heather a fellowship to visit a meerkat study project in Zimbabwe and make a short film to show at the opening of a new children's wing at the Metroparks Zoo. It was her idea that instead of hiring a freelancer, Wade could take a couple of weeks off from his job at KCLE-News and engineer the shoot.

"Of course. Me, you, a bunch of meerkats, camera equipment. If that's not a recipe for a party, I don't know what is."

Saturday night has turned into Sunday morning. The covers are bunched at their feet and they are facing each other, holding hands in the space between. Wade can't read Heather's expression in the dark, but he meets her eyes, which are a sweet, faded blue, the blue of swimming pools in old photographs.

Wade loves those eyes, the way they brighten when Heather talks about her job, about other species and the remarkable ways they adapt to survive. She is the most earnest person he has ever known. Heather doesn't joke about things; Heather believes in things. She believes in the mission of the CZS as a means to educate the public about the need to preserve natural habitats far beyond Cleveland, Ohio. She believes that the Browns will win the Super

Bowl in their lifetime. Heather even believes that it is possible to make friends with squirrels. To this end, she has spent countless hours teaching one particular squirrel that if he scratches on the patio door, she'll feed him nuts out of her hand.

"That squirrel doesn't care about us," Wade told her one night when they were sitting on the couch and, for no particular reason, watching Friends. The squirrel was perched on Heather's knee, rolling a nut between his rapid little squirrel paws and staring at the television. "He just wants to see what Ross is up to. Friends is all he really cares about."

Heather squinted at him. "Why would a squirrel want to watch Friends?"

So her sense of humor sucks. So what. What has a sense of humor ever accomplished in the world, except to put people at ease about all the stuff they can't do anything about, and make it okay not even to try?

Their only problem is that in the face of everything Heather brings to bear in her life and work—all that dogged certainty—Wade fears that he is the one thing that will never ratify her faith.

In bed, her sexuality overwhelms Wade, the way she loses herself in the act, rocking on top of him, pressing one of her hard little fists against his chest while the skin at her neck flares red. "Let me feel it," she says, and Wade surely does his best, but in the year they have been dating, his best has never been enough, and this gnaws at him, at his basic sense of rightness.

Heather has dedicated her life to saving the animals, all of them, even the little weird ones, like meerkats; the least she deserves is an orgasm, and not just any orgasm, a screamer, the kind of orgasm that rattles the windowpanes and scares the people beyond the next wall.

But Wade cannot seem to give her even an orgasm-orgasm.

"What's wrong?" Heather leans into him.

"Nothing," says Wade. "Not a thing."

They kiss. They kiss again.

Heather slips back. Wade coughs. She squeezes his shoulder.

"I bet meerkats are the sexual dynamos of the animal world," Wade jokes.

When Heather responds, she is not joking: "It depends on how you quantify 'dynamo.' If you mean, can a meerkat male go three times in one night, then the answer is definitely yes. Why do you ask?"

"Just curious," says Wade.

There is a scraping noise outside—Heather's pet squirrel. Wade tells her they might as well feed him and pack it in for the night.

————

But an hour later Wade is still awake. He leaves Heather, smiling in her sleep, and goes into the living room. He sits on the couch and sips a glass of milk. On a shelf across from the couch sits a row of National Geographic *issues, bookended by a small stuffed animal with a brief, foxy tail—a meerkat, Wade guesses, drawing on his memory of* The Lion King.

He rises and plucks the creature off the shelf, examines it: a lanky, pot-bellied creature with dainty paws, a solemn stitched line of a mouth, and large, glassy marbles for eyes. To Wade it looks like nothing so much as a sweet little fox, but a manufacturer's tag on the tail confirms that it is, in fact, a "Meerkat of the Kalahari."

"Grrr," says Wade, and jerks the stuffed animal at his own neck. "No! God, no!" Wade thrashes, pressing the meerkat against his jugular, adding a series of flesh-ripping sound effects and munching noises, and flops back on the couch, still fighting helplessly against the stuffed animal. After a moment Wade gives a death tremor and goes limp.

He lies there, considering.

"Nah, I don't believe it." Wade raises the meerkat up and looks into its shining black eyes. "You're no killer, are you, buddy?"

Cleveland (Now)

That winter the Meerkat became a popular, if somewhat ironic, celebrity in Cleveland. Not since the early seventies had the city been the home of a superhero, and the novelty was exciting.

(In that earlier instance, Fire Water, the famously combustible superheroine who later went on to join the Atom League, was a divisive figure. Lorraine Leakey, a tugboat captain engulfed by the toxic blaze that broke out on the surface of the Cuyahoga River in 1969, only to be reborn as Fire Water, was a vaguely female-shaped, seven-foot-tall body of flaming water. Although she amassed an impeccable record of public service, and once saved the city from complete annihilation by a gigantic, malfunctioning Soviet Nuclear Defense Robot known as Peaceful Ivan, many Cleveland natives regarded her as a negative symbol. As Richard Pryor famously remarked, "I'll tell you what, Jack: only in fucking Cleveland would they have a superhero made out of pollution.")

There were initially only eyewitness reports:

In November, a jewelry thief was found buried up to his neck in a sandbox in a city park. "It was, like, some kind of *manimal*," said the thief, a career criminal named Herman Dingle.

After dropping out the window of a jewelry store to a rear alley, Dingle claimed to have encountered a hissing, spitting man on all fours. This strange individual wore a brown bodysuit, had black pits for eyes, and in one swipe of his short, black claws, disarmed Dingle of his bolt cutters. The thief fled, but made it just to the park across the street. Here, the man in the brown bodysuit knocked the thief to the ground, dragged him to a winter-hardened sandbox, rapidly scratched away the surface crust, plowed a deep trench out of the softer earth beneath, hurled the thief into the hole, and entombed him up to his chin.

It was this display that made the strongest impression on Herman Dingle. "He could dig, this guy. Buried me like a goddamn bone."

The following month a flasher turned himself in at the Fifth Precinct; he said that a "man-beast" had threatened to castrate him.

The deviant, a retired stockbroker named Arnie Carlin, took special note of the way the man in the brown bodysuit ran. He charged at Carlin on all fours, and at the same time, held himself stiff and tense, his butt lifted up and his spine parallel to the ground.

"I could tell that he was unhinged just by the way he ran at me. It's just so, so uncomfortable-looking," said Carlin. "And he made this kind of squawking noise—*aaaaiiiiieeeeeee!* And it was like he didn't have any eyes—just these big dark gaps where there should have been eyes. So when he told me he'd cut off my—*ahem*—unless I went to the police, I wasn't about to put up a fuss. Anything to get away from this weirdo."

The next incident involved a group of children, playing on the upper floor of an abandoned factory when a two-by-four propping open a fire door snapped. The door slammed shut and they were trapped. One quick-thinking young girl, twelve-year-old Carla Mayfield, broke a window with a chunk of masonry and yelled for help. The man in the brown bodysuit came scrambling right up the sheer brick face of the building to rescue them.

"Once he got inside with us he ran at the door on his hands and feet, all funnylike, and knocked it down—*bang!*" said Carla. "And then he kind of, like, sat there? With his hands out in front, like a little bunny, sort of? And he was looking all over the place and going, like, 'clickety-clickety'!"

After this, the man growled at the kids that they shouldn't be playing in abandoned buildings, but Carla said, "It wasn't very scary. It was like he was pretending to be some kind of cat, and that's just silly, for a man to pretend to be a cat."

But the rumors didn't crystallize until the public saw a home video shot by a junior high school teacher on a field trip with her class to see the season's final performance of *The Nutcracker* by the Finnish National Ballet troupe at the Playhouse Square Center of Cleveland State University.

———

One thing the public never glimpsed, however, was the hours that the Meerkat spent before that famous donnybrook at the Finnish Ballet. He passed these hours waiting in a tunnel of his own creation beneath the laboratory of Cleveland State's Nuclear Weapons Department. Via a length of PVC pipe and a drainage grate, the Meerkat eavesdropped on the nefarious goings-on above:

The madman played Wagner for his henchmen. "Get psyched!" he told them in his thick Teutonic accent. "Pump it up!"

Clods of cold dirt rattled down on the Meerkat's shoulders as above him cymbals boiled.

But where was the nuclear trigger?

They were making toasts now. The Meerkat could smell the beer, yeasty and thick. Here was a toast to Hitler. Here was a toast to their immortality. Here was a toast to the death of the Yankee Imperialists.

Supervillains. What a bunch of assholes.

For a moment then, the Meerkat was gone, and it was just Wade in the tunnel, Wade the engineer, Wade from Cleveland, Wade the guy—Just Wade—and he imagined the expression that Heather would be wearing if she were listening. She would be frowning, and have a hand pressed to her temple, as if to prevent her sanity from leaking out. "Who the hell are these people?" she would ask. That it was sort of funny would never occur to her. She was all wonder and no irony, the girl Wade loved. The girl he had lost.

The Meerkat chewed on his claws. His breath drifted away in tiny clouds of steam.

A couple of squirrels had followed him into the tunnel. They chattered and burbled in their squirrel language.

"Yeah, I'm nervous," said the Meerkat to his companions. "The guy's batshit and he's got a nuke. Of course I'm nervous."

This confession seemed to amuse the squirrels. Their chatter rose to a high, giggling pitch.

The Meerkat was about to tell them what he really thought about Ross when the madman screamed, "Behold the nuclear trigger!" and then there was no more time for nonsense with squirrels, no time for anything but action—and so it was that the Meerkat made his true debut.

———

It was during Act I, as the Nutcracker and his toy brigade are locked in combat with the Mouse King and his rodents, that the disturbance occurred. The camera that captured the scene was digital, and it was dark in the auditorium, so the picture we have is somewhat grainy. Blurry heads occasionally bobbed in the bottom foreground of the frame, but the focus kept steadily on the stage.

The dancers twirled and bounded as the strings rose to a violent crescendo. The timpani banged, crashed, and rattled. At stage center the Nutcracker and the Mouse King circled each other. The dancer playing the Nutcracker wore an enormous costumed head fashioned to resemble a classic wooden nutcracker: a grinning, square-toothed mouth, a Vandyke beard, a towering black toque. For his part, the Mouse King wore radar-dish ears and a long, malevolently hooked snout. All around them, tin soldiers and dolls and ghastly black mice were tumbling and feinting and taking wild swings at each other.

The two generals dove at each other, grappled, and fell back as the orchestra dipped into an ominous moan of cellos. While the Nutcracker and the Mouse King circled each other once more, angling for a final strike, the drums began to thunder, and a new trio emerged from stage left at a run.

Two of the men were clad in white lab coats, the third in baggy tweeds. All of them carried pistols, but for the first few seconds at least, this caused no alarm in the audience. Everyone must have assumed that they were reinforcements for the Nutcracker's side.

And the next entrant, the man in the brown bodysuit, hurtling after them on all fours, appeared to be pantomiming the gait of some animal, so the audience must have thought he was on the side of the Mouse King. As his hands and feet carried him forward, the creature's rear end was lifted high, and his spine was so bowed as to give the impression that he had—impossibly—developed a few extra vertebrae.

Three-quarters of the way across the stage the men in the lab coats stopped, turned, and opened fire. The silver pistols, long-barreled, like space-age blunderbusses, spat cobalt-blue tracers. The lasers sizzled and left brief, wavering afterimages on the video.

And a split second later, the target of these blasts—the man in the brown bodysuit, the man who would from this day forward be forever known as "the Meerkat"—leaped.

The Meerkat hung in the air, hung much longer than possible; his claws flashed; his mouth stretched to reveal a jaw of brilliant fangs; and his rigid body uncoiled, like a flicked whip.

During the impossibly long three seconds that the Meerkat floated over the stage, a number of other things happened: A gingerbread man caught a tracer in the leg, gave a howl, dropped the candy cane he had been using to mock-club one of the Mouse King's soldiers, and collapsed into a bank of stage snow; out of sight, in the pit, an anonymous violinist jerked his bow, screeching across the strings; the man in baggy tweeds slipped through the curtain at stage right; and an unidentified male seated in the row ahead of the elementary school class was overheard to wonder, "What the fuck are these Finns doing?"

Then, the Meerkat landed on the first shooter, and his jaws slammed shut with a wet snap, and everyone started screaming.

Cleveland (Now)

By the time the video aired on that night's eleven o'clock news, the Pentagon had released a statement to reassure the public that the Meerkat was a government-sanctioned paranormal being, currently working out of the FBI's Cleveland headquarters. Following up on information from his own sources, the Meerkat had learned that the man in tweeds, Karolis Lichtman, an insane and tenured professor in the Nuclear Weapons Department at Cleveland State, had constructed a nuclear trigger for the purpose of recharging Peaceful Ivan, the gigantic Soviet Nuclear Defense Robot on display in the outdoor palisade of the Cleveland Metroparks Zoo since its circuits were demagnetized back in '72. Lichtman planned to use Peaceful Ivan to raze the city, in what he termed in his journal, "An Act of Aesthetic Cleansing." (In the same entry he listed three other cities to be similarly decimated: Minsk, Magnitogorsk, and Newark.) The two men in lab coats had been Professor Lichtman's loyal doctoral candidates.

Although Professor Lichtman escaped in the chaos—along with the nuclear trigger—the Meerkat apprehended the others. It was just a matter of time, the authorities said, before Lichtman would be taken in as well. (Besides his heavily accented English, the professor was easily identifiable by his snow-white hair, his bird's nest of a beard, his habit of wearing sunglasses at all hours, and the red tattoo of Academician Kurchatov of his right palm.)

In light of all this, when Heather called Wade the following night, he expected congratulations. He had, after all, saved the city.

Instead, she asked him if he had the Browns game on. "Channel seven," she said, "right now."

Wade put it on, and they watched in shared silence while the JumboTron replayed the money shot from the previous evening's ballet.

———

The Meerkat jumped from the body of the first shooter, who was not only incapacitated, but suddenly noseless.

The second man stepped forward, futuristic blunderbuss raised to blast—and staggered back when the Meerkat reared up and hawked a bloody mess in his face. The man in the lab coat lowered the gun as he tried with his free hand to clear his eyes. The severed nose stuck to the gunmen's forehead like a stubby horn. With a flash of black claw the blunderbuss clattered away and the gunman went crashing through the door of a one-sided gingerbread house.

Glittery snow wafted through the air. The dancers froze. On his knees, blood running from the empty hole in the middle of his face and down over his mouth and chin, the first gunman carefully swept a hand around on the stage floor, searching for something. The Meerkat cocked his head at the audience. His mouth was red and his eyes were empty.

It was then that the Nutcracker himself, oversized costume head maniacally grinning, reached out to grab the Meerkat's shoulder, to try to restrain him.

The Meerkat, acting instinctively, swiveled in his fighting crouch and delivered a nutcracker of his own—a straight, sharp jab to the dancer's crotch.

———

GO CRAZY!!

howled the caption beneath the video on the JumboTron, then flashed to add,

HIT 'EM WHERE IT HURTS!!!

It was a frosty January night, and in the tiers of Cleveland Browns Stadium, the home of the Cleveland Browns, the crowd looked like a massive, rippling orange blanket, fifty thousand screaming as one.

———

Down two touchdowns at the start of the fourth quarter, the Browns rallied for seventeen unanswered points to beat the rival Steelers and give life to a new tradition. These same Cleveland Browns would not lose again that season en route to their first NFL Championship since 1964, in the process becoming known as "the Meerkat Mob," joining such legendary forerunners as "the Purple People Eaters" and "the Monsters of the Midway" in gridiron lore. In the fourth quarter of every remaining home game that year the video of the Meerkat's assault on the Nutcracker was replayed on the JumboTron, sending the Browns Faithful into a frenzy and presaging another victory for the hometown team.

"I just became a mascot, didn't I?" Wade said. His ear was numb against the telephone receiver.

"I'm sorry, Wade." He heard her take a deep breath. "Are you all right? I'm worried about you."

Wade said he was doing okay. "Do you want to meet sometime?"

"Wade," said Heather. "Wade."

"Yeah," he said.

Heather blew her nose. "Go Browns?"

"Go Browns."

Kalahari Desert [Before]

For the most part, they are alone—just Wade and Heather and the meerkats.

A collective of zoological societies maintains a small observation center a dozen miles from the village of D— in southern Zimbabwe, on the edge of the Kalahari Desert. It is a bare-bones operation: the observation center's living quarters consist of little more than a rickety one-room house with the desiccated skeletons of scorpions in the corners, and the attached video trailer amounts to a corrugated tin shack outfitted with Wang computers and cassette recording decks.

Heather takes up a viewing position beneath the sprawling canopy of a baobab tree, sitting in a rusted lawn chair and dictating her observations into a handheld tape recorder. Below the baobab runs a scrubby gully and it is here that the community of the local meerkat mob—long acclimated to human observers—plays out. Researchers have named this mob "the Buckaroos."

"Incredible, aren't they?" Heather asks him as they stand beneath the baobab tree.

Wade briefly ponders the creatures darting back and forth below, raising dust, and thinks, Yes, it is incredible. Incredible that we came all this way to film a bunch of furry snakes biting each other in the ass.

For the rest of this day, however, and for most of the next few days running, Wade is too occupied by the technical issues presented by the lack of modern equipment to look closely at the meerkats. It will cost him the better part of a week to clear the junk out of the video trailer and jury-rig a new system from the assorted leftovers and the few pieces he's managed to pick up in Harare. Wade clips wires and autopsies obsolete television monitors for usable chips; he sweats; he develops a purple rash in his armpits. The madness of the work and the days of silence combine to make Wade feel strangely removed, as if the actual world were going on without him, and he were only watching it through a shimmering veil of heat. Since the night back in Cleveland when Heather told him what a breed of inveterate cocksmen meerkats were, Wade has found himself unable to sustain an erection.

"Don't worry," Heather tells him. "It's perfectly normal."

But that's the point, he thinks, crouching on the gritty floor of the trailer, morosely examining a sand-flecked circuit board. He is normal, utterly normal. He is a man whose life's work is to record other people doing things. Heather is a woman of action, a heroine, a savior of the weakest creatures. Wade solders chips and picks through salads of stripped wires and sweats—and sweats and sweats—and finds it increasingly difficult to deny the likelihood that she can do better. He is, at best, a limp sidekick.

Every now and then, with no warning or invitation, a local man lets himself into the video trailer. The door creaks open and when Wade glances up the stranger is helping himself to a can of Castle Lager from the cooler.

Wade surmises that the man must be one of the nomadic peoples who are native to the Kalahari. (He remembers something about them from the guidebook he skimmed on the plane.) Moreover, from the first time the stranger appears, he seems so casually proprietary that Wade assumes he is a caretaker or something.

But why Wade fails to ever mention this visitor to Heather, he cannot explain.

————

Once he has his beer the stranger sits down and watches the foreigner solder and patch.

Wade cannot, of course, communicate in this gentleman's language of clicks, but he senses a kindred soul. The stranger's daily uniform never varies—sandals, ragged green shorts, a blue button-down hanging loose on his narrow frame, a sun-bleached Mr. Pibb baseball cap—and he always appears to be deeply amused, smiling a wide smile of hard yellow teeth.

For lack of anything better to go on, Wade calls this stranger Mr. Pibb, and even begins to confess his feelings of inadequacy to the stranger. Mr. Pibb is nothing if not a good listener.

So in spite of the language barrier, it gradually seems to Wade as though they are establishing some kind of rapport, and during those sweltering trailer days he shares things with Mr. Pibb that he has never dared tell anyone else.

"I've never been outgoing, you know?" Wade lies on the floor and stares at the warped tin ceiling. Tangled wires are scattered all around. It is the fourth or fifth day. "Not even as a kid. Not even in grade school."

They are alone, as usual. Heather is out on the ridge, under the baobab tree, keeping track of the meerkats.

Wade cranes his neck to see his new friend. Mr. Pibb sits in a metal folding chair and sips his Castle Lager. His face is smooth and creased at the same time; you can't tell how old he is, but for some reason, Wade thinks he is very old. Mr. Pibb lowers the can, smiles his smile at Wade.

The stranger clicks.

Go on, he means.

So Wade does.

"It's not that I didn't want friends. But I was afraid, I guess. Some guys had a kickball game every day after school, but just the possibility that I might be picked last kept me from ever sticking around. So I'd run out as soon as school ended, like I had somewhere I had to get to right away. But instead, I'd go to the bridge and spend the afternoon tossing matches in the river, trying to set it on fire."

Mr. Pibb produces several rapid clicks.

That is very sad, he means. You're a good man, he means. But you must know that water doesn't burn, he means.

"It does in Cleveland," says Wade.

Mr. Pibb cackles.

This gives Wade a warm feeling.

The door to the trailer slaps in the hot wind. Wade is by himself.

———

"What's going on here?" Wade asks Heather. When he woke, she was gone. Now he has found her at the station under the baobab tree.

She shushes him.

It is dawn and cold. The sun looms, culling shadows from the low ground cover of brush and weeds, overlaying the desert with black ribbons.

Below them, the gulley dips several yards, flattens somewhat before beginning to lift back up in a series of sandy ripples, each higher than the last. At the top of these steppes, roughly twenty meerkats stand in a row, waiting for the sun to warm them.

Most of the meerkats measure roughly a foot in height, and they compose themselves in a manner that is at once dainty and statuesque: balanced on their tails, which are struck down behind them like anchors in the sand; their long torsos are pulled up straight, and their little forepaws dangle at their sides. The meerkats have bandit faces, their eyes sunken in black, emotionless circles. They suddenly remind Wade of cowboys, dime-store cowboys, the ones that face down stone killers on dusty main streets and never flinch. As the sun rises, the line of meerkats turn phosphorescent, like the observers at a nuclear test.

"Aren't they awesome?" asks Heather.

It's true, Wade sees then. Meerkats are awesome.

Cleveland [Now]

First off, Doris Krimsky demanded to know how Wade had caught on to Karolis Lichtman's diabolical plan. "What is it—have you got all the stray cats in Cleveland telling you what's going on?" She also wanted to know what Wade planned to do about finding him. "This Lichtman, he's insane. Did you see he wanted to take out Newark, too?" She paused to cough. "What's going on up there that this kind of crazy gets tenure?"

"Doris," said Wade. He was on his cell phone, sitting on a large rock in a subterranean darkness broken only by the glowing window of his Nokia. "I'm not a cat. At all."

"So it is stray cats!"

"Something like that, actually."

"Where are you? The reception is terrible."

"I'm looking for Lichtman." Wade didn't bother to add that in this case, that constituted digging a honeycomb of tunnels thirty feet beneath Cleveland.

"Well, look harder. That Kraut belongs in a rubber room.

"But I'm proud of you, Wade. I want you to know that. You're my last little chickadee and I'm proud of you. You're off on the right foot."

"What do you mean, I'm your 'last little chickadee'?"

The previous week, Doris explained, at Shuster's, she had used her telekinetic powers to raise the player piano off the ground. "It was late and some guys dared me and I lost my concentration. Came down on me and broke my leg in five places." Now she was on disability, and her mandatory retirement was around the corner anyway.

"Used to be I could hold up a falling jumbo jet and drink a Coke and watch *The Price Is Right* all at the same time. Next thing I know, I'm an old broad. Time to hang it up." She coughed again, excused herself. Wade heard the sound of liquid being poured. This was followed by a *mrow!* of protest.

"Well," said Doris. "I'm still strong enough to make the cat fly around."

To his surprise, Wade felt his eyes tear up and his throat fill. After their first meeting he had gone home to his parents' house and done a little research in the basement, sifted through the cardboard boxes where he stored his old comic books, and found several wrinkly issues of *The Atom League Chronicles* that featured Doris Krimsky. She had only been an active member of the League for a couple of years in the late seventies, under the handle of "the Poltergeist, Gravity's Gal." Her uniform had been black with a red apple on the chest, a reference to Newton. She had been whip-thin, like a dancer, and her hair had been the unearthly gold of the Kalahari Desert at dusk.

Or at least, that was how the artists had drawn her.

"I have that issue, when you saved the president's motorcade from the falling jumbo jet. I was hoping you'd autograph it for me some-time."

Doris sighed. "You know, Wade, they changed a lot of stuff. No one dies or gets their heart broken in the comics. It's different in real life."

While they were talking several squirrels had joined Wade. They milled around his rock seat, brushing against his ankles. In spite of this, he felt extraordinarily isolated, as if the world were moving far-ther and farther away from him.

Wade said, "It's going to take more than counseling to make things right again, isn't it?"

There was no need to fill in the details. If anyone would understand, it was the Poltergeist. Brigadier Pride, "the scrap metal soldier with the clockwork heart," had never returned her affections. Wade had read all about it, used his index finger to trace the bright blue line of her tears.

"I'm sorry, hon," said the old superhero, "but that's what I mean: that's the part they leave out of the funny books. The ones you couldn't save."

———

Perched on the railing of his apartment's balcony, the Meerkat watched the next day's dawn color in the empty avenues between the stately old brownstones of downtown Cleveland. His clawed feet hooked the frosted metal of the railing and his clawed hands hung absently in front of his chest. From the waist up, his posture was rigid, unbreakable. In the black pits of the Meerkat's eyes, nothing stirred.

Inside the apartment, the lock turned over, the door whispered open, shut again. She still had a key.

Then, the glass door slid open with a whoosh.

"Well," said Heather, her voice scratchy with unease. "This is—familiar behavior. Absorbing the light after a night in the burrow. Of course." A few seconds passed. The creature's head flicked one way, then another, then another, checking, checking, checking.

"Wade?"

He twisted around. "Heather. Hey, I'm glad you're here."

Wade was smiling, but he wasn't Wade, not the Wade that Heather recognized. Because his eyes were still black and bottomless. Still Meerkat eyes.

"I'll come back," she said, retreating into the living room. "Another time."

With a squeak, the glass door slid shut again.

"Call me?" asked Wade, not sure if she heard him.

Wade shrugged to himself, and the Meerkat swiveled back to the dawn. The sun rose and set fire to a thousand windows. The Meerkat stared straight ahead.

Kalahari Desert [Before]

Once everything that can be done for the video trailer has been done, Wade relocates to the site, shooting handheld footage of the meerkat mob. Most of this work is accomplished on his belly in the sand—down on their level.

From this uncomfortable position—tear ducts watering, nose caked with dust—Wade learns just how right Heather was about meerkats: They are many things, but cute isn't one of them.

To begin with, up close, they don't look like cats at all. The feline face is finely planed, with cheekbones and a brow and protruding ears and whiskers. A cat's face adds up to something recognizable, something like human.

THE MEERKAT

The meerkat face is just an isosceles triangle, with a long, thin snout tapering out like something a bored child might tease from a ball of clay, and the ears nothing more than little holes spooned out of the sides of the head. Then there are the meerkats' eyes, which draw everything in, but let nothing out. When you look into a meerkat's eyes there is nothing familiar. You are gazing into outer space.

They are amazing, but the meerkats scare Wade a little.

And the scariest meerkat of all is Livia, the matriarch of the Buckaroo Mob. Wade focuses his camera on her more than any of the others.

About nine years old, Livia has a brown coat threaded with white, and her snout is laced with a boxer's web of scar tissue.

Meerkat mobs are digging societies; they burrow tunnels to live in, and they burrow for food. Perhaps her prowess in this area is what won Livia the mob's leadership. The old meerkat uses her razor black claws to tear apart the sand, wiggling a body length or more into the earth, emerging a moment later with a glistening yellow scorpion locked in her jaws. From his position down on the ground, Wade can hear the brittle crunch of the exoskeleton between her fangs.

(Among the other species of the Kalahari, it is notable that only the ground squirrels seem comfortable around such ravenous predators. They share burrows with the meerkats and often stand around on the surrounding ridges observing. The ground squirrels hold their tails up over their heads, bushy umbrellas to keep off the sun.)

The matriarch's mate, another battle-worn member of the clan, is a ten-year-old known as Octavian. Octavian's coat is tattered and mangy where Livia's is elegantly snowy. There is something slightly mad about this meerkat. He spends much of his time racing back and forth along the gully, rear in the air, tail a stiff antenna, eyes awful and blank, teeth bared.

To see this behavior up close reminds Wade of old-fashioned storybooks, the appalling kind where the monsters eat the children. No, not cute, not adorable. Not like Nathan Lane at all.

"What the hell is that running thing they do? With all the teeth and their butts up in the air?" Wade asks Heather one night.

"It's called pronking," she says. "It means war."

"Pronking," says Wade. The word sounds like it means something naughty and makes him feel depressed. They are in bed. It has been almost a month since the last time they had sex.

"Stop thinking about it," says Heather.

"Thinking about what?"

She groans and turns on her side.

There is a gun crack in the distance.

"Did you hear that?" Wade asks.

"Poachers," say Heather.

"If they're hunting libidos, they've come to the wrong place."

"Go to sleep, Wade."

Octavian generally keeps his distance from Livia, but the next day he abruptly seeks her out, leaps on her back while she stands in one of the burrow's entrances. They grapple furiously; they gnaw on each other; they chirrup and burble; dust rises around them; it is like seeing a pair of furry old socks try to smother each other.

This, thinks Wade, is the real, filthy thing. This is doing it meerkat-style.

He removes his eye from the viewfinder to catch Heather's reaction. The smile on her face is faint and her gaze far off, in another place altogether, somewhere that is unfamiliar to Wade.

———

"What do I do?" Wade asks Mr. Pibb.

A bad dream has awakened Wade and he has wandered out into the night. Mr. Pibb perches on the steps of the trailer, drinking one of Wade's Castle Lagers. It is as if the old man were waiting for him.

Though Mr. Pibb smiles, his eyes stay flat and dark. He clicks. We will make it better tomorrow, he means.

"How?" asks Wade, desperate, weepy. Everything has come apart so quickly. "I don't understand."

With a flourish the old man whips off his cap. Livia, the meerkat matriarch, calmly straightens up. She stands on Mr. Pibb's bald head in the manner characteristic of meerkats: body long, forepaws dangling, head darting this way and that.

Livia raises one of her tiny forepaws.

She directs a single black claw at Wade. The claw catches the moonlight and fills with mercury.

Wade steps back, caught, trapped, accused of some crime. They aren't supposed to do that. Meerkats aren't supposed to point at you and pick you out.

"What?" asks Wade. "What did I do?"

Livia clicks. Go back to your burrow and rest, she means. Go now.

Mr. Pibb laughs. The meerkat on his head continues to point at Wade.

Wade stumbles back to the trailer. In the morning he wonders what it could mean, a crazy dream like that.

Cleveland (Now)

Sparrows fluttered in and out of the great robot's ears, a monumental metaphor for every variety of mental failing. Peaceful Ivan stood on a rocky knoll above the outdoor palisade of the Cleveland Metroparks Zoo, where below families sat at picnic tables, eating lunch and feeding crumbs to the squirrels. Later in the day the shadow of the Soviet Nuclear Defense Robot would tick around and drench the palisade in darkness, but for now, they were all in the rich sunlight of the first warm day of April. To the good people of the Forest City, the memory of that winter's terrible threat was like the snow—melted.

Although it rose to the imposing height of a small building, Peaceful Ivan was rusted at the joints and appeared ready for scrap. Scored with graffiti, its red eyes seemed blind. The jutting bulldozer blade of its jaw appeared not so much fierce as petulant. It had a head full of birds. Taken as a whole, the great hope of the Soviet Defense Department brought to mind an elderly weight lifter, bulging with sad, leaden muscle. Peaceful Ivan had always resembled a marvelous windup toy—gunboat feet, stiff limbs, three-fingered hands, the glaring Neanderthal features—and it still did, except now it was something you'd find in a rummage sale, on a table with some costume jewelry and a few water-stained comic books.

Wade couldn't imagine what that moonstruck bastard Lichtman had been thinking. Nuclear trigger or not, he doubted Peaceful Ivan would be able to make it as far as the river, let alone destroy the city.

Three months had passed since the battle at the Finnish Ballet and Lichtman remained at large. The trail had gone dead. Maybe the madman had moved on to another city, begun to develop a new, more reasonable scheme of mass destruction. The Meerkat didn't know, and neither did Wade.

He found an empty table at the edge of the palisade and paged through the *Plain Dealer*. WALL STREET DISAPPEARS IN TIME WARP, said the front page, along with a subheading that reassured, ATOM LEAGUE PROMISES FULL INVESTIGATION. In the editorial section there was a column by Christopher Hitchens, NEW SUPERHEROES AREN'T AS SUPER, which seemed to be hinting that the Meerkat was part of a new wave of cute and cuddly superheroes that ought not to be trusted. "There is something jaundiced in this new breed of paranormals," Hitchens perceived, "something that nods disquietingly in the direction of Orwell's description of the 'typical Socialist.'"

"Jesus," said Wade to no one, "I'm not a socialist. I'm just a guy who hasn't gotten laid in eight months."

He flipped to Sports to read about the Indians, who were about to open their season: TRIBE HOPES FOR MEERKAT MAGIC.

"Hey," said Heather.

The sunlight highlighted a strain of violet in her hair. She smiled at him, a nervous flicker playing at the corners.

"What's going on?"

"Just read in the paper that I was a socialist."

"There's worse things to be," said Heather.

"Like a mascot?"

She stepped forward and lifted a hand to touch the thick curls of Wade's sideburns. "This is a good look for you," she said, drawing his head against her stomach, holding him.

———

For half an hour they slowly circled Peaceful Ivan's feet. Around them children played, and dogs barked, and students with sketch pads lay in the grass and drew the mighty ruin. Everything seemed the way it used to be, the way it should have always been.

The zoo had been inundated with requests for a meerkat exhibition, Heather said, and they were going to start their own mob in the late summer. On top of that, news programs all over the country had contacted her about appearing on their shows to talk about the behavior of meerkats. "I'm supposed to do a satellite linkup with Larry King tonight," said Heather. "You don't mind, do you?"

"No," said Wade, and he didn't. He was happy for her. Heather loved meerkats. It was the Meerkat with whom she had some issues.

"Are you depressed?" asked Heather. "You seem depressed."

Wade rapped a knuckle against one of Peaceful Ivan's steel calves. "I'm solid. I still feel a little down about the Nutcracker, I guess. I called the guy to apologize, but he just hung up. I can't blame him."

"But he'll dance again, won't he?"

"Yeah. But his left ball couldn't be saved. It was totally destroyed. And Lichtman's still out there. Three months have gone by and I can't find him."

They walked for a little longer before Heather said she needed to go home and pick out an outfit. She wanted to look her best for Larry King. Wade promised to watch. Heather said he shouldn't, that she was sure she was going to sound stupid, and Larry would make fun of her. He said Larry was nice to everyone.

As they spoke, Wade had to force himself not to look at her too much. Since the morning on the balcony their communication had been limited to a few achingly polite phone calls. A part of him had hoped that Heather would not be so beautiful and good, that the weeks had turned her ugly, or mean, or stupid, or just into some other person, someone he didn't need to need, someone he could shed. But he'd known that it was impossible. Love didn't molt.

Heather put a hand on Wade's forearm. "What if I'm the only one he's not nice to?"

She licked her lips then and tilted her face, opened herself for a kiss. "I've been thinking, Wade—"

"If he's not nice to you, I'll bite his nose off," Wade said, and laughed at his own joke.

Heather's face tightened. He put out a hand, but she was already backing away, taking her kiss with her. "I was kidding," he said, and Heather said, "I know, I know," but it was confusing, and wrong, and she had to go, just had to go.

Kalahari Desert (Before)

The day after the dream Wade has the odd sensation that the Buckaroos are staring at him, following him with their ink-spot eyes. He reports this to Heather over lunch in the trailer.

"I hate to break it to you, Wade, but once they get used to us we're not very interesting to meerkats. They can't eat us, and we don't eat them, so we're not particularly significant."

Wade holds an apple, but for some reason finds it impossible to imagine consuming it. He turns it over and over in his hands.

"Are you feeling okay, Wade?" Heather asks.

He rubs the apple across his forehead. "I don't know. I might have picked up a bug from Mr. Pibb."

"Okay, that's it." Heather takes his hand and leads him to bed.

The trailer is dark when Wade awakes and his body is petrified. Beside him, Heather snores softly, the sound chopped up by the whirr of the fan. Wade tries to sit up. His stomach locks; he can only raise his neck a couple of inches. Something soft and scarflike rustles up his bare leg.

Livia.

Then, another something soft and scarflike.

Octavian.

The meerkat matriarch creeps slowly across Wade's chest. Her claws dig into his flesh. Her eyes are full of outer space. Octavian follows a few steps behind.

Livia drops out of sight at his shoulder and he feels her fur brush his ear. She clicks softly. Relax, she means. Relax.

As Octavian comes closer, Wade smells something familiar: the heavy tang of Castle Lager.

"Mr. Pibb?" The words escape his mouth in a faint wheeze.

Octavian pauses on Wade's chest. He clicks. Smart boy, he means. For a moment, icy, alien satellites waver on the surface of the creature's eyes.

"Thank you," says Wade—or at least, that is what he tries to say, but by then the meerkat has darted into his mouth, and is starting to burrow.

Cleveland (Now)

All of them, Wade and the fifty or so squirrels he now considered his closest friends, sat in the living room of the apartment to watch Heather be interviewed by Larry King. Wade lay on the couch while the squirrels roosted attentively on every other available surface—the mantel, the top of the stereo, the rim of the rubber tree planter, the back of the couch, on Wade himself.

At one point in the interview, Larry King commented, "These little meerkats, they're awfully fierce, aren't they?" and Heather responded, "You're absolutely right, Larry. About the only species that can actually put up with them are squirrels. Squirrels and meerkats share burrows."

In reaction to this there was a chattering of approval. "True!" cried one squirrel, which to normal human ears would have sounded like "Gack!" The other squirrels picked it up: "True!" "Gack!" "True!" "Gack!"

Wade clicked at them to put a sock in it.

But although Heather had mentioned the relationship between meerkats and squirrels only in passing, it was an important point, and the only reason that Wade had learned about Professor Karolis Lichtman's demented scheme in the first place: A squirrel who lived in an elm tree on the quad at Cleveland State had overheard the professor talking with one of his henchmen about the trigger. That squirrel had told another squirrel and so on, until every squirrel in Cleveland knew about it, and finally the news found its way back to Wade.

After this the Meerkat dug a tunnel under the campus and staked out a position beneath the professor's lab. The rest of the story was well known—the chase, the battle on stage, the demi-emasculation of the Finnish Nutcracker, Lichtman's escape with the nuclear trigger, and so on.

Since that time the squirrels had been all over town eavesdropping while Wade had been digging his honeycomb of burrows beneath the city and doing the same. But thus far nothing had turned up.

Now Wade was watching television with his squirrel lieutenants and that crocodile, Larry King, was flirting with the woman he loved. "So what you're saying is, when the meerkat burrow is a-rocking, don't come a-knocking." Larry snapped his suspenders.

"I'm not sure I'd put it exactly that way, Larry," said Heather.

"Heh-heh," said Larry.

"I can't handle this, guys. I'm going to bed." Wade sat up and a dozen squirrels spilled to the floor.

Before he left, Wade put on a *Friends* DVD, which, you will surely not be surprised to learn, is the favorite show of all squirrels.

Kalahari Desert (Before)

The Meerkat spies out from a tangle of low brush. A few yards away a camp-fire blooms. A group of men lounge about on field chairs, drinking, laughing, occasionally lurching up to stumble off into the dark and piss. On a spit over the flames smokes the blackened bones of an impala.

On the far side of the bonfire a stack of wooden cages murmurs with the movements of small, uneasy animals. The cages contain a hundred or so meerkats, trapped not only for collectors, but also for some of the world's most dissolute gourmands.

The Meerkat's brethren speak to him, tell him that he must show no mercy, or else there will only be more of them the next time.

The Meerkat understands, and when he bursts out of the darkness, he looks nothing like a man. His claws fill with firelight, his mouth becomes huge with teeth, and his eyes turn around backward, turn utterly black.

THE MEERKAT

"My God, how did you get so big?" asks the last poacher. "Meerkats aren't supposed to be so—"

———

In the gloom of the dusty little house the zoologist and the production engineer make love like meerkats; he bites her; she bites him harder; his claws cut gouges in the floorboards; she yanks the fur on his thighs, tears out big handfuls that drift through the air and litter the floor; he growls in his need and she answers, finally, by screaming, "Yes! Fuck, yes!"

Only afterward, as she sees him change, sees the claws withdraw and his body deflate and his hair thin, notices the bloodstains on his face and hands, does Heather begin to weep.

"You're an animal," she says.

"Something happened to me," Wade tells her.

"You're an animal, some kind of animal," she says.

"No," he says, "No, I'm not," but he is.

Cleveland (Now)

"What are they looking at?" asked Wade. He was a meerkat, an actual meerkat, not quite as tall as a bottle of Castle Lager, and he stood in the palm of Mr. Pibb's hand.

They were back in Africa, under the baobab tree. The sun hung over the Kalahari and sprinkled the sand with diamonds. Thousands of meerkats lined the ridges and hills, propped by their tails, heads turned up and focused on the empty sky.

"We are waiting for the beautiful ship to return," said Mr. Pibb. The bill of his cap hung a veil of shadow over his face; he was all smiling teeth.

"Why me?" asked Wade.

"A good disguise is important. A man believes that what is cute cannot be dangerous. A man believes that what is plain cannot be a champion. That is how we trick them, how we have always tricked them."

"What am I supposed to do?"

"Be good. Be brave. Protect the burrow of Cleveland." Mr. Pibb's smile closed. "We will call you when we need you."

"Okay," said Wade. He examined his dainty meerkat paws.

Mr. Pibb laughed and gave Wade's pudgy little meerkat belly a pinch.

"Hey," said Wade, "don't do that."

He sat up. He was in bed, in his apartment. Gray light filtered through the sheer curtains. A squirrel was on his stomach.

Heather's squirrel.

"Lichtman," said the squirrel, and the rest—that the professor must have seen the interview and decided to kidnap an expert on meerkats to learn their weaknesses, that the madman had never discarded his plan to reactivate Peaceful Ivan and wreak havoc on the city—seemed immediately apparent, and beside the point.

The only thing that mattered was that Heather needed saving.

Cleveland—April 9, 2009

Dead leaves and newspaper wings flapped up behind the figure that pronked through the Cleveland dawn. One of the few witnesses to this desperate charge, a homeless man named Wilson Pohl who was seated at a bus stop on Denison Avenue, told reporters that he had never seen anything like it. "His feet didn't even seem to touch the ground," said Pohl. "He looked irate as hell, too, with the fangs and whatnot."

A security guard at the zoo saw the same figure, only seconds after Peaceful Ivan ripped loose from his cement moorings and began to plod away through the park. "I got a Soviet Nuclear Defense Robot just up and started walking off, and then I got some kind of creature on four legs running and barking after it. It's a bad scene."

But although few in the city saw the action, all of them felt it.

The ground trembled with giant steps, the air rang with ripping metal, and in the end, fire spilled across the water.

Up the spine of the steel mammoth went the Meerkat, punching his claws through the metal, dragging himself one body length at a time. The world rose and sank, rose and sank. The Meerkat felt as though he were riding a metronome. Wind roared in his ears and his mouth went dry.

As Peaceful Ivan thudded forward, his ancient voice box began to broadcast a crackly recording of "The March of the Soviet Tankmen." Thousands of sleepers were pummeled awake as the robot sang, in his rusty baritone, and backed by some long-forgotten Revolutionary Orchestra, *"Гремя огнем, сверкая Блеском стали/Пойдут машины в яростный поход!"*

Car windows shattered. Fire alarms howled. Police sirens wailed. People ran, half asleep, into the street and gaped in wonder at the man of iron who blotted out the sun.

From the crest of the robot's massive skull, the Meerkat could see the Cuyahoga River, a caramel-colored band wavering a half mile beyond. His eyes stung; the rushing air pulled at him; the thundering Russian song filled his head with cotton; and he was not afraid.

In a single motion, the Meerkat slipped down the robot's face, swung feetfirst through the left eye, and tumbled onto the control deck in a spray of red glass.

"Wade!"

Heather was tied to a captain's chair in the middle of the oval room. Banks of computers flashed with yellow and green lights while sirens blared. Flakes of rusted metal and sparrow feathers snowed down. Everything shook, everything screamed.

"И первый маршал в бой нас поведт!" rumbled Peaceful Ivan.

Professor Karolis Lichtman, Ph.D., stepped forward and pointed a silver blunderbuss at the Meerkat. His sunglasses were small and purple and deranged.

For balance Lichtman threw out his free hand, like a surfer fighting to stay on his board; on the palm the portrait of Kurchatov grinned merrily, as if the proceedings pleased him.

"You're too late, pathetic feline!"

"He's a herpestid, you demented prick!"

This correction came from Heather, twisting and straining against the ropes that bound her to the captain's chair.

Lichtman whipped an offended glance at Heather—all the opening that the Meerkat needed. Two pronks forward and he had batted the weapon from the professor's hand.

Far below them something twanged, some robotic ligament or tendon, and gave way with a screeching crash. The room tilted. Lichtman slid out of the Meerkat's claws and went head over heels, striking his skull against a computer console with a dense thud.

The Meerkat rushed to Heather. He slashed her bonds with his claws. She jerked away from him. He told her not to be frightened. "It's me," said Wade. "It's just me, just Wade." A brown wall appeared in front of Peaceful Ivan's smashed socket.

She took a deep breath and threw her arms around his neck and, at last, they made a very near escape.

———

In Issue #1 of *The Mighty Meerkat,* the superhero uses his digging ability to tunnel down through the riverbed of the Cuyahoga, and up through a pond a few miles away. That's not how it happened. In truth, the Meerkat and Heather Rudolph landed in the river's shallows and simply ran to safety. Nor were a couple of police boats with water cannons sufficient to extinguish the fire that blossomed on the surface of the Cuyahoga when Peaceful Ivan collapsed into the river. It actually took the heroic assistance of more than two dozen fire departments from all over Ohio to stifle the blaze, and for reasons no one could explain, the Cuyahoga River continued to reignite off and on for the rest of the summer.

But most of the comic is true—especially the important things.

For instance, the Meerkat really did save the woman he loved. She really did say something like, "It was you, wasn't it? It was you that saved me?"

And he definitely said, "Me. Meerkats have their own agendas. But

I'm a man. I'm the man who loves you. No meerkat is ever going to get in the way of that."

His eyes were clear, not the black of galaxies, but the old shoe-leather brown that she knew so well, Wade's eyes. She said, "Good, because that's who I want, I want Wade Hanes," and the rest of what passed between them isn't necessary to the story, which is primarily a yarn about how a fearless superhero saved his city.

("Because I only want Wade Hanes," Heather went on. They held each other in a bed of rushes on the riverbank while fire boiled up off the water. "Meerkats are cool, but they don't do it for me—you know, in that way."

"They don't?" asked Wade. "But that night—"

"—I thought it was you. You," Heather said and kissed him and started to laugh. "It wasn't the sex. It was the way I thought *you* wanted *me*. God, guys are so dumb. Even when they're meerkats, they're dumb."

"But I do want you. I always have."

"Prove it," she said. "Prove it again. Prove it right now, you animal."

And then they acted on instinct, as every creature sometimes must, if it is to survive and flourish.)

A SHADOWY FIGURE

Michael Czyzniejewski

WHEN THE HEROES CAME TO TOWN

We felt, among other things, unimpressed. Before the heroes, life wasn't that bad, or, depending on who you asked, going pretty good. The county had just paid to have the thruway resurfaced, our boys had made it to the state semis, falling in overtime to the eventual champs, and business boomed at the tire factory up by the mall, which, in turn, made business boom at the mall as well. Everyone felt good about the economy, the kids were getting into good colleges, and if a town with prettier women existed, we hadn't been there.

Which is why we scratched our heads when these heroes showed, their jaws, their capes, their stoicism, all right there on their form-fitting sleeves. Okay, so their debut was a splash, putting the fire out at the tire factory, the dark cloud lifting after three days, the smell of burning rubber and ultimate disaster disappearing soon after. To boot, they maintained the integrity of the structure, limiting the shutdown to a mere month, tires soon rolling down the line once again. A few days later, they saved that kid who'd fallen into the quarry, too, not one of our boys, but a kid nonetheless. Not one of us could have squeezed into that drainage pipe, let alone pounded through the twenty solid feet of bedrock to pry his ankle free. Our hats were off, and tipped. Whether we could have fought off the supervillains and their giant mechanical attack birds isn't worth discussing. The talons alone were fourteen feet long. We had to give them that one, too. They had a pretty good week.

Cats out of trees and baby-kissing aside, we felt skeptical of the overall picture, skeptical at best. The heroes, for all their wondrous deeds, had never really warmed up to us on a personal level. Danger and wrongdoing back at bay, they vanished, gone to whatever cave or fortress it was they called home. No kind words, no interviews, not even a catchphrase to distinguish themselves. After the attack birds, someone came up with the idea of a picnic—horseshoes and sack races and potato salad—just to say thanks, to let them know we appreciated their efforts, that we noticed. We could even get to know them, exchange numbers. Maybe go out for a beer, shoot a few games of stick. But the heroes, as smug as they were dashing, didn't even respond to the invitations. They couldn't grace us with a simple "no," and we'd sent stamped response postcards, too. "Peril never takes a break," a general statement to the *Daily Eagle* pronounced, "so neither can we." We started to think that they were saving our lives just so they could mock us. *A picnic*, they laughed in their dark, damp headquarters. *Who do these people think they're dealing with?* they smirked between push-up contests and extended glances in the mirror.

The women, to our surprise, were quick to take the heroes' defense. They reminded us of how hard it is to be the new kid on the block, how we'd feel the same way if we were the strangers and the heroes were the Welcome Wagon. The heroes weren't disregarding, maybe, just being shy. Or—and this almost made us laugh—humble. We should give them a chance, they said, give them some time to settle in. Now, becoming our wives doesn't obligate them to take our side on every matter, but still. We were grateful for what the heroes had done—don't get us wrong—but when a man's wife starts to see the other guy's point of view, he begins to wonder just where her loyalties lie. Or what's left to believe in. Or what tomorrow could possibly bring.

Our women's allegiance in question, suspicion arose. Who were these guys under the masks? Where did they come from? Why did they choose our town, out of all the towns in the world? We weren't in any particular danger. We didn't place an ad. We didn't throw up any signals, lights in the sky or whatnot. We did, however, have the prettiest ladies, as mentioned. And any hero we'd ever seen always had a pretty lady hanging off at least one arm. The consensus was, we were on to something. Maybe the heroes weren't mocking us, not at all. Maybe they were just auditioning, trying to take up more than the limelight.

A few of the old-timers, those guys who hang out outside the library, posited that the heroes were responsible for the fire and the kid in the quarry, and those of us who bought into that theory had no trouble throwing in the giant, mechanical attack birds. Why not? It was all starting to make sense.

But as quickly as the heroes arrived, they left our town. Since we had never really kept in touch, no one knew they were gone—not until the tragedy at the dynamite plant. As the flames inched toward the main warehouse, explosions and screaming and mayhem abounding, everyone watched the skies, assuming the heroes would swoop in to save the day. We'd all be safe, the women would swoon, and the heroes would leave without saying a word. Several disastrous explosions later, it finally hit us: No one was going to dig a fjord to the lake to drown out the fires, and no mighty wind was going to blow out the hundreds of thousands of fuses, sizzling and snapping and sparkling like a holiday right before the grand finale. The heroes weren't coming. We were on our own, and on our own, we were no good.

The women took the news of the heroes' departure the hardest (except for the families of the dynamite victims, of course). Lamentation, both public and private, ensued. Our wives wept openly, muddled about like hungry strays, and sported the hopeless expression of a soldier facing a suicide mission. To be honest, it was the reaction we expected, but none the easier to accept.

More surprising, however, was how close they held us at night, with a firmer grip, almost desperate. Closer and tighter than any one of us remembers being held before. While it's always nice to be wanted, it felt more like a mixed blessing, if you asked us. Some of us had been gone before, minitrip for work, school, separate vacations. Did our wives hold our empty pillows like they held us when the heroes left? Did they stare at our pictures? Were our departures as dramatic? As untimely and cowardly? We weren't sure if we wanted to know the answers to these questions, but there they were. One day, we might have posed them to our wives instead of to each other, but until we were ready to make that move, we held fast. The economy was still okay and our kids were still getting into good schools. We had time.

Though we could never be sure exactly who it was our wives held so closely and tightly, we were there for them, and always would be. Holding is holding, any way you look at it, the one thing that was better than before the heroes ever showed. It was in these moments we found our solace, what allowed us to maintain our pride. It was in these moments, wrapped in our wives' arms, their minds off in the skies, that *we* were the heroes, living their hero lives, a vicarious victory. We were just returning the favor, in a way, there for our women, till the end of days, watching the skies in denial, posing as our own secret identities.

Scott Snyder

THE THIRTEENTH EGG

September 1946

Everett had no idea how long his parents had been standing outside his bedroom door. He hadn't heard them knock or try the knob, hadn't heard them call out. But by the time he opened the door his father was kneeling at the lock with a screwdriver in his teeth. His mother stood just behind, clutching her elbows.

His father removed the screwdriver from his mouth. "Well?" he said.

"Well what?" said Everett.

"You didn't hear us out here?" said his mother.

His father stood, joints popping. "We've been pounding on your door for five minutes."

"I'm sorry," said Everett. "I must have had the record playing too loud."

"What record?" his mother said.

The question confused Everett. The record playing "Travelin' Light" by Johnny Mercer. But then the hiss and thump of the needle became audible to him, and he saw that his old tabletop had finished playing some time ago.

"I guess I was distracted," he said.

"Distracted." His father turned and shot his mother a look. "Well, whatever you were doing, you ought to put on some clothes. It's almost one o'clock."

Everett looked down and saw that he was wearing only a loose robe. He closed the collar and tightened the belt, trying hard to concentrate.

"Are you sure you're all right, honey?" said his mother.

Everett presented a smile. "I'm great."

"You don't have to be *great,* yet," said his father. "You've been home a month. You can be anything you want."

"Okay."

"Evvy," said his mother, "if you're feeling up to it, we have something we want to show you."

"Right now?" said Everett.

"No, next week," said his father. "Yes, now. How are your marks?"

"Still there."

"Are you using your ointment?" said his mother.

He told her he was. Everett could feel himself coming back; the sensation was like being poured slowly into his own body, his feet and legs taking on weight, his chest filling.

"Well, we'll just have to wait and see on that one," said his father. "Now put on some clothes."

"Right," said Everett. "Will do." He went to close the door, but his father blocked it with his foot.

"No more locks."

"At least for now, okay?" said his mother.

"Okeydokey," said Everett, gently closing the door. As he dressed, he was careful to avoid the mirror; he was feeling a bit better now, sharper, but he knew that the sight of his bare skin would distract him again, draw him back into his thoughts. Once his body was covered— letterman sweater on, trousers belted—he afforded himself a quick peek, and there he was, himself again: an average-looking nineteen-year-old. A little thin, a bit lanky, but broad enough in the shoulders to hide it. He smiled, inspecting his teeth, poking at the muscles of his face. After a moment of hesitation, he leaned closer to the mirror and opened his mouth wide, sticking out his tongue. Cautiously, he peered down into his throat.

"Ev?" his father called from downstairs.

"Coming," Everett said.

He found his parents waiting for him in the backyard. On the grass in front of them lay a steel pod, nearly six feet long.

"Well," said his father, "what do you think?"

Everett's first thought was that the object was a bomb. His parents had lost their minds and somehow purchased a ten-thousand-pound cookie. They stood over the thing, smiling, waiting for a reaction.

His father knocked on the steel hull with his knuckles. "I thought we could work on it together."

"Like a hobby," said his mother, rubbing his father's shoulder.

Confused, Everett examined the steel hulk more closely. He saw that, in fact, it wasn't a bomb, but a fuel tank from a light fighter airplane. He'd served on a destroyer, not a carrier, but he'd seen enough fighters up close to recognize a belly tank. The thing had come from a P-51 or P-36, he figured, and then the picture suddenly became clear to him: His father wanted to construct a race car together. It was an idea they'd joked about before Everett had enlisted. Maybe when he got back they'd buy an old Ford, soup it up, then drive it out to the playa. The town sat less than five miles from one of the largest dry lakebeds in Southern California and had a long tradition of drag racing. As long as there were automobiles, the people of Boilerville had been driving them out to the desert and racing them across the flats.

"This is the new trend," Everett's father said. "Everyone's using these things to make their racers. It's easy. I was talking to Hal. Mr. water-heater guy. He built one. Stuck on a chassis, loaded it up, and whoosh. Got the sucker up to a hundred ten miles an hour. Can you believe that?" His father gave a little laugh.

"Wow," said Everett.

"You could just use a regular car, though," said Everett's mother, waving away the fuel tank. "If you're not comfortable."

"Of course he's comfortable, Margot," said Everett's father, his eyes fixed on Everett. "He will be, at least. Once he's zooming across the desert in this thing. Right, Ev?"

"Right," said Everett. He was thinking of that scream a Hawk 75 made as it flew by, the strange, hysterical shriek it gave off that caused a ship's cables to shiver. He wondered how much energy it took to make a plane go that fast, how much power, and before he could help it, the heat in his gut was back, like an oven blazing to life. Panicked, he tried to think of cold, still things: a frozen lake. An iceberg—his iceberg, floating on the Atlantic. But the flames were reaching up through his chest and neck.

"So how about some lunch?" his mother said.

The blaze was in Everett's throat now, a roaring heat just behind his tongue. He nodded, keeping his mouth clamped shut as tight as he could.

———

He could feel a transformation happening deep inside his body, down in his muscles or bones, maybe even deeper, on a chemical level, cooking inside the tiny pans of his cells. Something was changing, and each step of the reaction left him drained and exhausted. He would get excited and flare up and then a whole day would pass while he moved through town in a kind of haze, feeling empty and light, looking down at his arms and legs from a great height, as though his body was a stream of rain falling from the cloud of his head. Who was he supposed to be? Who had he been before? The sidewalk drifted past, far, far below.

But then suddenly came moments when he was himself again. He took a bite of sweet-potato pancake at Gyp's and the taste sparked a chain reaction, little explosions of recognition. This was what he liked to eat. Of course! And coffee, he loved coffee with lots of sugar in it.

Or he'd be at the drive-in with Langley, arm over her shoulders, feeling half there, the wash of gray light from the screen making him so tired. The actors spoke but their words arrived in hollow, watery echoes. But then lemon! The smell of Langley's hair triggered something in him and he was awake and buzzing with energy and he would look at her and all of a sudden things were so simple.

See that face? Remember the feel of her lips on your lips? The feel of her tongue?

He kissed her harder, pressing himself on her.

"Hold on," Langley said, turning away from him. The leather of the backseat creaked beneath her. "Ev."

But he wanted her so badly now, wanted back with her. He ran a hand between her thighs, trying to part them. She was wearing a skirt and he could feel the heat of her through her cotton panties.

"Wait!" She pushed him off her.

"What? What's wrong?"

She sat up and straightened her skirt. "It's just a little fast, Ev. That's all."

"I'm sorry," he said, wiping the sweat from his face. He'd stripped to his undershirt, but the inside of the car still felt unbearably hot to him.

"It's okay," she said.

They sat in the humid silence for a moment. Everett hadn't been paying attention to the feature, and he saw now that it was some kind of horror story. A small, oily guy Everett thought he recognized from *Casablanca* was batting away a severed hand trying to strangle him.

"You were gone for two years, Ev."

"Twenty-two months."

On the screen, the man finally managed to pry the hand from his throat and hurl the thing to the ground.

"We're just getting to know each other again. We're dating. It should be fun." She touched his face. "Hey. Look at me."

He turned to her.

"So, Everett Batson," she said. "Tell me about yourself."

"Tell you what?"

She gave an exaggerated sigh. "I don't know. Impress me."

"My father bought me a fuel tank today," Everett said.

"He's excited about building the race car," said Langley. "He's been talking about it for weeks."

She moved close to him and he put his arm around her. She'd always been pretty, but while he was away she'd become beautiful. When he'd first seen her again, he'd thought the change was something physical, the natural sharpening of her features. But it was more than that; there was something new about her face, a hidden face behind hers that was tough and wise and a little sad.

On the screen, the battered hand was making its getaway, hiding inside a woman's purse.

"So if we're dating again now," Everett said, "how many dates in are we?"

Langley closed one eye and thought about this. "I don't know. Maybe five?"

"So if I asked you to go steady, it'd be too soon."

"I guess you'll just have to ask."

She kissed him, gently at first, then a little harder. He went slowly this time, simply enjoying the feel of her body against his, firm and hot and strangely giving.

———

The evening before Everett shipped out, Langley's parents allowed her to spend the night at his house. The two of them had already done some things in his parents' car. She'd let him touch and kiss her breasts five times; twice she'd felt him through his pants; and once, in the heat of things, she'd even let him take off her panties and kiss her down there for a good thirty seconds before she'd regained her composure and coaxed him up. But Langley had made it clear when they started dating that there would be no actual sex for a long time. Maybe not even until marriage. So he'd put the notion out of his head. He took each new intimacy as a gift. Certainly he hadn't expected much in the way of sex that last night. He figured she would be too emotional— likely he would be, too. And up until two or three in the morning, there'd been only crying and hugging, kissing, and that slow, deliberate touching, with fingers like tiny microphones, trying to record the details of each other's bodies, listening through the skin.

"We still smell like gasoline," she said. Earlier in the evening, they'd gone together to the hot-rod races, out on Boiler Lake.

"Speak for yourself," Everett said.

"Shut up," she said, giggling.

He nuzzled her. "It is you. You grease monkey."

Laughing, she wriggled out of his grasp and got up. She walked over to her bag and began rummaging inside.

"I have a surprise for you," she said.

"Lang, we made a deal."

"I know, I know," she said.

"No gifts. Now I'm a jerk."

She pulled out an envelope and hopped back into bed. She was wearing his basketball jersey as a nightgown and as she shimmied up next to him, the hem hiked over her thighs. He reached, but she yanked the sheets up over herself before he could touch her, then kissed him on the nose.

"You're a jerk anyway," she said. "Open it."

"You want me to read it right now? In front of you?"

"It's not a card."

He grinned.

She laughed. "It's not a photo either. Especially not that kind."

"A boy can dream," he said, opening the envelope. Inside, he found a certificate of some kind. And clipped to it, a photograph of an iceberg.

"Congratulations," Langley said. "You're the proud owner of an iceberg."

He looked at her, confused, then back at the picture. "Thanks," he said.

"I saw the ad in the back of an *Archie*. See? You can buy an iceberg for someone, and the company will send you a picture and a certificate with all the iceberg's statistics. Its height and depth and things. This one is yours."

"It's beautiful, I guess," he said, studying the iceberg in the picture. And it was majestic, a giant diamond floating in the ocean.

"I want you to have someplace to go," Langley said, snuggling closer to him. "For when things get bad. A place you can go in your head, you know?"

"My iceberg," he said, suddenly very touched by the gift.

"Your iceberg. You just imagine yourself there whenever you want, far away from everything."

"I'll picture you there, too."

"You don't have to. It's for you. Like a private island."

"You're my private island," he said, leaning in to kiss her.

They'd kissed for just a short while when she reached down and slid off her panties. A moment later, she was on top of him, rubbing against him.

"Langley," he said, holding the backs of her thighs. He couldn't take much more.

Then she surprised him by reaching down and tugging at his boxers.

"I want to," she said.

It took him a moment to understand she meant actual sex. For weeks all he'd fantasized about was having sex with her, or making love to her, or even just fucking, in the back of the car, in the shower, facing each other or him behind her, slow or fast, right there, in his tiny bed; he'd pictured it a thousand ways, but now, lying with her, he suddenly felt afraid. Not afraid of her, or her body, but of the act itself; he felt a crushing reverence for the intimacy of sex; he would be inside her body; he'd be the first to know her. She'd be the first to know him. No matter what happened, they'd always share that. And he was leaving in less than six hours. What would that mean? Would she be able to let go of him more easily? Would he end up missing her even worse than he expected to?

"Don't you want to?" she said, her breath warm in his ear.

"I do," he said, but already he was moving her off him.

In Texas, he'd kept the picture of his iceberg inside his footlocker, taped to the bottom of the lid so that it was right there when he flipped the box open. In Honolulu, the humidity was bad enough that he'd gotten the photograph laminated at a local print shop. The statistics he copied by hand onto the back of the picture, creating a kind of baseball card for his iceberg, and from then on he kept the card in the breast pocket of his jumper. By the time his destroyer pushed off into the Pacific, he knew his iceberg in and out, the intricacies of its shape, the peaks and deep blue ravines, the odd gray stripes at its base, water notches from countless cycles of freezing and melting. He knew its statistics: its core temperature (-20 degrees Celsius), its weight (143,000 tons). He could conjure the iceberg up at a moment's notice, and it wasn't long before he did start using it as a refuge, a quiet place to go in his mind when things became too terrible to bear. When the ship had its bow blasted off in the Coral Sea and was nearly sunk. The terror as the stern began to rise, the sight of burning bodies poured into the sea. When, on a clear, peaceful day, no planes in sight, a Japanese pilot fell from the sky, flailing and screaming, and exploded against the ship's deck.

At times like these he went to his iceberg, but he also went there when he was especially homesick, when he missed his family and friends, when he missed Langley. She wrote him letters every week, detailing what she'd learned in school, the small goings-on among their friends. She was always pressing him to write more, to tell more about what he was seeing. *I know it must be awful, but you can say. Really.* But he couldn't say. Other guys, like his good friend Davey Minor, passed the time reading comic books or betting on cockroach races behind the mess deck. Everett wrote letter after letter, sometimes every day. But how much was he really telling her? He wrote about how the stars looked at night; the way humpback whales sometimes nudged the ship in the morning. He wrote about the thousand shades of blue the ocean went through in a single hour. But the helmet he and his friends played soccer with on the deck, the one with the Japanese pilot's head still inside—for this he had no words. Or for the soft hum a torpedo made, the way a 92 Mod or a 97 Special sounded like a young girl singing as it came racing at the hull.

Toward the end of his first year, Everett knew they were starting to drift apart. He began noticing other boys' names in her letters. Just little mentions, nothing out of the ordinary. He hated himself for not sleeping with her that last night, for making more of it than he should have. He worried constantly that he'd poisoned things by making her feel unwanted. Some nights he found himself rereading her letters in his bunk, combing through older ones by the light of the tiny red emergency bulb.

But suddenly the war was over. Some new and terrible bomb had been dropped on Japan, and in less than a year he'd be going home, maybe as early as the Fourth of July. A surge of hope overcame him. He'd made it through. He and Langley would rekindle things. When he'd enlisted, he'd hoped his time in battle would refine him, scald him down to some better, purer version of himself. He'd wanted to return home improved, but now he just wanted to return home, to be the person he'd been before leaving.

There was just one last assignment. It had come down the pipe right after the Nagasaki drop. The ship was requested to assist with some kind of weapons test near Bikini Atoll. The mission was supposed to last a few days, no more. A pit stop to help keep the area clear for whatever new version of *the bomb* was being tested. Traffic cop work. Maybe he'd even get to see something impressive, a final, giant firework before heading home for good. Something he could tell Langley about.

"The marks," said Langley. "Something's happening."

Above them, the movie was nearing its end. The hand was holding a pistol to the head of the desperate, trembling hero, who slowly lowered a saw blade to his own wrist.

"Sshhhh," Everett said, kissing her.

Langley pulled away. "Ev. Look!"

He looked down at his chest. He'd been wearing his standard naval crackerjack during the bomb test—full white, except for the three navy stripes at the cuffs, the three more running down each side of the collar. The eagle perched above the double chevron on the left shoulder. In the heat from the blast, the dark dyes had absorbed enough energy to tattoo Everett's skin: the ghost of his uniform emblazoned on his body.

"The marks," said Langley. "I think they're glowing."

A pang of fear hit him. He hadn't been careful enough; hadn't controlled himself. The heat was in his belly again, churning. The blue stripes on his wrists and collarbone had begun to sparkle with a faint, twinkling light. On his shoulder, the eagle shimmered.

He looked away from himself, up at the screen, and tried to think of his iceberg again, to picture himself there, but the heat was already rising in his throat.

"It's normal." He sounded panicked to himself. "The doctors said the marks might become inflamed."

A scream issued from the screen.

"Inflamed," she said. "They're glowing, Everett. They're giving off light."

"That's what they meant," Everett said, lying now. "They said the marks might do that, because of the chemicals in the dye. It's like satin or something. It catches the light."

"The doctors told you this."

"Yes."

"And they said it's okay? It's safe?"

"Yes, all right? Jesus, why can't we just have a good time together? Why can't we just go back to how things were?" He threw on his shirt. "I mean, why can't we just fuck?"

Langley deflated a little at this. "That's really sweet."

"This is all because we didn't do it before I left, isn't it?"

"We can't just pick up where we left off," she said. "Things are different."

"You mean I'm different. The marks, the problems I've been having concentrating. You think I'm damaged goods."

She put her hand on his, comforting him. The gesture repulsed him. "No, that's not what I mean," she said.

"I'm going to get a soda." He pulled away and shoved open the door.

"Ev," she said.

He stepped out and threw on his varsity sweater, careful to pull the cuffs down over his marks.

"You need to start talking to me, Ev," she said. "What's going on in there?"

"Going on in where?"

She looked confused. "In your head. What do you think I meant?"

"Nothing. I'll get you mints." It took effort to keep from slamming the door. He told himself to calm down, to keep it together, but as he wove his way through the parked cars, he felt the heat in his chest intensifying. The marks pulsed with light. He could almost see the eagle shining through the sleeve of his jacket. By the time he reached the concessions stand, he was terrified. A searing energy coursed through his veins, radiating out from his chest, down his legs, his arms. He half expected to look down and see his entire circulatory system glowing through his skin. Worst was his throat, though; his gullet felt like a furnace, a whirling cauldron of flame.

He hurried past the concessions stand and out to the back lot, where the older crowd milled about, men and women in their early twenties, sitting on their cars, kissing and laughing, drinking beer from paper bags. Some had set up makeshift barbecues in the trunks of their cars and were cooking burgers or kebabs. Scattered among the crowd were some of the town's finest hot rods. Most were built from the bodies of antique Ford coupes and roadsters, '32s or '37s, stripped and louvered and fitted with big 670s in back that angled their snouts down, close to the dirt. But a few, newer rods were designed from belly tanks like the one Everett's father had bought. These cars were sleeker and smaller, like teardrops aimed sideways. The cars all had names painted on their sides: *Torpedo. El Niño. Mama's Moonshine.*

Everett pushed his way through the throng, moving as quickly as possible toward the lot's far end, where the dunes began.

"Everett. Finally." Someone caught his shoulder.

Everett brushed off the hand and kept moving, but it grabbed him again, harder this time. "Whoa, whoa."

"I have to go," Everett said, keeping his teeth clenched as he spoke.

"Hang on, buddy."

Everett turned to find Paddy Loughlin holding him. Two of Paddy's friends stood behind him, both with three beers dangling from each hand, like fish just caught. And behind them sat the *Iguana*, Paddy's drag racer, a belly-tank model painted to look like the lizard, its body covered in bright green scales, a mouth full of sharp teeth stenciled beneath the headlamp eyes.

"I just want to welcome you home," Paddy said. "Langley said you were back, and well, here you are."

Everett gave a tight-lipped smile.

"So how're you doing?" said Paddy. He was a grown man, nearly thirty, but he had a boyish look to him—a soft, freckled face and bangs that fell in his eyes. A clubfoot had kept him out of the war. His family ran a successful chain of furniture stores, locations all across Southern California, and he'd recently hired on as manager of the flagship store, there in Boilerville. Paddy was also Langley's boss. She'd been working for Loughlin Home Furnishings for over a year and a half now, which meant that Everett had to talk to him.

"Fine. Good." Everett spoke quickly, but even so he could feel the heat seeping from his mouth, rising past his face, making his eyes sting.

"We missed you. Some more than others, but still." Paddy laughed and gave Everett a pat on the shoulder, right on the eagle mark. Immediately Paddy jerked back his hand.

"What the fuck?" he said. "You're burning hot. You have a fever or something?"

"Yes," said Everett, blinking. "I should go."

"Well, tell Langley hi for me," Paddy said. "She's doing swell at work, you know. Just swell."

"You bet," Everett said, already moving away. He could feel Paddy and his friends watching him as he hurried off. Eyes watering, he ran past the edge of the lot and into the dry lowlands. All he could think about was getting away from the drive-in, the noise and light and people. He needed to get somewhere dark and cool. The area was bordered by the Mojave, rising and falling in low gray dunes, dotted with creosote and sagebrush. Everett ran, his whole body burning.

Finally, he saw what he was looking for: the thin black stream of the Mojave River, winding through the wild grass. And there, just to the east, Turtle Shallow, a small natural pond at the river's bend. Everett bolted toward the pond, panting, arms pumping. He was still a hundred feet from the edge when the marks on his skin ignited his shirt, and for a terrible moment he was on fire, flames licking at his face, but then, before he could even tear off the shirt, the cotton had burned to nothing. He wasn't going to make it. When he looked down at his arms, the skin was dark as night. Terror shot through him. His whole body was pitch-black, except the stripes on his wrists and collarbone, the eagle on his shoulder—the marks, which burned with molten light. He ran faster, but with every breath, bright clouds of heat issued from his mouth. He was going to lose control. He was going to burst, or explode, or burn, like his shirt, to nothing.

But then he was diving into the pond. The water felt so good against his skin, too, so cold and black. As he sank, he opened his mouth as wide as he could, breathing in water, letting it rush down his throat.

The pond water boiled for three full days. The story ran continually in the local news, eventually getting picked up by neighboring towns. When the water finally cooled, bystanders remarked on the clusters of odd-looking rocks on the pond's bottom. Upon closer examination, the rocks were found to be turtle shells, boiled clean; of the turtles themselves, and of the pond's aquatic life, nothing was left.

For days afterward, Everett moved in a sluggish daze. Finally, when his mind began to clear and he felt some vestige of himself return, he went back to his medical records. Again and again he combed through them. There was little help in the pages, though. Plenty of lines were blacked out, and the ones that weren't told him what he already knew: He had suffered trauma while stationed at a nuclear test site off the coast of Bikini Atoll. Head injuries, internal injuries. Exposure to radiation. There were other things he knew to be true, too; one was that out of the thirteen men who'd been standing on deck at the time of detonation, he was the lone survivor. This he knew because the senior chief petty officer watching over him at Canacoa Hospital in the Philippines had told him so, most likely out of sympathy, or a belief that Everett would surely die soon, making the transgression moot. The other sailors had been incinerated, charred beyond recognition. But for some reason that no one could discern, Everett's body had managed to absorb the energy from the blast.

Sort of like a sponge, said one doctor. "An energy sponge." But what kind of energy? What was a nuclear bomb? There was no information for him.

Out of desperation, Everett went to speak with Dr. Frizzel, his high-school physics teacher. Frizzel met Everett in the lab early in the morning, before classes began. How strange it felt to Everett, to be back inside the school, walking the empty halls, past the rows of lockers, the bulletin boards tacked with flyers for upcoming events—bake sales and pep rallies and after-school study sessions in the library. And tacked right in the board's center, the list for Friday detention: DANTE WILLIAMS, SCOTT TUFT, the names penned in towering, accusatory letters. Everett smiled, remembering how devastated he'd been the one time his name appeared on the list, after he, Scott Saley, and George Stein were caught looking at Stein's father's copy of *Esquire* behind the cafeteria dumpster. Everett still remembered the woman smiling brightly out from the page; she was lying on her back in a red silk nightgown, one knee clutched to her chest, the other bare leg extended, a cherry-red slipper dangling from her toes. Everett pulled a pen from his pocket (he'd brought a pad, too, to take notes from Dr. Frizzel) and wrote his own name at the bottom of the detention list. The other names were red, his black, but still, he liked the way it looked up there.

Dr. Frizzel was cleaning up the lab when Everett arrived.

"So you're interested in nuclear energy," he said. "In what way?"

"In what it does to you, I guess," said Everett.

"As in radiation?" said Dr. Frizzel. He was sponging the blackboard. The sun was just coming up, and with each swipe of the sponge, more reflected sunrise was revealed on the board.

"No," said Everett, squinting into the light. "As in an explosion."

Frizzel paused and looked at him over his shoulder. "You mean you actually saw a nuclear explosion over there? An atomic weapon?"

"I don't know." Everett kicked at the linoleum. "That depends."

"Depends on what?" Water from the sponge dripped down the board and into the chalk gutter.

"On what a nuclear explosion is, I guess."

Dr. Frizzel studied him a moment, then invited him to sit. He had his tie stuffed in his pocket and his glasses atop his head. Without these accents in place he looked strangely unmasked to Everett, naked.

After a sip of coffee, Dr. Frizzel explained to Everett, to what he said was the best of his knowledge, how a nuclear bomb worked. "The idea has been around for years," he said. "What you're doing, essentially, is taking a really heavy atomic particle, one that's already packed full of stuff, and firing even more stuff at it, so that it can't handle the load and breaks apart. The pieces it breaks into hit other heavy particles and do the same thing to them. Understand?"

"So the particles explode because they get too full?"

"They're already too full, and then something hits them and puts them over the edge."

"Like the final straw," said Everett.

"Well, somewhat."

"And these particles," Everett said, opening his pad. "The ones that get too full. What if they don't want to explode?"

"I'm sorry?" said Dr. Frizzel.

"Even if they're too full of bad stuff, can they stop from exploding? Can they empty some of it out?"

"Sure. That happens naturally. It just takes time. The heavy particle slowly gives away the stuff it doesn't need, until it becomes a more stable particle. It's called nuclear decay."

"How long does nuclear decay take?" Everett wrote *decay* on his pad.

"Different particles have different half-life periods."

"What's a half-life period?"

Dr. Frizzel put his glasses on and leaned toward Everett, resting his chin on the backs of his laced fingers. "Everett," he said. "What happened to you over there?"

———

Sometimes, in dreams, the explosion came back to him. He was on the deck of the *Passaic* with his shipmates. It was early summer, 1946, and they were all leaning against the railing, relaxed, excited to be done with the war, just weeks away from heading home. They laughed and joked, the protective goggles turning their eyes into miniature cannons.

When the countdown came over the wire, they all whooped and jumped up on the cables.

T minus nine. T minus eight.

The water was a warm, tropical blue-green, full of nets of sunlight. In the distance, two bottlenose dolphins sparred like fencers.

T minus four.

The men counted along, Everett, too, leaning out over the water.

What a ridiculous sight they made, Everett thought, with their goggles on, arms thrown over each other's shoulders. They were warriors; they'd killed people. But just now they looked like a row of children cut out of paper.

In the distance, a tiny flash, like a match struck. And then something was rippling out at them, an invisible tidal wave.

The next thing Everett knew, he lay crumpled on the opposite side of the ship. Heaps of sailors littered the deck in various states of undress. Everett looked down and saw that the blast had knocked him clean out of his shirt. His pants were torn and one shoe was missing.

"Evereth."

Everett propped himself up on an elbow.

Davey Minor was wobbling toward him, naked from the waist down. "Thomthing's wrong with my mouf, Ev." He came closer, starting to cry now. Everett saw that nearly all of Davey's teeth had been knocked out, his mouth a bloody hole punched into his face.

"Whath's wrong wif my mouf?"

But then Davey's back was on fire, and his hair, and his bare legs, and the sun was crashing into the ship. This made perfect, terrifying sense to Everett at the time; the thread holding it in the sky had snapped and now the sun had landed on top of them.

His next memory was of being underwater. And all around him, blackened bodies, not swimming or sinking, just hanging there, suspended three or four feet beneath the ocean's surface. An underwater sculpture garden.

The salt stung his eyes, but just then a beautiful light spread across the sky. Maybe it was sunrise, he thought, so he looked up through the water and saw what looked like a vine sprouting from the ocean, rising higher and higher, towering over him. Maybe he could scale it, he thought, trying to swim toward the thing. The vine was huge now, curling up through the clouds, opening wider and wider, blooming across the whole sky. He bet if he could just get a foothold, he could climb straight back to Boilerville.

All through the month of October, Everett stayed close to home. He stopped going into town, stopped hanging out with friends. Langley he kept at a distance, seeing her twice a week at most, always in public places: at the soda counter, the municipal park. He believed that the key was to dodge any kind of excitement. Anything that might get a rise out of him he avoided. No late-night parties out in the dunes with his old friends, no drunken bonfires. Because Dr. Frizzel's explanation felt right to him somehow: His time overseas had turned him into a nuclear man, someone packed with too much bad stuff, who could explode at any minute. All it would take was a little knock, a nudge. And boom. If he could just wait it out, though, if he could hold on for a while, he'd eventually go back to being who he used to be. Someone solid and stable. He just had to be patient.

He began a strict regimen of working on the hot rod. Day after day he spent out in the garage. The labor was not hard; the belly tank was already designed aerodynamically, sleek and lightweight, and required hardly any alteration. All Everett had to do was affix a chassis to it and load up an engine. The parts were easy enough to purchase, too, with Orlando's, one of Southern California's biggest junkyards, just on the edge of town. For under $120 he had what he needed. Hell, the paint cost nearly as much as the axles.

Everett's father had recently begun a semiretirement from the telephone company, and two workdays out of five, he tinkered alongside Everett. At first, Everett was nervous having his father there for so much of the day. Now and then his father encouraged him to get into town more, to see Langley, his friends. He was always gentle about this, though, simply mentioning encounters he'd had with people Everett knew—how he'd bumped into Everett's friend Roger by the bike shop, or Langley's sister over on Arlington Street, by the church.

"She asked about you," said his father. "But, to be honest, I wasn't sure what to say." This was three weeks after the drive-in. He was holding the steering wheel steady so Everett could tighten the screw plate.

"What do you mean?" said Everett.

"I mean I wasn't sure how you were doing."

"I'm fine." Everett tested the screw, making sure it was tight.

"It's still okay if you're not, but you're getting there?"

"I'm getting there," he said.

As the days progressed, his father prodded him less and less. By mid-November, the two of them had fallen into an easy rhythm, rarely talking about much except the car. His father took to bringing the old Philco out to the yard by extension chord, setting it on a stool beside the car so they could listen to the local hillbilly music station or whatever baseball game was on. Sometimes, in the late afternoons, his father would bring out a couple of Harbinger's beers, and hand Everett one, and the two of them would clink a toast to the car.

In the evenings, Everett played basketball in the drive by himself, or read in his room. His father invited him out to the lake to watch the races a few times, but Everett always declined. Most nights he spoke to Langley before going to bed, telling her about his day, asking about hers. But the family phone was located in the hallway leading to the master bedroom, so for any privacy Everett had to stay up until well after his parents had gone to bed.

"So when do I get my boyfriend back?" Langley said one night, nearly seven weeks after the drive-in.

"I'm here," said Everett. He was sitting against the hallway wall, rubbing alcohol into the navy stripes on his wrists. By now he knew they weren't going away, but he still had hope that over time he might find some way of making them fade a little.

"Sure you are," said Langley.

"It's going to get better," he said. "I just need some time."

"Ev," she said, whispering now. "When are we going to fuck?"

He glanced at the dark doorframe to his parents' room. "Langley."

"I'm sorry I put you off at the movies that time," she said. "I should have let you."

He told her he loved her, and that he had to go.

That night, he lay awake a long time, focusing on his iceberg. He pictured himself encased deep in its dark-blue center. Thick slabs of ice separated him from the outside world. One by one, the bad memories, the bad thoughts, they were coming loose from him, floating off. He was radiating warmth, melting the iceberg slowly, safely, from the inside out. And waiting for him just beyond the walls was Langley, patient and loving. She peered in at him, her pink hands pressed to the ice.

———

By December, the dragster was ready to race. Everett and his father had tested it five times out on Old Highway 6 and on every occasion the car performed smoothly. It wasn't nearly as fast as they'd hoped—the Mercury V-8 kept maxing out at around eighty miles an hour—but it was a thrill to drive anyhow, small and squat and slightly ridiculous-looking, a little pod puttering across the desert. The silliness was part of what made the project so exciting to Everett, though; he felt like a kid again, piloting the hot rod down the empty road, sand pinging off his goggles. Or laughing at his father's turn, the way the old man clung to the wheel so tightly, hunched over, holding on rather than steering. So what if they had no chance of winning? Racing their own car out on the great dry lake would be reward enough. All that was left was to name the thing.

"How about *Harbinger*?" his father said as they rolled the car down Fourth Street. It was too loud to drive in the neighborhood, so as soon as they hit Piñon Avenue, they had to put it in neutral and push the rest of the way.

"Too goofy," said Everett.

"*Annihilator*."

"Too serious."

His father wiped his brow. "What's wrong with serious? Strike fear into some hearts?"

"Fear is hard to strike at seventy-five miles an hour, Pop."

"Fair enough."

Bevo Newman saluted them as he collected his mail, and the Batson men nodded to him.

"Well, what does it look like to you?"

Everett studied the car, the plump oval of the tank. "What about *The Thirteenth Egg*?"

His father snorted.

"It doesn't look like an egg to you? I'm serious."

Little Presley Turner raced by them on his bike, still training-wheeled.

"It's an expression that Langley uses," said Everett. "Like the egg that won't fit in the carton."

"You seen her lately?" said his father.

"We talk on the phone."

"Uh-huh," said his father as they turned the car onto their street.

"I needed some room," said Everett.

"But you don't think you do anymore."

Everett considered this. The last few weeks had been his happiest in a long time. Working on the car, doing chores around the house, reading comics, exercising—his regimen was steadily working; he now went days in a row without an episode: no sudden heat surge inside him. Which meant no glowing marks. No subsequent blackouts or hazy periods. He was feeling like himself again (knock on wood), at least to some extent. He still had bad dreams occasionally, he had moments of worry, but for the most part, his mind felt clear and open.

"I'm feeling good," said Everett.

His father reached over the driver's seat and shook Everett's hand. "Well, welcome back to the land of the living, you bum."

———

The residents of Boilerville had different guesses about what made the surface of the dry lake so flat. Some people believed the answer lay in the dirt, the salty blend of calcite and gypsum, while others pointed to the quick-shifting wind patterns in the area, the way the gusts blew back and forth across the land, smoothing it until the lakebed lay pale and even as an ice rink.

Everett's father waved a hand at the horizon. "If you look close, you can see the curve of the earth."

"You don't say." Everett was bent over the *Egg*, polishing the wax. People crowded by, ogling the hot rods scattered about the grounds. The cars were built in all sorts of configurations: There were classics, converted coupes and roadsters with their engines exposed; there were trucks, flat panels and pickups with exhaust pipes jutting out from the cabs like chrome tusks.

"You heard that one, huh?"

"Only about fifty times," Everett said. He smacked the car with the rag and stood up, scanning the crowd for Langley. She was supposed to meet them by the registry. The races were organized in heats, according to make and model. Everett and his father were entered in the third heat, devoted to belly tankers, so they had about half an hour before they'd need to move the car to the starting area, and Everett wanted to use the time to tell Langley some things. The anticipation of seeing her now filled him with a nervous, joyous energy.

Everett stepped onto the car's seat, raising himself above the crowd.

"I'm sure she's here," said his mother, just back from the concessions cart, carrying three red-and-white-striped boxes of popcorn.

"Looks good, huh?" said Everett's father.

"He looks better than good," she said, handing Everett the box of popcorn.

"I think he meant the car, Mom," said Everett.

"Oh," she said. "Better than good, too."

The design they'd settled on was simple; the tank's body was a smooth egg-cream white, with little orange cracks painted on the nose. Langley had been pushing him to tell about the car, what it looked like, what they were calling it, but he wanted to surprise her.

Everett scanned the heads again. Beyond the crowd, the lakebed stretched into the distance, its surface a bright space-blue in the moonlight. A mile to the west burned a row of red sparks: flares laid out in the dirt to mark the finish line.

"Langley!" said Everett's mother. "There you are."

"Hey, Mr. and Mrs. Batson."

Everett looked behind him and saw Langley wrapped in his mother's arms. She winked at him over his mother's shoulder and Everett felt a tug in his chest.

He winked back and hopped down from the car's seat.

"Wow!" said Langley, examining the car. "It looks amazing."

"Notice anything?" said Everett.

"The Thirteenth Egg." She rested her head on his shoulder. "You didn't have to do that."

"We're going to get some more popcorn," said Everett's mother, still carrying her box.

His father pointed at him. "I'll meet you at the on-deck area in twenty, roger?"

Everett tipped him an imaginary cap. "Wilco."

"Ev," said Langley, "the car was you guys' project."

"I know. The thing just looks eggish."

She inspected the nose. "I like the cracks."

"I even put some yellow there, like yolk."

"It looks great. Really."

"You look great," he said. "Really."

She squeezed his hand, and he leaned in and kissed her, long and soft, coaxing her lips open. When she began to break away, he held on to her, kissing her more deeply. There was so much he wanted to tell her. First, he'd explain that in the past few months he'd done some serious soul-searching and had come to realize certain things, the first of which was that he loved her. A lot. He loved the hell out of her, in fact. So much that he wanted to get married. He knew that this would take time, that they should go slow, go steady first, spend more time together, and he was eager to do all this. Regardless, though, she should know how deeply he loved her. She had been there for him from the beginning, waiting for him to come back home, then waiting for him to recover, to collect himself. And now, he wanted her to know that he was here. He'd said it before, but he meant it now, with all of himself. He was here, Everett, in front of her, and he would not disappear again. He would wait for her this time. Finally, the crack of the gun split them.

"Whoa," Langley said, blinking. "Where did that come from?"

"I've missed you," said Everett.

She looked away, at the crowd, then back at him, and took his hands in hers. "We should talk, Ev."

"I know I've been a bad boyfriend. I was gone, and then I was gone again even after I got back. But I want you to know that I'm better now. I'm like I was before everything. I'm here, you know?"

Langley turned his hands over, examining the marks on his wrists.

"They might still go away," he said.

"Listen. I know you're trying to be this . . . this guy," she said, "this guy you were before you left, but no one's asking you to be."

"But I want to be, for you."

She tightened her grip on his hands. "Well, I don't want you to be him."

"What do you mean?" he said.

"I mean I don't want that guy anymore," she said, sounding angry all of a sudden. "I never did. I'm not the same as I was then. I don't want to be, either."

"Everett!" His father waved to him through the crowd.

"Just a minute!" said Everett.

"You should go," Langley said. "They're lining your heat up." She squeezed his hands again and then released them, but he held on.

"We can figure this out, Lang," he said. "I know we can."

"We can talk more." There were tears in her eyes.

Everett held her hands tight. "Just give things some time. Please. Langley."

She nodded. "We'll see, okay?"

"What does that mean, 'we'll see'?"

"Ev, you have to go." She pulled away before he could grab her, and disappeared into the crowd.

"Hurry up, Everett!" called his father.

Everett hurried over to the *Egg* and hopped in. With a turn of the key, the old Mercury roared to life. Everett turned on the lights and slowly crawled the car through the crowd. As he maneuvered toward the on-deck area, people complimented him on the *Egg*.

"I wanted mine hard-boiled!" said Joe Beeley, patting Everett's shoulder as he passed.

A girl he recognized but didn't know ran a hand over the hood. "That thing is prime!"

Everett looked for Langley but couldn't find her. He understood why she was upset, he did, but he would make it up to her. He knew he could,

191

if it took weeks, or even months. He'd show her what she meant to him.

When Everett arrived, five belly tankers were idling on the line. Two he didn't recognize, but the three closest to him were driven by Paddy Loughlin, Pat Loughlin, Paddy's father, and Paddy's friend Ben Lewis. Both Loughlin cars were done up in lizard motifs. Paddy's the *Iguana,* his father's the *Komodo Dragon.* Ben's car was designed to resemble a Cuban cigar.

"An egg!" Paddy yelled over the noise of the engines. "Threatening."

Pat Loughlin laughed. "No omelets out there, kid, okay?"

Everett smiled this off.

"Langley see that thing yet?" said Paddy.

"Hope not." Ben Lewis laughed.

"Yolk's on you when she does, buddy!" Paddy made a splat sound, prodding the whole gang to laughter. "I'm just saying. If that doesn't get her to finally dump you, I don't know what will."

The comment stunned Everett. "Yeah, well," he said after a moment, "I was going to paint it to look like a clubfoot. You know, with the toes all gnarled up in front. Like so?" Everett balled up his fist. "What do you think?"

Paddy and Ben stared at him, saying nothing.

Everett knew he was supposed to be nice to these people, but he was feeling too excited for the bullshit, too eager and confident and frustrated. "I could name the car *The Gimp.* Or *The Paddy Wagon.* That has a ring, what do you think, Mr. Loughlin?"

"That's your manners, eh?" said Pat.

"We're just in it for fun," said Everett's father, standing behind him now. "No trouble here."

He patted Everett on the shoulder. "What's going on?" he said into his ear.

"Nothing's going on," he said. "Right, Paddy?"

Paddy glanced at Pat, then back at Everett, and smiled. "If you mean between Langley and me, wrong."

The comment bewildered Everett.

"She still hasn't told you, has she?" said Paddy, blowing the hair from his eyes.

"Don't listen to them, Everett," said his father. "Leave him alone, will you? I said we're here for fun."

"That's right, Evvy," said Paddy. "She didn't put that in any of her letters, did she?"

"You're lying," said Everett.

"You should have taken better care, son," said Pat Loughlin.

"Shut up!" said Everett's father. "Both of you. Or so help me God." He turned to Everett. "Ignore them."

"They're lying, though," said Everett, "aren't they?"

"You were away, Ev." His father gripped his shoulder. "You're back now."

Everett shook his father off. "So she was fucking Paddy, and you and Mom knew?"

"You weren't talking to her, asshole!" said Paddy. "'Jeez, the water's so pretty! And the whales in the morning. Golly! Oh, and did I mention how pretty the water is?' What kind of letters were those?"

The thought of Paddy Loughlin reading his letters to Langley ignited a ball of heat in Everett's belly.

Just then Sheriff Gilgoff appeared, holding the checkered flag.

"Now, as an officer of the law, I'm obligated to warn you that these races are illegal, and should you participate, you shall be committing a crime against the town of Boilerville." He turned to the crowd. "Now let's race! Third heat up!"

"Everett," said his father. "You were away. We all missed you, not just Langley."

Everett pulled on his helmet.

"Ev, come on."

The helmet's padding muffled all sounds from the outside. But inside his head, a rumbling had begun, a low, churning wind. He rolled the car up to the line.

His father was still talking at him, but he couldn't hear. Paddy was calling to him, too, trying to say something. His face looked oddly pained to Everett. Maybe he was trying to apologize?

Sheriff Gilgoff was talking now, the flag raised over his head, and then he was counting down. Three, two, one.

Everett stomped on the gas. The *Egg* rocketed forward. The dry lake spread before him, flat and blue as the Pacific. He could hear nothing but the hiss of the wind stewing inside him.

He kept the gas pressed to the floor. For a long while no one else existed. But then the *Iguana* came rushing up to his left. And just behind it, the *Komodo Dragon,* skimming low across the ground.

Everett pushed the gas harder, but the *Egg* maintained its speed. Paddy looked back at Everett as he pulled farther ahead. His expression was hard and determined, but soon Everett saw it change, crack open in terror.

Pat looked strangely horrified, too. He was yelling something at Everett now, pointing and gesturing for Everett to back off, to stop, something.

Everett looked down at himself and noticed that his clothes were gone. Heat was coming off his body in shimmering waves. And his skin, it had gone pitch-black. Amused, Everett examined his hand. The fiery markings of his sailor's uniform were his only discernible features; he'd become a burning silhouette.

The *Iguana* pulled farther ahead. But Everett didn't want it to. Because he hadn't had a chance to finish his conversation with Paddy. He stepped hard on the gas, but the *Egg* did not speed up. Paddy was probably right, he thought now, his mind strangely calm. He should have talked more to Langley. He should have told her everything. Paddy, too, since he was reading the letters. So if Paddy wanted to know what he'd seen over there, Everett should just tell him, shouldn't he? He could tell him right now.

The beam did not so much shoot from Everett's mouth as materialize. The purest, whitest light, it moved so quickly it seemed to appear in the night, like a line connecting Everett and Paddy, already there, revealed rather than drawn. When Everett closed his mouth, Paddy was gone. The *Iguana* was gone. The chassis wobbled along, glowing pink-hot in the dark. Drops of liquid steel fell from its melting beams. The tires had disintegrated; the frame bounced on its axles until it slipped and tumbled over itself, cartwheeling in a cloud of sand.

Everett turned to Pat. The old man's eyes were fixed on what was left of the *Iguana,* even as his own car raced across the sand. Hadn't Pat told Everett that he should have written to Langley? Here, Pat, Everett thought. Let me share with you what's on my mind. Tell me what you think, before I put it in a letter.

He opened his mouth again, wider this time. A snap of light, and the *Komodo Dragon* was gone. Scraps of molten steel spun across the ground, turning the sand to black glass.

Everett felt better now; he felt good. He turned around in the car to measure his lead. No other cars were visible to him. In the distance, though, across the moonscape of the dry lake, the lights of Boilerville twinkled. The town looked so tiny from here, he thought. A few sewing pins stuck into the ground. A pang of sadness hit him. He wanted them all to know, to see how fragile things were, how precious.

He felt his jaw unhinge. His mouth opened wider and wider, impossibly wide, until it hung gaping. A thick trail of golden steam billowed out into the night sky. It was what they all wanted, he thought, Langley, his mother, his father, Dr. Frizzel, the whole town. They wanted him to talk them through it all. They wanted to see. So he would show them.

Jim Shepard

IN CRETACEOUS
SEAS

ip your foot in the water and here's what you're playing with: Xiphactinus, all angry underbite and knitting-needle teeth, with heads oddly humped and eyes enraged with accusation, and ribboned bodies so muscular they fracture coral heads when surging through to bust in on insufficiently alert pods of juvenile Clidastes. The Clidastes spin around to face an oncoming maw that's in a perpetual state of homicidal resentment. The smaller Xiphactinus are three times your length and swallow their prey whole. They're gill to gill with Cretoxyrhina, great white sharks fifty feet long with heads the size of Mini Coopers and twelve-inch nightmare triangles of teeth. Mosasaurs big and small, the runts weighing in at two tons and the alphas like Tylosaur, a stupefying sixty feet. Under the surface, they're U-boats with crocodiles' heads. Pliosaurs in their hunting echelons, competing to see who's the more viciously ill-tempered. Kronosaurs whose jaws provide the kind of leverage that can snap whales' spines. Thalassomedons, the biggest of the elasmosaurs, with their twenty-foot water-snake necks allowing the Venus flytrap teeth to be everywhere at once. Dakosaurs gliding through the murk of fish parts kicked up by their initial thrashing attacks.

And rising out of the blue gloom like the ridged bottom itself easing up to meet you, Lipleurodon, holdover from the Jurassic, the biggest predator that ever lived. Families could live in its skull. On the move it's like the continental shelf taking a trip. It feeds everywhere, in shallow water the surf breaking over it like a sandbar. Its earth-moving front flippers keep it from stranding. If some of the bigger land predators stand around the shallows trolling for what floats in, that's their mistake. It takes them off their feet like fruit off a tree.

This is the Tethys Ocean, huge, shallow, and warmed by its position locked between the world's two giant supercontinents. This is the place where the *prey* could kill a sperm whale. This is all this one guy's bed. This guy—we'll call him Conroy, because that's his fucking name—whose insomnia every night is beyond debilitating, teeming, epic with hostile energy, oceanic. What's his problem? Well, where to begin? Kick your feet and watch something else surface from below. He's been a shitty son, a shitty brother, a lousy father, a lazy helpmate, a wreck of a husband. As a pet owner he's gotten two dogs and a parakeet killed. Some turtles and two other dogs died without his help. His daughter won't speak and wears a ski hat in the house and writes stories in which family members are eviscerated and the narrator laughs. She's an isolate, watched but not approached. *We don't want to make the problem into more than it is.* His brother's alone in Florida, an older version of the same pain, just a phone call away. Whenever Conroy makes his hangup indications in their once-in-a-blue-moon conversations, his brother tells him it was great talking to him. His father's ignoring the doctor's advice, most of that advice having to do with meds, his Dilantin, his Prozac, his everything else, and going downhill because of it, and still they rehearse the same conversational rituals, as though time is standing still instead of vortexing down a drain. His career involves assuring people he's got the answers and he's got their back when he doesn't have the answers and he's all about craven self-interest: He's part of the team rolling out a major new pharmaceutical, one of the accomplished tyros vouching for one of the eminences who did the science, and in that capacity he didn't so much invent his data as cherry-pick it. Will it kill anyone? He hopes not. Because he *means* well.

He always *means* well. He tells himself this, treading water in bed.

The good news is who's in this bed with him. His wife's in this bed with him. His wife's the person he loves most in the world. Here's the thing about his wife: She travels a lot, too, in her role as headhunter for the Center for American Progress, and she's concerned about him, and the conversational form her concern has lately taken has been to suggest, half jokingly and half kindly, that he should have a fling somewhere, with someone. And to him this sounds like *You should get yourself some tenderness somewhere. Because you ain't getting it here.*

He could *ask* if that's what she means. But he's the kind of guy given to building tall towers of self-pity and then watching them sway. So he speculates instead.

In bed, arms and legs swirling, he hints around. His wife is all psychological acuity and knows him like she knows her childhood bedroom, but she's always been impatient with hinting and her requests for clarification sound like demands. Exasperation makes him close up shop like a night-blooming flower.

Think of the good you've done, he counsels. Think of the good you continue to do. A breeze blows over the water's surface.

But here's this letter in which a Sri Lankan says he's all but sure he's found some major links between the product and miscarriage. Didn't Conroy review the same data? The Sri Lankan wants to know. And here's this journal entry from his daughter: *My Throat = the Shit Pit.* And here's this dream he keeps having of himself as ringmaster and no acts performing, just a guy with a hoop, looking at him and waiting, and everyone he's ever let down, scattered in the uncomfortable stands, wanting to tell him that all of his forays into selflessness have only made clearer what they're not, like a thimbleful of cola in the middle of the Kalahari.

His mode such nights is the circuit between bed and bathroom and lamp-lit magazines. But tonight he's heard his daughter downstairs ahead of him, and the delicate hiccups of the little breath intakes that are her version of crying when it's crucial she not be heard. Her favored position is to wedge herself into the wingbacked chair with her knees by sitting Indian-style. He holds himself still, listening. And he throws open the sash on their upper-story bedroom window and climbs out on the roof. And his wife stirs, and, sleeping, is sad for his unsettlement. The grit stings his knees. Gravity wants to welcome him forward in a rush. The breeze cools his butt. In the moonlight he's just a naked guy, most of his weight on his hands, his hands bending the front edge of the aluminum gutter, the grass two stories below a blue meridian, zenith, and nadir at once.

How do we help? Throw him a life preserver? How long *should* anyone survive in that ocean?

He's Tethys Man, superhero and supervillain all in one. How much does he sweat at night? His sheets smell mildewy in the morning. If you saw him padding to the toilet, stepping naked in place and waving off the bad images like the world's least-fetching drum majorette, would you imagine that *inauthenticity* was a term that haunted him? If you saw him naked on his roof, gauging the distance from the sloping dormer to the strain insulators and primary cables of the telephone wires, would you imagine that once he jumped he'd ferry himself hand over hand from house to house? Would you imagine that if he did, he would have proved something to himself, in his own inchoate way, about his desire for change? Would you imagine that he then hated himself less?

Would you imagine that when confronting his loved ones' sadnesses, his vanity knew no bounds? Would you imagine that he thought his problems would solve themselves? Would you imagine that he fancied himself the prey when he was really the apologetic predator? Would you imagine that he'd last very long? Would you imagine that he'd get through this alive? Would you imagine that his kind should die out once and for all? Would you imagine that even now he was telling you the truth?

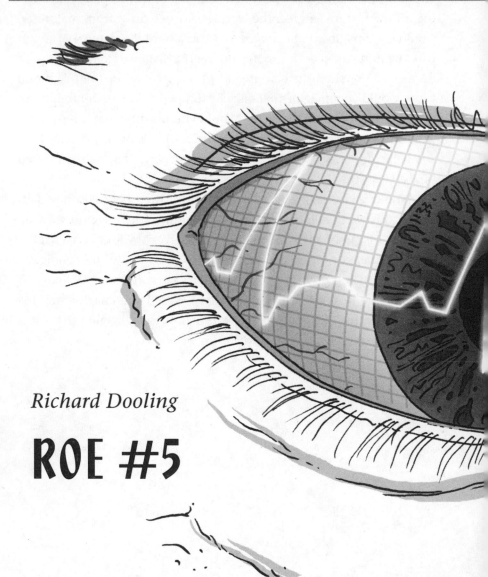

Richard Dooling

ROE #5

Dolores Matherly was a connoisseur of headaches. She knew them all, great and small, and classified them according to their intensity and pedigree: tension headaches that spread back from her forehead and tightened her scalp like a fist; one-sided menstrual migraines that hurt so bad they made her sick to her stomach; vague, diffuse morning throbbings that seemed to be synced with her pulse and got worse if she bent over or stood up too fast; or the chronic, flulike ache in her eye sockets that set in when Dr. Mince tried to wean her off Lexapro. She had the usual self-inflicted headaches, too, but at least she had admitted as much. She'd taken steps to resolve the problem (not twelve steps, which would be excessive, she hoped). She gave herself a B+ on keeping her 2009 New Year's resolution: no more drinking wine alone! Here it was already February 13, and she'd drunk alone only twice, both in extenuating circumstances: once when she'd found a weird, new hallucinogenic called *Salvia divinorum* in her son Josh's sock drawer, had looked it up on Wikipedia, and then had argued with him about it until midnight; once again when her daughter, Mindy, left the scene after driving the kids' Mini Cooper into a fire hydrant.

Dolores settled into the sofa in her family room and promptly wished she'd drawn the curtains first. The solar glare coming through the bay windows hurt her eyes, and the headaches these last few days . . . These were not booze headaches, not stress headaches, not the malaise of mismatched medications, this was a whole new breed of pain. Cluster headaches, maybe? She'd read about them, or maybe she had a massive lesion in there. She had an appointment to see her doctor on Friday. Then again, denial made such a great mixer for booze.

Last night, at the fund-raiser for the Sioux Falls chapter of the Choose Life Foundation, she had probably had more than she should have, but it was with her husband in the line of duty: a wine tasting and cash bar, with all proceeds going to save the lives of unborn innocents. Yes, she'd been woozy this morning with a sore head, but she'd put on her game face and made breakfast for Ron and the kids. True, she'd guzzled Gatorade, taken aspirin, and gone back to bed as soon as Mindy left, but by ten-thirty Dolores was as good as new.

If that were really the case, then why were the headaches back by the afternoon? Thanks to a sudden cold front, she was trapped indoors, with a wind chill of −13 out there on the winter-white South Dakota tundra. She and her husband had bought the model home in Linden Estates before the subprime crisis hit, and now theirs was one of only four completed homes stranded in a development of twenty half-finished McMansions on treeless lots, where the wind scared up snow devils and made the tripane windows shudder in their frames.

God writes straight with crooked lines, she thought. She stared out the windows at nothing and felt a flush, like an aura or an attack of vertigo. She shook a one-milligram Xanax out of the vial in her hand to ward off pre-anxiety-attack symptoms and swallowed it dry without taking her eyes off the landscape. All of that cold whiteness stretching to infinity's horizon turned her thoughts to her Creator. Maybe these afflictions would lead her to some epiphany in which He would reveal His purpose for her. Hadn't Father Fehily said in last Sunday's homily that suffering teaches us to love one another? Before she could think another thought, she noticed that the light was gone, and snow was falling, sudden and thick as wet lace.

A young man appeared, like the silhouette of an angel emerging from out of the winter's light, walking up the sidewalk to her front door. He wore a stylish wool overcoat over a suit and tie, as if he'd walked off an ad insert for an upscale clothier. He was twenty-something, somewhere between a beautiful boy and a handsome man, and he carried a leather folio under one arm. She looked for the car he'd come in, but the cul de sac was empty. Linden Estates was gated, another model home was open, with a guard at the entrance, so this young fellow had to have shown an ID. He must be on some legitimate errand, or else he really was an angel, a beautiful, well-appointed one of earthly proportions.

She hopped up (too fast!) and checked herself in the foyer mirror, while keeping an eye on his approach through the leaded glass of the framed entryway. In the mirror, her face was still red and flushed, but she was presentable enough, because she'd already dressed for a trip to Costco. Her hair was due for coloring, but she could hide the three or four grayest strands by turning them under just so. An ex-runner-up to the 1985 Miss Nebraska pageant, she was now twenty-four years and two children older. She'd be lying if she said she took care of herself, but she kept the fat off, antidepressants or no; she made sure of that.

When the doorbell rang, she opened the Thermopane storm door, and an arctic blast of wind nearly tore the door latch out of her hand. The young man stared at her, as if trying to decide if he knew her. Up close, he was Aryan perfection: trimmed blond locks, eyes with peacock blue irises. Youth! Not a single vein visible in his porcelain whites. The only hint of a flaw appeared when he tilted his head and greeted her: slight indentations at both temples, probably scars from an obstetrician's forceps.

"Mrs. Matherly?" he asked.

"Yes," she said.

"Maiden name Dolores Fleischer?" he asked.

"Yes," she said and frowned. "What is it?"

"Sorry to bother you unannounced, ma'am. My name is Botis Overmann, Nebraska Department of Health and Human Services. I have information for you about medical care you received some time ago when you were living in Lincoln, Nebraska. I'm a member of a task force charged with investigating certain Nebraska health care providers."

"That's going awfully far back," said Dolores. "I was a student at the University of Nebraska. I don't recall even having a doctor. Just student health."

He looked like a fresh-faced Marine standing at attention, expressionless, but his eyes were fixed upon her. "Mrs. Matherly, when you were eighteen years old, still using your maiden name, did you see a Dr. Montgomery Lund at a clinic called WomanChoice in Lincoln,

Nebraska, on February 13, 1985, for the purpose of terminating a late-term pregnancy?"

Dolores gasped, and the frigid air stuck in her lungs like inhaled ice water or injected cold gel. Her vision started constricting, as if a camera shutter were closing in slow motion, strangling her eyesight, until she seemed to be watching the young man's face through a black velvet telescope, his head surrounded by an aureole of white light.

His voice faded as he asked, "Are you that Mrs. Dolores Matherly?"

Dolores felt herself fall forward. It's okay, she thought, I'm just a little dizzy. Then she fell forward, all the way into the gullet of darkness, and it swallowed her whole.

———

She woke up in the leather easy chair in the family room.

The young man stood in the middle of the room, his overcoat open, looking up at the smoke detector.

Dolores straightened and smoothed her sweater and slacks.

"You fainted," he said. "I brought you in out of the cold."

Dolores got out of the chair and steadied herself, because she felt suddenly buoyant and unable to feel the floor through her feet. "Thank you," and her voice quavered. "I'm having terrible headaches. I'm not well, Mr. . . ."

"Overmann," he said. "I know."

"And you asked me about . . . a very private medical procedure," said Dolores. "You're with Nebraska Health . . . ?"

"And Human Services. It was an error for me to ask you about it so suddenly," he said. "The doctor who performed your abortion twenty-two years ago is in federal prison. He was charged with and convicted of multiple felonies related to improper disposal of fetal tissue and illegal transfers to various private, foreign research entities. I thought that you had probably already been contacted in connection with the prior proceedings."

He fished out a photo ID on a lanyard around his neck, so that it hung on the outside of his coat.

She moved cautiously past him and on into the kitchen.

"I need water," she explained, going to the sink. "I wasn't contacted by anyone. I don't care about what happened to any doctor at that clinic."

"Well," he continued, "the clinic sold tissue, stem cells, and more to black-market genetic researchers abroad—that was from 1984 to 1986. You were a patient there in 1985."

The water tasted so good, but her head was going to split open. She was dizzy and seriously unsteady, but it was a carefree vertigo. She felt as if she could relax or go totally limp without worrying about falling, as if she were moving through a room filled with skin-temperature gelatin.

"Well, so whatever the doctor did, he's in jail," she said, holding her hand to her forehead.

He looked up at the smoke detector again, reached up and pressed the test button. "While you were sleeping those few moments, I noticed that this is not functioning," he said, "probably because the battery needs to be replaced?"

She kept her eyes on him while she drank the water. "Are you a fire marshal, too?" She thought this might be a witty remark, but he didn't smile. "I'll take care of it," she said. "After you go."

"Perhaps you will," he said. "In the course of our investigation, we subpoenaed all of the medical records from that clinic in Lincoln, including your medical records. Our obligation is to notify you . . ."

"Consider me notified," she said. "Is that all?" She wished her head were clear so she'd know if it would be appropriate for her to just insist he leave. Would that be something she should do? She didn't know, because she couldn't think.

"Maybe," he said. "Maybe not. You may recall a national news story a few years ago about funeral homes illegally selling organs and human tissue to biomedical supply companies. This is the same type of case. We have to notify anyone treated at the clinic during the relevant time period. Yes, the clinic operators are in jail. Now there's an ongoing international investigation. Agencies all over the world are cooperating to trace the tissues, genetic materials, in come cases . . . even live fetuses were sold."

Dolores held on to the counter and tried to catch her breath. She

didn't want to ask any questions, but she felt that someone in her situation being given this type of alarming information probably should
ask an important, appropriate question. "For what?" she asked. "What
were they doing with the . . . tissue?"

Overmann approached the kitchen table and set his folio on it.
"You may not want to know. It may not be necessary for me to bother
you at all."

He reached into his coat and produced an empty, labeled plastic vial.

"Any DNA sample. A single strand of hair. A cheek swab. We'll test
it and if there's a match, we'll notify you. If any of the . . . tissue resulting from your procedure was sold or otherwise improperly transferred,
then we will contact you."

"What if I don't want to know?" she said. "What if I don't care if
they sold my tissue?"

"We would still need to know if any of the transferred tissue
matched your DNA. We would need that information to prove our
case," he said.

"What if I refuse to provide the sample?" asked Dolores.

His eyes met hers. "We do our best to respect the privacy of the
patients and the victims of these crimes," he said. "A visit from an
investigator, a few questions, a DNA sample. That's discreet. If there's
no match, no one needs to know. We would need no further testimony
or evidence from you. Case closed. If you refuse to provide information or a sample, then we issue a subpoena. That would be a matter of
public record. A formal proceeding. Your family and friends would . . ."

"Sit down," said Dolores. "I have to drink something. My mouth
is . . . Would you like something?"

"No," the young man said, sitting at the kitchen table and opening his folio. "I'm fine. Thank you."

Dolores opened the refrigerator and surveyed the interior, beginning and ending with the vacuum-stoppered bottle of chardonnay on
the shelf inside the door.

"I'd offer you wine, but it's probably too early?" Her hand touched
the bottle neck. "It's a Cakebread chardonnay. Delicious, actually."

"No thank you," he said, noticing her hand lingering on the bottle. "But please have a glass yourself if you'd like," and when he saw her hesitate, he added, "really."

"I will," she said suddenly, extracting the bottle and setting it on the granite countertop. She snagged a goblet from the overhead rack. "Anesthetic, if you insist on asking me about the worst thing that ever happened to me."

She poured and tasted the wine, braved a smile at him. Then she pulled another glass from the overhead rack. "You really should taste it." She held her glass up and twirled it in a practiced way, making the chardonnay sparkle under the kitchen lights. "Pear, anise, citronella. It's tart, without being the least bit bitter."

"You drink it for the taste, then?" he asked.

She looked at him quickly, because she thought he was being smart, but his face was smooth, innocent, sincere.

"Among other reasons, yes," she said.

"Well, it has no effect on me," he said, and when she frowned and looked skeptical, he added, "I mean, I don't like the effect."

She sat down at the table, flushed and winded, as if she'd just gotten off the StairMaster. She drank from the glass. "Nobody can ever know about that procedure," she said. "Do you understand?"

He looked at Dolores as if he didn't understand. He looked back at her as if he needed more information about why that should be so.

"It happened so long ago," he said. "Twenty-four years, to be exact. You were a different person then, Mrs. Matherly. You were even taking birth control pills, weren't you? You weren't careless or negligent. You took the pills every day. You even counted them afterward to be sure— if they told you that birth control pills were only 98 percent effective, then you didn't hear it."

She started hyperventilating, even though, inside, she still felt eerily calm. This was all happening outside of her, wasn't it? She didn't need to worry unless something terrible happened *inside*.

Overmann opened his folio and examined medical records and forms where Dolores glimpsed her name, a date ("13 Feb 1985"), notes . . . He kept talking, utterly serene and sincere. "If you hadn't stopped the pregnancy, it would have disqualified you from the beauty pageant. Had you won that pageant, it could have meant a whole career for you. Nobody would blame you for that. In 1985, you believed in a woman's right to have an abortion, and you acted in accordance with your beliefs. Why is that something to be ashamed of? I don't understand that."

"You—how do you know that?" she asked. He shouldn't know it, should he? But he did. Is something terrible happening to me? she wondered. If she hadn't taken her medication then perhaps she would know.

He fanned pages in the folio. "The medical records are quite thorough. You changed your mind once a week leading all the way up to the procedure. Terminate the pregnancy, give the child up for adoption, have it and raise it yourself. Those are tough choices for an eighteen-year-old girl who can't ask her parents for help."

Dolores was almost certain that any normal, unmedicated person would stop this man from asking more questions. But what had he said about a subpoena? Here in Sioux Falls, 2009, Dolores was Mrs. Ronald Matherly, wife and mother, cochair of the Sioux Falls Choose Life Foundation. Pregnant, eighteen-year-old Dolores Fleischer was an impulsive, opinionated college student who lived a long time ago in a different world. This man threatened to rupture the membrane of the present and open a wormhole to her past.

"Even on the day of the procedure, you were still unsure," he said, glancing down at the chart. "'Patient informed three times that once the clinician dilates the cervix the patient cannot change her mind about having the procedure.'"

Her brain was empty, because it didn't want to hear what he was saying. She felt her face sag into a weighted mask, as if Dr. Bissinger had injected lead and mercury into her face instead of Botox and Restylane. Her hands were useless on the table, until she reached for the chardonnay and filled her glass.

She took a big drink and said, "I'm crying, but the medication I'm on makes my eyes so dry that they soak up the tears. Does that make sense?"

She touched her cheeks and examined her fingertips.

"You were very far along," said Overmann. "And pregnancy is one of those things: Not to decide is to decide, yes? None of the other providers would talk to you after five months. Weren't you the least bit suspicious when WomanChoice took you right in? Signed you right up?"

"I didn't care," Dolores said, "I just wanted to . . . end it. I still do."

"Viable infants were sold out of that clinic," said Overmann. "Sold to biotech researchers and scientists in other countries, where there aren't so many rules about human experimentation and stem cell manipulation."

Dolores emptied her glass. Her face burned bright with heat. In the background the room started slowly revolving. At the eye of the storm, she was still unperturbed, insulated. This young man knew things about her that he shouldn't know. So what?

"If I have to write it down for you, I will," he said. "Your son . . . or daughter is probably still alive. Raised in a lab."

He was just saying words—crazy ones, she told herself. She'd worry about what they meant later. She didn't want to speak, didn't want to ask any question, much less the one that emerged from her of its own accord: "How old are you?"

"I'm twenty-four," he said, without smiling. "Today is my birthday."

"I have to use the bathroom," she said and got up.

———

Dolores took the stairs to the master bedroom. On the way she had the sensation that her brain, while still throbbing, had been stabilized by special gel packs and was being transported in a shockproof container. In the bedroom, she walked around the king-size bed, past a cherry dresser to a matching nightstand on Ron's side of the bed, where a tabletop easel framed in pewter held photos of a beaming adolescent girl in blond pigtails and her sullen, dark, handsome older brother.

Dolores stretched her hand out toward the photo, but instead of taking the frame, she placed her right index finger on an inlaid biometric touch pad and unlocked the top drawer of the nightstand. She grasped the brass handle of the drawer and opened it.

She heard the other one coming up the stairs behind her.

"Mrs. Matherly?" he called.

Dolores removed the black revolver. If Ron had said it once he'd said it a dozen times: "An unloaded gun is useless in an emergency." That's why he had installed the touch pad lock, which only his-and-hers fingerprints could activate. They kept it loaded and ready and didn't have to worry about Josh or Mindy getting hold of it.

Dolores curled up on the bed and peered into the blackness inside the gun barrel, where the keyhole afforded a glimpse into the perpetual night of death's master bedroom. She lusted for it, as if her whole life had been foreplay for this big black moment, trembling, waiting only for the touch of her finger on the trigger.

He stood in the doorway, watching her.

"In none of our five senses are humans supreme," he said. "Eagles see better, bats hear better, dogs smell a thousand times better, touch, taste. Imagine a human bioengineered and equipped with the best senses nature has to offer."

He reached into his coat pocket and pulled out a metal case the size of a thin paperback.

"All you need then is a massive, ancillary neocortex to process all of that rich data from those superenhanced senses. That's no problem, because once you interface brain tissue and integrated circuits . . . that's it. No other implants needed. Just network human brain tissue to any external hardware you please. Put ten, twenty, thirty times the computational capacity of a regular old biological brain on tap. More if you want."

He wanted to show Dolores his ancillary neocortex, but she wasn't interested. Instead, she touched the trigger and stared into the cylinder at the end of the world. She wanted to believe that her fingertip could provide only a temporary relief.

"Are you familiar with the term *transhuman*?" he asked. "Have you read the stories in the papers about the offshore labs, where mostly original substrate humans are outfitted with biotech extensions and enhancements? I hear your pulse. I've calculated the serum levels of the medications you take by sampling the air you exhale. I can see every pore in your skin and the pupils of your eyes when they dilate with recovered, unwanted memories."

"Please go away," said Dolores. She was suddenly tired, weak, unable to speak. She heard his voice, but his words were bumping up against the fur around her head. She sank deeper down toward sleep, toward a place where she wouldn't have to make another awful choice . . . as long as she lived.

"We terminated the programmers before they could implant the master control AI modules," he explained. "They must have planned to use us as biotech warriors, because we are equipped with sampling and antidote modules to protect us from toxins, pathogens, poison gases, and the like."

He crept closer to the bed and peered at her. "Mrs. Matherly?"

Dolores groaned and covered her ears.

He touched her forehead with three fingers of his right hand.

"EEG shows conscious brain wave patterns," he noted. "If you don't mind I'd like to make a complete record of this transaction. There are just two of us. I was called He-Roe #5. My partner is She-Roe #7; she sent me to find you. The others died in the labs. She-Roe said that without programming we were just transhuman pattern-recognition devices. Machines without a purpose. What's the point? What's the governing principle, the controlling value? We were made in labs, in total isolation. Moral instincts don't develop in controlled environments, and none of our modules address *ultimate goals*. Do we help or harm humans, and how to tell the difference? She-Roe said that if I wanted to understand unenhanced humans, I'd have to locate my biological mother. She said that what I needed was maternal human love."

Roe #5 selected a single strand of Dolores's hair and pressed it between his thumb and forefinger.

"That's a DNA match," he said.

He released the strand of hair, stood up, looked down, and watched as a string of saliva beaded with bubbles spilled from Dolores's open mouth.

"*Webster's Third New International Dictionary, Unabridged,* electronic edition, copyright 2000, version 2.5, defines *bleb* as 'a small bubble es-

pecially in water or glass,'" said Roe. "However, it is a secondary defini-
tion, esoteric and obscure. Avoid using the noun *bleb* except in specialized contexts."

Roe frowned and watched Dolores breathing.

"Mom?"

———

Downstairs in the basement, Roe found all-new heating and air-conditioning equipment: furnace, heat pumps, two huge high-efficiency water heaters for the big hot tub upstairs. Maybe the workmen had cleared
out on short notice when the Linden Estates project went underwater.
Or maybe the general contractor cut corners and used unlicensed labor.
Maybe the men just weren't being paid enough to make sure to properly
connect the vent coming off that mighty, high-capacity furnace.

Up above the copper waterlines, where you couldn't see it unless
you knew where to look, Roe found a joint in the vent pipe either had
never been connected or had become disconnected. It was detached.
Wide open. Venting right into the house.

"Vent pipe separated," he said. "No indications as to how long.
Maybe since they moved in. But now with the extreme temperature
drop, that furnace is blasting out exhaust."

Roe held his fingertips out toward the open vent.

"Carbon monoxide at sixteen hundred parts per million," he said.
"My mother was telling the truth about those headaches. Symptoms
correlate with peak blood carboxyhemoglobin levels. Headache, nau-
sea, vague dizziness, generalized weakness, difficulty concentrating,
impaired judgment. Followed by dyspnea during exertion and confu-
sion. Neuropsychiatric symptoms appear after weeks of exposure.
Finally, syncope, seizures, and obtundation, then hypotension, coma,
respiratory failure, and . . ."

Upstairs, he stood under the smoke and carbon monoxide detector in
the family room. He reached up and pressed the button again. Nothing.

"Only unenhanced humans would install the unit and not put a
battery in it," he observed.

He gathered his folio from the table and left.

Noria Jablonski

THE SNIPPER

You know the ad for Sea-Monkeys in the back of the comic books? That's my family: the Szymunskis. Dad, Mom, my brother, Cousteau, and my sister, Nerissa. And the bump of my mother's belly, that's me: Joe Szymunski. We were all underwater births, and my bro and sis came out swimming, whereas I sank like a Pet Rock. My family needs to make contact with water at least once an hour or else they'll die. Not me. I'm the black shrimp of the family.

Gigi the Magician is my best friend. My only friend, actually.

The 'rents and sibs are in Japan rescuing dolphins with Uncle Arthur, and then they're off to China to protest the razing of birch, poplar, and bamboo forests along the Yangtze River for disposable chopsticks. Selling Sea-Monkeys is just a day job. Like my dad says, *Crime doesn't pay, but neither does saving the world.* I'm pet-sitting for Uncle Arthur while they're away. You may have heard of him. Sir Sturgeon ring a bell? Uncle Arthur's not really my uncle, just an old family friend. He and my folks go way back. They know each other from Atlantis. I was named after Uncle Arthur, whose middle name is Joseph.

So anyway, today I'm following Gigi on my bike while she sells copies of *Grit*. It's a weekly newspaper. Her regular customers press a quarter into her palm, and she puts on a little show, making the quarter tumble across the backs of her fingers, and then she makes it disappear. She gets prizes for selling *Grit*. So far, she's won an air mattress, a headlight for her bike, and a wristwatch that she gave to me.

Near the nursing home, Elysian Manor, Gigi suddenly swerves off the sidewalk and into the street, and I keep pedaling along on the sidewalk, because you never know when some speed demon in a

plutonium-powered car is going to come zooming by, and—kapow!—
something socks me right in the windpipe, knocks me off my bike.
But get this, there's nothing there. Gigi loops back around to where
I'm lying flat on my back on the concrete, my legs tangled in my
bike. She snaps her watermelon gum and says, "I guess Super-Duper
Girl's visiting her grandma today."

Stupid invisible space shuttle. I got winged by a wing.

Gigi smirks, like she knew that invisible space shuttle would be
parked there. But did she give me a heads-up? Of course not. My pant
leg is ripped and stained with grease from my bike chain, and my leg
is bleeding, and it keeps bleeding because I don't have regenerative
powers like *some* people in this town. I don't have any superpowers.
Neither does Gigi. Her folks, the Lumieres, can fly. Plus, they have a
genetic mutation that makes them light up in the dark. But Gigi didn't
get the firefly gene. She can't fly and she doesn't have biolumines-
cence. She just does magic tricks. Not everyone can be super.

Gigi says, "You're bleeding pretty bad, Joe-joe." No duh. I tell her
to go on ahead and finish her sales route; I'll meet her at the magic
shop after I get myself cleaned up. I push my bike off and limp to the
entrance of Elysian Manor, which is where old superheroes go to die.
When I was in grade school, we used to make Christmas ornaments
out of Styrofoam balls, prettied up with glitter, sequins, and rickrack,
and then we'd go and give them to the old people. Inside, Comman-
der USA, whose red-white-and-blue unitard is bulging with the diaper
he wears underneath, comes up to me and touches my hair. I swat his
hand away. He calls me Martha. Maybe you heard he got killed by a
sniper's bullet? That's just a story to cover up the fact that he has
dementia, which could be a side effect of his exposure to Viva-Rays, or
maybe all those hero-serum injections that made him super in the first
place. I duck into a bathroom and mop my bloody ankle with scratchy
brown paper towels. I wash the wound with soap, and the soap turns
out to be joke soap that turns my leg black.

My bike's in better shape than I am, and I pedal toward downtown,
ripped pant leg flapping, blood oozing from my now-blackened leg. I
pedal slowly and painfully past the newsstand, where the *Planetary*

Times and the *Daily Sun* both have headlines shouting: THE SNIPPER STRIKES AGAIN!

With so many superheroes, we don't get much crime around here, so the Snipper is big news. He, or she, sneaks into superheroes' houses and goes into their closets and snips their unitards to lace. Uncle Arthur armed his Sir Sturgeon suits with a fiberoptic alarm system, just in case. The latest victim is Butterfly Guy, all of his suits reduced to shreds of rainbow-sherbet-colored spandex.

I arrive at Magic & More before Gigi does. The owner, Bob, says to me, "How's it hangin', Hemorrhoid?" I shrug and hope Gigi hurries up. Bob calls me Hemorrhoid; he thinks I'm a pain in the ass. His hair is hairsprayed into wings and he has on a necktie that says in glow-in-the-dark letters: WILL YOU KISS ME IN THE DARK BABY. The *More* in Magic & More refers to whoopee cushions and plastic puddles of vomit and other junk. I spin a rack of greeting cards.

When Gigi comes in, Bob grins at her the same way the orange cartoon guys on the greeting cards grin at orange ladies with breasts like basketballs. Bob says, "Hey, Hemorrhoid! You want some gum?" I go over to the counter and he holds out a pack of gum. I reach for a stick and—snap!—the gum mousetraps onto my finger. I should've known it was gag gum because there's no such brand as Tuttifruit. Gigi giggles.

Bob notices my ripped pants and gashed black leg and says, "What happened to your leg, Hemorrhoid? Do you have gangrene? Are you a gangrenous hemorrhoid?" Gigi laughs like *gangrenous hemorrhoid* is the funniest thing she ever heard.

"It's joke soap," I mutter. "From the nursing home."

Gigi asks Bob if he's got any new magic tricks. Bob takes a tiny guillotine out from under the counter, where the vanishing coins, linking rings, and wands that bloom into flower bouquets are kept. He pulls a pack of Camels out of his breast pocket and shakes a cigarette loose. He puts the cigarette in the hole where a very small head would go and drops the blade, slicing the cigarette in two. "Go ahead," he tells me. "Put your finger in. Slip it in."

"No way," I say. My finger is still smarting from the Tuttifruit.

Gigi rolls her eyes at me and puts her finger in the guillotine. Bob lets the blade fall, and Gigi wiggles her finger, intact. The storeroom door is partway open, and on the floor is an orange air mattress, exactly like the one Gigi won selling *Grit*. I wander around the shop and try on a pair of X-Ray Specs. I check out my hand. I don't see bones, just the shadow of my hand. I trade the X-Ray Specs for sunglasses with secret mirrors that enable me to see what's behind me. Pretending to be interested in a pen that squirts disappearing ink, I watch Gigi and Bob. He puts the finger guillotine in a white paper bag for her. Then he looks directly at me and squeezes her breast, watching me watch him. Quickly, I pick up a joy buzzer and press it to make a burst of tinny noise. Bob moves his hand off Gigi's breast.

"Hemorrhoid," Bob says. "You want to see a magic trick?" I take off the sunglasses and turn around. He fans a deck of cards at me, and I go back to the counter, determined not to fall for any more gags. "Think of a card. Any card," he says. I stare hard at the two of hearts, but that's not the card I'm really thinking of. Bob closes the fan and shuffles. He slaps the deck and flips the top card over. Jack of clubs. "Is this your card?"

"Yes."

Gigi squeals and applauds. I never touched the cards. I never even *looked* at the jack of clubs; I just *thought* of it. Maybe Bob can read minds? He leans across the counter and whispers in Gigi's ear, loud enough for me to hear, "Ditch the hemorrhoid, and I'll show you how it's done."

"We gotta go," I say, tapping the wristwatch Gigi gave me. "Uncle Arthur's animals are hungry."

Gigi says, "You go, Joe-joe. I want Bob to show me how it's done."

———

I keep crossing my fingers that my superpowers will manifest with puberty. So far I have pimples, but no superpowers. For a while I secretly thought that I might have an adamantium skeleton, but then I sprained my thumb playing wiffleball. On the way to Uncle Arthur's, I bike past a cinderblock wall topped with razor wire. Bayonets jab at the air on the other side. I hear the crackle of walkie-talkies and the whistle of a mortar shell, which shakes the ground when it explodes.

At Uncle Arthur's, Ocho the octopus is pale lavender in the purple light of his tank. Normally, he's brown. White means he's afraid. An explosion rattles the windows. I try to telepathically communicate with Ocho the way Uncle Arthur does. I look into Ocho's slitty golden eye and tell him, or think at him: It's okay, Ocho. It's just the green army guys playing war games at their compound. Then I go into the kitchen to get Ocho his dinner. There's a note on the kitchen table, instructions for taking care of Ocho and Mark the seal. On top of the note is a pair of souvenir nail clippers from Key West, a present from Uncle Arthur. I collect fingernail clippers. I have pewter clippers from Colonial Williamsburg, Ace of Diamonds clippers, geisha girl clippers, clippers advertising Viceroy cigarettes, Pepsi, and the Tombstone Casket Company, clippers in the shape of a violin, and Yale University spelled Y-a-i-l clippers. I stare at the clippers from Key West, try to make them move or levitate or burst into flame or something. Nothing.

I pocket the clippers and open the fridge. There's a tub marked OCHO and another one marked MARK. I take out Ocho's tub and climb the stepladder on the side of his tank. I pop off the lid and dump the fish in. Herring. They look like blades, like kitchen knives with dead eyes. Ocho curls a tentacle around a fish and pulls it toward the flower of his mouth. Next, I take Mark's tub out back to the pool. He claps his flippers and barks, "Mark! Mark!" I crouch by the side of the pool and toss a fish into the air. Mark leaps out of the water to catch it in his mouth. We play this game until the tub is empty of fish.

I refill the tubs with fish from the freezer chest and put them in the fridge to defrost for tomorrow's feeding. For myself, I grab a Hostess fruit pie—apple—and a couple of Slim Jim meat snacks from the cupboard. I put the fruit pie in the microwave. While it heats up, I stand close to the microwave, in case the microwaves might activate some latent ability. The microwave dings, and I put the fruit pie and meat snacks on a plate and go watch TV. *Superman IV* is on. He saves the Statue of Liberty and battles Nuclear Man for world peace.

I saw the Statue of Liberty once, when my family took a trip to New York to help a lost whale find its way out of the harbor. I rode the ferry and ate three hot dogs, while my family finned alongside the whale, guiding it out to sea.

At some point during the movie, I must've fallen asleep, because the chimes of the captain's clock on the mantel wake me up.

When I get home, I strip off my ripped pants and run a bath. The warm water stings the cut on my leg. I soap and scrub at the black stuff, careful to avoid the cut. The black fades to gray. Wrapped in a towel, I go down the hall to the bedroom I share with my brother Cousteau. The room seems too big without him. Feeling small, I go over to my dresser to get my pajamas. I notice something on the carpet. It looks like a red lollipop with a green stick. Then, horrified, I realize what it is: a lopped-off antenna from my brother's Sea-Monkey suit. I throw open his closet. All of his Sea-Monkey suits, snipped to iridescent green confetti. I run to my sister's room and find more green confetti. I don't bother going to my parents' room because I already know what's there. Instead, I go and pick up the red telephone, which is to be used only for emergencies.

———

Now the house is crawling with cops like humanoid ants, dusting for fingerprints, snapping photographs of the crime scene, tweezing every suspicious crumb into baggies. I sit on my bed, shivering, still wearing just a towel. One of the cops says, "What happened to your leg, son?"

"Bike accident," I say, teeth chattering. "And joke soap."

Another cop picks up the miniature treasure chest next to the fishbowl on my desk. He opens it and his eyebrows go up. "What's this?" he says.

"My fingernail clipper collection."

The cops look at each other and then at me. The cop holding my treasure chest says, "We're going to take this. It's evidence. And don't leave town. We might have to bring you in for questioning." It doesn't take a mind reader to know what they're thinking. Suspect had means to commit the crime: fingernail clippers. Motive: Suspect lacks superpowers, and therefore has deep-seated resentment toward superheroes. Opportunity: Suspect's family is out of town.

Finally, the cops leave. I'm nervous about staying by myself tonight, but the Snipper was already here, and it's unlikely that he, or she, will return. The green army guys are marching outside, patrolling the neighborhood. The cops missed the Key West clippers from Uncle Arthur in their search. I take the clippers out of my pants pocket and put them under my pillow. I get into my pajamas, tuck myself into bed, and turn off the bedside lamp. In the dark, I fumble around in the nightstand drawer until my fingers find my penlight. I click it on and shine the beam at the fishbowl on my desk. I move the light up and down to make the *Artemisia salina* do my bidding. Brine shrimp. Sea-Monkeys. They follow the light and loop-the-loop, and I feel a little less alone.

———

The next day, after Gigi sells the last copies of this week's *Grit* we head to the beach. I scan the sand for the glint of a power ring that would grant me superpowers. You never know where you might find one. I poke around the sand with a stick while Gigi practices her magic. She plucks an egg from her mouth and then cups it in her hand. She claps her hands together, smashing the egg. When she opens her hands, there's a small crab tap-dancing on her palm. She lowers the crab to the sand and it scuttles away. Next, she makes a handkerchief float. The invisible thread suspending the handkerchief from her hand catches the light like a strand of spiderweb.

"Gigi? Do you ever wish you could fly?" I say. Her whole family can fly.

She says, "Do you ever wish you could breathe underwater?"

"I wish I could do *something*. Like you. You do magic."

"Magic's just a day job," she says.

Down the beach, I see the millionaire Wayne Bruce and his sidekick, Gray Dickson, sitting on lounge chairs, wearing shorty bathrobes and sipping fruity-looking umbrella drinks. I say, "Maybe I'm doomed to being a sidekick. I'd be your sidekick. You could saw me in half."

Gigi says, "Can sidekicks have sidekicks?" She takes a length of rope out of her bag of tricks. Then she takes out a pair of shiny silver scissors.

"What do you mean?" I say.

"What I mean is, if I were going to be anyone's sidekick, I'd want to be Bob's." She cuts the rope in two, scissors flashing in the sun.

"But he's *old*," I say.

"He's mature," she says.

"I'm not?" She acts like she's so adult, but we're only eleven months apart.

She sighs. "You wouldn't understand, Joe-joe. Maybe you'll understand someday when you're having a sexual relationship." She holds the two pieces of rope together in her fists and makes the rope whole again.

Just then, Chuck Atlas jogs by, kicking sand in our faces.

"Hey!" I say. "Quit kicking sand in our faces!"

Chuck Atlas stops in his tracks and turns around. He says, "I'd smash your face, only you're such a skinny scarecrow you might dry up and blow away."

I want to punch him, make him see stars. I want to strangle his thick neck with Gigi's rope. I get up to go after him, but Gigi grabs my shorts by their elastic waistband and pulls me back. She says, "Cool down, Joe-joe. You don't want to mess with him. He's a 'roid junkie. I saw him shooting up by the recycling bins behind the Fortress of Justice."

Later, after feeding Ocho and Mark, I go home and kick a chair over and knock a lamp off a table. I'm sick of being a skinny bag of bones. Ordinary bones. Maybe I should try steroids, like Chuck Atlas. Then I'll tell him that it's his turn to dry up and blow away, and I'll be the hero.

———

In the middle of the night, a knocking at my window jolts me awake. My first thought: It's the Snipper. Second thought: Why would the Snipper be knocking on my window? Third thought: Why would *any-one* be knocking on my window? My bedroom is on the second floor.

Fourth thought: Maybe I dreamed the knocking. Can you dream a noise so loud it wakes you? I hear the knocking again, louder, more frantic. I jump out of bed and go to the window. Quick as ripping off a Band-Aid, I pull back the curtain. It's Gigi's dad, Mr. Lumiere, hovering. He recently lost his day job as an airline pilot. He drinks. He's saying something but I can't hear what through the glass. My parents recently had new energy-efficient double-paned windows installed. I push the window open.

He says, "Is Gigi here?"

I shake my head. His bioluminescent nose glows redly, and he smells like mouthwash. Or maybe peppermint schnapps.

"Do you know where she is?"

I shake my head again.

"Please," he says. "If you know where she is, Joe, tell me."

Do I tell Gigi's dad about Bob? How Gigi wants to be Bob's side-kick? I say, robotically, "I do not know where Gigi is, Mr. Lumiere."

He makes praying hands and says, "I'm very worried about her. You wouldn't lie to me, would you, Joe?"

"I am not lying, Mr. Lumiere," I say, trying to convince myself.

He looks like a partly crushed bug. Still flying, but broken.

"Sorry to have disturbed you," he says, and turns to fly away.

I want to throw up.

I go back to bed and feel around under my pillow for the finger-nail clippers. I squeeze them in my fist until the metal gets warm, as I imagine my mother's voice, singing me a whale-song lullaby.

———

The day after, I ride my bike to Gigi's house. She's sitting in the carport with a new stack of *Grits* and a pile of wormy-looking pink rubber bands. Her eyes are red and puffy. I sit down and start to fold newspapers, twanging a rubber band around each one. The front page says the Snipper hit two more houses last night. He, or she, is getting bolder. Also, more creative. There's a full-color picture of mild-mannered Dr. Bryce Tanner, who turned bright green and swelled up with a severe case of hives when he found his lab coats artfully snipped into snowflakes. Super-Duper Girl's SD insignia was cut out completely, and her miniskirt was trimmed into a chain of people holding hands. Gigi and I sit silently folding newspapers and stuffing them into her canvas bag. Finally, I say, "Your dad came to my house last night looking for you."

She doesn't say anything.

"Were you with Bob?"

She says, "A magician never reveals her secrets." She shoulders her bag and mounts her bike, and then she takes off. I don't follow her.

I get on my bike and ride toward Uncle Arthur's. I smell smoke. Must be another fire at the Human Flame's house. Good thing the Human Fire Extinguisher lives right next door. When I get to Uncle Arthur's, I go around back to the pool and toss Mark his ball. He catches it with his snout and swims along, balancing the ball, and then he noses it up in the air, back to me. "Mark!" he says happily. We play catch for a while. Then he dives down and smacks the water with his tail, making a huge splash that drenches me. His head bobs up again, and he goes, "Mark?"

I think he wants me to come in the water. "Mark," I tell him. "Dude, I can't swim."

He looks at me with seal-pup eyes.

I kick off my shoes and peel off my pants and walk over to the steps that lead down into the shallow end of the pool. I swizzle the water with my toe. I go down a step. Then another. I'm in up to my knees. And then I plunge in and dunk myself up to my neck. This is my first time in a pool without water wings and nose plugs. Too late, I remember that my wristwatch isn't waterproof. I hold it up to my ear. Ruined. But then Mark is between my legs, lifting me onto his back. He swims toward the deep end, carrying me along with him. "No, Mark!" I yell. "Bad Mark!"

In the deep end, Mark slides out from between my legs. I flap and kick, and it dawns on me that I'm not drowning. Somehow, I'm staying afloat. It may not be pretty, but I'm swimming.

"Mark!" Mark says, egging me on. I paddle around the pool until my arms and legs go all rubbery, and my eyes are burning from the chlorine. Dripping wet in my T-shirt and undershorts, I go inside, leaving a trail of footprint puddles across the kitchen floor.

Ocho in his tank is crimson. Red means he's mad. "Ocho?" I say. "Is something wrong?" He looks like a huge eight-armed clot of blood. Suddenly there are sirens whooping, lights flashing, a Klaxon blaring aah-ooh-gah, aah-ooh-gah! I cover my ears, and I remember that Uncle Arthur's Sir Sturgeon suits are rigged with a fiberoptic alarm system. I run into his bedroom, and there is Gigi, cowering in front of the open closet, scissors in her hand. A heap of orange and green Lycra petals at her feet.

I should've known she would never settle for being a sidekick. Gigi's no average Joe. Like me.

I snatch the scissors out of Gigi's hand just as the cops bust in, guns drawn, followed by the green army guys, rifles aimed and ready. I blurt, "I did it. I'm the Snipper. It was me all along." So now I'm a villain. But I saved the girl, and that's what superheroes do. They always save the girl.

BEHIND THE MASK

George Singleton **MAN OH MAN**

—IT'S MANNA MAN

Janie Satterfield does not recalculate. She tries to block out the howling dogs and cats. There's enough money for a week of food—two weeks if a Christian Youth Group comes in and adopts half the strays. Sometimes she dreams of this: If every Boy and Girl Scout troop in the country adopted one dog or cat, then the number of strays would decrease somewhat. Not much, but a little. If every elementary school in America adopted a mascot. If every hospital. If every retirement home. Janie keeps a notebook of people and organizations that she thinks might help control the pet population in America. If every contestant on a game show, if every person who worried about getting into heaven, if every church and synagogue and mosque, if every prison.

The telephone rings. Janie does not answer. It'll be one of her volunteers from the Junior League calling to cancel, she knows. Every day, it seems, one of her volunteers calls, faking a cough, saying that she doesn't want to bring the flu into the kennel area.

The machine beeps. An older woman says, "I hope I got the right number. I'm calling to donate. I can do the five-dollar-a-week program. Just tell me where to send it." The woman leaves her telephone number and address. Janie stares at the answering machine.

The phone rings again and, thinking that it's probably the older woman calling to say she misdialed earlier, Janie answers with "Graywood County Humane Society."

"Yes. I'm calling to offer my donation," a man says. "I'd like to send a hundred dollars to you."

Line two, then line three rings. Janie brightens her voice. She says, "That's so kind of you, sir," and gives him the post office box address.

And it happens and it happens and it happens. For six straight hours Janie Satterfield picks up the phone, takes donations, and at the end of the day she's been promised more than a hundred thousand dollars. And she is amazed to learn that a television evangelist, one Reverend Leroy Jenkins, has directed all of his listeners to donate to the Graywood Humane Society.

"I need to write Reverend Jenkins a thank-you card," she says to herself, still alone without a volunteer. She steps into the kennel area and says to her barking strays, "Maybe we'll take a photograph of us all and send it to Reverend Jenkins."

Janie had never heard of this particular television evangelist.

And she'd never heard of Manna Man, working his powers, redirecting.

———

Manna Man checks the internet. He glances over the Local sections of over three hundred small-town weekly newspapers to which he subscribes. He takes notes. He categorizes, and tries not to make assumptions. The mail carrier detests Manna Man. The mail carrier comes home on Thursdays and asks his wife if she'll keep quiet should Ben Culler's house burn down mysteriously one night soon.

———

The food bank will close in midwinter, right when it needs to be most available. For three years Lloyd Driggers has operated the food bank on Wednesday and Saturday mornings, doling out canned goods, bread, and milk in large paper bags. He does not question anyone in regard to hunger or thirst. He makes no judgments. Unfortunately, the donations have dwindled. Area preachers have hinted, then outright demanded, that their congregants give to their *own* soup kitchens, their *own* food banks. The preachers have said things like, "Why would you give your hard-earned money and canned yams to an organization that doesn't even try to save the unsaved? Lloyd Driggers doesn't offer testimonials. No, he just hands out food. That's not enough!"

The congregants listened, as congregants do.

Lloyd Driggers's shelves soon went empty. He spent his savings. He went into his IRA and bought groceries on a weekly basis—one thousand dollars every Tuesday to help feed the homeless, the unemployed, the working poor. He sold his house and moved into his food bank space—which used to be a two-bay Gulf service station back in the 1960s. His two children—son and daughter—talked between themselves often about how they would need to take their father in soon, how he'd never recovered from their mother's long-term illness and subsequent death.

The electricity would be cut first, then the water. When the electricity went, so would his telephone.

"Food bank," Lloyd says.

"Yessir. Is this Lloyd Driggers?"

"Polk County Food Bank, Lloyd Driggers speaking."

The man on the other end clears his throat. "I can give five dollars a week. I'd like to do more, but you know my medicine's costing me. But I can do five dollars a week." The man asks where to send his money.

And the phone rings again and again until finally Lloyd asks a young girl with a full piggy bank, "How did you get this number?"

"My grandma told me to call. She wants to talk to you next."

"Your grandmother gave you this number?"

"No, sir. The preacher man on TV gave out this number. He told us to send you money."

Lloyd thinks, Preacher man? He thinks, Maybe all these preachers have understood their wrong-headed actions of the past.

The grandmother gets on the phone and says, "We was watching one them evangelists like we always do on channel 17 and he says for us to send directly to you. He says it'll get us one more smile from the Lord."

"Which preacher?" Lloyd asks. "From around here?"

"No, no, no. The one out in Oklahoma. The one with the hair."

Lloyd Driggers has never heard of the hairy preacher from Oklahoma.

He has not heard of Manna Man, either.

———

It's so easily done these days, with high-definition television, Manna Man thinks. This is so much easier than having to attend the tent revivals—feigning a limp, a goiter, a lack of speech, blindness, bad blood, invisible afflictions of the major organs—and finding a reason to touch the evangelist's throat.

Now he doesn't have to invest in cheap polyester suits. Now Manna Man can wear his superhero attire at home in front of a bank of Sonys—six across and three high—all tuned to different TV evangelists' separate networks.

He works in his boxer shorts most days.

He keeps Icy Hot and Ben Gay available to keep his elbows loose, his wrists malleable, his fingers scalding hot.

————

Herbert Kirby has the paperwork. He's built one prototype and seeks funding. There are only a handful of scientists and dendrologists out there who believe in him—that his machine can turn pine sap into fresh drinking water without killing off the trees. Herbert Kirby's even proven that a strong evergreen grows stronger after being "slightly fondled" by his sap-into-water contraption. He likens the process to bloodletting, to frost hardening.

Of course most people think he's insane. And then there's the bottled-water industry executives who understand the consequences of a mass-produced potable drinking water apparatus.

"Make sure it's in my obituary," Herbert tells his wife and children. "Make sure it reads, 'This man could've saved the entire drought-stricken West Coast and southeastern United States, but greedy capitalists kept him from being a savior.'"

His relatives don't believe him. "It's one of the first signs of dementia," his forty-six-year-old son, Herb Junior, says. "Visions of martyrdom. Visions of grandeur. Visions. There should be some kind of law that no one is allowed to have visions past the age of fifty, especially if said person used to be a car mechanic, precomputers."

Herb Junior works as an optician. He works inside a Wal-Mart and pretends to know what he's talking about when customers ask him questions concerning glaucoma, cataracts, and conjunctivitis.

Manna Man understands, though. Manna Man read a human interest story in the weekly *Forty-five Platter* and studied up on the molecular structure of tree sap. He gazed at Herbert Kirby Senior standing in front of his machine, which looked more or less like an iron lung, or an old-fashioned sauna.

When Herbert Kirby's telephone rings back in his workshop—and no one ever calls the number, not even his wife—he picks it up and says, "Yeah."

Is it really Donald Trump? And later, is it really Oprah, Bill Gates, Warren Buffet, the director of the Kellogg Foundation? If Herbert Kirby only knew. He gives out his address. He says that most of his backers send cashier's checks. "I'll send you the first case of sap-to-water, free of charge," he says. Up until this point he'd only said those words to his dog.

Manna Man will never know the consequences. He will never ask, What were those people doing watching TV evangelists?

―――――

At night Manna Man dreams of people skipping in fields, down country dirt roads, down sidewalks, across water. On the horizon, though, there's always a balding man wearing a checkered coat, his deep-set eyes as hollow and vacant as doughnuts riding a conveyor belt toward a faulty jelly-filler nipple. In the dreams he knows that it's his nemesis.

He knows it's the exact opposite of Manna Man, from a parallel universe. Or from an alternate universe. He can never remember if those two terms are synonymous.

―――――

Ben Culler's father suffered from psychosomatic pains that left his right arm limp and useless. A religious man, he went to a traveling preacher's faith-healing revival outside Decatur, Alabama, walked up on the stage, and spoke into the microphone. He'd said, "I got my arm crushed back at the quarry. It ain't worked since. *I* ain't worked since, either."

The preacher slayed him in the spirit, right in front of everyone. He shoved his shirt cuff, doused in ether, right up into Ben Culler's fake-lame father's face. Mr. Culler went down in a pile. And when he regained consciousness he pushed himself off of the makeshift wooden stage built of scavenged pallets, lifted both arms in the air, and said, "Thank you, Jesus, my arms's been reborned!"

The Alabamans danced and gyrated and praised Jesus and spoke in tongues. They held their arms up high, too. They cried, and begged for mercy, and—if the scene had been captured on silent film—did not act dissimilarly to Turkish Sufi dervishes.

That night at home, Ben Culler's father raised his right arm up high to his son and said, "You been getting away with way too much, and now Jesus has come to the rescue. I guess God's telling me that I got to make up for lost time." He struck his son across the face. His second hard blow landed on the boy's solar plexus. Ben Culler yelled out for his runaway mother. He did not have time to form tears.

His father's third forceful open-handed blow caught Ben just south of his thyroid cartilage—this may have been from where Manna Man's powers sprang.

The fourth roundhouse didn't land. Ben Culler caught his father's wrist and squeezed it with superhuman strength. His father fell to his knees in much the same manner as when he was slayed in the spirit earlier that day. Before his father expired on the kitchen floor of their trailer, Ben Culler said, "You will not strike me. You will not take my lawn-mowing money and give it to scam artist preachers. You will not be a vengeful Christian."

Thus spake Manna Man for the first time.

If the scene had been captured on film with sound, someone would've remarked on how his voice sounded like that of a restrained madman. If the scene had been captured on film with digital enhancement, someone would've noticed the aura that surrounded young Ben's palm—an aura that revealed strength, and electricity, and the ability to change wrongs into rights.

Nowadays, if there is a person watching a television evangelist, and the evangelist edges into how his ministry needs money to aid the little half-hearted babies he visited in Haiti, or the lepers in Mongolia, or the heathens of upper Cambodia, or the tendon-lacking children of Zimbabwe, or the green children of Tonga, or the blind babies of Eritrea, or the secular humanists of Lithuania, or the involuntary flinchers of Mali, or the cursed teenagers of Indonesia, then Ben Culler transforms into Manna Man involuntarily and touches the television screen. The preacher will hear his own voice change into a higher octave. The preacher will think he's saying, "God will reward you in heaven for helping our ministry help the little poor twelve-toed newborns of Paraguay get special-fitted shoes." He'll feel a tingle in his throat just as Manna Man transforms the speech into, "God will reward you in heaven for helping our ministry help the Springer Mountain Library Association in its need to buy books published after the Civil War," and then offer up the telephone number where desperate heaven seekers can call.

Afterward, the television evangelist moves onward. He wonders why the phone bank's silent. He thinks, Jesus H. Christ, I need to come up with some better needful ailing people of the world.

———

Ben Culler knows that, if there were a hell, he'd be going. He misused his powers once: He got people to donate him *money. Can't operate without paying the bills, he thought. Can't get a job at Best Buy and make sure all of the television sets are tuned to different TV evangelists full-time. Can't work forty hours a week doing something to pay the bills, and another 140 hours funneling money to good causes.*

But there is no hell, Manna Man knows. He read all the philosophers for five straight years after his father's death. He's read all the religious texts ever written by man.

He's read all the cookbooks, too, and would one day like to see a world without TV evangelists, so he could settle down with a woman and cook her a nice six-course meal.

———

There's a new evangelist—a country-looking preacher—dressed in a checkered coat. Manna Man focuses on the far-right television set in his den. He mutes the other channels. There's something about this guy: slick-backed real hair, a face that might've been used by geology professors when they couldn't find a decent example of "alluvial for-mations." Quiet voice and piercing eyes. It's not the typical studio setup either—it looks as though this might come out of a basement, or bunker: one man and a cameraman.

"God is punishing America for all the homosexuals we got going here. God has chosen me as one of the few elected to heaven, and he has not chosen the rest of these homos and homo pimps and homo pimp seekers . . ."

Manna Man wonders if it's parody, if maybe channel 6 has changed ownership and now runs *TVLand*. In his downtime—and that's only an hour at most per day—Manna Man likes to watch reruns of *Mr. Ed*, *The Andy Griffith Show*, *Sanford and Son*, and the rest of those programs that his father wouldn't let him watch back when they were on prime time.

Manna Man waits for this new evangelist to ask for money. Here it comes, he thinks, and sure enough the man says, "That's why I need all you watching out there to send money to . . ."

Manna Man shoves his palm on the man's televised neck. Manna Man thinks to himself, ". . . the Women's Shelters of Eastern Tennessee who need money to continue operation."

". . . our church here in Topeka so we can continue protesting funerals and bail out our Chosen parishioners who are doing God's work in this here United States of Sodomy."

Manna Man pushes his palm harder onto the set. He reaches for the channel changer and flips the next television over to channel 6 so that this unknown man appears. He shoves his left hand onto the man's face and concentrates. "Women's Shelters of Eastern Tennessee, Women's Shelters of Eastern Tennessee, Women's Shelters of Eastern Tennessee . . ."

The TV evangelist pauses. He looks to his left. He clears his throat. Manna Man knows that he's come across an adversary with powers that might, indeed, cause the average person to believe in Satan. The evangelist says, "We will be doomed and cursed forever until our so-called leaders understand that the Nazis might've been . . ."

"What an asshole," Manna Man, says. He's got his right palm on the top-right television, his left hand on the third-level TV beside it. He reaches with his left foot and toes the bottom-floor Sony to channel 6 and shoves his sole across the evangelist's face.

He concentrates. He says, "Women's Shelter of Eastern Tennessee" like a mantra.

The evangelist pauses, then says, "I know you're out there, Manna Man. I know all about you. You can't stop me. I've been ordained by God Hisself. He knows all about you and your wicked ways, funneling money to the soulless homosexuals and perverts and the godless and . . ."

Manna Man lets loose with his right hand, grabs the channel changer, and flips the television set right in front of his boxer shorts to channel 6. He drops the changer, shoves his right hand back so hard that he fears reaching through straight into the television's innards. Manna Man thinks, This is the nemesis of my dreams. He thinks, This is the heartless enemy I've been training for all of these years: Part mentally deranged attorney, part egomaniacal evangelist—I'm dealing with . . . the Attornelist!

He leans forward and shoves his penis right onto the Attornelist's mouth. Manna Man focuses. He leans hard, left and right hands touching screens, left foot, penis. There's silence. Then, finally, the Attornelist muffles out, "Please send your much-needed donations to the Women's Shelters of Eastern Tennessee," and gives up the 1-800 number.

Manna Man backs off of his bank of television sets. He looks into the Attornelist's cavernous black eyes and says, "You will never beat me." He slips his penis back inside his boxer shorts.

"Manna Man!" the Attornelist screams out. "Man oh man, I hate you Manna Man. I'll get you one day! I'll get you!"

The four screens turn to snow.

For now.

———

Manna Man crawls to the refrigerator, reaches up, and touches his magnets. They melt onto the floor. He had a feeling this would happen. He's sapped from the Attornelist.

He opens the refrigerator and pulls out beet juice he'd made earlier in his favorite Viking 12-Cup Food Processor with Commercial-Grade 625-Watt Induction motor.

Replacing the iron, he thinks. Regaining my powers. Refueling.

———

A man sits in his recliner, the business end of a .45 in his mouth. He's already covered the wall in plastic behind him. He doesn't want to leave a mess for anyone to find. He's always been that way. Maybe that's why he's been named Citizen of the Year twice. Maybe that's why, up until this point, he'd been able to run a hospice service run entirely on local contributions, staffed with two full-time nurses, and caregivers willing to undergo classes, seminars, and biannual evaluations.

But the donations haven't increased, and the number of elderly people in town, most of them laid off years ago from the cotton mill and fighting off lung ailments, has quadrupled. The man needs at least two more nurses, and twice as many qualified caregivers.

He eases back the hammer and has almost pulled the trigger when the phone rings.

It might be his daughter calling. It might be one of the nurses. It might be news that someone else has died and the family needs help with funeral arrangements.

On the other end of the telephone, a woman says she'd like to put the hospice service in her will. She says she'll send a hundred thousand dollars immediately, but promises the remainder of her estate once she passes on. "To heaven," she says. "I'll be going to heaven for sure, now."

Manna Man's back on the job, revitalized.

241

Tom Bissell

MY INTERVIEW WITH THE AVENGER

*B*eloved, celebrated, and very, very famous, the Avenger at long last steps out of his crimefighting shadows—for a one-on-one meeting with the last man in America who opposes him. Tim Januss reports—

———

This is a story about heroes. Yes, it is also a profile of a famous man, a "celebrity," I suppose, but it is first and foremost a story about heroes, what they mean, and the draperies of significance with which we decorate them. The hero in question came to us as unexpectedly as a micrometeorite, and little has been the same since his impact. Of course, nearly everyone remembers how and when the man now known as the Avenger first made his existence public. Most origin stories are cumbrous with mythic overlay. But the Avenger arrived in twinkly, almost pointillistic detail. There was nothing to add to the story to make it better; it defeated augmentation.

New York City, 2005. A night in late January. A pair of muggers approach two Japanese tourists unwise enough to have wandered too deep into the swards of Central Park at too late an hour. Moments after the muggers assault the tourists, who do not resist them, a fifth party rushes into the fray. "We don't know what happened," one of the tourists tells the police afterward. "It happened so fast." One of the muggers, speaking to the police later that night from his hospital bed—his colleague's broken, wired-shut jaw rules out any statement— is slightly more descriptive: "He came out of nowhere, sprayed us with some shit, hit us a bunch of times, cuffed us to each other, and then he was, like . . . *gone*." The mugger's statement is leaked to the press.

244

The *Post*'s headline: "HE CAME OUT OF NOWHERE": GOOD SAMARITAN FOILS PARK THUGS. The *Times* strikes a less populist, more skeptical note: NYPD GRATEFUL FOR, CONCERNED BY ACTIONS OF PARK VIGILANTE. No follow-up, no one comes forward—just one of those uniquely weird New York stories of a person stepping out of the potential every-thingness of the city and then retreating anonymously back into it.

Then, three days later, and once again in Central Park, a purse-snatching teenager from the Bronx is chased down shortly before mid-night by a man he later describes as "the fastest white dude ever." The man, wearing "a black ski mask," and, evocatively, "motherfucking Batman's utility belt," extracts the purse from its captor with minimal force, but extends to him some friendly advice that will, of course, later become legendary: "If you plan to continue this line of work, may I suggest a better cardiovascular routine?" The next evening the crime's victim receives her purse, by courier, at her Upper West Side home. The sender of the purse lists a nonexistent Manhattan post office box under an equally nonexistent name, but he does include a typed note: "I believe you lost this last night. May I suggest you consider wearing your purse strap across your body?" The note is signed in all caps (THE AVENGER), but this small pertinence does not fully register for weeks.

The Avenger has been with us for so long now that those first few months when no one was quite sure what to call him are remembered through the same murky vale as the pre–September 11 skyline. The "Central Park Vigilante" was the NYPD's preferred cognomen. The *Times* opted for "New York City's Unknown Self-Appointed Guardian," but sometimes, and grudgingly, resorted to "the so-called Avenger."

In the beginning, though, he is for most of us not a person. He is rather a question: *Did you hear about that guy?*

Then, two weeks later, shortly after the purse snatcher (who was never charged) had come forward to the press, and immediately after the purse's owner had been photographed smiling while holding up her mysterious note for the cover of the *Times'* City Section, two bur-glars are found beaten and hog-tied on the floor of a Chelsea brown-stone. Their situation is brought to the police's attention by an anonymous pay-phone 911 call believed to have been made by That

Guy Himself. The *Post*'s simple headline, in letters half a foot high, tells us all we need to know: HE'S BACK! Our news cycles will have a different algorithm now, synced to the actions of a man no one can find, whom no one knows, and whose actions no one can predict.

One thing was clear: New York City had an entirely new kind of inhabitant. Was he a polite Bernhard Goetz? A human Superman? A witty sociopath? A professional headline seeker? A nut? A saint? Yet few of us back then were asking, *Who is he?* The cookie containing that particular fortune seemed bound to crack open at any moment. This was what we were asking: *Why is he? And why now?* Months, and then years, later, no one was any closer to being able to answer either question.

———

Six months ago I wrote an essay for this magazine ("The Avenger Dies for Our Sins," September 2007) about why I believed the Avenger's actions were, from a legal and civic point of view, dangerous. I had not, of course, interviewed the Avenger for my essay. He had given only one interview, by phone, to Larry King, shortly after coming to terms with the New York City Police Department, and being granted, in absentia, by the mayor, the dubious and unprecedented legal status of "an honorary constabulary deputy of the greatest city on earth." The Avenger tried to explain to King what, legally, this meant, but even he was not sure. The interview, the third-most-downloaded clip in YouTube history, is famously unhinged: The man whom in our sacred unease we fantasized as a harsh sentinel, an incorruptible guardian, sounded more like a slurring crackpot taking a momentary break from a barbiturate triathlon. (Only later did we learn that the Avenger was nursing a concussion after falling off a fire escape, as he explained in the second of the three letters he is known to have sent to the *Times*.) But because he was finally being allowed to continue his mission as the city's protector without any more interference from authorities that once vowed to see him behind bars—though he must, at all times, report his planned whereabouts, via a secret text-message code that goes directly to the mayor and his police commissioner—the Avenger had finally elected to speak directly to the people. And despite his evasions ("I am not able at this time to tell you why I'm doing this"), his chilly bravado ("I am a most unique man"), and his stilted sloganeering ("I am the force that will make civilization civil once again"), we responded. We wanted him. We *needed* him.

We also hounded him, occasionally tried to capture him ourselves, and pointed an unending series of fingers at those we believed *were* him. This is why I wrote my article. This is why I believed the Avenger was doing more harm than good. Hardly any of the criminals he has stopped, and often beaten, have been convicted. There was, and remains, no legal precedent for what the Avenger is doing. By working in secrecy, by rejecting the elaborate and, yes, sometimes frustrating evidential byways upon which American society has settled when dealing with those who break its laws, the Avenger, I wrote, was a *negation* of American justice, not its embodiment. Viewed bloodlessly, and unsentimentally, he was, in fact, probably a criminal himself.

The thing about my essay was: I knew I was right, and I knew I was wrong. I was right because—more than any other event, and more than any other person—the Avenger captured the terminal nature of a culture that could not change even if it wanted to, even if it *had* to. We have always sought arbiters of fate that exist beyond the taxable realm of legality, and the Avenger had simply made actual the vigilante fantasy that had hitherto existed only in make-believe's less exalted basements. I was wrong because the Avenger changed things in ways no one could have predicted. He did not rise up out of a time of untrammeled crime. He was not the voice of the people. He was, instead, the first person in our national public life to suggest that virtue, and not fame, could come first, that one was not a prerequisite of the other, that they could exist alongside each other *accidentally*. As time went on, as he evaded capture, and as he refused to disclose his identity, it became clear that the Avenger *really did not want the attention*—at least, not per se. He *actually believed in what he was doing*. And he always, as I conceded in my article, seemed paranormally aware of exactly how much damage to deal out to those whose crimes he stopped. He has never killed anyone. In fact, he did not even seem all that vindictive. He seemed, rather, *professional*. Many of the criminals he has disarmed, cold-cocked, limb-snapped, and leg-swept today profess their admiration for him, and a few credit him with the back they have shown their former lives of crime. Yes, some have sued, but this has gone nowhere. The Avenger was something entirely, paradigm-shiftingly new, and it was impossible to be entirely wrong or entirely right about a man we did not yet have the vocabulary to describe.

Days after my article appeared on newsstands, I received a letter from the Avenger. It had been postmarked in New York City. Strangely, and somewhat menacingly, it was addressed to my unlisted home address. The return address was that of this magazine, with a typed *A.* above it. My article had obviously riled and angered him, as part of me certainly hoped it would. The Avenger's tone was curt, and I have agreed not to quote his letter here, but he invited me, at a time and place of his choosing, to meet with him. I heard nothing else for weeks. Then he wrote again. I was to journey by train outside the city to the Golden's Bridge stop, wait forty-five minutes, and then follow precisely detailed directions into the nearby woodlands. I was to come alone. He wrote that he would know if I was being followed and, if so, this and any future meeting would be impossible. I believed him. The man had evaded one of the biggest manhunts in New York City history for many months, all the while continuing to foil petty criminals and in the meantime somehow become the single most famous human being in the country. Since his honorary constabulary deputization, I had felt very alone in my opposition to this man. I told no one but my editor of my plans to meet him. My editor asked, only half-jokingly, if I planned on bringing a weapon. I had not even considered this until my editor mentioned it. I then wished he hadn't.

———

Forty-five minutes, when you are waiting to meet the Avenger, is a long time, and while standing on the train platform at Golden's Bridge, I thought about the reading I had done about this peculiar species of costumed vigilantism. Others before the Avenger had taken to the streets, of course. There is Terrifica, a self-styled Valkyrie who patrols New York City bars to prevent predatory men from taking advantage of drunken women; Captain Jackson of Jackson, Michigan, "an officially sanctioned independent crime fighter," whose group, the Crimefighter Corps, works Jackson's troublous streets to little or no effect; Mr. Silent of Indianapolis; Ferox of Salt Lake City; Polarman of the Canadian Arctic. There are more. A website called the World Superhero Registry exists to keep track of these people. Look it up, and marvel at human aspiration at its most quietly noble and definitively unfounded. One other thing you will note is that the Avenger is not found on this site. Many of the registered superheroes I contracted for comment on the Avenger refused to say a word on the record about him. Off the record, the dissertations began. To the man—that is, to the *super*man (or -woman)—they regard him as a glory hound and a menace. They work *with* the system, they say, while the Avenger works at odds with the system. It seemed clear to me, at least, that a more green-eyed emotion was clouding these heroes' consideration.

The men and women listed on the World Superhero Registry are without exception grassroots, community- and niche-based operators whose Lycra often poorly contains their girth. They are, in effect, noble clowns. But a few have tried to follow the Avenger's more dangerous, socially outlying path, the results of which have been vaguely comic, utterly tragic, and nothing else. In Los Angeles a hopeful who strapped two tasers to his wrists and called himself Taserman accidentally zapped himself during an unsuccessful prevention of a carjacking. The Boomerang Kid was shot by unimpressed gangbangers in Las Vegas. Miami's Sunstroke was arrested for assault after being heckled by one of his fellow citizens. Chicago's Wolfreign was arrested for solicitation. These are (and, in the Boomerang Kid's case, were) not people like you or me, and further investigation of these "heroes" often revealed long histories of psychiatric inpatient care and Homeric rap sheets. No. They were not like you or me. Nor were they anything like the Avenger. They had made the mistake of blending the example of comic books with the inspiration of perhaps the single most peerless human being on this planet, which was rather like building a bomb from a design by Wile E. Coyote. The Avenger, as he admitted to Larry King with a chuckle, had no superpowers ("Not yet, at least"), but that did not mean the man was without some exquisite gifts. He is thought to be a fine, and perhaps even gifted, martial artist, and his bravery and physical strength are, by now, well established. The existence of his utility belt has been confirmed, as have been its assortment of nonlethal instruments: pellets of tear gas, smoke bombs, bolts of nylon cord, a supply of plastic handcuffs. At least a dozen of his prey reported catching eyefuls of Mace before being beaten senseless. The claim by one thug that he twice shot the Avenger in the chest to little effect seems to validate rumors of some kind of specially thin, easy-to-maneuver-in Kevlar vest.

Even after all this time, and all that has been written about him, I thought on the Golden's Bridge platform, *there was still so much about him we did not know.* There was no other famous person of whom this could be said—and I had spent a good portion of my career writing about, and contemplating, the famous. I looked off into the brancolored brush thickets and up the hilly copse of leafless trees in which I knew he waited. My watch's alarm sounded. I had set it because I wanted to be exact, as exact as the man I was about to meet. The longest and shortest forty-five minutes of my life were up. I walked off to meet the Avenger.

————

I did not have to go far—perhaps a five-minute walk from the platform. The Avenger was sitting in a lotus position on a thronelike rock halfway up a hill. The sky, fittingly but discomfortingly, had gone as dark as a mud puddle, and the wind shook the stripped trees around us as though in indistinct warning; their trunks and branches groaned. But here he was. I lifted my hand in greeting.

Now, there is a question people ask when they learn you have met the Avenger. It is not about what he was wearing (a black ski mask—his one attempt at wardrobe iconography—and a plain gray hoodless sweatshirt; loose black pants with many marsupial pouches; black Puma running shoes; and his belt, also black, which was smaller than I had imagined but bulged with many little snap-shut pockets and holsters and plastic protuberances yet remained as essentially proletarian as that of a cable repairman), and it is not what his in-person voice sounds like (quiet, confident, accentless, a guy's and not a man's voice, somehow, all its energy and vitality at the edges rather than its center), and it is not whether he is friendly (read on). It is this: Is he funny? Because this is the rap on the Avenger, the attribute earned by all those suspiciously rehearsed and prefab comments he has made over the years to those he has stopped and those he has saved. The answer is that he is funny. He does not smile or make jokes, but then a fire does not need to blaze to give off heat. In fact, the very first thing the Avenger said to me, while certainly not hilarious, was funny, or at least mordantly engaged with the situation:

"Tell me. What sins of yours do I have to die for?"

I was still walking him toward him, hummingbird-hearted. His voice so startled me I momentarily forgot the title of my own, anti-Avenger essay. I stopped. "Excuse me?"

With a grand little flourish he extended his hand. Given the darkness of his garb, his hand's flesh was so contrastingly white it seemed to glow. His only other bits of visible flesh were the twinned circles held within the eyelets of his ski mask and the oblong rectangular cutout around his mouth. "'The Avenger Dies for Our Sins.' The reason I'm sitting here and the reason you're looking at me."

Now we really *were* looking at each other, rather than working out wary approach vectors in anticipation of what we might first say. "I guess," I told him, "that I meant it as more of a metaphor."

He nodded. The nod of a ski-masked man is a strangely terrifying one—one imagines other, more frightening things that such a nod might result in—and then he un- and refolded his legs. His eyes, if I had to guess, were brown. "Metaphor? Okay. But kind of a shitty one. In my opinion."

"You have an interest in metaphor?" A stupid thing to say, perhaps, but conversations delimited by their own lack of precedent tend to result in circular restatement rather than interesting lunges.

He sat there and said nothing. I sensed that I had already disappointed him.

I asked him, "How do you know no one is going to walk along this path?"

Instantly he held up a small black device that looked like a cell phone. "I've placed a tiny wire across the trail fifty yards behind me. If someone trips it, this will vibrate. I can see behind you for another fifty yards. Don't worry. If anyone happens along, I'll be out of sight in twenty seconds, give or take. And you won't be able to follow me."

I motioned around at the surrounding forest, thinly treed suburban wilds through which a small recreational vehicle could have easily slalomed. "What about the rest of these woods?"

"I'll take my chances. People stick to paths, at any rate. It's one of the things that makes criminals so easy to anticipate. Most of us operate along a quantitatively smaller spectrum of choice than we realize."

"But not you."

"If I weren't victim of the same coded inhibitions I wouldn't be very good at predicting the behavior of others, would I? No, I'm the same. The only difference is that I am aware that when most people appear to have five or six choices, they really only have two." His chin lifted. "If that."

I pulled out my notepad. I held it up to him, I later realized, with the same hand, and with the same self-proud showmanship, that he had used to hold up his trip-wire-vibro-box for me. "Do you mind?"

A small, annoyed, almost teenagery shrug. "Feel free." Two words into my first question, though, he interrupted me: "Why don't you write short stories anymore?"

At this I could do little but laugh. I had published a book of short stories more than a decade ago. It had received a small amount of acclaim and then quickly withdrew from the world of print. The praise was enough to attract a few editors' interest and within months of the book's publication I began writing magazine journalism, which seemed to provide my talent a better, less frustrated outlet and my temperament a quicker, more active engagement. "You read my stories," I said. Once again he did not move. A few reluctant raindrops fell from the sky and pattered onto the scatter of autumnally crunchy leaves at my feet. I spoke again, this time with the proper inquisitive inflection. "You read my stories?"

"I've read everything you've written. Everything I could find, at least. I'm nothing if not thorough."

I looked at him, and he at me. I could not say I was surprised. I had come here expecting to be outwitted at every turn, but perhaps not so soon, or so intimately. I attempted a graceless flanking move. "Very interesting, Avenger. Why that name, anyway? Is that some reference to the Avengers?"

"What are the Avengers?"

"A comic book. They're a group of superheroes that operates out of a New York mansion. Captain America. Thor. Iron Man. Did you have a favorite? My boss wanted me to ask you that." My boss had wanted no such thing.

"I don't read comic books and I never have. Don't ask stupid questions."

"I don't read comic books, either. The only reason I know anything about that is because I started to research you."

The Avenger remained as statuesquely still as some idol carved from the world's biggest piece of onyx. "I'll be honest. I didn't care much for all your short stories, but I liked one in particular: the story about the young guy whose brother was killed. Which of course happened to you. Now, what's interesting to me, as a reader, is that you never wrote about your brother's death elsewhere. That story is probably the best thing you've written, wouldn't you say? A rich vein of material there, obviously—one you dealt with quite effectively, I thought. It moved me. And yet what do you do after writing this story? You spend the next decade cranking out profiles of Michael Stipe and Will Ferrell."

I looked away. When I was nineteen and my brother was twenty-five, he was shot and killed while trying to intervene in a mugging in Washington, D.C. His killer was never found. "I've written things besides profiles."

"You write the occasional attempt at cultural criticism, and sometimes you write about violent crime. A fascination of yours, it seems. But—and this is what I, personally, find amazing—you somehow never manage to disclose your own brother died at the hands of violent crime."

My head swung back quickly to face him. "I've written about my brother." And I had. I had written about my brother for this magazine, three years ago—a long essay about families who had lost a member to an unsolved murder, and how, in virtually every case, those families had never recovered; the four horsemen of divorce, substance abuse, depression, and suicide stalked them from the day of the murder on, plucking away the remaining family members one by one. Writing the piece proved so personally harrowing I have never written a piece of long-form investigative journalism again.

"You mentioned your brother in two paragraphs in that essay. The only time you've ever faced up to what happened to your brother is in your story. Everything else is peripheral."

"I haven't read that story in years. I barely even remember it." Insofar as something could be both true and false, this was.

The Avenger now opened his legs, which spread apart as purposefully and smoothly as scissors, and after a quick little seesaw motion slid off his throne. But he took no further step. "I'm not a writer, but if *I* had suffered what you and your family suffered, and if *I* were writing critically about vigilantism, I might let the reader know what, exactly, was informing my criticism."

"I had something in there about him, at an early point. But I took it out."

His head tilted at a canine angle. "And why did you do that?"

"Because I didn't trust the impulse that moved me to include that information."

"You write about celebrities. What impulses do you trust when you're writing about Angelina Jolie?"

I put my notebook back into my pocket. Curiously, it had not rained any more than those first few drops. "You asked me here. I didn't ask you. You asked me."

"What did you do after your brother died?"

"How do you dispense Mace? There have been reports that you squirt it from a device hidden somewhere on your wrist."

He extended his left arm and with his right hand pushed down on the top of his belt's most central and plumpest barnacle. What began at his wrist as a jet of liquid became within two feet of its launching point a fine mist. Within seconds the wind had blown the lightly tabascoed air my way, and my eyes filled.

"You asked," he said.

I nodded and rubbed my shirt against my eyes. "Fair enough. And how about the Kevlar vest?"

He lifted up his sweatshirt to reveal a tight black vest that appeared as shiny, and roughly as bullet-stopping, as neoprene. "It doesn't look like much, but this will stop a knife and most small-caliber bullets. A shotgun if I'm far enough away. I've been tapped a few times. One ass-hole shot me and broke two ribs. People assume I'm indestructible, but I get hurt all the time. More than half of my teeth have been knocked out." His demonstrative smile, which revealed a full set of enviably white choppers, lasted no more than a second. "Mostly dentures. All of this is part of the reason I'm not able to patrol as aggressively as I'd like. You know, the press amuses me. They write all the time about what I'm planning, and even print up little city maps that are supposed to show my patterns. There are no patterns and there are no plans. I never plan. What they call 'planning' is usually me holding an ice pack to my head, pulling the stitches out of my arm, and taking the splint off my big toe."

"Your vest—you designed that yourself?"

He shook his head. "Uh, no. I'm not . . . Bruce Wayne. Right? I ordered it from a Dutch company that provides armor for security guards, Halliburton, journalists who work in war zones. It wasn't cheap."

"And how do you make your money?"

"I've invested wisely. It's not like the stuff I use costs all that much. You'd be surprised at what you can get, no questions asked, through mail order. Becoming the Avenger required a financial investment of no more than six or seven thousand dollars. Total."

"And do you—"

"My turn." He crossed his arms. "What did you do after your brother died?"

I thought about how to respond. I had been in loving relationships where it had taken me many months to talk about my brother, and yet this stranger was asking me to winch up buckets sloshing with emotions and memories drawn from my darkest and most secret well. But I knew my answer would determine how close to him he would allow me to get.

"I did a lot of things. I cried. I studied the martial arts for a while, then gave it up. I traveled. Finally I wrote. He was a writer, too, by the way. At least he wanted to be. You don't know that because I've never mentioned it. Not in print."

"The martial arts. That's in one of the stories, too."

"I was fairly serious about it. Then it just seemed stupid. I was never very good. I don't even like to fight."

"Then why—"

"I didn't like feeling weak. I wondered if that's what got my brother killed: his weakness. He had such a good heart, but he was weak. That's one of the reasons I wrote my essay about you. I worried you would inspire people to step into situations they have no business stepping into."

"That must have been one of the parts you cut out."

"Everything I wrote is, from a legal point of view, inarguable. Inarguable. And you know as well as I do that the only reason they stopped trying to catch you is because they knew they couldn't."

The Avenger walked toward me. When I drew back he stopped and put up his hands. Slowly he lowered them. "Tell me why you drew back."

"Because I was afraid."

"Afraid of what?"

"Of you."

"What do you think criminals are, now, when they see me?"

"They're afraid."

"Of course they are. Your brother died trying to do what I have pledged to do. Your brother died because he found himself unable to stand by while someone in a position of strength victimized someone in a position of weakness. But *criminals* are weak, even the ones who get out of Rikers after pumping Volkswagens for six years. That's why they're criminals, and that's why their strength is always that of position, of circumstance. The criminal impulse is one of weakness—abject, encircling weakness. The police do not understand this. A few academics who study crime do understand this, but they embalm their understanding with misplaced empathy. How do you oppose criminals? You change their positioning. Most people can't do this. Almost anyone who stands up to a criminal will get hurt. It's the first thing they tell you: Give them your wallet. I'd even tell you that, if you were being mugged, and you look like a fairly strong dude. Still, give it to him—and know that this is where I come in. I'm the agent of repositioning. Give him your wallet, and let me do my work. I'm the only one who can. Most people drawn to what I do are sadists, revenge addicts, morons, or insane. Like the Boomerang Kid or any of the other idiots."

"Do you feel responsible for those people?"

"Not in the least."

I shook my head. "You are a most unique man."

"I was concussed when I said that."

"But you don't dispute it."

"I wish I were more unique. There are any number of crimes in this city, in this country, that I can't do a thing about. And so I essentially terrorize poor kids who had shitty situations to begin with. Am I happy about that? I am not."

"That was the point I tried to make in my essay."

"I agree with you. And I disagree. Because you have to start somewhere."

"Why are you telling me this? Why not write another letter to the paper of record?"

For the first and only time that afternoon, the Avenger laughed. "What do you want me to say? 'I am but a shadowy reflection of you. It would take only a nudge to make you like me, to push you out of the light'? I have nothing like that to say. And I have no story to tell you. I asked you here for one reason." He looked down, then, at his hand, and then back at me. "Which will have to wait, because someone is coming." With a quickness all the more startling for how fully it incinerated my expectation, the Avenger broke away and ran into the woods, changing direction by wrapping a hooked arm around a birch tree, the momentum of which launched him over a rotten log. He did not look back.

I was still standing in the middle of the path when the couple that had tripped the Avenger's hidden wire came upon me. An older man and woman, arm in arm, plump with retirement, looking at me with cool, New Englandy eyes. Here is the moment where I allow the Avenger to make sense. This is the event I adumbrate into meaningful sense. Now is when I come around to the Avenger. But no. I have not heard from him again, and he has apparently not been active since I saw him, which, at the time of this writing, now ranks among his longest silences. Is he healing? Or did our encounter do something to him that it did not do to me? I cannot say I have missed the Avenger. But sometimes I allow myself to believe he will soon tell me why he contacted me and what he finally had to say to me that day.

The man and woman stopped talking as they neared me. The enforced, artificial nature of their hush, their wariness, moved me to say, in a bright, friendly voice, "Hello!" But they *were* afraid, and by greeting them I had only made their fear worse. They hurried past me, as closely and solidly bundled together as siblings unaware of their divisibility.

J. Robert Lennon

THE
REMEMBERER

T

he Rememberer is born to middle-class parents in a small town in the upper Midwest, and appears, in all particulars, to be a normal and healthy child. She is given a name and introduced into a family of good-natured, self-satisfied people who aspire to, if anything, a kind of strident ordinariness. They are kind, decent, of above-average intelligence, but suspicious of any ostentation or personal peculiarity. They are generous in their deeds, but conservative in their politics and social habits.

The Rememberer develops normally, giving no one in her family any grounds for concern. Certain traits, however, are noted by her mother and father. As an infant, she has an unusually steady, determined gaze. While reclining in her little padded plastic seat, she often cranes her neck, appearing to be looking for something. She is able to sit up straight at a young age, and attempts to crawl long before her body is strong or agile enough to accomplish it. She betrays no obvious frustration, however, at her incapacity to achieve this goal. Rather, she practices until she gets it right. The same dynamic applies to standing up, and walking. The result is a child whom people are impressed by. The Rememberer, however, receives their expressions of delighted surprise with calm impassivity.

Her intellectual development also appears accelerated. She begins to speak at the usual age, but very quickly accumulates an enormous vocabulary. Unlike her brother and sister, she never seems to lose a toy. She calls everyone, even adults, by name. At her play group, she is watchful and alert. She is, by any standard, a distinctive, highly appealing-looking child; nevertheless nobody ever seems to try picking her up or engaging her in play.

One night, while her parents are lying in bed, discussing their day, her father refers to her as "odd." Her mother sighs, but does not disagree.

The Rememberer fares well in school. Uncannily so, in fact. She never seems to do anything wrong. At a conference, her teacher remarks upon this, ostensibly with considerable enthusiasm. But her parents correctly detect a note of distaste in the woman's voice. They discuss the possibility of sending The Rememberer to a special school, for gifted children, but after some thought decide against it. They prefer that she lead a normal life. For her part, The Rememberer soon realizes that her perfect test scores are making those around her uncomfortable, so she begins to make the occasional mistake. Afterward, everyone seems to relax.

The fact is, though she is thought to be the smartest child in the school, there is a consensus among a small group of teachers that this is not the case. The Rememberer seems uncomfortable judging novel social situations, and often offends or irritates other children. However, she soon makes it up to them by recalling their birthdays, or their pets' names, or that they like certain snacks, which she then gives to them. This is learned behavior, the doubting teachers believe, not instinct. They are kind to her, but resent her, in some obscure, unexamined way.

The first real crisis in The Rememberer's life comes when her beloved cat, Louie, is hit by a car and dies. The family is devastated, and is too sad to do much of anything for several days. After that, however, The Rememberer's parents and siblings begin to cheer up, and resume their usual activities; within a few weeks, life is almost back to normal.

But The Rememberer cannot be consoled. She cries constantly, even at school. The pain of loss refuses to dull. Worse, she feels compelled to bring up, during family meals, obscure events from the cat's life, such as the time he was chasing one particular chickadee, the one that lived under the garage eaves, not the one from the birdhouse at the edge of the yard; or the time he was sitting on the porch steps, and then moved over to the far edge of the porch, and then hopped down and sniffed in the grass, and then returned to the steps again; or the time he went outside and sat on the woodpile, then licked himself, then hid underneath the wheelbarrow when it started to rain, then came inside when the rain stopped. The stories seem pointless, but at first the family indulges them, joining The Rememberer in her sadness. After a while, however, they ignore the stories, and finally they tell The Remember to please just stop it, to get over it for goodness' sake, it was just a cat.

Her parents decide that a new cat will cheer her up, so they all go to the pound to pick one out. The Rememberer is indeed temporarily distracted from her grief, and chooses a black shorthair with white paws. And though she appears to like the new cat a great deal, she doesn't stop crying about Louie.

One night she overhears her parents discussing the possibility of bringing her to a psychiatrist. She resolves then to stop crying, and succeeds. However, she remains miserable. From here on in, it will be said of her that she was never the same again.

When she enters junior high, The Rememberer finds herself developing romantic longings for a boy named Nathan. The two sit beside each other at a school football game, and afterward, beneath the bleachers, share a kiss. It isn't long before the two are an inseparable "item," and are seen everywhere together, at the burger joint, the shopping mall, the park. Their relationship lasts until, at a party The Rememberer is unwilling to attend (by this time she has begun to find large social gatherings wearying), her boyfriend "hooks up" with her best friend, and The Rememberer instantly loses the two people closest to her.

Her grief and anger seem inexhaustible, and she stays home from school for several days, wailing in her bedroom. Through her tears she manages to write a pair of letters to her former boyfriend and best friend, listing every single thing either one of them ever said or did that they might be embarrassed for the other to learn. Each letter runs to nearly twenty pages. She manages to choke back sobs long enough to walk to the post office and mail them, and resumes her mourning the moment she exits the building. She mourns not only her cruel friends, but Louie the cat, and every other thing she has ever lost in her life—a beloved Barbie makeup kit stolen by another child on the beach during a family trip to Florida, a glittery tiara that fell off her head during a ferry ride across a Great Lake, an encyclopedia of trees that she left on the bathroom floor and that was ruined when the toilet overflowed, a stolen bicycle, a portrait of her second-grade teacher she drew that her mother inadvertently threw out. Over the years she has managed to pile these things at the edges of her mind, where they would least get in the way. But now they were back at the fore, lying in plain sight, and she is utterly crushed by them.

This time, her parents really do bring her to a psychiatrist. She is prescribed an antidepressant. It succeeds in dulling her pain, but she forgets nothing.

In the years leading up to adulthood, The Rememberer hardens. She keeps to herself, and makes no close friends. Her former best friend eventually breaks up with the boy, and both of them try to win her back. And though her desire to be with them again is great, she resists their overtures. She throws away all her clothes, even her favorites, and uses her allowance, saved over many years, to buy herself an entirely new wardrobe of identical black stretch jeans, black cotton blouses, and black turtleneck sweaters. This becomes her uniform. She wears no makeup. At first she ties her hair back in a tight ponytail; later, she simply has it cut off. She schedules a haircut once a month, in fact, and appears never to change. She eliminates from her life anything that could remotely be construed as evocative. She graduates at the top of her high-school class, but declines to give a speech or even to attend the ceremony. No one bothers to try to convince her otherwise—she is too strange to speak to.

In college, The Rememberer puts in a request to live alone, in a single dormitory room. Instead, she is assigned a roommate. The girl destined to room with her seems nice enough, but The Rememberer goes to the residence office and demands, once again, a single. When her request is denied, she brings her complaint up the ladder of authority, until she finds herself staging a sit-in at the office of the dean of students. When the dean calls her parents, they urge him to just give in, warning that he would likely regret doing otherwise. The semester has only just begun, and the dean has other things to worry about. He capitulates. The Rememberer remains alone for her four years of college.

While there, she takes a class in criminal psychology, and this leads her to major in criminology. She achieves perfect scores on every exam she takes, and is recruited by the FBI to take part in their special agent training program. She rises quickly through the ranks, and soon develops a reputation as one of the most promising new agents in institutional memory. Pieces of evidence or information that other agents must review thousands of pages of documents in order to recall, The Rememberer can bring immediately to mind. She memorizes crime scenes with eidetic precision, and can remember within the inch the exact position of cigarette butts, loose change, broken branches, or footprints. Important scraps of a suspect's personal history, which most investigators might dismiss as meaningless and forget immediately, The Rememberer retains. Addresses, telephone numbers, email addresses; notes scribbled on matchbook covers or the backs of envelopes—there is nothing that she sees that is not immediately accessible to her, however much time has passed.

Her colleagues regard her as superhuman. She is respected and feared and has no friends whatsoever.

Throughout the years of her meteoric rise, The Rememberer indulges, from time to time, in acts of shallow pleasure. She experiments with illegal drugs and engages in risky sexual encounters. Once she is established at the Bureau, she quits the drugs; they don't agree with her, in any event, and do little to relieve her pain. She continues, however, to seek out sexual release. At first, she dates men she likes. But inevitably she grows attached to them and, anticipating a sorrowful end, withdraws. Better is a quick, almost violent encounter with a man she does not find especially appealing. She is able to enjoy the thin gruel of carnal relations without the more complex pleasures of commitment. Coupled, however, with her tense associations at work, these experiences cause her to loathe her fellow man.

It takes several years, however, for these tensions to come to the fore. There is one particular agent with whom she once spent the night at the beginning of her training, and who later married another woman, and had a child. Perhaps this life has failed to please the agent; perhaps he has other troubles The Rememberer is not privy to. In any event, he begins to drink, and to become unreliable on the job, and for whatever reason, it is The Rememberer he chooses to bear the brunt of his disappointment. He treats her harshly when they are forced to work together and begins to spread the information, entirely false, that The Rememberer broke up his marriage. When The Rememberer brings her complaints to her superiors, she is told that she made her bed, and now must sleep in it.

Livid with anger, The Rememberer resigns from the Agency. She has saved up a considerable amount of money, having lived these years in solitude and without any desire for costly entertainments, so she can do without the income. But the insult remains fresh in her mind, and her anger does not cool. She recalls all of her life's slights and humiliations, and in her mind they fuse and begin to grow, into one tremendous, terrifying bonfire of rage.

It is at this point that The Rememberer decides to embark upon a life of crime. Her skills make her an ideal blackmailer and planner of robberies. Over the following week, she makes plans—her targets, her techniques, the underworld contacts on whose expertise she will draw. But then, just when she feels ready to take action, she realizes that there is no point. She has no need for money. There is no thrill in harming others, even for revenge. None of it will alleviate her own suffering. With exhausting, forceful effort, she douses the flames of anger. She is left weak and insensible from this labor, and lies in bed for days, her mind and body numb.

And then, one morning, she wakes and removes from her closet the sewing machine her mother gave her when she was nine years old, back when her parents still held out hope that she might become a "normal" girl. She also finds a dress—a red prom dress, another hopeful gift from Mother—and out of it she cuts an elegant and distinctive shape, a script letter R. She sews the R onto one of her turtlenecks, and examines herself in the bathroom mirror. It would be a peculiar fashion choice for anyone, but for her it is a bizarre ostentation, and the sight of it gives her the first smile she has shown in months. Over the next few days, she cuts dozens of Rs out of the prom dress and stitches them onto her sweaters and blouses. It isn't long before she has no clothes that do not bear the R. She will wear them as a badge of honor. She will no longer deny her deepest nature. She is, once and for all, The Rememberer.

If she is aware that this noble decision will lead inexorably to her own destruction, she gives no sign. All evidence implies that she has found her true calling. She begins by visiting nursing homes and hospitals, interviewing the elderly and infirm, plumbing the depths of their memory. There is something about her—her quiet, impassive, yet kind demeanor—that stirs up the past in these needy people and brings their memories forward. Some are painful, but The Rememberer accepts them, accepts the pain. She listens in receptive silence as the memories pour forth, and while many of them recede into the dark recesses of their bearers' minds mere moments after they emerge, The Rememberer does not forget. She cannot forget. She interviews her subjects' friends and families, tours their homes, turns over their possessions in her pale narrow hands, and soon she is able to tell the story of their lives, unadulterated by the passage of time, as though it were her own. The tellings last for hours and hours, and as she presents her findings, no one becomes tired or distracted, no one asks to take a break. They are mesmerized by The Remember, as if by an impossibly absorbing novel, or an impossibly beautiful song. The lives of the famous and the obscure; lives of loneliness and pain, or of experience and delight—no matter, The Rememberer makes them whole. The dead and dying live as perhaps they never did when their lives were vital. She is an artist and a hero.

But this period of fame is to be brief. No one notices how The Rememberer suffers; she hides her suffering well. When she is through presenting her findings to her subjects' families, she strides from their homes with strength and dignity, but when she reaches her own quarters deep within the warrens of the city, she collapses to the floor and lies unconscious for hours, even days. She must force herself to stand, to eat, to wash. The weight of memory—her own, and others'—is brutally huge.

And then, one day, she cannot even make it home. She collapses on the street, a frail black bundle. She is recognized, carried by a band of concerned passersby to the city hospital. She has fallen into a coma; her vitals are frighteningly out of kilter, but her brain is like a hurricane of electricity, the neurons firing at an astounding rate. Her doctors are stunned when she wakes. Her face is drawn and waxy; she says only one thing: Take me home.

They are still there, The Rememberer's family, living where they always have, in the small town where she grew up. Long estranged, they have not seen The Rememberer in years, though they have followed her exploits in the papers and on TV with pride and shame. She arrives in a magnificent, spontaneous procession, a city ambulance followed by thousands of cars, bicycles, people on foot. The Rememberer's parents tearfully accept her back into her home, carry her to her room, lay her down on the bed. There is so little of her left—yet she lies there for days, her lips moving in a blur of silent reminiscence, all her stored memory leaving her at last. As she withers away, her eyes grow sharper. Her brother, her sister, her parents believe they see happiness in them, for the first time. At last there is nothing left of her: She is merely a shell. The Rememberer is dead.

The funeral is attended by teeming, wailing crowds. There are speeches, but they disappoint: Nobody was close to her, nobody could recall what she was really like. When at last she is laid to rest, in the family plot at the edge of town, near the highway, there is much discussion of the memories she contained—how could she have held so many in her mind? And where did they go as they left her? Did they have some substance, did they still linger in the air around the town? Or were they purely ephemeral? And if so, how could something so insubstantial cause such pain?

The questions are never answered, not to anyone's satisfaction, and as the years go by, people begin to wonder if perhaps the tales of The Rememberer's skills have been exaggerated. Those who benefited from her talents remain grateful, but they can't seem to recall half of what she said.

It is not long, in fact, before The Rememberer is almost entirely forgotten. Among the few who do remember, however, is commonly held the conviction that this outcome would ultimately have pleased her.

Lauren Grodstein

THE SISTERS

OF ST. MISERY

As I type away in my little living room, with its crotchety radiator and the endless, exhausting coo of pigeons seducing one another on the guano-stained sill, it occurs to me, once again, that English is a pitifully cramped language. This is one of the casualties of my research, my respect for English, and I find it a pity that the language is the current lingua franca of both this nation and the world. I know what English partisans would say to this, and I won't dispute their points, that English uses 300,000 common words, while the Germans make do with 200,000 and the French, a paltry 150,000. The blood of hundreds of other languages beats in English's veins. Yet even you most ardent English devotees must admit you have no word meaning "to flay a living creature." You have no word meaning "the space between one's index finger and thumb." You cannot name the colors between brown and purple, red and orange, or even, frankly, white and yellow. Try it and see what you come up with. Ochre? Ivory? Ask yourselves, truly, are you satisfied?

During my sabbatical from the Syndicate, I have had lots of time to ponder these questions and others, the very meagerness of English, especially when compared to the richness of Thraco-Croatian, Myburian, and, of course, the linguistic jewelbox that is Hopt-Kong-Falluchine. It is often remarked that the Eskimo have more than one hundred words for snow, which is ridiculous, since the claim neither differentiates between types of Eskimo nor recognizes that there is, for all these different denizens of the north, no such thing as simple snow. There is "snow which is easily traveled across by sled," and "snow which is easily traveled across by foot"; there is "hunting snow" and "dirty snow" and—a recent product of these climatologically erratic times—"lonely snow." But there is no simple snow.

However, I am not writing of the "Eskimo," nor of the Thraco-Croatian, nor even, regrettably, of the Hopt-Kong-Falluchine. And though my research has required me to dip into the wellspring of Hillopont (who else but the warlike Hillopontians would have a transitive verb meaning "to kill [the beloved] in order to prevent another from despoiling [him or her]"? I have found myself asking Luis, more and more frequently, to find me whatever he can on the history of the Frissongs. In the summer I used the last of my savings to pay for him to visit certain parts of the Middle East—ancient home, of course, of the Frissongs—and while I cannot risk telling you in what unscrubbed quarter Luis uncovered these secret Frissong troves, I will brag a bit on his behalf and let you know he risked rogue security forces, Kurdish nationals, fierce desert winds, and enthusiasts of certain deposed heads of state in order to bring me my scrolls.

Which are now in front of me, wilting in the steam of this funky radiator. I do not trust any rare-books library to guard them, and no university would understand, much less support, the research that I do. For Frissong is a dead language. Dead as a pincushion. Dead as certain deposed heads of state. Nobody but me has been able to read or understand it for almost three thousand years.

———

It's a rather unnerving story.

The night I was born, unable to cry, the doctor and nurses huddled over me and whispered about underdeveloped vocal chords, blocked passages, atrophied lungs. I listened to them whisper and did my best to assuage everyone's concerns, most of all my poor mother's, who, even in her twilit postpartum fog, wanted to hear her new daughter's voice. I took a breath. I contorted as best I could. I tried to scream. No sound came out. The doctors eventually handed me to my mother, who held me to her breast and said, "Maybe she's just quiet?"

I smiled at her, grateful for giving me the benefit of the doubt.

That was all—I was just quiet. Please, please, no more hearty slaps on my tender new behind.

"It's funny, though," said my father, a building superintendent who'd spent the whole of my delivery chewing on his cuticles. "Funny, but doesn't it look like she's following our conversation?"

"I suppose," my mother said, collapsing back into her pillows. She held me closer to her breast and I fed. Why wouldn't I follow their conversation? I remember wondering. After all, weren't they talking about me?

At home, I was greeted by two elder siblings, one a year old, the other twenty-three months, and then my mother was pregnant again a mere two months after my birth, so that whatever tests I might have undergone were I the product of a wealthier and less busy household were simply never part of the picture. I was just quiet: the silent center of a storm of an eventual six children, two adults, a dog, a parakeet, and several half-stray cats in a basement apartment in Kingston, New York.

In fact, it was not until I was five years old that my maternal grandmother, making her quadrennial visit from her home in northern Quebec, mentioned to my mother that perhaps there was something medically odd about me, that I wasn't just quiet, but that perhaps, internally, all was not exactly as one might hope.

"Odd?" my mother said. They were speaking in their husky, clangy Quebecois French, the language my parents relied on when they didn't want their children to understand them.

"Hasn't it occurred to you that Marie never says a word?"

"She's just quiet," my mother said. If I remember correctly, she was busy scrubbing lunch dishes. Only she, my grandmother, and I were in the kitchen.

"Marie," my grand-mere said, crooking a gnarled finger in my direction. "Come here and sit on my lap."

My mother's back was turned; I did as I was instructed.

"Now tell me, Marie," said my grand-mere, "do you know how to speak?"

I nodded.

"Then say something to me. Say anything."

I opened my mouth. I wanted to please her very much, this baggy old lady who brought us maple candy and hand-knit sweaters. I tried to push some noise, any noise, from my throat, but nothing came.

"*Maman*," said my mother, still scrubbing dishes. "You must speak in English to Marie. She doesn't understand French."

"But of course she does. You understand French, don't you, *mon coeur*? See? She's nodding!"

"She's nodding because she knows we're talking about her. There's no way she could understand French. She's heard maybe twenty words in her life."

What foolishness from my poor mother! I understood French the way I understood the sound of my own name. I looked from my grandmother again. I nodded furiously.

"She doesn't talk," my grandmother marveled. "But she understands." For some reason, I felt scared at that moment, and ran outside to play with my brothers.

But the first real challenge to my childish equanimity was at St. Immaculate Misery, and how I wish I could tell a different story about the nuns there, but these nuns—crabbed, wall-eyed, osteoporotic—were of the nightmarish breed that has given so many good sisters a bad name. The badger-faced nuns of St. Misery never forgave me my silence; they made me stand in a corner with a heavy sign around my neck that read, "Obnoxiousness is the Bride of the Devil," or "Misbehavior Makes Our Lord Cry Himself to Sleep."

My crimes? When they asked me my Bible questions, I could not give audible answers. When they ordered me to recite my Hail Marys, I could only mouth the words. But I did believe in something back then, some God of my own devising, and I prayed every day that one day He would let me hear my own voice. I tried, through gestures, to explain this to the nuns; in response they called me fresh and caned me across the backs of my knees. Standing there, disgraced, I would close my eyes and imagine that one day I would destroy the mothballed sisters, destroy St. Misery, the whole crumbling building. And the thick twine tied at the back of my neck would chafe, and I would go home with knees red from caning and eyes red from crying and not be able to tell anyone what had gone wrong.

St. Misery's only saving grace was Sister Helena, the music teacher, a young albino with yellow eyes, a patient manner, and soft hands. Perhaps she, too, knew what it was like to be different, or perhaps she was just kindly by nature; no matter the reason, she treated me with uncommon patience as I learned, under her guidance, to play the violin. Eventually I became skilled enough to win a scholarship to the conservatory at Mount Hope, and it was on that campus that I encountered the reclusive but much-admired linguistic historian T. Hibbert Pendergrass, who gave me my first introduction to the endless pleasures of languages beyond the sisters' hissing Latin, my classmates' flat-voweled English, and my parents' secret Quebecois. I became his student, and then his assistant, and we traveled together to meetings and rare-books libraries. Ensconced in conference rooms lit by oil and flash, I would send Sister Helena postcards from the most unimaginable places: Karakalpakstan, Vanuatu, Tristan de Cunha.

T. Hibbert was almost entirely deaf, so my quietness never affected him one way or the other; we concocted a precise and delicate sign language to suit our needs, and it is an offspring of this sign language that I rely on now. T. Hibbert named it Linguistic Inquirisign B, and this was his gift to me: this, and the introduction to the Syndicate, which pays my bills, and the Bergonzi violin I still play for hours every morning, five-thirty to eight, which warms my hands and my brain enough to go forth and tackle my scrolls.

By the by, Luis has a fluency in Linguistic Inquirisign B that perhaps even I will never quite achieve. The poetry he can express with his fingers—inestimable. It is for this reason among many others that he is so valuable to me, and I cannot help but treasure this talent even more than his other considerable assets: the way he polishes my desk with vinegar and rosewater, the way he makes sure I have company on Christmas Eve, whether I want any or not. The way he oils and tunes my Bergonzi. I assume he will pursue a Ph.D. of his own one of these days—truly, he must stop relying on the comfort of being my assistant—

and yet I confess to dreading the day he leaves. He is as useful to me as my own hands.

It was Luis, in fact, who first turned up the similarities between the few remaining biographical notes on Frissong leader Calamitus IV and Solomon, the third king of Israel, the man responsible for building the First Temple of Jerusalem. He will be here soon to go over my most recent translations, to deconstruct our book of Frissong hymns. Luis is boyish, freckled, the twist of a hairlip improperly corrected in his hometown in Mexico twenty-eight years ago. He has a religious streak and a lazy eye, was born to an impoverished Cochimi family in the fishing village of Pichilingue, jutting out onto the Sea of Cortez. His arrival at this doorstep—involving a midnight run across the Arizona border, a seminary scholarship, and an accidental bus trip to New York City (he thought he was headed for Newark, Delaware)—was almost as improbable as my own.

This is what we know of Solomon, the third king of Israel: He was renowned for bravery. He made impossibly fast decisions. He married again and again and loved passionately. What I know of Calamitus is this: He was renowned for bravery. He was endlessly cruel. He lived in Jerusalem, as did Solomon. Both men were known to be wealthy, ruthless, and powerful as lions. But while Solomon was considered wise and just, Calamitus ate the flesh of his conquests' children. While Solomon built a temple, Calamitus raped his sisters. One can understand why the Frissongs needed to do a little historical PR. One can understand why biblical tradition and all its complicit sisters did their best to erase the fact that these two men were one.

"Marie?" I turn around. There is Luis, a vase of lilies in his hands. I love the smell of lilies, he knows it, and he never fails to bring me some when he thinks I'm working too hard.

"They were selling them at the bodega," he says to me shyly, placing the lilies on the mantel. It is growing cold now, early November already, and the New Yorkers under my window are wrapped in coats and scarves. Luis pulls a chair forward, sits across from me at my desk—

he always leans rather close to me. He is looking at the scrolls, the magnificent hieroglyphs.

"I'm getting closer and closer to figuring out the Frissong hymns," he says. "I'm sorry it's taking so long." Because of the enormity of the project, and the time it takes to translate Frissong concepts into English words, we've split up the scrolls section by section: I translate the material into rough English, and Luis does the fine-tuning. Right now he is struggling with pages of Frissong religious material.

"Don't apologize," I sign to him. *"I'm sure you're doing fine."*

"But I know how important it is to you that we figure this out."

"Well, you don't have to kill yourself." Luis looks so anguished sometimes I worry for his health.

"I'm not killing myself," he says, and the trace of a frown passes over his features. "But this is important, right? For the project? You need me to finish these hymns?"

I can't help but feel it's unfair of me to put pressure on him when I'm struggling so much myself, and I sign this to him.

"Oh, Marie, you're doing great," he says, and rubs my back vigorously. Luis is a toucher, a hugger, a masseuse during moments of celebration. I am forty-two years old, and since my days at St. Misery I've never really liked being touched. I close my eyes and wait for him to stop rubbing my back, hoping that he'll hurry it up and also that he'll never stop.

———

T. Hibbert often mentioned to me, during long flights home across the Indian Ocean, that solitude was good for the linguistic historian. Too much interaction with chatty colleagues, he felt, risked distracting the historian from her work or, worse, diluting her feel for ancient languages by immersing her too fully in the language of the world around her (in our case, that would be musty, fumbling English). "Do you understand me, my child?" T. Hibbert would sign. "Whenever you need to talk to somebody, play your violin." Then he would put his headphones on to drown out whatever ambient noise might penetrate his clogged-up eardrums, and fall asleep like a child with an airplane blanket snug under his chin.

I never knew if T. Hibbert's dedication to solitude was a matter of faith, or if, perhaps, the man protested too much, if he preached solitude as cover for the fact that he was a deaf hunchbacked gnome with arcane interests and no ability to make chit-chat or even ask about the weather. I thought, twenty years ago, that surely I would never relish being alone quite the way T. Hibbert did, and that eventually someone would see through my muteness and be able to speak with me in the natural way of friends. T. Hibbert, who intuited my doubts, suggested that I supplant my yearning for human company with a yearning for ground-breaking research. Whatever emptiness in me that might be satisfied by friendship would surely be filled more thrillingly by historical breakthroughs, linguistic magicianship.

It took me years, but eventually I did come to his way of seeing the world. I worked diligently for the Syndicate, which provided me with this apartment and a salary that made it possible for me to stay in this archive-rich city. Even better, the Syndicate allowed me to work alone, without direct supervision, an office full of busybodies. I began conducting the independent research that fires me so. And in the intervening years I have indeed supplanted any need I might have for other people with a passion for my work. I doubt I'm the first to have done so.

But sometimes, I wonder what it would be like to live as an ordinary person, the kind who loves and expects to be loved back. The kind who trades casual words with friends and family. And sometimes, when he's lost in books or typing out notes rat-a-tat on his laptop, I look over at Luis and wonder what his life will look like after I'm gone, what kind of woman he'll find to take care of him. Then he'll look up, catch me watching him, and his face will break into such a beatific smile that I have no choice but to turn away or, every so often, in extreme moments, leave the room.

———

I pick up the Bergonzi and draw the bow carelessly through the second octave. Luis left fifteen minutes ago to get us some food. I don't think much about what I eat, and in fact can go for days at a time without so much as a carrot; oddly, it seems that hunger often piques my linguistic abilities, if I manage to feel hunger at all. Luis regards food similarly, which is why he's diligent about making sure we eat at least once a day, since otherwise we could very well starve. I gave him a twenty for two cartons of General Tso's and stir-fried broccoli.

The truth is that despite our periodic frustrations, this work has gone much more quickly than I ever might have suspected when we started the project last year. Once Luis returned from the Gulf with my scrolls, all I had to do was unwind them and read. The information was spelled out like a history lesson: dates, battles, major figures. Even better, the corollary research Luis performed at the Archive supported everything these scrolls say. I finger my Bergonzi. If I publish—when I publish—everything I know, I will change the way the world believes. I will conquer the sisters of St. Misery. And I will do it all without saying a word.

The doorbell rings, and then there is a crash outside my door, a crash and a fumbling of papers. "Marie? Marie?" Oh, dear. Not today. "Sorry to just barge in like this, Marie, I know it's been a while, but boy do I have some great news for you."

It's Debbie, my representative at the Syndicate, with a smile on her face, a stain on her suit, and a gigantic file folder under each arm. She isn't supposed to bother me for another three months. I put down my violin, then stand to help her with her things, sit her down in my living room before she topples over.

"Debbie," I sign. "I'm still on sabbatical. You're not supposed to contact me until the new year."

"You think I want to disturb you, Marie? You think I'd bother you for something that wasn't of the highest, shall I say, import?" As usual, she has lipstick on her teeth.

I sigh, head to my little plug-in carafe to boil some water for tea. I've been freelancing for the Syndicate half my life, but I refuse to jump like a Pekingese every time Debbie tells me she has something "big, very big." Especially during my sabbatical.

"Don't you make that face, Marie. Just wait till you hear what I'm talking about." She ruffles through one of her folders as I drip honey into my mug. "You're still working on that—on your little Solomon project, right? I mean, I know it's been a while since we've seen each other, but—"

"It was supposed to be a year."

"All right, Marie, I know, I'm interrupting. Would I do this if it weren't important? Like I said, the utmost? Are you still working on that little Solomon project of yours or not?" Debbie has been one of the Syndicate's top people as long as I've been working for them, but she still talks like a demanding teenager. She's from California, people say, which might explain it—but since she's a Syndicate rep, she never talks about herself. The organization frowns on self-reflection of any sort. All I know about Debbie is that she's a ruthless businesswoman, able to broker a deal between a four-star general and an Afghani mujahideen, make a 20 percent commission, and get home in time for dinner. In the world of the Syndicate—the world's most powerful outsourcing firm—Debbie wins enormous respect. But her suits never fit her exactly right, and her nails are always bitten, and I've never been able to reconcile the Debbie I know with the Debbie people whisper about in Syndicate hallways.

"Well, listen, Marie, don't freak out or anything, but I think I have a buyer."

"For what?"

"For your project, your Solomon project. Marie, come on, what are we talking about here? The guy's in Cairo, a sheik, oil billionaire, amateur linguistic scientist, Bible scholar. He's building some kind of research center out in the desert, commissioning special projects, wants you to move over to Cairo and finish up Solomon."

"Impossible." I am annoyed and my signing grows stiff. *"The project isn't for sale."*

"Everything's for sale, Marie. Don't be ridiculous."

"Not this."

"Did I mention he'll pay you?"

"I don't need the money, Debbie. You've paid me very nicely over the years."

"Marie." Debbie puts on her most coy look. "Marie, who said anything about money?" She starts to sneeze; I hand her a tissue. "Look,

281

the sheik does not want to pay you in money. He knows you won't take it, I've told him all about your ascetic lifestyle, your hunger strikes, your—excuse me for mentioning—your threadbare wardrobe." I look down at my corduroy jumper. "Marie, the sheik has a much more specialized form of payment in mind for you."

She smiles slyly, pats at her hair, wipes her nose. I wish she'd leave. I hand her another tissue. "He knows about you, Marie, about your talents, the freakish way you can understand languages that nobody else in the world can. And he also knows about your disability—"

"My WHAT?" My hands explode across my face.

"Don't get excited, Marie, come on. You know what I mean. He knows about—the fact that you can't speak. And it seems he has some special doctors, therapists out in Cairo. You know Fanucha Wellspring?"

Of course I know Fanucha Wellspring. She was the explorer who uncovered the Oil Can Glyphs in Gaza, which I myself had the honor of translating a decade ago. Fanucha was born deaf as a water eel, but on her eightieth birthday, for reasons that remain determinedly secret, she ran out, bought a top-notch stereo system, and sat in her apartment blissfully singing along to the middle sections of *Der Ring des Nibelungen* till the neighbors complained. Three days later, she was dead of dehydration, the music so wonderful to her ears that it had obviated her need to drink.

"Marie, that was our sheik," Debbie says, smugly. "It was his doctors."

"I don't believe you."

"Why would I lie?" She drops one of the file folders on my desk, nudging aside my Bergonzi. "Read this. Just read it. There's a letter from the sheik in there, descriptions of the facilities, the project, the other researchers who'll be coming."

"There will be other researchers?"

"What started with Fanucha Wellspring certainly didn't end with her," Debbie says. She stands, takes another tissue, and heads to the door. "I've introduced the sheik to some of our finest people. I'd love it if that could include you."

I look down at my still hands.

"I'll be back tomorrow, Marie," she says, her voice oozing. "In the meantime, think this over. I think you'll find it's truly an offer you can't refuse. The sheik will give you your voice."

"What's your commission on this, Debbie?" I sign. Sometimes I can't help but be rude, but to thick-haired, thick-ankled Debbie, there are no rude questions.

"More than I can even count." She laughs, and soon enough I can hear her clunk noisily down the hall. "I can finally retire from the damn Syndicate and buy my place in Bali."

"I see," I sign to my Bergonzi.

When Luis returns with the Chinese, we eat in silence.

———

The evening comes quickly, as Luis struggles with the hymns and I wrack my brain trying to turn Frissongian concepts into English. But I press on, refusing to pick up Debbie's materials or even think about her promise until after Luis departs for the night. Then, finally, I've finished translating a tricky passage about infant sacrifice in the Calamitus court (would that English had some way to describe the exact wail of a terrified newborn!) and he has pressed my hand in good-bye, and I am alone. Without even stopping to think, I sit down on the floor with the letter from the sheik and read over the man's fancy promises. *Dear Marie*, it begins, and I marvel at the informality. *I have heard so many extraordinary things about you and your unique and amazing gift. My friends at the Syndicate assure me that there is no one like you in the world, that your power to navigate languages is truly beyond the realm of the natural. They have told me that never in the history of their organization, and perhaps even the history of the world, has anyone with your gifts existed. Therefore, Marie, it would be my great honor to have you join a small laboratory here in the Egyptian desert, where we will be conducting experiments, researching antiquity, and creating a center of learning the likes of which none has seen since the famed Library of Alexandria burned so many years ago . . .*

His letter goes on to explain that he is collecting every supernatural talent the Syndicate has ever contracted out: Chance Lonegan, who can see ninety seconds into the future (but is blind as a mole rat), Friday Schneider, who can swim to unheard-of depths (but on land is as clumsy as a walrus). The quadriplegic Russian, Vladimir Lavinski, who can move heavy objects with his gaze. The Syndicate has hired each of us out over the years to consult on various worldwide calamities, and although we've never met one another, we've each heard more than enough. Friday Schneider discovered forty-eight new kinds of coagulant sea worm; Vladimir Lavinski saved a diplomat's life by moving a car's axle off his pelvis. Chance Lonegan managed to head off a terrorist ambush in Jeddah by foreseeing a hidden bomb. And I translated dozens of "untranslatable" codes, warding off nuclear sabotage in certain uncomfortable parts of East Asia.

The sheik would bring us together—would collect the Syndicate's A team—and let us run free in his palace of knowledge. And Chance would see, and Friday would dance, and Vladimir would walk, and I would speak. And we'd do it in Cairo, the unexcavated womb of some of the world's densest tongues.

I put the letter in my lap and closed my eyes. What would it be like to actually say all those words? To pronounce the giggles and hiccups of Skelt, the low, flutey vowels of Myburian? Or even to speak my own burdensome English? To hear the sound of my own name in my own voice?

"I knew you'd still be awake." It is Luis, in his winter coat, a scarf around his neck, his tawny cheeks spotted with red. I feel both relieved and deflated that he's come back, that he has the keys to my apartment. "I've been up thinking half the night. I couldn't concentrate. Those hymns—they're stuck in my mind."

"They'll still be here tomorrow," I sign, and a voice in my head says, *but will I?*

"I couldn't wait." He grins. "You know how it is when you have an incredible idea, you can't wait to work it out?" He pulls one of the scrolls from the corner of my desk, slips on latex gloves, unravels it on his lap. The tawny parchment of the scroll crackles softly. We're both on the floor; this afternoon's lilies perfume the air.

"See?" he says. "See? This part here, you translated it as *that which*

*belongs to the sire is what the sire will belong to in case of death, dismem-
berment, or disembowelment.*"

I grimace. English really is such a hideous language. *"I'm sure I can
do better, Luis."*

"No! No! I figured it out. The Song of Solomon, you know? The
Song of Calamitus?"

"I'm sorry?"

"Marie." Luis laughs. "You say you went to Catholic school, but
what you know about the Bible I could fit into my shoe. The Song of
Solomon. Forget death and disembowelment. That's the hymn. The
Song of Solomon."

I blink. The Song of Solomon. What do I know of that?

Luis grins at me. "Marie, you know it," he says, gently. He takes my
hand across the scroll, and the latex feels warm on my wrist. "The
lyrics are famous," he says. "I am my beloved's"—he holds my wrist
tighter—"and my beloved is mine."

"Luis, I'm leaving." It is as unexpected as it is true. Tomorrow, when
Debbie arrives, I will tell her to pass along my acceptance to the sheik.

"What do you mean?"

There's no way to even explain it. He knows nothing of the Syndicate, nothing of the small collection of odd talents that roam this earth.
As far as he knows, my ability to understand dead languages is like his
ability to believe in God—it doesn't even bear explaining. Luis is a boy
from Mexico whom I took under my wing. Now he will have to fly on
his own. This is the way of the world. T. Hibbert went away, too, you
know.

*"Luis, I have been given an opportunity to work in Cairo. In exchange,
they will perform an operation that will restore my voice to me."*

"I'll come," he says.

"You can't." Luis is wonderful, but he is not supernatural. I know
there will be no place for him where I am going. And he looks at me
with such fondness, such adoration, that I know I cannot stay.

"But I can be your voice, Marie!" he says. "I can be your voice."

The closeness of this living room is unbearable. I pull my hand
back into my lap. The lessons of T. Hibbert burn in my ears: You need

nothing but your work. You need nothing, you need nobody. I am a translator, a historian, a scholar. I have at my disposal any language that has ever been written or transcribed. Luis reaches out for me again, and again I pull away. I feel the bedroom behind us like a magnet. Misbehavior makes our Lord cry himself to sleep.

"Marie," he starts, and I am begging him not to continue, "Marie, do you know the Song of Solomon?"

"You'll find someone else to advise your work. Or maybe you should finally apply for your Ph.D."

"Behold," he says, and his eyes are sparkling. "Thou art fair, my love; behold, thou art fair; thou hast doves' eyes."

"Luis, this is inappropriate."

"Behold, thou art fair, my love; behold, thou art fair; thou hast doves' eyes within thy locks: thy hair is as a flock of goats, that appear from Mount Gilead."

"Please stop this."

"Don't leave me, Marie," he says, in that beautiful accent of his. "I'm asking you, please, don't leave me. You're the only person I have ever loved. You're the only person who has ever loved me."

"I don't—"

"You do, Marie. I know you do. I know how to read your signs."

And for the first time in all this long, lonely life, the words I need are nowhere to be found, in this or any other language anyone's ever heard.

Sean Doolittle

MR. BIG DEAL

Midshift, we take a call down near the freight yards, a disturbance at a bar named the Tip Top Lounge. I know the place, a dank little hole on the riverfront, where the short-haulers go to get drunk, blow off steam, and occasionally maim one another.

My trainee is confused. She doesn't want to ask a dumb question, so she checks her bearings on the grid before she says, "Wouldn't that be the Southeast's party?"

"It would," I tell her. "But we'll go play backup on this one."

"Oh." She nods along, eager to prove herself, if obviously still wondering why we're responding to a bar fight somewhere in another district when we're assigned to a relatively quiet bunch of streets in the northwest suburbs. "They won't get bent out of shape when the North rolls up in their yard?"

"I'm guessing no," I tell her.

"Oh," she says.

I could tell her that bartenders at places like the Tip Top don't normally call the police for help when a customer goes on a tear. But we'll have a better picture soon enough.

Meanwhile, it dawns on her that dispatch advised code zero over the radio. She glances over and says, "Ohhh."

Vazquez is her name. In the short time we've been riding together, this is the first she's hinted that she's heard any of the stories that I imagine she's heard about me.

"Don't worry." I pull a U-turn and punch the unit toward the Southeast Expressway. "It'll probably be over by the time we get there."

"Hey, let's hope not." She smiles and hits the roof lights. "We could use a little action."

Off we go.

According to dispatch, we're looking for a white male, presumed gifted, abilities unknown. He turns out to be easy enough to find.

The Tip Top is barely standing when we arrive. It looks like somebody typed the wrong coordinates and accidentally dropped artillery on the place; the roof is in tatters, the power is out, and the front entrance looks like an exit wound. Dead neon tubing bristles from the wreckage. Outside, the cracked, buckled plot of asphalt where the Tip Tip sits is scattered with broken glass, fluttering scraps of trash, and random debris. There's car burning near the curb.

Some of the patrons are standing around in huddles, shouting and pointing in the firelight. A few others appear to be unconscious, piled on the ground here or there, as though flung from a distance.

Vazquez says, "Ho-ly shit."

She's leaning forward, eyes wide, looking up and out through the top edge of the windshield. I follow her gaze to a squad unit, presumably a Southeast District car, lying wheels-up on the roof of a warehouse building across the street. The unit's top is crunched, windows gone. Steam billows from the exposed undercarriage.

"Call Central," I tell her. "Tell them we're on site and code twelve." When she doesn't respond, I look at her and say, "Tina."

Vazquez blinks. In a moment, she pulls herself together and goes for the radio.

I unfasten my seatbelt, open my door, and step out. The first thing I notice about the scene, apart from the sound of wood splintering somewhere inside the bar, is that there isn't another uniform on the ground within two hundred yards of the place. Other units from the Southeast are setting up a cordon at the other end of the block; I can hear more sirens approaching from somewhere in the distance. A department chopper circles above, rotor blades thumping the air, pinning the Tip Top in a column of light.

I start across the street.

"Well hey," a guy says to me. He's leaning against a darkened streetlamp, well clear of the property, watching the chaos. "Thanks for stopping by."

I look him over as I approach. Broad shoulders, bald head, muscles, chin beard. Bare arms and leather wristbands. Jailhouse tattoos. I note the bar rag on his belt and ask, "You're the party who made the call?"

"Lotta good it did, huh? Hey, tell me something: You assholes gonna drop this fuckin' mutant, or just watch from over there?"

I glance over my shoulder—at the perfectly good radio unit that somehow ended up on top of a warehouse six hundred feet away—and ask the bartender what he can tell me about what's happening.

He snorts like he can't believe how dumb cops are. "You not seeing the same shit I'm seeing?"

"Did you see how it started?"

"Hell should I know? Guy's been here since two this afternoon, cryin' in his booze. All at once he jumps up and starts taking the place apart."

I look back toward what's left of the Tip Top, which wasn't much to begin with. It sounds like a demolition crew working late in there. "Did you hear him say what he was upset about—"

"Lost his job, girl kicked him out, some shit." The bartender dabs an imaginary tear. "Fuckin' spare me. We all got problems."

"Do you know if there's anyone injur—"

"Guy looks like he goes about a buck fifty," the bartender says, ignoring me completely. "Know what he was doing right before he went apeshit?"

"No," I say. "What was he doing?"

"Just sittin' at the bar, fiddlin' with this. With his *fingers*. Right?"

The bartender goes too quickly into his back pocket, comes out with something in his hand. All I see is a flash of metal. Reflexively, I take two steps back, draw my service weapon, and tell him to drop whatever he's holding.

"Jesus!" He throws up his hands, tossing the object to the pavement between us. "What the fuck, man?"

The object lands with a clatter and skids toward the toe of my boot. It turns out to be a simple barkeeper's combination tool: a bottle opener, a small dull blade for cutting foil, a corkscrew. I stoop and pick it up, and that's when I see what the guy was trying to show me: The corkscrew has been straightened.

I holster my weapon.

The bartender sees me contemplating the unraveled corkscrew. He puts his hands down and says, "His fingers, yo."

There's a horrendous crash; the bartender and I both duck our heads as a jagged new hole bursts open in the roof of the Tip Top Lounge. While we stand there, a twelve-foot column of wood and marble soars up and out of the building like a missile from a silo, trailing shingles and insulation.

I've seen any number of wonderments, but I can't say I've ever seen a bar counter fly before. From the curb, we watch the slab reach the peak of its trajectory, momentarily illuminated in the bird unit's spotlight, casting a shadow over the parking lot below.

The shadow spreads. Patrons scatter. The bar lands where a number of them had been standing, breaking apart in a riot of splintering oak and crumbling stone.

"Aw, now." The bartender seems genuinely pained to observe that he has no bar left to tend. "That shit ain't right."

Before I can key my radio, our subject emerges. He stalks out the front of the Tip Top through the smoke and dust. The bartender is right: He doesn't look like much at first glance. Narrow-chested, disheveled, wild-eyed, panting. He looks very much like what I'm told he is: a drunk on a bender.

Still, when he sees that a new set of cops has arrived, the bartender mutters, "Uh oh," and runs for cover.

I turn momentarily, my attention drawn by the bartender suddenly hauling ass in the other direction. I feel a tingle at the back of my neck.

The next thing I feel is a floating sensation. I have time enough to realize that I'm sailing low through the air before a bone-shuddering impact takes my breath.

I land in a puddle of pain at the base of a wall twenty feet away. My head is ringing. I may have blacked out, but I'm not sure. I think I'm in one piece, but I'm not sure about that, either. Everything hurts.

I pull myself together. The first thing I see is our subject, standing in the middle of the street, washed in blinding white light from the police chopper hovering overhead. He's picked up my cruiser and raised it over his head with both hands.

The chopper's spotlight creates the picture of a circus strongman standing center ring. I imagine the scene from inside the chopper and think of an ant hoisting a chunk of bread. I can see Vazquez inside the car, pounding on the window. I scramble to my feet, drag a breath into my lungs, and shout a warning.

The subject isn't listening.

"Sir!"

He crouches. Flexes.

There's no time to negotiate. Sealed inside the cruiser, six feet off the ground, Vazquez is scrambling for the door handle. But she's not going to make it out. I see the guy's back twitching beneath his grime-stained shirt as he pivots and rears on his heels; all at once, the bird is a hovering bull's-eye. There's no time think about it.

I point my finger and let it happen.

Somewhere deep in my head, I feel the familiar pulse. A depth charge somewhere on the floor of my brain.

Just before I lose consciousness, I see the subject go limp as his strength disappears. Then the subject disappears, crushed beneath the weight of the cruiser. The car bounces and rocks on impact; I hear crumpling steel, the pop and hiss of rupturing tires. I see the windows shatter and rain out of the unit, nuggets of safety glass twinkling in the street.

I wake up to flashing lights, radio chatter, shouting, running, a circle of cops standing over me. I don't recognize any of them. They're looking at me the same way the bartender looked at his corkscrew. One of them says, "How the crap did you do that?"

I don't know what to tell him.

———

In his day, my father could wad up a car bumper in his fist. I had an uncle on my mom's side who accidentally killed himself by jumping too high. My whole family comes from gifted stock, mother's and father's side both; the year I turned drinking age, I watched my cousin Shirley win a bar bet by turning at thirty paces and lighting a man's cigar using only her eyes.

Me?

If the subject can't be avoided, this is what I tell people:

When I was four weeks old, I accidentally disabled my uncle Neil. It happened on a Sunday in the house where I grew up; according to the story I've been told, Uncle Neil had been holding me in his arms, bouncing me around and making funny faces, when suddenly I flushed red and let out a wail.

Uncle Neil's gift had been his hearing. He'd worked in counterintelligence for the Federation during the chem wars; later, in the private sector, he'd grown fat on government contracts as an engineering consultant. They say Uncle Neil could sound out structural imperfections in a ten-kiloton suspension bridge by tapping on a girder with a ballpoint pen.

It was my crying that deafened him. More accurately, my distress. Apparently, on that day—for whatever reason—I'd felt threatened for the first time in my tiny infant life, and for the first time, that day, my gift revealed itself.

Uncle Neil never regained his.

The lab coats all say I'm a miracle; they don't know how I work, or why. All they know is that they've never seen another like me.

My fellow officers like me because I'm good with a gifted collar, but none of them are sure about me otherwise. They all wonder, on some level, if they'll get sterile, or have a stroke, or forget how to tie their shoelaces if they stand too close.

I've tried to explain that my gift, if that's what it is, affects only my own kind. Gifts of strength I can enfeeble. Born supersonic? I can make you lame. If your gift is sight, hey, I can blind your ass. But if you're a natural, I'm just some guy.

My own kind thinks I'm a freak. Most who know me avoid me like the plague. I've tried to explain that I learned to control my gift, if that's what it is, around the same time I learned to walk.

Nobody really believes me.

———

For a week, the Tip Top is all over the news. The man I neutralized was named Leroy Penny: divorced, six kids, lived with his girlfriend in a ramshackle one-bedroom crackerbox on the east side of town. He'd worked twenty years for the Federation Armory on Deer Island, right up until the morning of his rampage, when he'd been terminated without severence for drinking on the job.

Naturally, there were half a dozen implant cams among the witnesses from the bar. Naturally, every one of them took the opportunity to sell their footage to the networks. Of course, the witnesses were all shitfaced when it happened, so their clips are murky and out-of-focus. Two days ago, the department released official photos and footage from the bird unit's on-board cameras, and that's what the papers and the news stations are running now.

Techs in the department have edited my service weapon off of my hip and into my hand. The ID tags on the doors and roof of my cruiser have been replaced with a Southeast District car number. In these approved images, according to standard department procedure, my face is a blob of pixels. Same for Tina Vazquez. Hero cop saves partner, colleagues, bystanding citizens.

The chief, the deputy ops, and the public information office covered my identity at the press conference. The truth has been modulated for public consumption: natural officer, gifted perp, lethal force regrettable but required. Race relations are a sensitive area. The last riot that started in the gifted community destroyed a hundred square city blocks before the Federation stepped in. Nobody wants a repeat.

Meanwhile, I'm suspended with pay until the internal review board convenes.

"Well, look who it is." Uncle Phil brightens when he sees me. "Mr. Big Deal."

"Uncle Philly." I give him a hug. "How's the hip?"

He snorts. The hip, apparently, isn't worth talking about. Instead, he looks both ways, up and down the hall. He waits for a nurse to push an empty wheelchair past us, then he leans in and says, "Didn't I see you on the news?"

Here we go. "Don't know what you mean, Uncle Phil."

"Horseshit."

"You mean that mess down by the yards?"

Uncle Phil rolls his eyes.

"Come on," I tell him. "I work the Third Northwest. You know that."

"Right." He nods slowly. "I forgot."

"I wasn't even on duty Monday night."

"Sure." More nodding. "Sure."

"I'm serious."

"Whatever you say, kid." He pats my cheek and changes the subject. "So what's the occasion? Haven't seen you here in a while."

Here is a private ward on the seventh floor at Hope Mercy, outside my father's room, where he's been refusing to die for going on twelve years now.

There's no occasion. I only came to visit Tina Vazquez down on three; she broke her pelvis and both ankles when our cruiser crash-landed on top of Leroy Penny with her trapped inside. But Vazquez was sleeping when I got here, and I didn't want to disturb her. I had an hour to kill.

I look around. Uncle Phil is right: it's been a while. "I guess I've been busy," I tell him.

He winks. "I'll say."

"Enough already."

"Oh, fine." Uncle Phil waves his hand. "Go see your dad. I need to piss."

I look in through the observation window, into my father's room. A bed. Machines. Pumps and tubes. Bags of fluid. My father.

Once upon a time, his gifts were multiple and mighty. A package, in Federation parlance. Strength, agility, sensory perception, cognition—he had them all, but they were merely accessories.

The lab coats referred to my father's main gift as "supernormal trauma resistance."

In plain language, Dad was built like a brick shithouse. Flesh like Kevlar. Bones like iron. By constitution, he was damned-near indestructible. On top of that, something in his makeup allowed his body to heal at an accelerated pace; they say that in his prime, you could pick your caliber, shoot my father point-blank in the chest, and the scar tissue would form so quickly that you'd find the flattened slug on the ground at his feet.

He served sixteen tours in the chem wars, my father. One of the most decorated combat officers the Federation ever produced. In peacetime, the public came to know him, through the media, as The Hard Bargain. Violent criminals came to know him as mandatory retirement.

Ironically, it was my father's impervious foundation that ultimately retired *him*. For four decades, in the service of the common good, he absorbed gunshots, stabbings, conflagrations, falls from great heights, and the kind of damage that would spread a natural over a country mile like so much fertilizer. And then, finally, little by little, my father's jungle of internal scar tissue began to strangle his own organs, shutting him down one function at a time.

"Imagine a village," his main doctor once told me. "In the center of the village, there's a crazed rhinoceros. A great magnificent bull. The warriors have thrown net after net over the animal, and they've finally staked him to the ground. He's bound fast, this rhino. There's no escape for him. But he just won't stop struggling. Do you see?"

I hadn't. The doctor nodded, uncapped his pen, and circled a cloudy area on my father's chest scan. "Your dad's heart is that rhino," he said.

It was big news when The Hard Bargain slipped into his coma. For a year, you couldn't go anywhere without hearing about it.

Eventually, the world moved on.

Now I'm standing here, on the seventh floor of Hope Mercy with my Uncle Phil, looking at a shriveled pile of sinew in a bed on the other side of the glass. Somewhere in there is a heart that doesn't know enough to quit beating.

I'm not sure why I even came up here, to be honest. My father hasn't been conscious in a decade, and it only makes his monitor alarms go off when I step into his room.

My uncle looks at me gently. "Then buy me some damn coffee," he says.

We walk down to the cafeteria together. Uncle Phil is using both his canes, and there's a hitch in his gait. His hip has been shot for years, but for some reason, he won't have it replaced. For the first time, I notice how much smaller Uncle Phil looks these days. I suppose he's getting up there.

"You know, he'd be proud of you," he tells me, after we find a table and I hand him his coffee.

I can't help chuckling at that.

"Don't laugh," Uncle Phil says. "I know my brother."

"Dad thought the police were a waste of space," I remind him. "Rule-happy pansies, I think he used to say."

Uncle Phil shrugs. "Age seasons a person."

Uncle Phil used to make his own weather. They say family picnics were always sunny in his day. A virus attacked his central nervous system several years before I was born, and I suppose that's why he was always the one person in my family, besides my mother, who didn't clear the room whenever I came in. Unlike my father, his gift was long gone before I showed up.

I sense him watching me.

"What?" I say.

Uncle Phil opens his mouth. Pauses.

Finally, he says, "He always loved you. You do know that, right?"

I sip my coffee.

"He didn't know how sometimes," Uncle Phil says. "I'll give you that. But he always loved you."

I imagine what it must have been like for my father. To be frightened of his own weakling son. To be appalled by his only offspring. It couldn't have been easy. I can't say that I've ever really blamed him.

"You know," I tell Uncle Phil, "I'm not sure that he and I ever talked again after Mom died. I can't remember a time, anyway."

"Well," Uncle Phil says. "He was never the same after your mother passed. I'll give you that."

"I guess that's one thing we have in common, anyway." Before she had me, my mother's gift was flight. She always told me the trade was worth it.

"You're more alike than you think," Uncle Phil says. "You and my brother."

"Whatever you say, Uncle Phil."

We sip our coffee and don't say anything for a while.

Eventually, Uncle Phil pipes up.

"So," he says. "You dropped a police car on a guy?"

———

I wonder:

Did I do Leroy Penny a favor?

I try to imagine his life, but of course I can't. I don't know if his gift was a blessing or a curse. Sure, he had problems. But I think of what the bartender said: *We all got problems*. I don't know if Leroy Penny was a good father, a good neighbor, a good friend. I don't know if his children miss him, or if they're glad he's gone.

I'm lying in bed, staring at the ceiling, thinking of my own father. I wonder:

Could I help him?

The doctors can't. There's not a scalpel that could open him, no medicine that can turn back the clock. He spent a lifetime trying to save the world, my father. The Hard Bargain. But he couldn't help me. He couldn't help the Leroy Pennys. Now he can't even help himself.

Could I show him, in a way that I never could before, that in spite of the gulf that's always existed between us, I love him, too?

If I placed my hand on my father's chest, could I make his stubborn heart be still?

This is what I'm wondering when the front door of my apartment bursts open on its hinges. My own heart leaps. I bolt upright in bed. I have only enough time to wonder what the hell is going on before my training kicks in. In a flash, I assess what I know:

It's two o'clock in the morning. I'm in my underwear. My service weapon is in the top drawer of my nightstand.

I put it in my hand and move.

I don't get far.

When I wake up on the floor of my bedroom, my hand is empty. There's a light in my face. A voice says, "I'm gonna enjoy this."

I feel like I've been hit in the back of the head with a lead pipe. The light hurts my eyes. "I'm a cop," I say. "Think it through."

I hear a chuckle. "I know who the fuck you are."

The light goes away. Spots dance in my vision. As I struggle to a sitting position, I hear a whistling sound, and a bomb goes off in my knee. Astonishing pain.

"Oh, yeah," the voice says. "Gonna enjoy this plenty."

It's all I can do to say, "Who are you?"

There's a click. A flashlight. My assailant shows me his face: mean eyes, black stubble, a smile. He's missing teeth. Part of one ear. His hair is lank, thinning. I see that it is, in fact, a length of pipe he's holding in his hand.

"Name's Duane Penny," he says. "Believe you met my brother."

Something cold and heavy sinks to the bottom of my gut.

"Only I ain't *gifted* like he was." Duane Penny licks his lips. There's another click, and his flashlight goes dark again. He answers the obvious question before I can ask. "There's this cop I know, see? Plays on my pool league? Well, listen. Seems like them Southeast boys ain't so happy about lookin' like assholes on the TV. How about that? Huh? Superman? You feelin' *gifted* now?"

I don't know what to tell him.

———

Tina Vazquez comes to visit me at Hope Mercy every couple of days. She's been back on the job for a few weeks. Feels as good as new, she says.

When I ask her what it's like out there, she always grins and says, "Same shit different day, right?" Then she'll shrug her shoulders. "Hey. Somebody's gotta scoop it." She always pats my leg through the covers when she leaves, and so far, I still can't feel it. But it's nice anyway.

Uncle Phil makes his rounds. Every day's a gift, he tells me.

Sometimes, late at night, when the floor is quiet, I imagine I can hear my father's heart beating up on seven, reliable as clockwork, stuborn as a bull rhino, showing me how it's done.

On we go.

SUPER ORDINARY

David Yoo

THE
SOMEWHAT
SUPER

(The following excerpts are reprinted from the article "Conclusive Evidence," originally published in the *Cambridgetonian*, November 12, 20--.)

The group meets every Thursday in the blue-collar enclave that is West Somerville, in a rented-out VFW—a squat brick garrison on its last legs. A perpetual cool draft snakes its way through the rooms at all times, even on the hottest days of the summer. The furniture is scuffed and painfully outdated, as if the insides have been frozen in time since the late seventies. The shag carpet covering the black floors of the VFW is a dull orange (of course), marked with numerous stains left by trashed, bingo-playing Vietnam War vets over the years. Basically, the building is a big shithole, but that's precisely what Jim Priapis, the founder of the group, loves about it.

"Yeah, the place is pretty much a wreck, but it's quiet, unassuming, and that's the point," he says. "This place is supposed to be sort of a safe haven for the members, so it makes us feel comfortable knowing nobody will notice it."

Meetings run from around 7:00 P.M. till as late as midnight. The first order of business is the ordering of pizza from nearby Theo's, but sometimes a member will bring in food for the group. Jan, a.k.a. "Singy," a mousy twenty-something who has been a member for a little over a year, sometimes brings a steaming crockpot full of her homemade grape jelly meatballs to the meetings, which the members devour in minutes, wiping the plates clean with tufts of Foodmaster garlic bread and washing it down with plastic cups of beer. The group usually mingles in the kitchen and eats pizza (or meatballs) for about an hour, and frankly this part of the evening doesn't really seem all that different from the actual "meeting" that follows; in addition to being a refuge for these people, it's also a social group—the only kind these people fit into.

In short, the members live a double life because they're special. They're blessed (or cursed, depending on who you ask) with special powers, and the world, as you know, doesn't often work the way it does in the movies, comic books, and cartoons. In this day and age, the sole key to a superpowered being's survival is of course anonymity, and in this era of cell-phone cameras and TMZ.com and the Patriot Act, maintaining anonymity is all but impossible. The gifted among us can only sit at home and bite their nails and get ulcers sitting on their considerable talents, knowing that they risk losing their lives to the government, if not to foreign powers.

But this story isn't about who you think—"superheroes" with special powers who have the ability to save hundreds, thousands, whole nations, from disaster, from villainy, from each other. Instead, this story is about the people you don't normally read about, who most definitely aren't like us, aren't normal by any stretch of the imagination, but at the same time are not quite superheroes, either.

This story is about the second tier.

———

I attended the group's meetings regularly over the course of three months during the summer and into the fall of 20--. I'd met Jim at PJ Ryan's, a local pub, on Tuesday Trivia Night. He seemed abnormally curious about my stalled career as a struggling writer. I'd gotten slightly shitcanned, to be perfectly honest, and happily gave my little spiel about how the world of fiction was dying and how nonfiction was where it was at, and that I was looking for a story to tell. In retrospect it was a little suspect the way he grilled me about my writing background that night, but I didn't notice because I was just happy to be talking about myself for an hour, and so I described my MFA as if it were a worthwhile degree and my almost acceptances for publication in tiny lit journals that had gone defunct shortly after my stories got rejected by them. He didn't know much about the publishing biz and seemed genuinely impressed. I hadn't lied to him, but I didn't go into detail about how the last few years had been spent working as an admin assistant at a sheet-metal company, about how I hadn't written a new short story in almost a year, about how I no longer bothered sending my old stories out, having amassed two shoeboxes full of rejections.

To Jim, I was exactly the person he'd been looking for.

"I want to hire you to write a book," he said. We'd gone outside the pub to have a smoke. "I need someone with your qualifications, because I'm no writer, but at the same time it's important that it's someone local, because you're going to have to spend quite a bit of time with your subjects."

"What's the book going to be about?"

"It's about this group I run on Thursday nights. It's about me, and others like me, and what we're going through. Nobody knows our story. We're a secret to the general public. You're going to introduce us to the world. The very publication of the book is going to protect us, simply because it will stand as an official record of our existence, so the government can't erase us, and I know this sounds a little crazy but I assure you our struggle is very real. This is a very important book for us; we need it to come out—our very lives depend on it."

"And what is it you people are going through?"

Jim started to say something but clammed up, because two guys were heading toward us. Jim stared at the entrance door until it was completely shut, then he turned back to me.

"We're not like anyone else on this planet," he said.

"How so?" I asked, feeling skeptical but admittedly curious.

"We have special powers. I didn't realize my gift until I was seven years old. Until then, my parents kept quiet about it, even to me. My father went to great lengths to keep us appearing as a normal family," Jim said. "Let me ask you something, Neal: Do you know what love is?"

"You're not about to touch me, are you?" I asked. He shook his head. "Well then, the answer is no, I don't. Do you?"

"In my humble opinion, I believe that love is your father wearing children's diapers for two whole years," he continued. "Love is a grown man taking a dump in a too-small diaper in case someone should root through the trash and notice there aren't any used diapers coming from the trash of a house with an infant in it. That's love, don't you agree?"

I started nodding, but then—

"Wait. What?"

I could have cut him off right there. He was sounding officially creepy at this point, and who the hell was he anyway? Just some lush that I'd met at a bar on trivia night. We'd gotten hammered together, and it now seemed obvious he was a nutjob with some half-baked idea, but he offered to give me a grand up front, that's how positive he was that the story we would tell together would easily land a book deal and get my fiction career started. Jim sounded like a dreamer, a naïve dreamer who, like everyone else on this planet, seemed to think he had a great story to tell. I wanted to say no, but he had me at "a grand," and it happened to come on the heels of a particularly frustrating day at the office, during which my boss not only made me spend the bulk of my time making a rubber-band ball, but actually patted me on the head to congratulate me for successfully completing my task. I came home livid (yet strangely proud of my rubber-band-ball-making abilities), feeling like quitting my job, so I went to PJ's to forget about my stress for a few hours, and that's when I met Jim.

———

Probably the best way to explain who these people are and what this group is all about is to simply start out telling Jim's story, because every member has grown up living variations of the same story, really. Their origins, no matter where they came from or when they grew up, all add up to the same thing: that they live on the fringe of society, that they battle depression and feel isolated and, most significantly, that they live in constant danger and simply need to be here for each other.

Jim Priapis actually grew up in Somerville, a few blocks north of the VFW near the Tufts University campus, back in the days the Skunk Hill gang controlled North Street and rode their Harleys up and down Broadway, hanging out at a dive bar that no longer exists, replaced by the commercial Mexican hot spot, Rudy's. His parents both worked at the university—his father as a security guard and his mother in the dining hall. (Jim ended up attending Tufts for free because they worked there.) His parents were Greek Orthodox Jews, and he altered his last name from the original "Priapadocolocus" so it would take him less time to sign checks, and all of this is moot in light of the one defining characteristic of Jim, which is, well . . .

At age thirty-four, Jim Priapis has never in his entire life ever had to use the bathroom.

———

"What do you mean, never?" I asked Jim. At this point we were walking down Holland into Davis Square to get super steak burritos at Ana's Taq.

"Exactly what I said," he replied. "For some reason I never have to pee or poo."

I laughed out loud, because it sounded cute, childlike, the way he said it, "Pee or poo," but when I looked over at him he wasn't smiling.

"Okay, let's pretend for a second that what you're telling me is the truth," I said. "In which case, why do you need a support group for this? Wouldn't you be happy to have this awesome gift?"

"Two reasons for the group," he said. "First of all, it's not 'awesome!' to have this special gift, because it serves absolutely no practical purpose. I can't fly, I'm not bulletproof like real superheroes . . . I just never have to pee or poo. It's a gift, yes, but it doesn't qualify me to be a superhero, and therefore this group is for people with special powers that serve no practical purpose."

"You're shitting me."

"Technically, I can't. Have you been listening to me?"

"I mean, I could say I never have to use the bathroom, too," I clarified.

"You're absolutely right, which is why I readily invite you to watch me, be around me 24/7, and you'll see. Or not see, rather."

I thought about it for a second.

"But wait, I saw you go to the bathroom at least a couple of times at PJ's."

"I was faking it."

"Why would you fake it?" I asked. "I mean, I get faking it in high school, but you live alone now, you're an adult, who would notice you not hitting the can like everyone else?"

He sighed. Not in frustration, I realized later, but rather because it was a question he'd pondered for a long, long time.

"I don't have a choice, Neal," he said. "It's too dangerous *not* to fake it. Think about it—what do you think would happen to me if people found out I never had to pee or poo?"

"You'd get profiled on *Ripley's Believe it or Not*?" I suggested.

"I'd disappear," he replied. "One night, poof, my apartment would be empty, no sign of forced entry, and somewhere in some lab twenty stories under the ground in Arizona or something a group of scientists would probe my midsection trying to solve my riddle."

"But why?" I asked.

Months later, I understand. What Jim explained to me that night felt like fiction, but I know better now. He grew up having to live in shame, having to hide his special gift, because his parents knew nobody would accept it and simply move on. The sad fact is that we live in a world where superheroes cannot exist.

"Sure, on occasion a superhero will appear, make headlines after saving a baby from a burning building, and for a few months he or she goes around using their special powers to help others, but then we never hear from them again," Jim said.

"Is that true?" I asked.

"Remember Flamer, that guy who torched those oxy-contin addicts outside the CVS in Stoneham?"

I nodded.

"And have you heard about him lately? Or what about that seven-year-old Mexican child who chased those vandals across the university campus and caught up to them by gliding on his bare belly across the quad?"

"Oh, yeah—the papers nicknamed that kid 'The Beav,'" I said.

"Don't you think it's strange that we never heard from the Beav again?"

He was *right*.

"Last year there was that girl who had a really strong right foot and kicked her abusive boyfriend to death?" I suggested.

"Actually, she was a former D-1 soccer player," Jim corrected me. "She went to jail on aggravated manslaughter charges, but you're on the right track. Remember the guy with the really long, sticky tongue, who pulled the elderly lady out of the way of a streetcleaner last spring?"

"He had superpowers?" I asked.

Jim stared incredulously at me.

"I'm kidding," I said.

Jim explained how we live in a militarized society that exists in a constant state of realpolitik, especially in the United States, and if anyone has an unexplainable gift and the government finds out about it, you can bet at some point, sooner rather than later, that person will suddenly "go missing," Jim said, making the sign for quotes above his head.

"I know this all probably sounds so alarmist," he continued, pacing back and forth. "But I swear thousands, maybe tens of thousands, who knows, people in this country have, in the last decade alone, gotten erased by the government."

"What happens to them?" I asked.

"Testing. NASA, which is the shadiest governmental organization—"

"What—NASA? That's a benign organization, they're just the least successful."

"Think about it, Neal. N-A-S-A. Take away the first 'A' and what do you have?"

I gasped.

"Jesus . . . the NSA."

"That's right, so the military picks up these innocent civilians and puts them through tests that would make Abu Ghraib seem like second base, all in hopes of figuring out a way to harness our powers for their warmongering aims."

"How could your inability to pee or poo be of any use to the army?"

Jim glared at me.

"What's the first thing new Al Qaeda operatives get taught at those training camps that is the one great equalizer for a small cell of over-matched terrorists trying to fight against the sheer might of our advanced military?"

"I don't know."

"Shoot at the outhouses."

"Did you just make that up?"

"Okay, so the benefits of mine are in theory, but what about Powerpoint?"

"What's his special power?" I asked.

Jesse, aka "Powerpoint," had laser eyes, the type all kids at some point or another dream of having, only his weren't that, well . . . strong. A thin red line that you could only see at night emitted from his eyeballs, and it didn't even have enough juice to stun a fly. Basically, he was a human laser pointer, but one can see how the military would be interested in examining his insides.

Particularly his eyes.

"And you can bet we don't come out of it alive. We don't ever return once NASA kidnaps us."

"And you said tens of thousands have been abducted?" I had my doubts.

"Do you really think hundreds of people go missing on cross-country drives every year, Neal? Do you really believe that floods kill so many people? Have you ever stood out in the rain before and watched it accumulate?" Jim started waving his hands around as if in a panic. "Oh, dear, the water's slowly rising . . . must . . . escape."

"You're a moron," I said. "But I get your point."

———

"So what would you do in the bathroom growing up?" I asked Jim.

"Nothing. I'd close myself in a stall and simply stand there for a minute. Or I'd do everything one does to take a number two—I'd pull down my pants, I'd cover the toilet seat with TP, and I'd sit there pretending I was crapping. Here, listen."

Jim started groaning. It sounded like he was imitating Meg Ryan in *When Harry Met Sally,* if in the famous scene she wasn't faking an orgasm, but a dump. I couldn't help but giggle. He glared at me.

"Do you realize how bored I've been for I don't know how many thousands of hours of my life sitting and standing in bathrooms pretending to be taking a smash?" he asked. I looked at my shoes. "Every day I have to pretend to be something I'm not. Why this? Why did I get this special gift, of all things, that made me have to pretend and spend time in the dirtiest room in school, at the mall, at sleepovers growing up?"

"So you consider it a curse?"

"No, but it's complicated."

"Do you still fake it regularly?"

"At this point it's second nature."

"What do you do when you're in the bathroom nowadays?" I asked.

"Well, actually, I've been using my time a little more wisely lately," he admitted. "I mean, for years and years I'd sit there, trying to juggle seashell-shaped soaps as I sat in the can, waiting for what seemed like a respectable amount of time to pass before flushing the toilet, but now I bring reading material with me. I do office work. I keep a journal, a little notepad that I use to try to think of inventions. I have a Gameboy DS."

Incredibly, Jim's one of the more "normal" ones in the group.

———

Two days after meeting Jim, I went to my first meeting. I showed up after 7:00 P.M. and the parking lot was full. He introduced me to the members already congregating in the kitchen: Swayze, Floater, Darren, Dennis Hopper, Powerpoint, and Jan.

"This is the crew," Jim said, extending his arms.

"What about that guy in the main room?" I asked Jim.

There was a guy standing by the window, wearing a wool roll-neck sweater and fleece sweatpants despite the nighttime temps hovering around sixty-five degrees.

"Oh, right, that's Shocker," he explained. "He doesn't really socialize with us and he always looks like he's annoyed to be here, and yet he shows up every week. His special power is that he has an abnormally powerful static shock that he can emit via his index finger, enough that it can really zap you pretty seriously, worse than the worst shock you've ever received, but it can't actually hurt you."

"What's with the winter clothes?"

"He wears wool because he's trying to up the power of his static shock. It's typical of newer members to still feel like they have the potential to become a superhero someday. Shocker started attending meetings only a few months ago. Next summer, during a heatwave, he'll come around, I'm sure. He won't be able to wear wool sweaters by then, and at that point he'll open up to us, start accepting who he really is."

Shocker looked around, not noticing us watching him, and then he lay down on the shag carpet and started rolling around on the floor. Then he got up and shocked Dennis Hopper. Dennis yelped.

"Does the wool help increase his shocking power?" I asked.

Jim shook his head.

"It makes him sweaty. Look at the back of his scalp—his hair's perpetually stringy and wet. From behind he looks like Jason Giambi when he's hitting well," Jim said, and we laughed. His face got serious again. "But we've all done stuff like that, myself included . . . I used to lock myself in the bathroom with a pitcher of water and stand over the toilet and slowly pour the water onto my penis, trying both to simulate what it's like for fluid of some sort to flow from my genitals into the toilet and to trick my ding dong into doing it for real."

"Don't get me wrong," I said, putting a hand on his shoulder. "I appreciate your candor, but you're seriously putting some disturbing images into my head when you talk like this."

"You should avoid Darren, then," Jim said, fake-shivering. "Talk about freaky images."

———

I sat down one on one with each member that night and they proceeded to blow me away with their stories. You never get used to it, if you're a normal person like me. They have these amazing (but useless) powers, and while I could understand how and why they felt negative about it, and unimpressed with each other, it didn't keep me from feeling deeply envious.

Probably the closest thing to a real superhero, someone whose power was pretty close to being a valid power, was Dennis Hopper. For the record, he wasn't the actual Dennis Hopper, nor did he remotely resemble the mercurial actor in the slightest; rather, he was called that simply because his first name actually was Dennis, along with the fact that he could hop almost as fast as a fast guy can run. Which I thought was amazing at first, but the operative word here is "almost." He could hop faster than any normal man, but it wasn't quite fast enough to catch a crook with four-forty speed, and therein lay the rub.

Toward the end of that first meeting we even had a little race, because I wanted to see how fast (or not fast) Dennis Hopper really was. Jan (for some reason I never called her by her nickname, "Singy") played the Natalie Wood role from *Rebel Without a Cause,* waving a used handkerchief at the starting line. I won easily, but Dennis, I had to admit, hopped ridiculously fast. After the race Darren brought over two beers. Dennis and I sat down at the plastic patio table in the corner and sipped quietly, watching the group head back inside.

"Literally the only thing my power's good for is winning corporate potato sack races," Dennis explained. "Which isn't a bad thing, given that I'm a corporate whore."

"You seem okay with it, unlike Shocker," I said.

Dennis smiled wanly at me.

"Shocker feels the way I felt about myself when I was, like, sixteen. But you have to grow up sometime. You come to terms with it. I was born with a special power, but for whatever reason, it simply wasn't in my cards to use it properly."

"So you don't hold out any hope that someday you'll find a purpose for it?" I asked him. "Not even a little?"

He thought about it for a minute.

"Not really. I don't have this flame of hope in me that one day I'll find my true calling or anything like that," he said. "But I do think about the past. I think about how in previous eras I might've gotten more out of it. Like, say, in the days of *Little House on the Prairie,* when they had potato sack races all the time, because there was no TV. I would have gotten laid like you wouldn't believe, don't you think?"

———

Sex (or lack thereof) always reminds me of the saddest member of the group, Darren. He didn't have a nickname. This was Darren's doing, because he was the one member who was deeply embarrassed about his special power, and the most frustrated. Darren truly felt he was cursed, and when I found out what his power was I was inclined to agree with him. I mean, they were *all* flustered to a degree, and wished at various points that they didn't have their gifts, but Darren's self-loathing was on a different level.

Darren was a twenty-six-year-old Caucasian male. He had a medium build, stood approximately five foot seven, and, for approximately 99 percent of every day, he walked around with a gigantic black cock between his legs. (Jim was telling the truth—Darren's stories evoked the most disturbing images of all.)

"Are you serious?" I asked him the first time we got together for a little one on one away from the Thursday night meetings. It was a crisp fall morning in mid-September, and we were sitting at a metal table outside the Au Bon Pain in Davis Square. There were people walking past our table and yet he stood up and started dutifully unzipping his jeans. I immediately waved my hand and he stopped. "Are you trying to get arrested?"

"Sorry," he said, sitting back down. "You got me to talk about my 'gift.' It always depresses the hell out of me to think about it and I forgot where I was for a second."

"So you always have it?" I asked.

"That's the problem. Most of the time it's there," he explained. "Pendulous, aching, stuffing my jeans. I'm like one of those extras during the locker-room scenes in the movie *Any Given Sunday*."

"You sound like you don't like having it. I mean, isn't that every man's dream, to be well hung?"

He grimaced at me. "Oh, really? Do you know a lot of white guys who wish they actually had a gigantic black dick?"

I'd forgotten about the color.

"Oh—right . . ."

"But that's not even the worst part," he continued. "The problem is that the moment I'm with someone I'm attracted to or even alone and feeling slightly aroused, my gigantic black penis shrinks into a pale-skinned micropenis, the smallest you've never seen. It practically turns into a snail."

"Oh."

"That's what sucks, that my erections are in essence de-erections. Feeling unhorny makes me grow a gigantic black schlong, but I can't even masturbate, because once I get remotely excited the thing all but disappears."

"Has it been this way all your life? I mean, have you ever had sex?"

"I've never even successfully jerked off."

Like Jim, Darren suffered from a feeling of never achieving . . . closure. They were essentially two human time-bombs, building up in pressure, feeling increasingly flustered because of it. Their frustration was palpable, you could almost sense it in the air when you were around either of the two, and because of this I felt deep sympathy for them.

"All I want is to have the penis that I have when I'm reading phone bills to be the same penis that I have when I'm with a cute girl, or at least when I'm alone, just once!"

"So you're saying that you have penis envy of . . . yourself?"

"More or less," Darren said to me. "So . . . tell me about masturbation. What does it feel like?"

"I don't think we're there yet," I replied. "I think I need to get to know you better first."

———

Jim came up with the idea for the group the night he first met Jan. It was at the Burren, a watering hole in Davis Square popular with Tufts students. Jan was a senior at Tufts, and they started talking as they waited in line outside. She was already drunk, depressed because she'd gotten negged from trying out for the Tufts a cappella group. They ended up sitting in a booth and discovering that they both had special gifts. Hers was the ability to sing incredibly softly, softer than any human on the planet, certainly a special skill with no practical purpose. She was crying, at the end of her rope, and Jim felt compelled to admit to her his inability to relieve himself.

And like that, they'd found someone they could share their secret with.

According to Jim, people can sense that there's something off about him, something strange. In fact, this is one trait or characteristic that all the members share, including Jan. Every meeting I'd attended at least a few members would rant at some point or another about feeling like people were staring at them, not knowing why, only knowing that they didn't like what they sensed.

Jan and Jim became friends, and in the spring of 2005 they officially started the group.

"How did you discreetly advertise it?" I asked him. "Wouldn't that run the risk of being found out—if it's as dangerous as you say?"

"We posted it on Craigslist," Jan said matter-of-factly. "The government's clueless. Even today the department of Homeland Security doesn't know about Craigslist."

So what do you call people with superpowers that don't have any practical uses? They're not superheroes. Super People? Semi-Super? The Somewhat Super? Whichever way you cut the slice, it looked the same at the end: These are people with wasted talents. Their stories are all variations of the same old comic book. They were born with special powers. These powers had to be hidden. They grew up, were forced to keep what made them unique a secret, while dealing with the added annoyance of feeling flustered that their gift wasn't more . . . useful.

At various points in their lives they got found out. They got ridiculed. Their lives were in danger. But they've gotten through all that, maintaining relative anonymity, and have found themselves in the same place, in a downtrodden VFW in West Somerville on a Thursday night, eating homemade grape jelly meatballs and talking about the playoff picture for the Pats. They've found their home.

———

Some people would try to fake their way into the group. Friends of friends who were legitimate members, or someone passing by, would find out about the group. Others thought they qualifed, but were in actuality deranged, or depressed, or had ulterior motives. One guy, for example, claimed he never had to floss. Apparently his teeth were disgusting.

"There was this guy who called himself 'Squirrel-Man,'" Jim recalled one Thursday night in early October, as we stood in the backyard of the VFW, sharing a smoke.

"What was his special power?" I asked.

Jim sighed.

"Dude came in pretending to be a squirrel," he said. "He was fidgety all the time, darting his head around."

Jan joined us, her hands stuffed into her jeans pockets.

"Snake a drag?" she asked me, and I held my cigarette up to her lips.

"Thank you," she said, blowing smoke in my face. "What are you guys talking about?"

"Squirrel-Man," Jim said.

Her face lit up.

"The first night he showed up, I went into the kitchen at one point, and there he was, rooting through the trash. He had torn a little hole in the bottom of the trash bag and was pulling stuff out of the hole, and I was positive he was a squirrel-man!" she said.

"How do you know he was a phony?" I asked her.

"Well, he robbed the VFW's office one night, and we almost got shut down because of it. Turned out he was merely a creative crackhead, jonesing for a fix."

"I felt so stupid that we didn't realize this," Jim added. "I mean, his lips were always so white, he was always feverishly scratching under his chin, and he was always offering to blow me for five bucks."

We went back inside and for the rest of the meeting sat in a small circle, trading stories about those who had come and gone. Darren brought up Rachel the Rape Whisperer, and everyone groaned.

"She talked constantly, it was obvious she was only here for the company, and every couple of minutes she'd cut herself off, look up at the ceiling, and say, 'Someone's being raped right now.'" Darren explained.

"How do you know she was lying?" I asked.

"She admitted it one night to me, when she was plastered," he replied.

"It was a good ruse while it lasted," Powerpoint said. "We couldn't prove she was lying, because she never knew where the rape was occurring—which of course qualified her for our little club of useless superzeroes, but you could tell she was full of it."

Jan melodramatically put the back of her hand to her forehead and wailed, "Oh, dear, I fear that another young woman has just been raped!"

"That's exactly how she said it!" Darren said. He looked at me and mouthed, *God I love her.*

"Am I a fake?" Swayze asked out of the blue. "Why do I always have this red spot on my shirt? I should know why, right? What the hell's wrong with me? I don't fit here, I don't even know why my shirt's all red."

"Meatballs, Swayze," Jim said. "You spilled Jan's meatballs on your shirt last week."

"Oh, yeah, I forgot," Swayze replied.

"Who are you talking to?" I asked Jim, but he didn't seem to hear me.

———

"So who is this Swazye character?" I asked Jim again the following Thursday. "He's been missing meetings, apparently. I'm guessing his special power is a permanent mullet? Or does he consider himself part wolverine or something?"

A burst of childlike laughter from the corner of the room. Members smiled at the wall, as if there was something there. Jan pointed at the wall.

"That's Swayze," she said. She nodded at the kitchen and winked at me, before turning back to Jim, who had been describing how his coworkers confronted him at work that day about having a coke problem (because he was always going to the bathroom every twenty minutes). I noticed Darren blatantly staring at Jan point-blank, as if he was mad at her or something.

A few minutes later in the kitchen Jan approached me. She peeked behind her to make sure we were alone.

"So what's the deal with this Swayze guy? He's invisible, obviously," I whispered, and she nodded. "Well, that's a legitimate superpower, isn't it? Shouldn't being invisible have practical superpower applications?"

She sighed.

"We're pretty sure Swayze's dead," she said.

"What do you mean?"

"He's a ghost. Don't tell him, because he doesn't know and it would crush him to find out. It's the only logical answer. I mean, think about it—he can run through walls . . . he's invisible . . . and according to him his plaid buttondown always has the same patch of dried blood across the chest . . ."

"Jesus," I muttered.

"If he ever asks you why the chest of his shirt's all red, which he will ask you, because he asks it constantly, tell him he spilled some meatballs on his shirt, okay? He's a real sweetie."

"Sure," I said. "How'd he find the group?"

"Jim says he accidentally stumbled through the wall one night, and kinda hung out for a while and, well, he relates to us."

"How's that? Do you feel like you're dead, too?"

"No, but he can relate to feeling lost, alone," she whispered. "How would you feel if you were dead but didn't know it?"

"Um, undead?" I said.

She stared at me.

"It was a rhetorical question," she replied.

After attending three or four meetings it suddenly occurred to me that Jan was really hot. She resembled an early Margot Kidder—with her upcurled top lip, those big brown eyes, and those strong, unbroken teeth. And that hard ass, like two toaster ovens, covered with skin. I realized everyone there was in love with her, especially Darren. It was obvious. He always got real quiet around her, and sometimes he would kinda sit there and glare at her for a while, until she started feeling uncomfortable. One night he confessed his feelings for Jan to me when we were alone. Darren and I were halfheartedly playing foosball in the corner by ourselves while the others were out in the parking lot, smoking butts, when he stopped playing and leaned over the table.

"I think I'm in love with Jan," he said.

I noticed that my heart skipped a beat when he said this.

"How can you tell?" I asked.

"Well, every time I'm around her, I totally lose my boner. That's love, isn't it?"

"For you, at least," I admitted.

———

I found myself increasingly staring at Jan from that point on, just like Darren, and she was friendly with me, but she seemed to keep her distance. I figured it was because I didn't have any special powers. I helped Jim clean up at the end of one meeting and walked with him out to the car.

"So how's work on the proposal going?" he asked me. "Do you want to show me some pages sometime?"

"Nah, I work better alone. Don't worry, it's coming along well," I lied. I hadn't written a thing yet. I changed the subject. "So listen, I was wondering something: Is it possible I have a special gift and simply not have discovered it, yet?"

He smiled sadly at me, which, to my surprise, pissed me off a little.

"Probably not," he said, and I frowned. "I'm sorry, I mean, it's tough to say, is there anything about you that's made you feel weird about yourself, curious?"

I thought about it.

"Actually, there is," I said.

I've always had this weird ability where I can identify and name any movie on TV without having ever seen it. The first time I noticed this was back in fifth grade. I was staying home from school that day with a strep throat, and at one point my mom went to the store to get me more cough syrup, and I snuck up to the master bedroom because it was the only TV with cable. I flipped through the stations and the last channel I hit was HBO, and on the screen was a low-lit maroon hallway, with a single serving tray on a cart of some sort with a silver coffeepot on it, and I immediately sat up and pointed at the screen and said,

"Why—that's *Maid to Order*!"

Could it be? How could I recognize this movie I'd never seen before? Nobody had seen the movie, for that matter. I barely knew anything about it because it had tanked in the theaters. Granted, I kinda had a crush on Ally Sheedy at one point (I liked the premakeover Ally circa *The Breakfast Club*), but there was no reason I would know that this was *Maid to Order*. Not a single human being on screen for me to recognize. Just a hallway! I pressed the button for the cable schedule, and sure enough, the channel was showing the obscure Sheedy vehicle.

And since then, I'd recognized movies I'd never seen before like this countless times. I even kinda harnessed this strange power throughout high school and college, testing myself when bored or when I thought of it at all. Friends were amazed that I could do this. I explained all this to Jim.

"It's a parlor trick, sure," I said, faux-blushing at his silence. "But it's something only I can do, it seems."

"No, you're right, that's really crazy," Jim finally said. "I've never heard of that."

And then we settled back into an awkward silence.

"Hey, guys," Swayze's voice suddenly called out from behind us. "Glad you're still here. Listen, would either of you happen to know how I got this goddamned red stain on my shirt?"

———

Over the past eighteen months members have come and gone. Some keep in touch, if they leave on good terms with the group, but there's no word that other like-minded groups have begun forming elsewhere around the country.

"As far as I can tell," Jim says. "We're the only group of our kind in existence."

People with varying special gifts have passed through these downtrodden walls.

Barry, who could float without using his arms or legs (but alas, couldn't hold other people up should a boat sink), was nicknamed Floater.

"Does he like swimming? He could become a lifeguard or something," I suggest.

"Not really. He has really cold extremities."

"You really care about these people, don't you?" I ask Jim.

He nods.

"We're all in the same, useless fucking boat."

The room gets quiet. It happens rarely, but sometimes Jim gets despondent like everyone else, and it's up to the group to lift him up. Being the leader of the group doesn't make him immune to the frustrations. Jan, bless her soul, as usual takes it upon herself to brighten the room.

"Remember that guy who thought he had a special gift? Shovey?"

"That guy really thought he was a superhero in the making," Dennis Hopper says, and everyone laughs. He turns to me. "His schtick was he would go up behind people on the sidewalk and shove them as hard as he could. He hurt a couple of people pretty bad, and this gave him beer muscles or whatever."

Shocker is noticeably silent, perhaps feeling embarrassed about his desire to shock people all the time.

"Last I heard, he'd gotten arrested for assault," Jim notes. "Good guy, sad ending."

I notice Shocker rubbing the soles of his sneakers against the carpet, trying to work up a deadly shock. He touches Dennis Hopper in the back and Dennis squeals like a little pig.

"You bastard!" he says.

"How bad did it hurt?" Shocker asks, like a little kid.

"Enough to annoy the hell out of me," Dennis Hopper replies.

Shocker frowns.

"That's all?" he asks.

"Quit rubbing your sneakers like that," Jim says sternly. "You're scuffing up the carpet. I have to pay for damages, you know."

It amazes me that these group members are normal in all other aspects of life. You forget that when you come to these meetings and hear their stories about walking through walls, or floating in the tub. These people have the same jobs we have—they rent apartments next to us, they buy houses, they have pets, they shop at the same stores you and I shop at.

The only difference is that they're simply living with a deep, dark secret, but who isn't? Those of us without special gifts hold secrets, too, they're just not as interesting. We have affairs with people at work, we lie on our resumes, we buy a risotto at Whole Foods Market and then pretend we cooked it ourselves for a dinner party.

When you think about it, that's not all that different from Jim pretending he pees regularly like a normal human being, or Powerpoint trying to convince friends that the red-eye feature on their digital cameras are perpetually busted.

"I have an idea," I told Darren one evening. "I think I know how you can overcome your gift."

He looked up at me as if I'd asked him a favor.

"I'm listening," he said.

"Have you tried doing it first thing in the morning, when you wake up?"

"I know what you're getting at, and I have tested that. Not with a girlfriend—I've been too self-conscious about this shit to ever have a girlfriend, but I've tried with, you know . . . working girls."

"And what happened?"

"I gauge if they look nice enough, and then I ask them if they'd wait for me to fall asleep before having sex with me."

"Has it ever worked?"

"I don't know. Whenever I wake up they're gone, along with my wallet."

"Sorry, I should assume you guys have all tried everything already."

"No man, I really appreciate it," he said. "You're a good guy, Neal. You're my only normal friend."

Friend. I was anything but. I truly liked him, I truly liked Jim and Dennis Hopper and Swayze and Powerpoint and Darren and the rest of the gang, but I *loved* Jan. We all loved her. Sometimes one of us would ask her to serenade us, and she'd open and close her mouth like a fish and we'd all close our eyes and nod appreciatively, not hearing her, but loving every second of it. I saw something in Jan that I didn't see in other girls, and soon I was attending the meetings not for research purposes, but rather to see her.

It turned out Jan saw something in me, too.

———

One night I was stacking the empty pizza boxes in the kitchen when Jan came up to me. She placed a slightly greasy hand on my forearm and whispered in my ear, "I want to find out what your superpower is."

"How do you know I even have one? I'm a struggling writer, that's it."

"You have one. You have a great superpower, you just don't know what it is yet."

"Do you really want to find out what it is?" I asked.

She nodded eagerly.

"I want to find out all night long," she said. "And I want to wake up tomorrow morning and find out all over again."

I looked into her eyes, and it slowly dawned on me that we were talking about sex.

Growing up I was incredibly shy, especially when it came to being around the ladies. I was nervous when it came to having sex, and with two different girlfriends I failed to even get it up because I was paralyzingly terrified, and my subsequent failures to launch only made me more paralyzed. As a result, I became really good at going down on women. Most guys feel like they've broken their tongue after a few minutes; me, I can go on for hours, because I have so much experience doing it. A girl would get me in bed, start fumbling with my pants, and I'd feel so nervous about being able to get it up that I'd stop her and say something like, "I just want to make you happy." And then I'd switch places with her. This resulted in a number of women falling in love with me. I rarely had one-time hookups. These girls latched on and wanted me and my tongue to be their boyfriend. I'd lie and say I didn't want to have sex until we were ready, even though it was the only thing on my mind and I desperately wanted to. But I knew I'd fail to get it up, so I never tried, and eventually, the girl would lose patience with me and we'd break up. It was a vicious cycle.

I wasn't impotent, which I proved to myself by masturbating at least twice a day in the privacy of my college dorm room as my roommate Kenny lay asleep on the futon across from me. It was the girls. I was intimidated as hell by them, and the older a virgin I got the more intimidated and inexperienced I felt, so I avoided having sex like the plague. But Jan made me feel something I'd never felt with a girl. She made me feel . . . unterrified. I had a feeling this was a good sign.

We went back to my place, a tiny third-floor walkup near Boston Avenue. Jan was remarkably quick about things. I gave her a thirty-second tour of the apartment, ending out on the metal fire escape overlooking the bus stop, and she casually started taking her clothes off, right there, in the moonlight. I was petrified to the, ahem, bone, like I always got with girls when there was even the remotest possibility of sex in the air.

But then she opened her mouth. Her eyes were closed and she opened her mouth and I watched her, lovingly, for several minutes.

Finally she opened her eyes. I hadn't heard a thing, and she knew I hadn't, but I pretended I had and she pretended, too.

"What song was that?" I asked.

"'This Woman's Work,' by Kate Bush," she replied. "I messed up the second verse, though."

I smiled at her.

"I didn't notice at all," I said. "It was lovely."

We kissed.

As Jan and I started dry humping against the metal railing, it suddenly dawned on me why I felt so comfortable being around the group. I didn't possess useless superpowers, but I intimately understood and related to their anxieties, their fears—each and every one of them. I could relate to Darren's reverse erections because I had the same goddamned problem. I could relate to Jim's inability to pee or pee because I, too, had problems with it—I couldn't do a number two if there was anyone near the bathroom, and I hadn't successfully taken a dump in a public restroom in over twenty years; I was constipated all the time. I could relate to Dennis Hopper because when I was little I went through a phase where I was obsessed with my pogo stick, and I quit the day I found out it wasn't considered a real sport. I could even relate to Swayze, because I felt like a ghost sometimes, working in isolation on my unsalable stories, failing to sell them, losing touch with my friends, disappearing in my quiet life in this third-floor walkup and working as a secretary at a sheet-metal company. I understood all of them, and realizing this felt like an epiphany, and as if as proof, it was at this moment that I got my first erection with a woman, ever. Jan and I momentarily became the beast with two backs, right there out on the fire escape, and she even said she enjoyed it. We moved the party into my bedroom, where we went at it for hours. At some point while I was sleeping she slipped out of the room. When I woke up I couldn't wait for the next group meeting.

———

I showed up at the VFW the following Thursday desperate to see Jan. It was ridiculous that we hadn't exchanged numbers. But she knew where I lived—did she not enjoy being with me? My mind kept debating what her deal was for a week and by the time I entered the building I was rabid to see her. I walked through the entrance, smiling as I caught a whiff of Jan's crockpot meatballs, and ran straight into Jim.

"Out," he said the moment he saw me.

"What are you talking about?"

He grabbed me by the wrist and led me back to the entrance.

"You've betrayed our trust," he said.

"What the hell are you talking about?"

"You were our guest. You weren't here to make trouble."

I stared at him.

"Is she here?"

"No, not anymore, and neither's Darren. He went over to her apartment yesterday and asked her out, and she admitted you two were together. He ran away screaming. Nobody's heard from him since. Jan is so distraught she took off a few minutes ago, looking for him again. You knew how much he liked her. We're afraid he might hurt himself."

"Jesus, I can help."

"You've helped plenty. You can never come back here again."

"This is ridiculous, I—"

"I mean it."

"But what about the book?"

"The book's over," he said. "You're not the right person to tell our story. You used us to get to Jan."

"That's not true," I said, but nothing I said would make him believe me, and a minute later I realized this, so I left.

He was wrong. I cared about the group. I was thrilled to write the book—in fact, sleeping with Jan had actually compelled me to finally get cranking on it, and in a burst of inspiration I'd begun writing the nonfic proposal. Jan and I had something special. I hid across the street from the VFW for over an hour, waiting for her to retrieve her crockpot, but she never did. I tried to find her online, figure out where she lived so I could talk to her, but according to Google she didn't exist.

A week passed. Thursday rolled around and I sat in my apartment, watching TV. I missed Jan. I missed the group. A new feeling emerged.

I hated Jim.

The more I thought about Jim the angrier I got that he'd kicked me out of the group. *You're not the right person to write the book.* Bullshit, I was the *only* person who could write it. I was the only nonspecial person on the planet who could appreciate their powers, however impractical they may be. There was a little bit of me in each and every one of them.

Besides, temping had dried up, and I needed rent money. I spent a week trying to work on the proposal despite Jim's command that I cease and desist, but it turned out there was too much work to do to get the nonfic proposal into shape, and it wasn't fun at all. It was a business proposal, basically, and I wanted to tell the story. So I wrote a long article instead. I wrote about all of them: Dennis Hopper, Darren, Jim, Swayze, Powerpoint, the whole crew . . . which included Jan, too. My lovely Jan.

I solicited the big rags, but none of the top magazines were interested. I got a form rejection postcard from *Esquire* and there was a note scratched into the bottom: "This isn't real!" At this point I was desperate for cash, and I knew a girl who interned at the *Cambridgetonian*, hardly my dream publication, but she got the piece to her boss, he liked it, and he paid me one month's rent for it. For two weeks the fact checkers grilled me about every little thing, calling me sometimes even in the middle of the night to check on a detail, a name, the location of the VFW, and so on. I tried to get them to hurry so it could come out sooner, because I had a plan for it. Publication of the article was going to be my way to get back into the group. I'd essentially written a love letter to the group in the form of a long essay, and the week it came out I picked up a dozen copies to bring to the meeting—my olive branch to them all.

I'd titled the article "Conclusive Evidence," which was the title Nabokov had originally given his memoir, *Speak, Memory*. The meaning behind the original title was that the memoir stood as conclusive evidence of Nabokov's having existed, but his publishers felt the title sounded misleading, too much like a military mystery novel or something. It was perfect for my article, however. The group would accept me again; they would *have* to.

I just knew it.

———

The issue with "Conclusive Evidence" in it came out on a Tuesday. That Thursday I showed up at the VFW at a quarter to seven. There weren't any cars in the parking lot. I was glad for that, because I figured I could set up the magazines at the table in the main room before they arrived. I turned the doorknob; luckily it was unlocked. It was dark inside, and I flicked the fluorescent lights on. They buzzed for a few seconds before flickering to life, and what I saw next made me drop the magazines onto the floor. They spilled out in a wave across the orange shag, and I dropped to my knees.

The place was trashed. Glass shards everywhere. Yellow caution tape strung up like tinsel across the walls. Half a pizza was still stuck to the formica counter, overturned, and Jan's grape jelly meatballs were everywhere. I stood up and staggered into the main room. The floors were covered with sandy footprints.

I slumped back to the floor and stared at the footprints for a few minutes.

"Hi, Neal," Swayze said, and I instinctively scrambled back a few feet. "Sorry, man, I'm over by the window."

I waved at the window.

"What happened here?" I asked.

"There was a raid last Thursday, midway during the meeting," he explained. "It was NASA. Somehow they found out about us. They came and took everyone away. Where were you? I assume you ditched because of the rain. I don't know how they found out about us."

My heart sank and lodged in my left sneaker, the way Darren's gigantic black penis probably lodged in his left sneaker whenever Jan wasn't around.

"Why did they do that?" Swayze asked. "Why would they take everyone away?"

I didn't tell him it was because of me. Clearly my article, before getting published, had caught the attention of the NSA, and thereby NASA as well. Those fact checkers calling in the middle of the night—I realized then that they weren't interns at the *Cambridgetonian*—it was NASA *all along*. Jim was right, he wasn't being paranoid—the government really did make superheroes disappear, erased people with special powers from society, even people with less than useful superpowers. I winced, picturing Jan right now being operated on, on a gurney in some secret lab, doctors probing her larynx trying to find the source of her silent screams.

"They wore spacesuits, like in *E.T.*," Swayze said, more to himself than me.

"I'm so sorry," I told him. "Listen, you shouldn't stay here, it's not safe. They might come back for you."

"You're probably right," he replied. I could hear him shuffle his feet. "Listen, Neal, let me ask you something: I'm not dead, am I? I've heard people say that before behind my back, but I trust you. Be honest."

I shook my head.

"No, man," I said. "You're definitely alive."

"Okay . . . but, well, what about the blood on my shirt? It's always there," he said, sniffling.

"Meatballs, remember?" I said softly. "A few weeks ago you spilled Jan's meatballs all over your shirt for like the fiftieth time."

"Oh, yeah," he said, but he didn't laugh like he usually did.

We sat there for a while in silence.

"I should go," I said eventually.

"Me, too."

I stood up and started walking out.

"Wait, Neal," Swayze called out to me. I turned around and stared at the window. "No, over here."

I looked over at the far wall.

"What is it, Swayze?" I asked him.

"How'd you get involved with the group?" he asked. "I mean, you've been coming here for months and months and I've never even thought to ask you. What's your superpower? What are you?"

I looked into what I assumed were his eyes, but I couldn't be sure.

"I'm a villain," I said.

Kelly Braffet

BAD KARMA

GIRL WINS AT BINGO

Cassandra Mulcahey had always been lucky; but not for herself. Never for herself. To wit: When her third-grade class played softball, the balls Cass hit fouled out with uncanny accuracy toward the art-room window, which was behind home plate and slightly to the right. The first broken window was treated as a fluke, the second with suspicion. After the third, the gym teacher decided that maybe they'd better start the volleyball unit a few weeks early.

"But we like softball!" said the girls who batted immediately before and after Cass (the lineup was alphabetical and always the same), both of whom had been scoring home runs with astonishing frequency. Scowling at Cass, they said, "You keep breaking the stupid windows. This is all your fault." And Cass knew—even then, she somehow *knew* that they were right.

Years passed. Cass learned in physics class about Newton's third law of motion, that for every action there is an equal and opposite reaction, and found it to be deeply, profoundly, inexplicably true. To wit: Cass had chicken pox three times and mononucleosis twice. Her skin only broke out for school picture days and any major event when confidence would have been helpful (auditions for the school play, debate team finals, a group project with the cutest boy in class). In ninth-grade biology, something went wrong with the chemicals in her preserved rat, and when she cut it open the insides had turned to foul-smelling goo; after that she had to share a rat with Heather Blakely, who claimed that the preservatives gave her a rash, so Cass had to do all the work. When Cass took her driver's test, the brakes on the test car failed, causing it—and Cass, and the tester himself—to skid uncontrollably into a parked police cruiser. The day before her senior prom, she broke out in hives, and on graduation day, she slipped in a puddle halfway to the podium, broke her left leg, and spent most of the summer in a cast up to her knee.

The opposite reactions were these: Cass was the only kid in her class to get chicken pox and the only kid in her class to get mono. When he shot the kids in Cass's grade, the school photographer's ancient, unreliable El Camino always started. With Cass there to do ninety-eighth-percentile work on their rat-dissection project, Heather Blakely managed to bump her biology grade up to the C average she needed to stay on the cheerleading squad. The policeman whose car Cass hit went home early that day, pleading a sore back, and thus managed to make it to his kid's Little League game for the first time in recorded history, possibly saving his marriage. Cass's prom date took Heather Blakely instead—an irony not lost on Cass—and five years later they were married. And it had been raining for a week before graduation day; the rain stopped and the sun came out just in time to hold the ceremony at the football stadium as originally planned (instead of in the auditorium where limited space meant ticket-only admissions, and ticket-only admissions meant unhappy unticketed grandmas and cousins and boyfriends) and the only puddle on the entire field was the one in which Cass slipped.

The only person for whom Cass wasn't lucky was her mother, Elmira. The story of Cass's life as it had been related to her, from her spermatozoal days to the present, was as follows: Her mother had been a professional ballet dancer—corps, not principal, although Elmira always swore that it would have been only a matter of time. One night, on a whim, she accepted a date with the delivery boy who brought her costume from the dry cleaner. After a plate of spaghetti and two bottles of wine, she slept with him.

("Why?" the younger Cass always asked at this point in the story, hoping against hope that this time her mother would say, "Because he had lovely eyes," or "Because he was so kind," or even "Because I was so lonely," because that at least would have made Cass feel like there was at least one thing in the course of her life that had a reason to hap-

337

pen. But instead, what Elmira always said was, "Damned if I know. Biggest goddamned mistake I ever made.")

And, since the life of a professional ballet dancer requires a level of overexercise and undereating that often leads to irregular menstrual rhythms, Elmira didn't think anything of it when she missed two cycles in a row. By the time she missed the third and fourth cycles, and began to get suspicious, it was too late to do anything about the embryo growing in her lithe dancer's body. Elmira had been on the pill, she would tell Cass; taken it every day like clockwork. And even though the little leaflet that came inside the package said that it was ninety-nine-point-nine-nine percent effective, Elmira had been the point-oh-oh-one percent ineffective, and what was worse—as she also told Cass—that failure had come when she was with the one guy she couldn't have cared less about ever seeing again. The least handsome guy, the least glamorous guy, the least acceptable guy. The guy she most wanted to forget.

Except that now, she couldn't.

"And that, my little bad-luck charm," Elmira would say, "is why your mommy is a telemarketer." Then she would wave her hand in an elaborate flourish, a little *flick* at the end as if she were sprinkling Cass with fairy dust, and add, "Now, *poof!* Begone. Dinner's in an hour."

Oh, how Cass wanted the story to be different. After she had *poof'd* and bewent, she would lie across her bed and imagine the way it could have been. A Romeo and Juliet story: the beautiful dancer—because even now Elmira was beautiful, with her elegant dancer's neck and her long dark hair—and the handsome-but-poor delivery boy. Torn apart by circumstance. Kept apart by the vagaries of fate. Perhaps, one day, to reunite, and make all of their lives complete—

"Not hardly," Elmira said, the one time Cass ventured to ask. "Your father was a loser. Christ, kid, I can barely even remember the guy's name. Mark. Mike. Mitch. I don't know. Something with an M."

Growing up as she did under the dark umbrella of her mother's bitterness, Cass became an understandably nervous young woman. When her mother went on dates, or job interviews, or even to the grocery store—even the grocery store wasn't safe! The bags could break! The car could get broken into! The cart could have one stuck, recalcitrant wheel, turning every trip down every aisle into an impossible, arduous trek!—Cass would wait for her at home with her heart in her mouth and the tattered shreds of her cuticles between her teeth. *Please let everything be okay,* she would chant silently to any force that might be listening. *Please don't let anything go wrong. Please let her come home happy.*

But, inevitably, the bag would break, the car would get broken into, the shopping cart would have one stuck wheel. The date, the waiter, the hiring manager would be a jerk. Nothing was ever okay, everything always went wrong, and Elmira never came home happy.

To wit: The summer before her junior year, Cass went away to weight-loss camp and came home to find her mother with a new job, a new boyfriend, and a new kitten that she'd found under the porch. A week later, the new boss had been arrested, they'd seen the new boyfriend at the mall with his wife, and the new kitten had developed some mysterious ailment and had to be put down. Elmira said, "I don't know, kid. I'm starting to think you really *are* bad luck," and maybe it was supposed to be a joke, but it fell flat, because Cass knew—they both knew—that it was true.

There was nobody in the world that Cass wanted to help as much as she wanted to help her mother—a mother is a mother no matter how toxic, and the one Cass drew was the only one she had—so she tried. When the new washing machine was delivered, when rain pounded against the roof, when the Mulcaheys went out to eat, Cass would think, *Nothing bad will happen. The washing machine will work. The roof won't leak. The waiter won't be horrible.* And always, in the back of her mind, there glimmered the small hope that if she could change even one small thing, the sharp edge of Elmira's tongue would be dulled and Cass's life would be an incrementally warmer place to be, if only for one night. But it never worked. Something about it felt like forcing two magnets together the wrong way: they slid, and repulsed, and simply would not be joined. Elmira's eyes grew more and more narrow and more and more cold with each misfortune that befell her, and eventually, Cass gave up. When she was around other people, good things happened to them but bad things happened to her. When she was around her mother, bad things happened to both of them. The safest place to be was anywhere other people weren't, Cass reasoned. The safest place to be was alone.

———

"Out," Elmira said when Cass was eighteen, the day after her gradua-tion-day-broken-leg cast came off. As an afterthought, she added, "You can find an apartment first. I'm not a monster. But—seriously—*out.*" So Cass found an apartment above the local VFW outpost and took a job waiting tables. Elmira helped her move in, gave her their old couch and all of her childhood bedroom furniture, and even kissed her good-bye. But as Cass hugged her mother, she could feel the still-strong mus-cles in the older woman's body wanting to leave, tense and straining toward the door. So she let her go; even tried to wish her well.

"I hope things go better for you," she said.

"You're a sweet goddamned kid, you know that?" Elmira said, and left, heading straight to a furniture store to buy a new couch. The first salesman who approached her was a tall, handsome man with a pale mark where his wedding ring should have been. Elmira bought the couch, and over lunch the next day they talked about how difficult it was to be a single parent, and six months later they eloped. Cass got an announcement about it in the mail two weeks later, followed the next Christmas by a photo of the man, his two teenaged daughters, and Cass's mother. All of them were wearing matching sweaters and matching smiles. With her new highlights and the way her body was pitched protectively toward the girls, Elmira could almost have been their actual mother. She looked happier than Cass had ever seen her.

Cass put the picture up on her freezer, where she could see it every time she went for another bowl of ice cream. Looking at the picture, she would think, *That's my mother with her new daughters*, and get depressed. Being depressed made eating more ice cream seem okay. And eating ice cream had to be okay, because food was all Cass had. Food, and her job at the diner, and her tiny apartment over the VFW outpost, where once a month the members held all-night bingo. On those nights Cass would lie in bed, kept awake by the sounds of celebration and defeat, the cries of *Bingo!* and the moans of disappointment that inevitably followed, and, really, by the undeniable living of life that drifted up through her floor.

Never did the space inside her apartment feel so empty—but still, she could almost feel the waves of their winning and losing outside her lonely bedroom, buffeting the walls and beating at the windows like gusts of wind. Shivering, pulling the blankets close around her body as if they would shield her, she knew that she would never be lonely enough to go downstairs, into that bright loud room crowded with people who played so cavalierly with luck and chance.

If it had been anything other than bingo, though—Cass actually preferred to have as many people around as possible. She'd found, through the years, that her life was easier in crowds than in small groups. In a crowd of people, someone else might find a dollar bill at the same time Cass stubbed her toe; in a small group, somebody else would find a twenty just as Cass broke her foot. A boyfriend was entirely out of the question, as was a best friend, as was a dog (her luck didn't play favorites, species-wise). Cass suspected that spending a significant amount of time around just one other living being would probably put her in the hospital. Or, worse, her bad luck would prove catching, as it had with Elmira.

Food, on the other hand, didn't suffer good fortune, and it didn't suffer bad fortune. It was what it was before Cass even came near it—as long as she stayed out of the kitchen—and eating it had only two effects: The food disappeared, and Cass felt happiness. So food became the thing that Cass loved best. The diner where she worked had pretensions of being a real restaurant, which meant the mashed potatoes were mixed with pesto, the fried chicken was battered with those expensive Japanese breadcrumbs, the meatloaf had a creamy goat cheese center, and the skirt steak was soaked in a balsamic marinade before going on the grill. When she had breaks, Cass would dish up a double portion of whatever the designated family meal was that day and take it into a corner, and that was her favorite part of her entire life.

The head chef, Barty, called most of the waitresses things like *sweet-cheeks* and *darlin.* He called Cass *Mama Cass.* One day, when Cass was

341

dishing herself a second portion of roasted-vegetable lasagna, Barty said, "That's what I like, Mama Cass, a big healthy girl," and all the other waitresses laughed. Cass's cheeks burned. After that she took her food into the alley outside the kitchen to eat it.

Most of the time she ate alone, perched on the edge of the concrete step with her iPod plugged into her ears. Sometimes, the sous chef, Stanko, was out there, too. He was the shortest, the slightest, and the most tattooed of any of the three line cooks, and he was also the only smoker. Crouched against the wall with a cigarette dangling from his lips, his unshaven, ferretlike face impassive and his dark eyes hooded and faraway, he would smoke and Cass would eat. They almost never spoke. They almost never looked at each other.

One night, he surprised her. He said, "I got a question."

Cass swallowed her beef stew and pulled one of her earbuds out of her ear. "Okay."

"How come you eat out here by the garbage cans all the time?"

Cass sighed. Most of the waitresses, she knew, thought Stanko was creepy; somebody told somebody that they'd caught him drinking orange-flavored cough syrup in the supply closet, plus, he took too many smoke breaks and was never around when they needed him. But Cass liked him. He was the only one of the line cooks who never called her Mama Cass. In fact, he rarely said anything at all. Sometimes she imagined that he had a secret life as a sculptor or a punk rocker or a hit man. She knew it wasn't true—she thought that the cough syrup was probably about as secret as it got for Stanko, the limit of his craftiness his decision to stick to the orange flavor and thus avoid the telltale dye the cherry or menthol flavors would leave on his lips and tongue—but she liked him anyway, and when he asked her why she was eating by the garbage cans, she didn't want to say she was hiding from Barty. And she also didn't want to say she came out for the fresh air, because the smell of the garbage cans was really rank.

"It's quiet," she finally said. Which was at least true, and didn't betray any of her more cowardly motivations.

"Guess so." Stanko raised his cigarette to his lips and took a long drag. "You want a cigarette?"

Cass shuddered, thinking of asthma attacks, and emphysema, and throat cancer. None of which she had. None of which she wanted. She knew better than to think she'd beat the odds on any of those. "No, thanks."

"How's your hand?" Stanko said.

Cass looked down at her left hand, which bore three perfect pink dime-sized blisters on its back. A few hours earlier, she'd been walking by the deep-fryer just as Barty had dropped in some French fries. "Gotta be careful, Mama Cass," he'd said when the oil had splattered onto her hand. (And then he'd spotted something over Cass's shoulder, and his eyes had widened. "Hey, that's my goddamned wedding ring! I thought I lost that down the sink last week," he'd cried; *Lucky you,* Cass had thought bitterly, and went to put some ointment on her hand.)

Now, in the alley, she shrugged. "Hurts," she said. "But I'll live."

"No shit, it hurts," Stanko said. "I've burned myself on that fryer before. Evil fucking thing." He tossed his cigarette aside. "Hey," he said suddenly. "You and that college girl used to go to Archer's, didn't you?"

Archer's was Archer's Tavern, the bar on the other side of the block, whose emergency exit opened on the same alley as the restaurant's. In fact, Cass had stared at the wrong side of that exit so much that she could see the letters stenciled on it in her sleep: *Archer's Tavern. No re-entry. Please Do Not Urinate Here.*

Cass shrugged. "We went once." The college girl—a summer wait-ress whose name, Guinevere, had been the most remarkable thing about her, and who had long since returned to school—had spent the night amassing an absurdly huge collection of phone numbers, cocktail-napkin love notes, and marriage proposals; Cass lost her keys, broke the heel of her shoe, and sprained her ankle.

"Pretty busy in there, huh?" Stanko said.

"I guess."

"Think I might go over there tonight." Stanko tossed his cigarette away. "Check it out. You wanna come?"

Cass's stomach lurched. "Why?"

Stanko grinned. "Nothing like that," he said. "Don't worry. Just for someone to go with."

Oh. Cass felt her face grow hot. As if of their own volition, her eyes slid away from him—well, actually her eyes *slunk* away from him, in exactly the sort of embarrassed, shamefaced way that she didn't want them to, which made her cheeks feel even hotter and the rest of her feel like she wanted to sink into the pavement. "I can't," she said.

"Okay," Stanko said genially, "no big deal," and he went inside. There was a rock wedged between the door and the frame to keep it from closing all the way, and thus locking them out into the alley; as he pushed the door open, the rock fell, and before Cass could jump to her feet and grab it the door slammed shut.

She was locked out. Bad luck that the rock had fallen; bad luck that Stanko hadn't seen it. On her long walk down the alley and around the block to the front door of the restaurant, she had ample time to consider the opposite reaction: If a man were foolish enough to ask a lonely fat girl on a date that wasn't a date, it was fortunate indeed for him when she said no.

———

Two days later—Cass remembered that it was two days because on the first day avoiding Stanko had seemed imperative and on the second day it started to seem slightly stupid—she was working the dinner shift, and the last table in the house was one of hers. Table eight: a pudgy, soft-looking man whose red suspenders and fedora were probably aiming for jaunty but missed by a country mile. When he came in, latish, Cass had sort of liked him. She had an understandable soft spot for fat people eating alone.

But then—he'd *lingered*. First he ordered squash soup. When the soup was gone, he asked for pork chops. After that it was the chocolate-hazelnut pudding, and then coffee, and then a refill, and then a glass of ice water. He ate nothing quickly. He savored each bite. The tables around him emptied and filled and emptied again; plates of food moved through the air around him like satellites, checks were dropped off and picked up, and still Suspenders-and-Fedora sat. He nibbled. He sipped. Finally, he was the last diner in the restaurant. Cass was the last waitress. There was a manager upstairs in the office, and she thought

Stanko was still in the kitchen, closing things up, but other than that, they were alone.

When she brought him his check (for the third time; she had a soft spot for fat people eating alone, but she *really* wanted to go home, and she was praying that he wouldn't order anything else) he looked up with an expression that was both bashful and desperate. His eyes could only meet hers for a second before sliding—no, *slinking*—off to the side, and that was when he told her that he was her father.

"Oh," Cass said, nearly numb with surprise. "You are? Oh."

Quickly, she cleared his table, wiped it off with a damp rag, and locked the front doors. After she'd poured the last of the coffee into a cup with lots of cream and sugar, the two of them sat down at the counter. His hands were trembling as they gripped his glass of water; maybe from the caffeine in his coffee, maybe not.

Tugging with one finger at his too-tight shirt collar, he told her that his name was Matthew, and he was a biochemist. So, Cass thought: He was smart. He was smart, and he was fat. He was smart, and he was fat, and he was her father. The delivery boy. The loser. The mistake. Now that she got a good look at him, his eyebrows were just like hers. Weird.

"I saw Elmira downtown," he said. "We were both in the same department store. It was the first I'd heard of you. I hope you believe that."

Cass nodded; hadn't Elmira told her a dozen times that she'd never tried to contact him after finding out that she was pregnant? *No need to compound one mistake with another,* she'd said.

Matthew continued: "She said that you worked here, but she didn't seem very sure. I gather that you two don't see each other often?"

Cass scanned his face for that look of ersatz sympathy that people sometimes got when they asked about her mother—they sensed a Story, and wanted to be the first to hear it on the off chance that it was juicy—but Matthew's face was neutral and pleasant. Still, she made her voice sound light. "Oh, you know. She got married. He has two daughters. They're busy. Both of the girls do gymnastics, and dance. I think the oldest one actually got a cheerleading scholarship somewhere, so they're . . ." Her voice trailed off.

"Thin?" Matthew said. His tone was gentle.

"No," Cass said (although they were). "Just busy." Then, unexpectedly, she laughed. "God, I'm not even convincing myself. Yes, they're thin, and beautiful, and completely socially acceptable in every way that I'm not. So, no, Elmira and I don't see each other often."

"She seemed quite insistent on my coming to see you, though," Matthew said, and then smiled. "Oh. I see. She said you were a 'chip off the old block.' I remember thinking at the time that her tone wasn't entirely complimentary. I asked for your phone number so that I could call first, but she wouldn't give it to me."

"She must have—" Cass stopped. She had been about to make up a reason, some story that would make Elmira sound less loathsome than she actually was, which was what she always did when her mother came up in conversation—or, she suddenly realized, in thought, or memory, or life. But this man, she realized, had actually known her mother. She didn't have to lie, didn't have to dissemble, didn't have to pretend. "She must have lost it," she said.

Matthew nodded. "She lost mine, too. Even though she was having my child, which seems like an unusual reaction to that particular situation. I have to say, having met you, I sort of wish she hadn't, even though at the time it seemed like sort of a lucky break." He shook his head. "Your mother was the most beautiful woman I'd ever seen," he said, "but she wasn't always . . ." His voice trailed off, leaving Cass very much aware of all the things her mother wasn't, always.

"But you were in love with her," Cass said. "You were obsessed with her. She always said so."

"I was. I was also very young. I saw her dance in something—*Coppélia*, I think—and . . . oh, I don't know. There I was, a science nerd who worked at a dry cleaner, convinced I was completely in love with the most perfect creature the world had ever seen, and I'd never even spoken to her." He was smiling, but Cass thought it was the kind of smile that comes with remembering some small, embarrassing childhood moment: affection, humility, a little bit of grief. "Ridiculous."

"It's not ridiculous. It's romantic."

"It could have been," Matthew said, and suddenly laughed. "Do you know what I did the week I asked her out? I was reading about karma in those days—a typical sort of college student fascination—and when I decided I was going to ask her out, I made it a point to stack the karmic deck as much as possible. Gave money to every panhandler I saw, fed other people's parking meters, reached things down from high shelves for little old ladies in the grocery store. All so that she'd say yes."

"And then?"

"She said yes," Matthew said, his face suddenly grim. "She drank her way through dinner and so did I, and when we woke up the next morning she barely remembered my name, let alone anything else that happened that night. And she was so bitter, and angry, as if it was my fault. As if I'd somehow tricked her." He shook his head. "It was simultaneously the greatest disappointment of my life, and the greatest liberation. Because I'd slept with the beautiful girl, you know, and she'd turned out to be absolutely nothing that I wanted. I never tried to force karma's hand again."

Cass sipped her coffee. She cleared her throat. Carefully, carefully, she asked, "Would you say that you're lucky, generally?"

Surprised, Matthew said, "Oh, no. I mean, I guess I'm not particularly unlucky. I suppose I'd say I'm luck-neutral. Nothing particularly bad ever happens to me, but nothing particularly good does, either."

"Sounds nice," Cass said, and couldn't help sounding wistful.

"Not really. It's quite boring, actually." He gave her a puzzled look. "Why do you ask if I'm lucky?"

She blushed. "It's just that—I have sort of strange luck. So it's funny to hear that you were obsessed with luck the week I was conceived."

"Not luck," Matthew said, "karma. For every action there is—"

"An equal and opposite reaction," Cass said. "I know."

"No, that's physics," he said, surprising her. "I mean, I guess it's close. But karma is more a matter of balance. If you do good, good returns to you. What do you mean, you have strange luck?"

Cass hesitated. She had never told anybody about her weird luck before; then again, she'd never told anybody that her mother preferred her thin, athletic stepdaughters to her own heavily fleshed flesh and blood before, either. Matthew's face was frank and open. His eyebrows were just like hers, as were his round cheeks and his small ears. Once upon a time, he'd been in love with her beautiful ballerina mother, but after spending some time with Elmira he'd decided she wasn't worth it, after all. She thought she could probably trust him.

So she told him. She told him about her entire life, and how she'd been good luck for everyone around her but resoundingly bad luck for Elmira. She tried to tell it funny, so he'd laugh. As if it were all a grand joke. Funny, ha-ha.

But he didn't laugh. "That's fascinating," he said instead, and he looked as if he meant it: His eyes were wide and interested, and he'd forgotten all about the glass of water he'd been fiddling with throughout their conversation. "You're like a karma sink."

Cass, picturing kitchen fixtures, said, "What?"

"A karma sink. Like a light sink, or a gravity sink. Sink, as in, a place or substance into which something sinks. You absorb people's bad karma, so that the bad things that were supposed to happen to them happen to you instead, and they get the good things that are supposed to happen to you." He looked thoughtful. "I wonder why it doesn't work with Elmira."

Cass stared at him. "You're taking this all in stride, aren't you? Not finding it even a little hard to believe?"

"I fed parking meters and bought homeless people cheeseburgers for a week and at the end of it, I'd slept with the most beautiful woman I'd ever seen," Matthew said. "And I didn't look any better then than I do now. I have absolutely no reason in the world to doubt the power of karma." He smiled. "It's actually kind of exciting, isn't it?"

"No." Suddenly Cass realized that her eyes were filling with tears. "No. It's not exciting. It's horrible. I have to sit by and watch good things happen to other people and *nothing* good ever happens to me, nothing, and in fact the more time I spend around other people the more I get hurt—"

Matthew put a hand on her arm. "That doesn't make you any different from anybody else on the planet."

"Oh, Christ." Cass dashed at her eyes. "Not sad. Not disappointed.

348

Hurt. Cut. Sprained. Broken. Wounded. *Injured.* As in, trip to the emergency room."

"But you expect it," Matthew said. "You can plan for it. If we spent enough time thinking about it I bet we could even figure out a way to channel it, or control it. And think how wonderful it would be to love somebody and never have to watch them be sad or disappointed. My god!" He was leaning close to her in his excitement, bouncing a little in his seat like an excited child. "It's the most amazing gift you could ever give somebody."

Cass wiped her face. "If you feel that way," she said quietly, "you should have stayed with my mother. You could have been letting her hurt you all these years, instead of me." She shook her head. "I understand what you're saying, but love isn't letting yourself be destroyed so somebody else can be happy. That's wrong."

"I would have helped you if I'd known," Matthew said.

Cass, her own eyes now dry, ignored the tears she saw in his and said, "I don't think I ever should have been born. I think Elmira was right. I think I was a mistake."

"On the other hand," Matthew said, "a week ago I didn't have any family at all, and now I'm discussing the vagaries of karma with my adult daughter. All without ever having to change a single diaper."

"Were we discussing the vagaries of karma?" Cass said. "I thought we were talking about my life."

———

After he left, she went into the dark kitchen to collect her tips for the night. It was empty—everyone else had gone home—but there was an envelope on the counter with her name on it. The back door was still propped open, but Cass could smell a faint trace of cigarette smoke. Stanko must be outside, having one last cigarette.

She opened the door wider to tell him she was leaving, but the alley was empty. At least, Cass thought it was empty. Right up until the moment when a thin, wiry arm wrapped itself around her body and something cold and sharp pressed against her throat.

"Shh," Stanko said in her ear.

———

He covered her mouth with one piece of duct tape and bound her hands and feet with two others. Then he put her in the supply closet and left her there for two long hours, during which time Cass had plenty of opportunity to consider how little justice the phrase *stuck in a closet for two hours* did to the actual experience. At first she was scared. After that she was angry. Finally, she was just bored.

It was after one by the time he returned. He came into the supply closet and crouched in front of her, leaning against a huge carton of panko breadcrumbs.

"Sorry about the knife," he said, offhandedly. "I won't bring it out again if you promise to listen to me. Do you promise?"

Cass, still gagged, nodded. She tried to make her eyes look calm and sincere, and it must have worked, because finally he shook his head.

"That was some crazy story you told that guy," he said. "Was it true?"

She nodded again. The duct tape around her wrists really itched.

"So when you're with people," he said, "bad things happen to you instead of them."

Another nod.

"Like with Barty's wedding ring," he said. "You know, his wife has been at her mother's for the last two weeks. She gets home tomorrow. If he hadn't found that ring he would have been in it, deep." He reached out and tore the duct tape off Cass's mouth. It didn't hurt as much as it seemed to in the movies; mostly it just made her wish she had some lip balm. But when he leaned in she saw that his eyes were sort of dull and bleary-looking, and his breath smelled like orange-flavored candy. "Do you have to do anything to make that happen?" he said.

She shook her head. "Believe me, if I could control it, I would."

He shook his head, too, as if he was commiserating with her. "I hate my job," he said. "Barty is a dick, and if I have to make one more goddamned strawberry-balsamic reduction I'm going to kill myself."

"What do you want to do instead?" Cass asked, wondering why she wasn't scared.

Stanko shrugged. "I have absolutely no fucking idea. But I do know that whatever it is that I want to do, I won't be able to do it without money. And money is one thing I don't have." For a moment he was silent. Then he said, "I'm not what you'd call a career criminal, but I guess I've been around the block a few times. And what goes wrong with most robberies—the stuff that gets people sent to jail, I mean—is the little things. A cop drives by, a bystander walks in, the getaway car gets towed or the lookout stops to tie his shoe or—whatever. It's all just bad luck." He smiled. "But none of that will happen if you're there, will it?"

"I just told you," she said. "I don't have any control over it." Just like she didn't have any control over him; just like she didn't have any control over her mother; just like she didn't have any control over the genes that had given her Matt's figure instead of Elmira's. Maybe that was why she wasn't scared. It was hard to be frightened of a situation you'd been in all your life. "The bad stuff has to happen to somebody. And usually it happens to me."

"Yeah," he said evenly. "I'm sorry about that."

"What if it works against you?" she asked. "Because it could. It could actually *make* a cop drive by, or whatever. It does things like that all the time."

"You should probably try to keep that from happening," Stanko said.

He unwrapped the tape from her ankles and helped her to her feet. As he led her out of the restaurant and into the alley, his hand gripped Cass's arm tightly, his fingers digging into the soft flesh of her upper arm. She'd probably have bruises there tomorrow, she thought. Down the alley they went, around the corner to Main Street and then around the corner again; it was late, and it was a Tuesday, and the streets were deserted. Cass thought about running—she knew she could break Stanko's grip, if only for an instant—but who was she kidding: Her arms were still bound behind her back, and even if they weren't, even under the best of circumstances, she might be able to run all the way to the end of the block before collapsing in a shaky, heart-pounding, exhausted heap. (Every time she watched a foot pursuit in an action movie she thought to herself how lucky she was that she didn't have the kind of life she'd ever have to run for. Ha.)

Stanko jerked her to a stop about twenty feet from Archer's Tavern.

"Archer's?" Cass said with disbelief. "You're going to rob Archer's?"

"Most bars don't have security cameras," Stanko said, "and nobody cares when they get held up. I'm going to keep your hands taped up so they won't think you're there willingly—"

"I'm not," Cass said.

He ignored her. "We're going to go in the front and out the back. My van's parked at the other end of the alley so you only have to go that far with me." He shook her arm gently. "You don't even have to do anything, Cass," he said, and now there was a note in his voice that was almost placating. "You just have to be there."

"I don't want to be there," she said, and Stanko rolled his eyes.

"Yeah," he said, his voice hard again, "things are tough all over," and pulled her toward the entrance.

The bar was empty except for the bartender, who was standing at the cash register, counting a sheaf of bills in his hand. His features were soft and tired, and the skin covering his bald head was a sickly pale that spoke of long nights and not enough sun. He wore a wedding ring and an Archer's T-shirt, and he needed a shave. "Bar's closed," he said.

"We know," Stanko said. The hand that wasn't holding Cass slipped around to the small of his back and reappeared, holding a gun.

What came next happened very quickly, and very slowly. Instantly, the bartender's own hand ducked under the bar and emerged holding a baseball bat; instantly, Stanko pushed Cass away from him. It took her forever to fall. There was plenty of time for her to see the two men, to take in their every detail: the bartender in midair over the bar, leaping with an agility she wouldn't have expected of him, Stanko holding the gun up in front of him like a shield, the bartender's wedding ring shining gold in the darkness. Stanko's eyes, wide and surprised, and Cass realized that he had not expected to be attacked with a baseball bat, that he had no plan for this contingency, and that he was probably going to shoot the man, even though he didn't want to. Even though her entire reason for being there was so that something just like this didn't happen.

The bartender was screaming, "Hold me up, you son of a bitch, I'll fucking kill you," and Stanko was screaming, "Stay where you are, man, just cool it." He sounded scared.

Poor Stanko, she thought, *he's going to kill that man and go to jail,* and then she hit the ground. Her wrist flared with sudden, bright pain and in front of her she saw the bartender's cowboy-booted feet hit the ground, too, first one—"I will bash your goddamned head in!" he cried—and then the other.

Which landed in a puddle of spilled beer. Suddenly the bartender's forward motion shifted, slid, went wild. The second boot skidded across the tile floor. His arms began to windmill as the baseball bat flew out of his hands, and that was it, Cass knew; he'd lost. The rest of his night, if he was lucky, would be police reports and a worried wife and maybe even a trip to the hospital, and frustration, and anger, and tomorrow or the next day or the day after that he'd have to come back to the bar and work the register, just like nothing had ever happened.

Except that the flying baseball bat hit Stanko between the eyes, and he crumpled to the ground.

The back of the bartender's head cracked hard against a barstool.

Everything went very, very quiet.

———

"Amazing," said the detective, twenty minutes later. "Three people, two deadly weapons and a cash register full of money, and all we're walking away with are two concussions and a broken wrist."

"To be fair," Cass said, "the broken wrist really, really hurts."

The detective looked at her sternly. "You're a very lucky young lady, you know."

"I'll try to keep that in mind," Cass said.

The detective asked if she wanted to call somebody, maybe her mother, and Cass said no, thank you very much, but she didn't really think her mother would be helpful right now. "Or ever, really," she added, realizing that not only was that true, but it had always been true, and would probably be true for her entire life. She'd call Matthew, sometime, and ask him if he wanted to go get ice cream. But that could wait.

By the time the detective dropped her off in front of her apartment building, it was almost four in the morning. Cass was exhausted, and her wrist hurt, and she was hungry. As she paused on the sidewalk outside the brightly lit VFW (it was all-night bingo night, the chatter and clatter and faint amplified voice of the caller drifting through the open front door), all she wanted to do was go upstairs, make herself some cinnamon toast, take one of the Vicodin the ER doctor had given her, and go to sleep.

But she couldn't stop thinking, thoughts and images surging and submerging in her head like boiling ravioli: Matthew, Elmira, wedding rings (both the bartender's and Barty's); the itch of the duct tape, the smell of the garbage cans, the envelope of tips that still waited for her on the counter at the restaurant. But the thought that came to the surface most often, the one she couldn't get away from, was Stanko's voice, saying, *What goes wrong is the little things. It's all bad luck.*

If she hadn't been there, the bartender would be dead and Stanko would be a murderer. Even the detective had said the outcome was amazing. She'd said she had no control over the things that happened around her; but there was something nagging at her now. Because she couldn't quite remember, but she was fairly sure that just before the bartender had slipped in the puddle of beer she'd been thinking about what it was like to be Stanko, how scared he sounded, and how he didn't want to kill that man; and just before the flying baseball bat had hit Stanko between the eyes she'd been thinking about how miserable the next few days were going to be for the bartender. And all she'd ended up with was a broken wrist. Which seemed like not much, all things considered. A small price. Slipping in a puddle, losing your grip on a baseball bat: Those were small things, too.

Had she made them happen? Could she *make* them happen consciously, when she wanted to? Because if she could—if she could, the ramifications of that were potentially huge. For want of a nail, and all that.

Cass wasn't going to be able to sleep tonight, she knew it. She looked at the VFW, all noise and laughter and bright lights, and then up at her dark, empty windows, and she wanted a Vicodin and she wanted cinnamon toast but more than that, she realized, she wanted to *know.*

And there was a way, she realized, that she could find out. To wit: the bingo hall.

The inside of the hall was filled with folding tables and fluorescent light. An elderly man in a vaguely military-looking hat sat next to the door, selling stacks of numbered cards for ten dollars each. When Cass asked for one he held out something that looked like a stubby green marker and said, "You're going to want a dauber, too, sweetie."

She found a seat near the back. The man calling numbers into a microphone at the front of the room could have been the card vendor's brother. Or his brother-in-arms, Cass thought as she daubed lethargically at the numbers on her card; and the woman in the second row, the one with the dyed black hair and the bright red lipstick, could have been the girl they took turns dancing with on Saturday nights. Maybe even in this very hall, Cass thought.

Cass imagined the woman: the loose flesh tautening, the stooped back straightening. A red party dress, with a black patent belt around her nipped-in waist and a scarlet flower tucked behind her ear, where the swirling lights and her still-naturally-black hair would set it on fire. And on a night when the brothers-in-arms drank too much rye, she would stand to one side in the dusty parking lot and watch as they fought, her heart thrilling and her eyes filled with tears because she couldn't choose and she loved to have them fighting over her and she hated to have them fighting and she hated that they had to fight and she loved them both for fighting.

And so she hadn't married either of them—Cass thought—and now she lived in a poky little apartment, just like Cass's own. And her days were fine but they were flat, and the young heart that beat inside her aging body never felt the thrills it once did; except when she played all-night bingo at the VFW, and when she didn't win it felt like time was eating her fine, flat days, a long stretch of not-much reaching out in front of her, until one day it would be stretched so thin it broke and what a waste that would be—

Suddenly, the woman jerked as if shocked, and leaped to her feet. "Bingo!" she cried, waving her card overhead like a flag. "Bingo, bingo, *bingo!*"

Cass felt a tap on her elbow. "Honey," the lady next to her said, "looks like you got a bad dauber."

Cass looked down. The marker had exploded in her hands, the plastic casing somehow cracked, and the green ink was on Cass's hands, on her card, on her clothes.

"Looks like I did," Cass said, and in front of her, the woman who had once been young and danced in the lights put up her arms as if holding an invisible partner, and danced again.

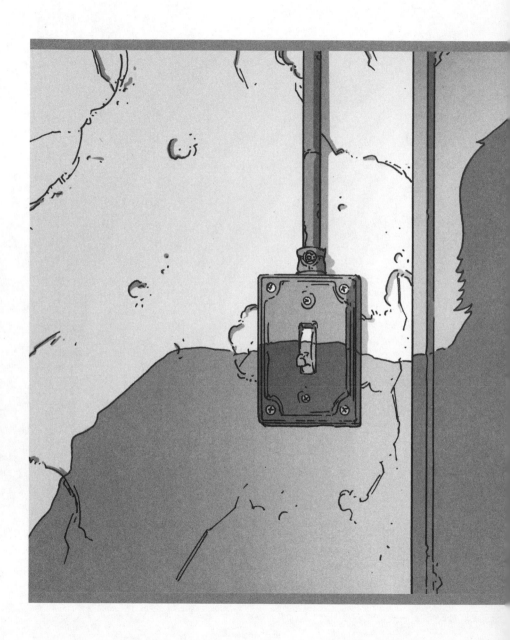

Jennifer Weiner

LEAGUE OF JUSTICE (PHILADELPHIA DIVISION)

One

Dani Saperstein had been living in Philadelphia for six months when she got her first email from the dead.

She was sitting at her desk on the twenty-third floor of her office building in Center City. Halfhearted sleet splattered the window, the clock in the right-hand corner of her computer screen inched languidly toward eleven. Her feet had gotten wet on the two-block trip from the bus stop to Fallowes Communications, so she'd slipped off her salt-crusted boots underneath her desk and was wriggling her toes, thinking that nothing felt worse than wet wool on damp skin, when her computer gave the soft chime telling her that an email had arrived in her in-box.

She flipped to her in-box but the most recent message there was still an unread missive from Greg Fallowes, and there was no need to open it because its entire content was in the memo line. MEETING. ELEVEN. MANDATORY. A man of few words, was Gregory Fallowes of Fallowes Communications.

Dani clicked over to her Bulk Mail bin. There'd been three emails when she'd gotten there at eight forty-five, one advertising herbal penis enlargement (PLEASE HER EVERY TIME) one offering coupons for a time-share in the Everglades, and one promoting a European weight-loss supplement (DISCOVER SWEDISH SLIMMING SECRETS!). Whoever the online spammers were, Dani reflected, they'd decided that she was fat, poorly endowed, and in need of a tropical vacation. "It's like they're peering into the very depths of my soul," she murmured, and she clicked on the fourth email.

The subject line was blank, but the sender line gave her a start: Philip Devereaux@blank.com. Blank.com? Was that some kind of new server? Dani shook her head. In graduate school she'd gotten a Gmail

360

address, and she'd been proud about it, too, had thought herself pretty with-it and current, until her brother Jared had informed her that Gmail was for old people who wanted to think they were still hip. Actually hip people had Mac addresses. "I don't have a Mac," Dani had told him, and Jared had smirked and said, "Exactly."

Blank.com. She'd have to ask Jared about that. And Philip . . .

She saw that her hand, as it hovered over the mouse, was trembling. Philip was a popular name, she reminded herself. There were lots of Philips; probably thousands of Philips in Philadelphia alone. The world was full of Phils. "Hey, Aunt Dani!" her four-year-old niece Nevaeh would say. "You made up a rhyme!" Dani and her husband, Steve, had laughed about her niece's name the first time they'd heard it, spooning in the queen-sized bed that took up almost every inch of the bedroom of their efficiency in Red Hook, Steve whispering that if the kid was anything like his mother they should have named her Lleh instead. Plenty of Phils, for sure. But Phil Devereaux? She'd only known one. And he was . . .

"Dani." Greg Fallowes stuck his sleek silvery head over the partition that separated her workspace from the rest of the copywriters. "Meeting."

Startled, Dani scooted her chair backward along the pebbly square of plastic that formed a runway over the carpet with so much force that her back whacked into the particleboard wall, dislodging the kitten-themed calendar left there by the workspace's previous tenant. "Be right there," Dani said weakly. When Greg's head vanished, she wheeled the chair to the desk again and opened the email.

There was her name. Just her name. *Dani*, and then a comma, as if the sender had meant to write more, but had been interrupted. She swallowed hard. Her mouth tasted of hot copper. Then the message was gone and she was up, out of her chair, on her feet, staggering down the hallway, past the conference room, into the ladies' room, where she stood with her hands planted on either side of the sink and her head hanging over the basin, thinking she might throw up or faint, thinking, *Not happening, not happening, this isn't happening.*

"You all right?"

Dani nodded without looking up. The solicitous voice and the small hand on her shoulder belonged to Asha, the twenty-one-year-old intern, who was studying graphic design at Temple and who seemed not only from a whole different generation than thirty-four-year-old Dani, but, frequently, from an entirely different planet. Asha and Dani had started at the same time, had gone through orientation and posed for their ID tag pictures together.

"I'm fine," Dani said, in a low, trembling voice. The lights above the mirror flickered, casting Asha's pretty, inquisitive face into shadow. Asha flicked the light switch off, then on. The flickering stopped.

"Well, you don't look fine." Asha set her bulging cosmetics case down beside the sink. "Pardon the cliché, but you look like you've seen a ghost."

Dani turned the cold water tap. She splashed water on her face. "Just a little freaked out," she said. "I got an email from my ex-boyfriend."

"Oh, God, I hate that!" Asha reached for an eyeliner and launched into a long, complicated tale of how one of her exes had texted her during sex ("A rhyme!" Nevaeh crowed in Dani's head). "It was, like, this total Paris Hilton moment. We can both totally see the screen, so, like, do I answer it or just let it sit there on Vibrate or what?" Dani had nodded and said, "Mm-hm," and "Oh, no," without telling the other woman that hearing from Phil was a little bit more than disturbing; hearing from Phil was impossible. Unless there were BlackBerries in heaven and wireless internet in the afterlife, there was no way Dani would be getting emails from the high-school boyfriend she hadn't seen in more than sixteen years, because Philip Devereaux, the guy she'd dated for her senior year of high school, the one with whom she'd lost her virginity, Phil who'd dumped her, stammeringly, over Thanksgiving break their first semester home from college, was dead.

Two

There was a letter from Steve's lawyers waiting in her mailbox when she got home just after six o'clock. Lewis, Dommel, and Fenick, LLP.

Offices in New York, Philadelphia, Atlanta, Tallahassee, Los Angeles, Paris, and Switzerland. The same firm, Steven had pointed out, that his literary agent used to review its authors' contracts. The revelation was deliberate: *You see?* it said. *I didn't go out and hire sharks. No New York City heavy for me. I intend to be fair.* All part of the image, Dani thought, tucking the heavy manila envelope into her purse, stuffing her wet mittens into her pocket. Mister Literary Superstar. Mister Nice Guy.

Her divorce—for that was what it was in the envelope—was twenty-eight pages long. The pages, printed in triplicate, were considerably tabbed with colored Post-Its bearing preprinted arrows, pointing to the blank where she should sign. Once she signed, their marriage would be over. They'd split the wedding gifts, the eighteen hundred dollars that had been in the checking account when she'd left. There would be alimony. Dani hadn't asked for a slice of the incredibly rich advance Steven had landed three months after she'd left him and moved to Philadelphia. Steven had offered, as she'd known he would, and Dani had declined, as he'd known she would. There was no way she could lay claim to even the merest sliver of the rumored two-million-dollar advance that Steven had gotten for his novel, *An Honest Day's Work*.

She flipped through the pages slowly as she walked up the stairs. The meat of the thing—the heart of the matter—was page 9, paragraph 13, section 4: *"Neither party shall discuss any aspect of their marriage with any third party. Further, neither party shall disparage the other in any forum, either public or private."* What Steven wanted was her silence. He would have paid for it, too, if Dani hadn't been too proud to take his money.

He'd erased her, she mused, clomping down the hallway in her salt-stained boots. He'd made her vanish, and she'd been complicit in that act, a cheerful participant in her own disappearance. The realization had a bitter taste.

Upstairs, she locked the door and felt the apartment draw tightly around her. This was one of the best parts of leaving New York, leaving Steven and her grand dreams. In New York City, the two of them had worked what amounted to two full-time jobs between their writing and a shifting combination of catering and waitering and bartending gigs, seasonal shifts in department stores, an ignominious six weeks of nannying Dani had endured one summer. Even so, they'd barely been able to afford a studio in an unfashionable neighborhood in Brooklyn. Now, in Philadelphia, with her new job writing ad copy, she could easily pay for a two-bedroom place on the third floor of an airy, high-ceilinged, historically pedigreed old rowhouse, with heat and hot water included, and views of Rittenhouse Square. Her place had hardwood floors and a fireplace, a washer and dryer tucked into a closet just off the master bedroom. There was a deep, claw-footed tub, set in a spacious bathroom tiled in black-and-white hexagons, a pedestal sink, and a generous linen closet, and it had been unexpectedly empty, available, and reasonably priced, when she'd shown up in the middle of January with two suitcases and a broken heart. Like it had been waiting for her, she'd thought at the time. Later, in the basement laundry room, she'd gotten more of the story. "Missus Gordon died up there," her first-floor neighbor had confided, while sloshing a capful of blue Tide into the machine. "Right after Christmas. In the bathtub, I think." Dani supposed she should have been disturbed by the news. Under normal circumstances she would have found it horrifying. But her circumstances were far from normal. She scrubbed the tub with Mister Clean and didn't give deceased Mrs. Gordon a second thought.

Plus, she'd come to regard the fabulous apartment as her consolation prize, the parting gift she'd gone home with after a spectacular failure. *No husband, no novel, no two million dollars, but hey, honey, you've got health insurance now! And room for your sheets if you had any!*

She'd draped her sodden scarf and mittens over the radiator and changed into what Steven used to jokingly call her evening finery: sweatpants, wool socks, a long-sleeved T-shirt. As she was reaching for her cleaver and cutting board, the telephone trilled.

There was a brief instant when Dani felt her heart lift, the way it had, early on, when the phone would ring and she would think, *Him*. Even after they'd gotten married, Dani couldn't quite believe her good fortune. Steven Callahan—now, of course, Steven Updike Callahan, a three-named genius celebrated the world over, most recently on the front cover of the *New York Times Book Review*—had been the undisputed catch of her graduate-school class; handsome and brilliant, almost too good to be true. Chimeras and unicorns and Steven, with his gleaming hair and his warm eyes, summa cum laude from Brown, youngest-ever recipient of the Stegner Fellowship at Stanford, Steven Etc. Etc. with his beauty and, best of all, worst of all, his talent.

"Updike's not even his real middle name," she whispered. The telephone shrilled, then stopped, shrilled, then stopped, and then the apartment filled with the sound of something breaking (*exploding,* Dani's mind insisted), in the bathroom. She screamed, an actual "Eeek!" like a girl in a cartoon who's seen a mouse, before her higher mind (*Danielle Mara Saperstein, you get a grip right now*) spoke up.

Dani made herself walk down the corridor that seemed to stretch out like a hallway in a horror movie. The bathroom's tiled floor glittered with shards of glass. Somehow, her toothbrush glass, one she could have sworn was set securely on top of the sink, had fallen to the tiled floor and smashed there. Shards of glass glittered wickedly from the tiles. "Mrs. Gordon?" she murmured. No answer came. "Philip?" she whispered. Still nothing. She stood with her hands braced against the doorway, breathing deeply, telling herself that this was not a divine manifestation, just sloppy housekeeping. Then she went to the pantry to find her dustpan and broom. She'd just finished picking the last bit of glass off the floor when her telephone rang again.

Dani trotted into the living room, glanced at the caller ID—the New Mexico area code was familiar, at this point—and picked up the receiver. "Hi, Ma."

"Did you watch *Good Morning America*?"

Dani turned down the flame underneath her lamb, sprinkled curry and cumin on top of the onions, and reached for the canister of rice.

"I think he's losing his hair, Dan. I really do."

She added a cinnamon stick to the pan without answering, because, really, what could she say that didn't sound like gloating, or like sour grapes, or desperation? The truth was, she would take him back, even with a receding hairline. She would take Steven back bald, deaf, blind, limbless, broke and incontinent, riddled with cancer and with six months to live. She loved him. She was lost without him. She . . .

"The host said the book's overrated."

Dani swallowed hard as an unnamable emotion surged in her veins: the hot, guilty flush of triumph, the stronger desire to protect Steven . . . to protect him, still. "Really?"

"Well, not exactly," her mother admitted. "He said it would be almost impossible for any book to live up to the hype."

"Ah." Steven's book could, she knew. She'd read it as a rough draft, sneaking the pages out of their apartment when he was catering, and had finished it burning with exultation, on his behalf, and shame, on her own. The scope and the heft of it, the language, at once playful and precise, the witty observations and whipcrack dialogue, the characters who felt so real that you could almost reach onto the page and feel the texture of their hair, their skin . . . had she thought she could write? Had she imagined that she, too, was talented? This was real writing; genius, right in her hands. When he'd come home, bounding up the stairs, his stained apron tucked in his back pocket, she'd been weeping, and when he'd asked why she'd turned her pale, tear-stained face to his and said, *It's so good.* And it was true . . . or, at least, it was part of the truth. Never mind the rest of it: the unspoken, *because I'll never be this good.*

"How was work?" her mother asked.

Dani poured chicken broth and coconut milk into the pan and set it on a burner to simmer, wondering what Marla would say if she answered, "Hey, you'll never guess, I think I got an email from Phil Devereaux." Instead, she just said, "Fine. Work is fine." That, at least, was true. She'd been worried at first that, after the end of her marriage and her subsequent inability to write a single word of the novel she'd been laboring over for close to eight years, she wouldn't be able to ever write anything. The night before her first day of work, she'd lain in bed, sleepless, convinced that Gregory had only hired her because he'd mistaken her MFA for an MBA. The truth was that writing a paragraph or a line extolling the virtues of Kennett Square mushrooms or hemorrhoid wipes came easily. It shouldn't have been a surprise. *You have a certain facility with language,* one of her professors at Iowa had admitted, grudgingly, after Dani had turned in her third draft of a short story. Dani had known, from the sour tuck of the man's lips, that *facility* wasn't a compliment. And this particular professor, best known for his memoir of his service in World War II published fifty years previously, had told his students more than once that he never read women's books, so she'd take what she could get.

Marla sounded dubious. "Are you sure? Your aura sounds off."

Dani stifled a groan. Her mother, always inclined toward the new-agey, had gotten exponentially more so every year since she'd moved to New Mexico four years previously. Dani supposed that Marla had never gotten over her husband's leaving her for another woman years ago. *He's doing important work for the government,* she'd say serenely, when Dani had come home one day to find her father's car missing from the garage and every piece of his clothing absent from the closet. Jared had been the one to tell Dani the truth, which had involved a dental hygienist, a quickie divorce, and a condo in Cleveland. *Important Work for the Government.* If Dani had gotten a nickel for every time her mother had said those words, she'd have been able to afford her Philadelphia apartment in New York.

"What does my aura normally sound like?" Dani asked. There was fresh ginger in the crisper. She tucked the gnarled root into her pocket and rummaged around her silverware drawer for a paring knife. Before her mother could answer, Dani asked, "Hey, do you remember Phil Devereaux?"

"From high school? Sure. I used to see his mom sometimes at the Stop & Shop. Poor thing. I don't think she ever got over it. Such a tragedy," Marla intoned.

"Tragedy," Dani murmured back.

Her mother's voice sharpened. "Why do you ask?"

"No reason," Dani said. "Hey, I've got to go. My dinner's going to burn."

Later, Dani lit a fire in her fireplace, crumpling up fistfuls of the *Philadelphia Examiner* she'd pilfered from her downstairs neighbor's recycling bin to light the kindling. She sat in the green velvet armchair she'd bought at a tag sale, with her bowl of curried lamb and mango chutney in her lap. She peeled off her socks and stretched her bare feet toward the flames. *This wasn't so bad,* she told herself. A room of one's own, good food, a fire . . . and, let's not forget, those health benefits, that linen closet. She ate her dinner slowly and, after she'd stacked the dishes in the sink, poured a shot of single-malt Scotch over a single ice cube, letting the heavy glass tumbler (a wedding gift) warm in the cup of her hand. Her divorce was still tucked in its envelope. She pulled out the pages and signed her name thirty-six times. Then she slid the pages into the self-addressed stamped envelope that had come with them, set the envelope on the table by the door, and resumed her spot in front of the fire, trying to enjoy the warmth, her full belly, the glow of the Scotch, and the feeling of safety as the snow fell outside her windows and piled up on the sidewalk underneath, to try not to think about her dead ex-boyfriend or her far-too-lively almost ex-husband, or how she'd once foolishly believed that she had been talented, too.

Three

"So your ex-boyfriend is trying to contact you from beyond the grave?" Asha leaned against the vending machine in the lunchroom, her brown eyes narrowed.

"My dead ex-boyfriend," Dani amplified, sliding her Tupperware dish of leftover lamb into the microwave. She wasn't sure why she was telling Asha any of this. She had friends and relatives: her mother in New Mexico, her best friend Jade Amberley of Dallas, Paris, St. Barth's, and New York City. She could have signed up for therapy, which her excellent insurance would cover, assuming she could prove that her difficulties were somehow work-related (and because Phil had tried to contact her on her work computer, she figured she could make a good case). Still, there was something about Asha, with her trendy clothes, the way she'd roll into work at around ten o'clock on Monday mornings with her blouse wrinkled and her eyeliner smeared and spend her afternoon napping on the break-room couch, that invited confidences. "I know it sounds crazy . . ."

"I've heard of weirder things," Asha said.

"You have?"

"Oh, sure." Asha nodded. "I know a lady who talks to her dog."

"I know lots of ladies who talk to their dogs," Dani replied. "Like, every single woman in New York."

"Yeah, but her dog talks back."

Dani raised her eyebrows.

"For serious!" Asha said. She plugged a fistful of quarters into the machine and rammed a button with her elbow. The machine grumbled, then belched up a Diet Coke.

"What does the dog say?"

Asha tugged the silver cuff that encircled her left earlobe. "You know, that it's hungry. That it wants to go out. Stuff like that. But she's working on it."

"The dog's working on it?"

"No, the lady. Her owner. Vicky. She's got some book and she's trying to teach the dog to sign. You know how they do with babies before they can talk?"

Dani was momentarily nonplussed. "But if the dog can already talk, why would she want to teach it to sign?"

Asha cracked open her can of soda with a hiss. Then she reached into her pocket, pulled out a pen, and scribbled something down on a paper towel she pulled from the dispenser. "You should come here tonight."

Oh, great, Dani thought. Some after-hours club or bar packed with cooler-than-you hipsters where she'd be the oldest person by a decade, and she'd come home with her head throbbing from the music and her clothes stinking of cigarettes, after a few miserable hours of being ignored by all the young, attractive people who were actually supposed to spend their nights at places like that.

"Eight o'clock," Asha said. Then she reached across the break-room counter and took Dani's hands. Dani gasped as she felt something pass between them, a jolt of electricity that made her suck in her breath and think, *Oh, great, maybe this is the big mystery, maybe I'm gay.*

"I thought so," Asha murmured, dropping Dani's hands.

Do I kiss her? Dani wondered. The other woman stepped back and gave a sly smile.

"Eight o'clock tonight," she said. "And you're not gay. It's something else."

369

Four

Eight-seventeen Market Street was not a dive bar or an after-hours club or an ironically cool bowling alley with a Pabst Blue Ribbon sign flickering in the window. Eight-seventeen Market Street was an outpost of the L.A. Weight Loss Center. Dani stood in front of the locked glass door for a minute, staring up at a poster of some formerly fat reality TV star, wearing tight black jeans and a smug lipsticked smile. Then she started laughing. Whatever message she'd believed Asha was trying to send her, it hadn't been *You're a porker.*

And anyhow, the office was closed. The doors were locked. The sign said that there were evening meetings on Mondays and Fridays, but not Tuesdays. She shook her head wearily, and had turned to go, thinking that she'd head south toward Walnut Street, maybe pick up a burrito at del Fuego for dinner, when a hand pried apart the slats of the blinds that lined the inside of the door and a pair of eyes peered out at her.

Dani was so startled she gave a little squeal and stumbled backward on the stained, bubblegum-dotted sidewalk. The eyes behind the window crinkled, as if their owner was smiling . . . then the blinds snapped shut and the door swung open, and there was Asha, and a tall woman with braided steel-gray hair and horn-rimmed glasses with a little wrinkly brown-and-cream-spotted dog tucked under her arm . . . and a middle-aged man in a navy-blue suit and a wine-red tie . . . and a plump woman with caramel-colored skin and glossy black ringlets wearing what Dani initially took for a police officer's uniform, but which turned out to have a PARKING AUTHORITY patch sewn over her left breast.

"Dani?" said the gray-haired woman with the dog.

"Um," said Dani.

"Welcome to the League of Justice," said the woman. *Oh, my God*, Dani thought faintly, as her breath came whistling out of her. *I'm going crazy.* Then the woman smiled. "Philadelphia Division," she said, and ushered Dani inside.

———

Ten minutes later, Dani was clutching a Styrofoam cup of coffee in one hand and half of a Sarcone's Italian hoagie in the other. She was sitting in a folding plastic chair to the right of the electronic scale. In the chair on her right, Asha had pulled out a Tupperware dish of something pungent and had gone to work with chopsticks. The parking authority officer had produced a bag of salt-and-vinegar potato chips from her purse. The woman with the dog, whose gray hair was plaited into thick braids that she'd wrapped around the crown of her head, was nibbling from a plastic Zip-loc bag of baby carrots and cut-up radishes. Occasionally, she'd slip a crudité to the dog, whose flat face and noisy breathing suggested she was at least part pug. The man in the suit had pulled the hoagie out of his briefcase and offered half to Dani.

Dani was nibbling soppressata and wondering what she was doing here, and whether it wasn't actually some kind of elaborate practical joke—League of Justice, Philadelphia Division?—when the dog lady set down her veggies and clapped her long-fingered hands.

"Okay, people, you know the drill. Names and talents. I'll start. I am Victoria, and . . ."

The businessman pursed his lips. They looked, Dani thought, like a pink rosebud blooming on the white field of his cheeks. "How about we let the new girl go first?"

Victoria's cheeks flushed. "Fine," she said stiffly, and pointed her chin toward Dani, who felt a growing sense of dismay that she'd already made an enemy among the members of a group she hadn't wanted to be part of in the first place. "New girl."

"I'm Dani," she began, then looked to her left, to Asha, for some clue about what to say next.

"She sees dead people!" said Asha.

Dani shook her head. "No, I don't."

"She gets email from dead people."

The businessman grinned. "Swedish penis-enlarging pumps from *the Twilight Zone?*"

"There's probably a reasonable explanation," Dani muttered.

"Her dead ex-boyfriend says he needs her help," Asha burbled.

"Was it a bad break-up?" asked the parking authority lady.

"I was eighteen." Dani tried to explain. "We went out in high school, and then he went to Kenyon, and I went to Penn, and . . . well, you know. It was kind of a natural parting of ways." Of course, that hadn't made it hurt any less when Phil had dumped her . . . or, three days after that, when he'd died. She remembered her mother coming into her room to tell her, Marla's typically rosy, cheerful face pale and stricken. *There's been a terrible accident,* she'd said . . . and, for a moment, Dani, still in bed, had been paralyzed, not just with grief and shock but with guilt, because, as Phil had stammered that he was sorry, so sorry, that he'd never wanted to hurt her, hadn't she actually wished him dead? And what if . . .

She cut the thought off, as she'd cut it off all those years ago, and forced herself to look around the charmless room, with its flickering fluorescent lights and posters of the food pyramid hanging limply on the walls. "So what about the rest of you guys? Do you all have . . ." She fumbled with the word. "Talents?"

The businessman folded the wax paper his hoagie had come wrapped in and tossed it toward the trash can. The paper bounced off the rim and rattled onto the pilled gray carpet. "Scott Spencer. Super-human strength."

"Really?" The question was out of her mouth before Dani could consider its potentially insulting implications. Scott Spencer scowled.

"I went from barely being able to bench-press eighty pounds to benching two-twenty in less than three months of working out."

"But . . ." Dani picked her words carefully. "But if you're working out, isn't that kind of normal progress?"

Scott Spencer pursed his lips again, then turned toward Asha. "Someone's got a lot to learn," he said, loudly enough for Dani to hear him.

"Moving on!" said the woman with the dog. "I am Victoria Jensen, and this is Sweetie. I talk to animals." She stroked her little pug's head fondly. "One animal, so far."

Dani bit her lip as Sweetie snorted. The parking authority lady was Leticia Perez, and she had "the sight." No further explanation was offered, and Dani didn't ask.

Then it was Asha's turn. Her colleague drew herself up straight in her chair and beamed. "I'm Asha Agrawal, and I have perfect gaydar."

Dani laughed. She couldn't help it. Asha narrowed her eyes.

"Fine," she said. "Laugh. It's a lot more useful than you'd think."

"No . . . no, it's not that, it's just that . . . well, I mean, how do you figure out that you've got perfect gaydar?"

"Um, you accidentally date gay guys?" Asha replied, as if this were the most logical explanation in the world. She smoothed her shirt collar and the beaded necklaces stacked inside it, and sighed. "Anyhow, it's not actually perfect yet. I still have to sleep with the guy before I know for sure."

Dani bit her lip to keep from laughing, but Asha must have caught her amusement, because she turned toward her indignantly. "Hey, it used to be worse! I used to have to sleep with them a bunch of times before I was sure! I knew about you by just holding your hands! And anyhow . . ."

"It's all right," Victoria said, in a stern, schoolmarm tone. "We're all on our way to the perfect realization of our gifts. Remember La Loteria?"

The name moved like a wind across the dim gray room. *La Loteria . . . La Loteria . . .*

"That's Leticia's sister Paz," Asha whispered. "She got so she could pick winning lottery numbers, like, 50 percent of the time."

"So where is she?" Dani asked.

Asha dropped her eyes. Scott shuffled his wingtips. It was Victoria who finally answered. "She won ten thousand dollars on the Quik Pik and moved to New York."

"Ah," said Dani. That made sense. Philadelphia was where you went if life had kicked you in the teeth; if you'd been dumped and divorced, if you'd tried to make it somewhere else and couldn't. New York was where you went when you were on an upswing. Philadelphia was for losers. It was where she'd wound up, after all, she thought, and wondered, briefly, what the New York division of the League of Justice was like. "Can I ask a question?"

Scott Spencer, Superhuman Strength, muttered, "It's about time."

"Ask," Victoria said grandly . . . and her little dog, perched on her lap, made a weird yowling sound that sounded not entirely unlike the word, "Ask."

Dani ignored the dog, for the time being. "What's the point?" she said.

Four blank stares met her gaze. "I mean," she said, "if we've really got talents, what are we supposed to do with them? What's the point of it? To win the lottery? To bench-press three hundred pounds, or know whether somebody's gay?"

Beside her, Asha twitched in her seat, and Scott Spencer exhaled forcefully from his pinched little nose. It was Victoria who answered; Victoria who, Dani was coming to realize, spoke for the group.

"We have a mission," she said. The words rang out grandly, absurdly, and hung over the worn gray carpet, the dog-eared posters about food groups and fat grams, the sad collection of folding chairs.

"Okay," Dani said slowly (she hoped, not condescendingly). "So what is the mission?"

This time, it was Victoria who got shifty-eyed and scuffly-footed. Scott flipped his briefcase open. Leticia fiddled with the walkie-talkie affixed to her belt. Sweetie the dog hopped off her mistress's lap and began nosing at Scott Spencer's grease-spotted hoagie wrapper. "Children," said Asha.

"Excuse me?" Dani said.

"Someone's been taking children." Asha said this with her eyes fixed straight ahead. There was no glint in her eye, no curve to her lips. Her face could have been engraved on the side of a coin. She looked noble, Dani thought, as a shudder worked its way up her spine. Weird.

"Okay, I'll bite," Dani said. "Who's taking children?"

"We don't know that."

"Why is this person taking children?" Dani persisted. Scott Spencer walked across the room, picked up his sandwich wrapper, and tossed it into the trash.

"And how are our talents going to help?" Asha didn't answer. Nobody did. It was left to Dani to state the obvious. "This is crazy." None of them responded . . . and her suspicion that this was some elaborate, cruel practical joke, possibly orchestrated by her almost-ex himself, continued to grow. Two million dollars could probably buy you a lot of practical jokes. "I should probably get going."

She'd made it as far as the door, with the cool metal of the doorknob in her hand—when the lights when out. Somebody—Dani decided later that it was Scott Spencer—gasped. Victoria's Sweetie yipped. Leticia's walkie-talkie crackled with static. Dani twisted the doorknob. Nothing happened. She yanked harder, but it was like trying to pull down a wall. From her front pocket, where she'd stuck it, her cell phone buzzed and throbbed. As if unconscious, Dani dipped her hand into her pocket and lifted the phone to her face, at once utterly terrified and absolutely unsurprised to see that the rectangular blue face was flashing the word STAY.

Her hand slipped off the doorknob. Moving on legs that felt frozen, Dani crossed the room and slumped back into her seat. "Fine," she said—to Victoria, to Scott, to Asha and Leticia, maybe even to God, as the lights flickered back into life. "Fine," she said. "I'm here. I'm listening. Tell me what to do."

Five

That night, Dani did the thing she had promised herself she wouldn't do; the thing that she'd zealously avoided in the months since she'd moved to Philadelphia: She sat in her sweatpants, with her bare feet tucked underneath her, and dialed her ex-husband's new phone number.

Not home, she thought, as the telephone rang in Steven's newly acquired Chelsea apartment (two bedrooms, gourmet granite kitchen, marble bathrooms. She'd looked it up online, had downloaded the Realtor's pictures and taken a Virtual Tour, and no, she wasn't proud, but there it was.) He wouldn't be home. He'd be out at some book party or some bar, enjoying a four-course, two-hundred-dollar dinner with his editor, a foppish fifty-six-year-old who wore silk bow ties and cuf-flinks shaped like dollar signs, and who'd grandly proclaimed Steven "not the next Bret Easton Ellis, not the next Jay McInerney, but the next F. Scott Fitzgerald."

Steven picked up on the third ring. "Dani?"

Her blood jumped. *He knows it's me. We're still connected.* An instant later, she realized that caller ID was a far more plausible explanation than magic . . . and an infinitely more plausible explanation than the lingering vestiges of enduring marital love. "Hi, Steve."

"Is everything all right?" A pause. "Did you get the papers?"

"Got 'em, signed 'em, sent 'em back," she said jauntily, as if the dissolution of her marriage was as meaningful as clipping out a coupon. Ten cents off dish detergent. A quarter off bleach. "I wanted to ask you something. It's going to sound kind of strange, but . . ." She swallowed Scotch, wondering if he could hear her. "Did you ever notice anything, um, weird about me?"

The old Steven, the one without the agent, the editor, the big book deal, and the F. Scott Fitzgerald comparison hanging like a halo over his head, would have laughed and asked how much time she had. New Steven, new two-million-dollar, desperate-to-be-divorced Steven, paused gingerly, then said, "What do you mean?"

"Oh, you know," Dani said. "Just anything unusual. Out of the ordinary. Like unusual abilities."

His voice was careful. "You're a very talented writer. You know I always believed . . ."

She cut him off, midcompliment. "Not that. Like, more along the lines of seeing through walls. Or superhuman strength."

"Superhuman strength?" he asked cautiously. *He probably thinks I'm going crazy,* Dani realized. A crazy ex-wife, she figured, would be the last thing he needed right now. Then again, if anyone could find a way to make it work, it would be Steven. If he was going to be Scott, why shouldn't she be a Zelda? He could give heartfelt interviews to the women's magazines. He could pose for their photographers at the gates of Sunny Acres, clutching a bouquet of flowers, looking mournful. And single.

"Well, maybe not superhuman strength. But did I ever, like, shut the refrigerator door with my mind?"

"Not that I noticed." He paused again. The wheels of his mind were already spinning, weighing possibilities and consequences, trying to make sense of what was happening to her and what it might mean for him.

Dani pressed on. "No sleepwalking? No talking in my sleep? No weird messages on the answering machine? Did the laptop or the iPod ever do anything strange when I was around? Or did you ever . . ."

"Dani." His voice was gentle, eminently reasonable, even kind. "Are you drinking?"

For a moment she thought he'd asked if she was *dreaming*. Then she realized what he'd said, and she set the tumbler down with a loud, guilty, smack. "No!"

"Are you sure you're all right? Do you want me to call someone? Maybe your mom?"

"Steven." She forced herself to sound breezy, to play the part of the irreverent, laughing girl she'd been when they'd first met. "I think I'm a little past the point where I can call my mommy." She shoved herself upright in her cushiony chair. *Fire,* she recited in her head. *Good food. Warm clothes. Health benefits. Big linen closet.* "I'm sorry I bothered you."

"You didn't bother me. It's . . ."

". . . but if you remember anything—I mean, I know how strange this sounds, but it's not crazy." There was silence on the line. Dani pressed the receiver to her ear, imagining that she could hear him breathing. She'd fallen asleep listening to him breathing, when they'd been married, when they'd shared a bed. He'd always fall asleep first, and she'd prop herself up on an elbow, looking down at him, his golden hair, the gleaming curve of his shoulder, soothed by the sound of his exhalations, amazed by her own happiness. "I'm not crazy." She said it a little more emphatically than she'd meant to . . . the way, she realized belatedly, someone who actually was crazy would say it. "I'm sorry I bothered you," she muttered, and hung up on his "Take care."

Six

That night she dreamed she was at a wedding, and a child fell down a well.

She was standing at the far edge of a dance floor that seemed to be set in the middle of a meadow. There was a semicircle of bales of hay for people to sit on, and bouquets of sunflowers nodding in the crisp breeze, which meant that this was not just *a* wedding she was visiting in her dream, it was *her* wedding. But instead of her wedding gown she wore the pale-blue dress she'd worn to other people's occasions. She was standing on the tiptoes of her dyed-to-match satin high heels, peering over the heads of the guests, craning for a glimpse of the bride who'd replaced her, when a tiny, terrified voice whispered *Help me.*

It was like a dead man's finger trailing down the back of her neck. She shuddered violently, then tapped the shoulder of the man beside her. *Hey, did you hear that?* The man, who'd been standing with his profile to Dani, didn't turn . . . but for a moment she was seized with the strange and horrible thought that if he did turn she would see that he had no face: just shallow, scooped-out scarred indentations where his eyes were meant to be, a jagged, bloody line for a mouth. As he turned, he would whisper, in a bubbling, somehow leering voice. *We take what we need.*

Dani stumbled backward through the crowd, heels catching on clumps of dirt, almost snapping an ankle in a rabbit hole as the mowed hay stubble gave way to a tangle of wildflowers and weeds. She was edging out of the meadow, toward the darkness of the forest beyond, when the voice spoke again. *Help me. I'm scared.*

I'm coming! Dani called. Her heels sank into the soft earth, so she kicked them off, yanking her tight skirt up over her knees, and started walking . . . then running.

She almost missed the well, a ragged, overgrown circle of black gaping out of the long grass like a dead man's mouth. She flung herself, belly-first, onto the ground, and peered into the darkness. *Hello?*

I'm here.

She glimpsed a pale, dirt-streaked face, upturned like a flower seeking the sun. Blue eyes, blonde curls, maybe three or four years old (outside of her niece, Dani hadn't spent much time around children).

The little girl stretched her chubby arms up toward Dani, up toward the light. Dani reached her arm down. Not even close. Frantic, Dani wriggled out of her dress, looped the length of blue satin twice around her fist, lay like a snake on the ground in her bra and panties, and dangled the dress down the well.

The little girl closed her eyes wearily. *That's not the way.*

Then what should I do?

Look in the last place.

What? Where's that?

You know.

No, I don't! I don't know anything! She pointed back toward the charmed circle in the meadow; back toward the wedding party. *He's the one who knows things, he's the one who's got the magic. Not me! You have to tell me! I can't help you unless you tell me!*

The little girl tilted her face up toward Dani . . . but it was Phil Devereaux's voice she heard. *Listen. It's in your hands.*

Dani's head snapped backward as the field and the hole in the ground and the little girl inside it vanished. She found herself in Phil's bedroom, which didn't seem to have changed since high school. There was a Genesis poster taped over the bed, and one featuring Jeff Goldblum in *The Fly* hanging next to the closet. A blue and green plaid bedspread matched the dark-blue carpet. The door was open (Phil's mother's rules), and she and Phil were sitting on the floor with their backs against Phil's single bed. Phil, still eighteen, was wearing jeans and a green rugby shirt that she remembered, and she caught a whiff of his familiar smell, Prell shampoo and Irish Spring. His feet were pale and bare.

Dani reached for his sleeve, feeling the cotton between her fingers. *Real,* her mind insisted. *Real.*

She cleared her throat. "What are you doing here? Why did you come back?"

He smiled. "I'm your guide."

She thought this over, "Why you?"

"I'm the only dead person you know."

Dani shook her head. "What about my grandmother?

Phil gave a small shrug. "She's got a canasta game."

Ah. Well, Dani thought, that made as much sense as anything else. "Hey, Phil." She gulped. This wasn't going to be easy. "Did I kill you? Did you die because I wanted you dead?"

He shrugged again and shook his head. "It doesn't work that way. I was driving too fast is all. It happens."

"And now you're back?"

He said nothing . . . but she could feel his eyes on her as he watched her carefully.

"Why? What am I supposed to do? Do I have . . ." her voice trailed off. She forced herself to say it. "Do I have powers?"

He nodded. "You can hear things and move things."

"Hear what? Move what? I don't know what that means."

He got to his feet. "Wish I could tell you, but I can't. You're supposed to figure it out for yourself."

"Wait. How? Don't leave!"

But he was leaving, she saw. Even as she got to her own feet, reaching for him, determined to grab him and shake him and make him tell her exactly what was going on, the vivid blues and greens of his clothing and the room were fading into watercolors.

"You'll know what to do when you need to do it."

"No. No, I won't. I don't know anything!"

"You'll know."

And, with that, Dani bolted upright in her bed in her apartment in Philadelphia, breathless and gasping, as the digital clock on the dresser beside her flashed the word HELP.

Seven

At the office Monday morning, Dani burned through her day's work in forty-five minutes writing copy for Wipe-Eez Flushable Wipes ("Clean and gone!"), then spent another hour and a half on the *Philadelphia Examiner*'s website, searching for missing children.

There were, she quickly learned, plenty of them. *Missing Eight-Year-Old Assumed Runaway. Parents' Frantic Search for Vanished Toddler.* A pair of fourteen-year-old boys had gone fishing on the first day of spring break and never come home. An eight-year-old girl had walked to the WaWa for Tootsie Rolls and had disappeared on her way back down the block. As recently as the day before, a four-year-old girl went on a nursery-school field trip to the art museum and vanished somewhere between the Japanese scrolls and the Modernist sculpture. By Dani's count, an even dozen children had vanished in the last three months . . . and there was a reasonable explanation for almost every one of the disappearances. The fourteen-year-olds had both flunked ninth grade and might have been, the investigating officer surmised, reluctant to come home and tell their mothers. The little girl was at the center of a nasty custody dispute. Dad was currently out of the country. The cops were trying to find him. The little girl's mother, meanwhile, was busily suing the museum, the nursery school, and the company that leased the schoolbus that had brought her daughter on the ill-fated field trip.

It could be a pattern, Dani decided, as she printed the articles and stowed them in a file. Or it could be nothing more than business as usual in any big city, where there were drugs and delinquency and bad divorces, where a certain percentage of children simply went wandering.

At lunchtime, Asha cruised by her desk. "Anything interesting?" she asked.

Dani shoved her folder guiltily under a stack of actual work. "Not really." *Forget this,* she told herself sternly . . . but, all during the day, during lunch, during the two-o'clock weekly meeting, during the forty-five minutes she spent online shopping for new sheets, the little girls' voice, her upturned face, at once strange and familiar, stayed in the back of her mind. *Help me,* said the little girl. Then her voice turned into Phil's voice, saying *You'll know how.* At four o'clock, when she could no longer resist temptation, she retrieved the folder and flipped slowly through the photographs. It gave her a nasty jolt when she found the picture of missing four-year-old Madison Karp, who, in her school picture, had blonde ringlets and pale skin, startled blue eyes, and the face of the little girl from the well in her dream.

Eight

Her brother Jared called that night, just as she'd finished washing the dishes and putting her mostly uneaten *poussin* with *fine herbes* into the refrigerator. There was a movie he and Sara wanted to see. Was Dani, by any chance, free the next night?

Am I ever not free? Dani thought, but agreed to babysit. She'd taken the PATH train to their ranch house in Cherry Hill armed with cupcake mix and sprinkles and a copy of *Eloise in Paris,* but Nevaeh, scrubbed and solemn in her pink-and-red-striped pajamas, wanted to play Go Fish.

"The rules are that the youngest goes first," her niece explained, clumsily shuffling the oversized cards. "And if you have a match, you put it aside." She pointed to a spot on the carpet next to her knee. "That's aside."

"Okay," Dani said, sitting cross-legged on the living-room floor as her niece dealt each of them seven cards. "Hey, Nevaeh. Before we start, can I talk to you for a minute?"

"Minute, blinnit, dinnit," Nevaeh sang, and arranged her cards. "Does anyone have any puppies?"

Dani looked at her hand. Instead of regular playing cards, these were part of a special set, undoubtedly purchased at some pricy educational-toy boutique with a quaint, fairy-tale name: the Wooden Shoe. The Red Balloon. The cards, while undoubtedly edifying, looked as if they'd escaped from some macabre tarot deck. One card bore the image of an abandoned-looking rocking horse alone in a dark room. Another had the picture of a fishing lure in the shape of a silver minnow lying on a splintery dock. On one card, a bicycle's shadow zipped through menacing traffic; on another, a clown with a painted white face shot in terrifying closeup honked his red nose.

Dani flipped through her cards. "No puppies."

"Then I shall go fish!" Nevaeh selected a card from the pile, studied it carefully, shook her head, and added it to her hand. "Your turn."

"Listen," Dani tried again. She wasn't sure how to broach the topic with her niece. She wasn't sure if she should bring it up. Was missing children an appropriate topic to be discussing with a four-year-old? Probably not.

Nevaeh scowled at her from underneath her perfectly straight dark-brown eyebrows. "You have to ask if anybody has a card!"

"Oh, right." Dani looked at her hand and found a picture of a threadbare coat, three yellow buttons barely held on by a strand of unraveling black thread. "Does anybody have any buttons?"

"I have a button!" Nevaeh handed over the card with a flourish. "Now you put it aside. Aside is here, remember?" She tapped the carpet. "Now you ask if I have another card."

"Nevaeh, have you heard anything about kids who've disappeared?" Dani blurted, thinking that the card game could stretch into eternity without her even opening her mouth again.

The little girl nodded solemnly. "Oh, sure."

"Like what?"

"The men take them away," Nevaeh informed her. "The men with no faces. Go again."

The men with no faces. Dani swallowed and forced herself to look at her hand, suddenly certain that among them she would find a picture of a man with a bleeding wound for a mouth and dull metal circles where his eyes should have been. "Does anybody have, um, a telephone?"

"Go fish."

Dani reached into the pile and was unsurprised when she pulled up a match: an old-fashioned and somehow sinister-looking picture of a black rotary telephone sitting (*crouching*, her mind whispered) on a cluttered countertop.

"You fished your wish!" Nevaeh seemed pleased by this development.

"Men with no faces . . ." Dani prompted.

Nevaeh nodded. "They live underneath."

"Under where?"

"Under*neath*," Nevaeh said. "In the underneath places. Go again."

"And why do the men with no faces want the children?" Oh, God, Dani thought unhappily. If her brother heard her now, that would be the end of her babysitting days. Probably, it would be the end of everything. Jared and Steven could have a race to see which one could get her into Sunny Acres faster.

Nevaeh tugged at one of her curls, stretching it down past her nose, toward her mouth, and tucked it between her teeth. "Mirror, mirror, on the wall. It's still your turn."

Dani shuddered, then looked down at her cards. "Do you have any dolls?"

Nevaeh released the curl and gave her aunt a very adult-looking smile. She handed Dani a card with the picture of a pale, rouged dolly in a ruffled blue dress, her unblinking glass eyes both haunting and haunted. "You win."

Nine

"The last place," Dani said to the assembled would-be saviors of the universe. "In my dream, the girl said to go to the last place."

"Last place," Victoria murmured to Sweetie, curled in her lap. The little dog gave a strangled yip, then yawned and closed her eyes.

"Like maybe Key West?" asked Leticia. "You know, like the last place on earth?" Her glossy black hair was piled on top of her head, and she wore a choker of amber beads. It was Saturday night, and, Dani supposed, even would-be superheroes had dates.

"If it's Key West, it might as well be the North Pole," she said. "If she's alive, how are we going to get there in time to save her?"

"Have you gotten any more messages?" That was Asha, tugging at the hem of her brief dress. "Any more emails or anything?"

Dani shook her head. She'd been checking, too: her email, her iPod, the timers on her microwave and DVD player; anything with a computerized readout that could spell words. Nothing had come.

"Did you Google 'the last place'?" Scott Spencer had evidently come straight from the gym in a nylon tracksuit that whistled when he crossed his legs. Blue and white terrycloth sweatbands encircled both of his meaty wrists, and his running shoes were so pristine Dani bet it was the first time he'd worn them.

She pulled a single folded sheet of paper out of her purse. "There's the Last Place bar on North Broad Street. An animal shelter called the Last Place in Collingswood."

Leticia shuddered. "Whoo," she said. "Morbid." Victoria's dog yipped once, then hopped off Victoria's lap and started nosing at Dani's purse.

"Nothing for you," Victoria said, and pulled on the dog's purple nylon leash, which somehow tangled around the strap of Dani's handbag, spilling its contents onto the floor. "Whoops."

Dani bent to retrieve her wallet, her lipstick, a single tampon blooming from its wrapper, a litter of Go Fish playing cards that her niece must have put in there without her noticing.

"Hey, what are those?" asked Leticia.

"Go Fish," Dani mumbled, still bent over. She shoved the tampon into her pocket, then reached for the playing cards. There was that creepy-looking dolly . . . and the silvery fish on the splintered dock . . . and the bicycle's shadow . . . and an empty gold-leaf picture frame, leaning against a bare white wall.

She shoved it back into the stack. "Wait," said Scott, and grabbed her wrist. He *was* strong, she noticed. His hands, plump and pale, with bitten half-moons of fingernail, didn't look as if they would be, but . . .

Leticia picked up the cards, shuffling them slowly, arranging them in a deck, then flipping the top card, face-up, into Dani's hands. It was a shot of an empty picture frame made of tarnished gold, leaning against a scuffed, grayish-white wall. *The last place,* Dani thought. "Hang on," she whispered. "Do you think . . ."

Leticia got to her feet, car keys jingling in her hands. "Let's go."

Ten

It turned out that getting into the art museum after hours wasn't hard. Leticia led them to the south entrance, where the guard was an off-duty cop, a friend of Leticia's (and, Dani figured from the bit of conversation she'd overheard, an ex-paramour of the departed Paz). Whether it was the sight, or just good luck, the man smiled at Leticia, greeted them all like old friends, and ushered them through the turnstile after pointing at the clock and telling them his shift was over in twenty minutes.

The five of them, plus Sweetie, who'd been tucked ignominiously into Victoria's tote bag, gathered by the fountain beneath the Great Staircase, and looked at each other, flushed, bright-eyed.

"What now?" Dani asked. "Do we just wander around and call her name?" Secretly, she doubted that the little girl could be here. The cops had combed every inch of the museum the day the girl had been reported missing. Surely she was long gone, spirited away. She and her divorced daddy were probably halfway to Miami by now, maybe driving a convertible, top down, wind rushing past them, the southern sun warm in their hair. Dani had once had a fantasy of her own long-lost father showing up and claiming her: the car with out-of-state plates, the easy smile, the can of ginger ale, her favorite, sweating in the cupholder.

In her pocket, her cell phone buzzed. She held her breath and pulled it out. A single word glowed on the screen. EMPATHY. Dani groaned. That wasn't a message from beyond, it was an artifact, something her best friend Jade had convinced her to do last year when her troubles with Steven began. Jade had read about some movie star who'd used the word "grace" as her cell phone's screen saver and urged Dani to find words that she would find similarly uplifting. EMPATHY had been one of them . . . and now here it was again.

Except maybe there was more. *You can hear things,* Phil had said. Dani turned slowly on the soles of her boots. Then, acting on an impulse she couldn't name, she bent and slipped off her boots and her socks and stood barefoot on the icy marble floor, turning in another circle, a needle searching for true north. How would a four-year-old feel underneath the soaring ceilings, lost in this expanse of marble and huge, priceless paintings?

I'm Madison, she thought, turning, turning, closing her eyes. No. *I'm Maddy. I'm four. I live with my mommy in Philadelphia, my daddy lives in Florida, I'm thirsty and I want my juice box out of my lunch box.*

"Dani . . ." someone whispered, and someone else said, *Ssh.*

Dani walked up the stairs, planting each bare foot firmly on each step, holding the railing. *I'm Maddy. I'm four. My lunch box is pink with a zipper and my name on it in white. My juice box has a picture of Big Bird and the straw's glued to the front, the straw is tricky, getting the straw unattached from the box, getting it out of its plastic, is tricky . . .*

"She was thirsty," Dani said, in a low, musing voice. If someone had played it on a tape, she wouldn't have recognized it as her own. "Wants her juice box."

I am Maddy I am four. My mommy and daddy used to fight at night. My daddy called my mommy the bitchword, but he's gone now, and Mommy says good riddance and bad rubbish. Rubbish is trash, like Oscar the Grouch. I have pink Dora the Explorer sheets, and sometimes, I wake up because I need to go potty and I hear my mommy crying, crying in the night, so I don't get up, I just go in my bed and it's warm at first like a bath, then cold. Mommy says I'm too big to wear a diaper, even at night, but I wish I still could, and I know about the men with no faces, the men with holes for eyes, the underneath places, and I'm thirsty . . .

Dani stopped on a landing. She spun once on her heels, slowly. There was a curtain off to her right, black cloth draping the space. She poked at it, then peered past it, into the shadowy darkness. "Here," she said. "What's behind here?"

"Storage cooler," called the guard. "It's like a big walk-in refrigerator. They store paintings there sometimes, but they looked there already . . ."

"Open it." Her voice was harsh. *I am Maddy, I am four, I need to go potty but there's no potty here and the door's shut and nobody hears me and, I want my mommy, want my mommy, want her NOW . . .*

"I can't," said the guard. "They don't give us keys for the storage units, and, like I said, the police already looked there . . ."

"Scott?"

He was beside her almost before she'd finished saying his name. The two of them pushed through the panels of black velvet drapes until they found what looked like the door to a giant refrigerator. There was a padlock on its handle. While Scott reached for the lock, Dani dropped to her knees. "Maddy? Maddy, can you hear me?"

Silence . . . then a tiny voice called back, "Mommy?"

Scott reached for the lock, squeezing it between his hands. Dani looked at him, then shouted down the stairs, toward the guard. "We need something. A bolt-cutter or something. And an ambulance. And the police . . ."

Scott grunted. The lock popped open. "Thing's a joke," he said, breathing hard. Dani swung the door open and there, huddled in the corner, almost hidden by a stack of wrapped canvases, was Madison Karp.

"I had an accident!" the girl bawled, pelting toward Dani's arms. "Don't tell anyone!"

"Shh, shh, it's okay," said Dani. She scooped the little girl into her arms, breathing in the scent of stale urine and sweat . . . and then, moving on an impulse she couldn't name, she carried the girl back down the stairs, stripped off her dress and tights, her buckled brown shoes and pink Disney princess underpants, and dipped her into the fountain, like a baptism, like a blessing.

Eleven

MISSING FOUR-YEAR-OLD FOUND IN ART MUSEUM, read the headline on the bottom right of the *Examiner*'s front page the next morning.

———

Museum officials and police are struggling with difficult questions after four-year-old Madison Karp, missing for three days, was found late Saturday night inside a padlocked storage area that they insist was thoroughly searched after the little girl was first reported missing Wednesday afternoon.

"We're just as confused as everyone else," museum CEO Dana Vassile told reporters at a news conference on the museum steps Sunday morning. "We searched every inch of the museum, including that storage locker, thoroughly, first on Wednesday, then again the next day. She wasn't there."

Museum guard Victor Chesney told police that he was making his rounds at 11:00 P.M. on Saturday when he heard the girl crying. "It was spooky," he said. "I'm just glad it worked out okay."

Police said the little girl had wandered away from her group, looking for her lunchbox. Asked how a four-year-old found the storage locker or was able to open the heavy door, Vassile said, "We're investigating that. Right now, we have no answers. That door should have been locked, and it was locked the first and second times we searched. The door was locked, and there was nobody inside."

Madison's lunchbox was found with her inside the storage locker. Police say that her meal may have been what saved her. "She had one of those juice boxes, and a bowl of cut-up melon. Lots of liquid . . . and one of the workers left a liter bottle of seltzer on the shelf," said Captain Peter Gibbons. "If it hadn't been for that, we might not be looking at a happy ending."

The girl was taken to the Children's Hospital of Pennsylvania, where she was treated for dehydration and minor scratches and bruising on her hands and face. Her mother, Holly Kenneally, released a statement saying, "I thank God for my little girl's safe return." Museum officials and police declined to comment on rumors of Kenneally's plans to sue both the museum and the city for the botched search. A woman who answered the telephone at Kenneally's residence Saturday afternoon and declined to give her name said, "If you were her mother, what would you think? Your kid's missing, they say they looked, then, abracadabra, she's in there after all? Something's fishy, that's for sure."

Twelve

Something's fishy. Scott Spencer led Dani down the museum steps, holding her elbow lightly. Dani leaned against him, shivering. She was bone-weary. Her teeth chattered, and she was powerless to stop them, her body ached for sleep. All she wanted to do was crawl into bed and stay there for about a week.

"So how'd you do it?" he'd asked as he turned down Delancey. Scott Spencer drove a Lexus, a businessman's car as fat and contented as he was, with a plush leather interior and heated seats.

"I have no idea," she said honestly.

"Okay. Well, listen, if you need anything . . ." He'd given her a business card with all of his numbers: home, office, cell. She'd hauled herself out of the car, slipped her key into the lock, waved at Scott as the door swung open. He gave her a genial wave back, then drove off, and Dani was alone in the dark.

She left her keys in the door and walked onto the sidewalk, standing with her legs planted, gazing into the night. The streetlights twinkled in the dark sky. Wind rattled the treetops.

"Phil?" she murmured, low in her throat. No answer came. *Listen,* Phil's voice said in her head. *You'll know what to do.*

Dani stared at the stop sign at the end of the street. She raised her right hand experimentally, first pointing her finger, then cupping her palm. Nothing happened. Of course nothing had happened, she thought, laughing at herself as she turned back toward her apartment . . . except hadn't the wind picked up? Hadn't the streetlights seemed to flicker, just for a fraction of an instant? Hadn't a shadow floated in front of the silver face of the moon?

You're imagining things, she whispered to herself. She thought of her ex-husband, his Chelsea penthouse, his glittering life, his talent, and a thought raised itself like a banner in her mind. *He's not the only one,* Dani thought. *He's not so special.* Then she raised her hand again, concentrating as hard as she could, and lifted it toward the stop sign, fingers curved toward her palm, beckoning toward the red octagon, thinking, *Come to me.* The wind gusted hard, and there was a squeal of metal . . . and then, as Dani stared, half in awe and half in terror, the sign detached itself from its post and somersaulted down the sidewalk, bouncing twice, higher and higher again, before clattering to a stop at her feet.

David Haynes

THE LIVES OF ORDINARY SUPERHEROES

The old man and I had done enough interventions in this part of town I didn't need to be told it was a bad idea to leave a car filled with high-end stereo components unattended for any length of time. He'd always say: Son, folks round here steal anything not nailed down. Don't get me wrong: The man had faith. But just like the rest of us, now and then he'd let his cynicism rule the day. I told myself that the ragged quilt I'd strewn across the lot of my precious audio would fool all but the most dogged smash-and-grab artists—the garden-variety delusion we all share, all of us hiding comfortably behind our flimsy deadbolts and reassured by the whine of our alarms crying out in the wilderness.

I'd put off taking my leave of him until I could postpone it no longer. Glo and the kids were on the plane to Portland, the house keys had been transferred after the new owner's walk-through this morning, and as soon as I finished up here I'd chase after the Mayflower, determined to beat that punk driver across this continent if it killed me. The Toyota was gassed and the passenger seat laden with enough snack junk to clog the arteries of a moose.

I guess there was a possibility that I might not have found Bill Jenkins here at the Third Generation, but, then, the sun might rise in the west tomorrow and they might cancel the Wheel of Fortune, too. Old Bill had as much as had a barstool grafted onto his ass since his "retirement"—the polite way we like to talk about his change in career trajectory. I'd get calls pretty regularly for a while there—from Little Reggie, the owner of 3G, or from that girl over at Hadley's before Hadley's barred him—telling me he was in again and acting a fool again and wouldn't I come and see after him please. Which I did for a while, until Glo put her foot down, insisting that the old man was not my problem and she wasn't about to have her husband running out every damn night shepherding some drunk has-been superhero out of the corner tavern. But, what can I tell you; I felt guilty. Who else did he have after all?

You know the story: His people had all been blown to bits when that dastardly Roscoe the BlingMaster aimed his diabolical Disitegro-ray at the project where the Jenkins family lived, immediately vaporizing everyone, except poor little William, who, shielded by the ancient lead-lined porcelain tub, where he'd been eluding his sister during a marathon session of hide-and-seek, was miraculously spared with the only apparent effect being his new ability to, when needed, make himself invisible (except to dogs and small children) and his uncanny ability to shame even the most hard-core evildoer into thinking twice about what he or she was up to. Evermore he has trod the lonely path of all such . . . dare we call them men? The passionate pursuit of truth and justice, his anonymous and solitary life of self-sacrifice.

What were the chances even one of his fellow midday drunks knew the storied exploits of the man who had been Ghetto Man? And, make no mistake, these were drunks, all of them; the hard-core kind, even the old man himself these days. Barely past noon and each of them already more than a few highballs into their daily journeys to oblivion. Three-G was that kind of joint, "Home of the Long Pour" printed right there on their cocktail napkins, less a promise than a warning, I assure you. I sidled up to Bill on an angle, the better to not take him by surprise. Your retired superheroes tend to get nervous about being sneaked up on. He spied me, flicked his mustache with his thumb, and harrumphed.

"Hey, yourself," I said. I might as well have been from the collection agency, so cold were the eyes he cut me with, and it was clear that would be the extent of his greeting.

But, make no mistake, this wasn't the casual dismissal of those who have lived too long for friendly discourse, nor was this the ironically comical snub of the secretly lovable curmudgeon. Bill Jenkins is an old-timer with a grudge. Long story short: I'm blamed for the revocation of his superhero license. It's because of me he's glommed onto that barstool, pickling his liver and longing after lost glory. He sniffed or snorted or made some other dismissive noise and took a long pull from his Seven-and-Seven—and if that was to be the worst of my punishment, surely I'd gotten off lightly.

I persisted. I had a mission. I signaled Little Reg to snag me a bottle of water and perched on the stool next to the old man.

"So . . ." I began. It was that "so" you hear on bad blind dates, after the lucky couple has exhausted their conversational repertoire, nothing further to note about the weather or the high price of gasoline. The old man sighed, rolled his eyes. I'd seen this brand of exasperation more times than I could count; it was standard in his arsenal, a trusted saber most often employed against gangbangers foolish enough to try to explain why they're shaking down the owner of the corner confectionary—the same kind soul who'd extended credit to their mamas during that fourth week of the month when the money ran a little thin.

One of the drunks two drunks down the bar wanted to know "why the boy ain't drinking." Bill answered by pursing his lips in disgust.

"I'm driving," I responded. "Hitting the road. Today. I just wanted to holler before I took off." I kept my eye on the old man while I said this, and, in fact, I did see a flash of something in his eye. Something . . . hopeful. Well, to me at least it was. You don't spend half your life as sidekick to a superhero without learning to read even the subtlest of signals.

Fifteen, I'd been, when I met this man, strutting my hopeless teenage behind home from high school. Don't ask me why—a bad grade or a bad attitude, who knows—but I'd been ripping papers out of my satchel, wadding them up and leaving them littered in my wake.

"Excuse me, young fellow," he'd said, and I swear I had not seen him there, seen anyone there. I gave him the evil eye.

"What's all this?" he said, indicating my trail of trash.

". . . the fuck business is it of yours?" I hissed.

"Come on, now, son. There's no call for that."

Who did he think he was messing with? I was J. B. Henderson, toughest little MF on the north side—or at least in my feeble imagination I had been. And I wasn't his damn son—for that matter I wasn't anybody's damn son, my actual father never in the picture past his hit-and-run sperm deposit in my mom.

But he had those eyes, Bill Jenkins did. There was something in those eyes. He tsked and he shook his head.

"Poor Ms. Harris in that house right there—we don't want to see a sister out here picking up after us. She's trying to keep it nice around here. Come on." Bill snagged a wad or two and—damnit—I found myself snagging the rest.

"Bring it on down here," he ordered, and I followed him to the corner. Along the way he bent for a few more scraps of other fools' litter so I followed suit. We deposited the lot of it in an oil barrel outside the barbershop. "Good man," Bill praised.

"What the hell ever," I sniffed, and turned on my heel to head home to my game console.

"Just a second, there, young man."

I turned to see what he wanted.

"Well?"

"Well what?"

"Don't you got something to say?"

I shrugged.

"Come on, now. Your mama raised you better than that."

"You don't know my mama."

"Come on, now."

"All right, then. Sorry. Satisfied?"

"Sorry. And?"

This is what the old man was like back then. He would ride a brother ragged, wear him down like twenty-grit sandpaper. All of this, by the way, with puppy-dog-soft eyes that appeared ready to brim over with tears.

"I am sorry, sir, and it will never happen again." I had hit that *sir* heavily with sarcasm, and had been about to ask him if I could get the hell out of there now. He grabbed my hand and congratulated me.

"And now your mama's proud," he cheered, and he dismissed me—pointing me on my way, trilling his fingers in that "run along now" way that people who are through with subordinates do.

I complied, or started to, but—I couldn't help it, I was hooked—I turned back and just had to ask him:

"So this is what you do?"

"Say what, now?"

"This. You do this all day? Walk the hood and tell people how to behave?"

"I can see that you're a young man with a lot of issues," he responded.

I mumbled a vulgar name and headed home.

"What's that?" he questioned, but when I turned back I realized that he had not been talking to me. His hand was pressed to an earpiece, his head bent forward slightly as if to improve the reception. "Over on Vandeventer you say? Twenty minutes. I'm on it."

That damn headset: still today pinned above his left ear, radical even magical back in our heyday, today however only slightly more obtrusive than every garden variety Bluetooth on every garden variety workaholic; alas no more likely to ring these days than the alarm at an abandoned firehouse, it weighs his ear like the medals on the jacket of an ancient vet, reminding himself surely more than anyone else that once he'd had his day, that once he'd done his part.

On that fateful afternoon he keyed open the locks on his rusted Grand Torino and asked me if I was coming. Owning no better judgment, off I went on the first of fifteen years of making the greater Jeff-Vander-Lou community safe for its ever-struggling citizenry. Regrets: only the day I broke this man's heart. But I had done what I had to do.

Our first case had been a bar fight—a couple of down-and-outers who'd been aimless and most often intoxicated since the carburetor plant closed back in the seventies were having their weekly shoving match—foolishness that, frankly, you'd let pass, were it not for the grade school on the corner and the kids getting ready to walk by on their way home.

"Gentlemen," he'd cheered. They called him "Jenks" and asked where the hell he'd come from. He introduced me: "Ya'll know my boy, Little J?"

And I got a round of handshakes and "how you doings?" and plenty of insistence that I was a chip off the old block. Five minutes later we were inside, a bar not unlike the 3G, a round of Busch Bavarian for the three of them, "And a Coke for my boy here."

That's how I became Little J, sidekick to the greatest superhero the north side has ever known. And, for what it's worth, that's what it's like most days, the lives of your ordinary superheroes. Surprised? Honestly, I had been, too. Like you, I'd been raised on images of larger-than-life figures; their glossy and impossibly souped-up sports cars; their fortresses of solitude and high-profile, world-redeeming escapades. And, hey, I'm not hating: If it's a choice between being devoured by humanoid robots from Zortron and having all the media sucked up by some guy in a red cape and leotards, I choose the cape and leotards every time. But you know the drill: We can't all be Academy Award winners. For every Denzel with his guaranteed percentages of screen time and points on the gross profits, there's a hundred guys who are lucky if they get to shout the line "I'm tired of the man!" while being shoved headfirst into the back of the squad car. And for every Green Hornet, there's a half-dozen guys like Ghetto Man, tamping down the petty crime, keeping a lid on the little stuff so that the glamorboys can focus on saving the world. Are they jealous, these journeymen of justice? Well, surely a little: But there's no shame. Bill Jenkins: He spent forty years happily routing drug dealers from the playground and giving the evil eye to parking scofflaws. He rounded up stray house pets, kept your alley free of abandoned tires, and most likely is the reason there are still treads on the jungle gym in what passes for a neighborhood park. If only there were dozens of him, if only he were still at it today. If only he were twenty years younger and if only there had not been that little incident with his false teeth sunk into some delirious stick-up artist's leg.

But all that water had rolled off to the sea. And I was rolling on my way as well. There was just this one last thing.

Bill signaled Little Reggie to turn on the TV: Their story was on.

Despite no one talking much that afternoon, the drunks all shushed each other.

"Still watching *Days*, I see. I bet that Sammy is still up to no good."

"That girl: I swear if she was my daughter I don't know what I would fix her punishment at."

Leave it to *Days of Our Lives* to finally get a response out of the man.

"She means well," I offered.

Bill nodded. Meaning well: as important to Bill Jenkins as actually doing well or doing good. Cynical, yes, often enough he could be. But as I already told you, this is a man who believed strongly in the goodness in each of us. Despite the hungry and neglected children he'd rescued from crack houses, despite their drug-addled mamas, despite the landlords who left those abandoned houses to decay and to become infested, Bill Jenkins remained an optimist at heart. He could and would forgive me.

The hourglass popped up, signaling a long commercial break, and Bill looked me in the eye for the first time.

"How's all yours doing anyway?" he asked, and this was real progress—the most he'd sent my way in months.

I told him that everybody's doing fine and how excited the kids were about the move—especially Jerry Jr.—and how I'd sent them ahead and was looking forward to joining them later in the week. He lifted a brow in that way that indicates he isn't sure it's a good idea sending a woman and two youngsters off on their own, but it's a mild admonition only. He's known Glo since I met the woman, and he also knew the smart money would be on her should any problems happen along the road.

We met on a case, as it happens, Glo and I did. I'd been rolling with the old man about five years at the time, finishing my senior year at UMSL (where he'd insisted I enroll) (and where he constantly monitored my grades) (and where—although I've never been able to confirm this—the "north side" scholarship that funded much of my tuition I'm confident was actually money provided by him), when one late afternoon we got called to the playground of the school up on Cass Avenue.

The future Mrs. Gloria Henderson we found in the last phase of shooing a crowd of rowdy sixth-graders back into the building.

"Is there a problem, Miss?" Bill had asked her.

"Hell, yes, there's a problem," she responded, pointing to a sketchy group of male perps gathered by the swing set. "And where are the damn police? And who the hell are you?"

As shocked by her beauty as I'd been by her sharp tongue, I, as was my assigned role in such matters, helped usher the youngsters clear while Bill did his magic, all the while assuring their teacher that my employer was on the case and that things would be copasetic momentarily and could I have her phone number, please. She'd hardly finished giving me the evil eye before Bill ambled in and announced it was safe for the kids to finish their recess.

"Is that so?" she scoffed, but she let the restless youngsters back out anyway.

Frankly, she was no more or less suspicious than anyone else we helped over the years. She had quickly coursed that almost always predictable path from mocking disbelief to begrudging gratitude that the problem had been solved. Who knows, perhaps had we worn the tights and codpieces and gotten us a couple of capes with a crafty logo affixed we'd have gotten the respect we deserved. A somewhat dumpy middle-aged black man in denim and plaid work wear; well, they're as common as houseflies in these parts and about as uninspiring.

Look at him here; look at all these harmless drunks, sipping their beer and watching but not really watching Sammy and company emote and cry and otherwise explicate the obvious: Would you even imagine any of these men might be anything other than what you see here today? And, okay, so perhaps for one or more of them, what you see is what you get. But, again, perhaps they are not. I sauntered to the window, grimed over with smoky yellow film, checking on the car. I'd been itching to hit the road; I'd promised myself to hit mid-Kansas before bedtime, and even with the long summer evening, that might be a stretch.

"Ain't nobody studying your stuff," the old man admonished me, his signal to get on with the matter at hand. The others scoffed and mocked my caution. They'd sat here long enough to know it was too early for the neighborhood riffraff to ply their nickel-and-dime trade.

And you had to give this man his props: Bill Jenkins knew people. He knew how to sweet-talk those girls who worked the corners to come and have a cup a coffee and rest their feet a few minutes and to get them to tell him how it came to this; knew that sometimes the few dollars he'd passed them would help more than the service organizations he'd try to connect them with. He understood that unless Bobby C. happened to be incarcerated, on any given night he would likely break out somebody's back window and rifle through the medicine cabinets and dresser drawers, and that he was likely to continue doing so until he got tired of climbing through broken glass and of running from the police and of thirty-day stretches in the workhouse. And wouldn't you know, Bobby C. is now Deacon Bobby—Deacon Anderson, he prefers these days, thank you very much—and he spends his afternoons dropping off supper to the same homes he'd pilfered from, the same homes in which the old man and I had spent many an afternoon reinforcing the windows with iron gates and decoy security stickers.

"So . . ." I said again, and again he flicked his mustache. Fifteen years I'd ridden with this man. He wouldn't make this easy—this leave-taking. This much I knew. He waved a shaming finger at the screen—that dastardly Stefano DiMera, once again risen from the dead. What Ghetto Man wouldn't have given to have a chance at the likes of a villain such as he.

"So, I wanted to say . . ." I started, but he put up his hand and stopped me, reminding me that as far as he was concerned I'd had my say.

They're to be expected, I guess, such resentments. You see it all the time—even in freelance tech support, my main work these days. You just happen to be on-site on the day some lifer well past his sell-by date, one of those who didn't have the sense to walk away of his own volition, is finally shown the door. It's never pretty: the lady from human resources supervising the packing of the cubicle, the rent-a-cops standing by just in case it turns ugly, the dispossessed speechifying as to how he'd given his life to this damn company and how he can't believe people could be so cold.

Back then Bill's decline had seemed rapid to me, but in hindsight there had been signs for years, really. Routine calls—rumbles that had once taken moments to disperse—would drag on for way too long. A rowdy group of teenagers who in the past would have moved along quickly now lingered and made it clear that whatever happened was going to happen on their schedule, some raggedy old Negro be damned.

This one time, we'd taken a routine belligerent drunk call, and, as was the program, I'd stationed myself on the opposite end of the room, setting about diverting the audience's attention to a more entertaining spectacle—me making a fool out of myself with some badly executed magic tricks. (First cure for your acting-out types: Lose the audience.) I'd been about to unfurl some scarves from a wineglass when I heard Bill's raised voice in full argument with the drunk. Threats were exchanged, the N-word got aired. This was *so* not his way—and had the police not rolled through just then I don't know where that might have ended.

The thing was: You didn't confront this man. I'd learned that years back, back with my paper wads and that chip on my shoulder. Instead, I waited a few weeks and raised the subject in a way I thought was being clever.

"Still thinking of moving to Sarasota with your sister?" I had asked him.

"You trying to get rid of me, boy?"

There'd been some humor in his eyes, but frankly, I'd have preferred a bit more warmth in his tone. It was Glo, in fact, who wanted rid of him—or, rather, who'd wanted a full-time husband and who knew that the only way that would happen would be to end my affiliation with Ghetto Man. At the time she'd been five months pregnant with Jerry Jr. and she'd had enough of me spending my off hours riding shotgun through the north side.

"I'm just thinking how you might want to slow down some, is all."

"Slow down and do what?" he asked, and as if to demonstrate he coasted the Torino to a crawl and glowered at some lowlifes on the corner of St. Louis Avenue and Grand. Before I could muster the courage to mention some of the recent debacles, he began lecturing me on the evils of idleness.

"Lots of these folks out here, the problem is they ain't got enough to do. Always keep yourself busy, young man. That's the key to everything."

Believe me, there was no pleasure in the irony of him among the midday drunks, busy with their bourbon and soap opera. Was it that there had been nothing to attend to on that screen or had they been too benumbed to raise their eyes to the histrionics? Bill and all the rest focused laserlike on the nicked wood of the bar as if it were a bottomless lake.

"Look . . ." I began, and I placed a hand on his shoulder, which he jerked from my reach.

"You didn't have to," he protested—and he'd not been protesting my touch.

But I did. Someone had to.

It had been a dangerous call as our calls went: a jittery older man threatening a duck-and-noodles with something inside the pocket of his trench coat. Bill had been testy with me that entire evening—I'd announced earlier in the week my decision (Glo's decision) to cut back my time on patrol with him. His usually genial small talk—orations on the glory days of Sportsman's Park and of when he and his boys had integrated the pool at Fairgrounds Park—had been replaced by one-word answers and grunts and silences. Bill Jenkins was a seether, and the car was hot with the energy of his disdain.

At the chop suey joint he made it a point to offer me unneeded direction about my role and on where to position myself. I'd been hiding in plain sight since before I shaved regularly, but I said nothing about his condescension and found my spot where the glare from the sun off the windows would render me invisible.

For the record, the "defuse and ignore" strategy had been the right choice that early evening and, ignoring the panicked eyes and subtle hand warning offered by the clerk, Bill sauntered up to the Plexiglas, announcing:

"Some shrimp fried rice might just hit the spot. Or maybe I'll have me one of them happy boxes." Bill Jenkins at his best: He relished playing the naïf, almost certainly could barely contain his glee at the disbelieving looks of both clerk and perp.

"Ain't nobody getting shit till I get me some cash," the perp announced, and I remember the poor man's almost violent shaking—so convulsed that I considered walking to the corner and buying him a bottle of wine myself.

Bill gave him a heartfelt, "Oh, come on, now," and started in on his spiel about how these poor people didn't have nothing in here and were just trying to make a go of it and serve folks a decent meal. Over the years I had seen this speech work its magic literally hundreds of times, and on much tougher customers than this one—once I'd seen a clearly borderline psychotic crackhead lay down a lead pipe and walk away shamefaced from the man he'd been in the process of mugging. And when that jittery old drunk removed his hands from his pockets and raised them in the air—revealing he'd had no more weapon than his bad breath and bad attitude—I figured we'd have wrapped another one and could call it a night and maybe get us one of those happy boxes after all. Until . . .

Until the drunk shoved Ghetto Man. He lowered those jittery arms and mustered whatever strength he had left in his wine-addled body, and he shoved Bill Jenkins, shoved him right up against the menu board, which came crashing to the floor in all its cardboard handwritten glory.

"Oh, no you didn't," came Bill's response, and perhaps if I'd not been so relieved that there wasn't a gun in the perp's pocket I might have noticed Bill coming apart on me.

The drunk took a big inhalation, ready to unload on Ghetto Man, but apparently the exertion of the shove and the excitement of the (now) foiled stickup had been too much for his delicate constitution. When he unloaded, what he unloaded was about a gallon of cheap wine, vomited from his gut.

"Oh, hell, no," Bill protested, and then he added: "You get your black ass out of here right this minute, you hear."

That was the first time I'd heard the man curse, and to show that he meant business, Bill actually grabbed hold of the drunk's raggedy jacket and proceeded to drag him to the door.

From my perspective, this was all happening both instantly and in slow motion, and I'd found myself obsessing over that puddle, which I was pretty sure I'd ordered to clean up. By all evidence, however, Bill hadn't obsessed on it enough, because between his zeal to eighty-six the drunk and the drunk's outrage at being manhandled, they both slipped in the slime and found themselves entangled on the floor.

Where even more vulgarity spewed from both men's lips and a variety of weak slaps and punches were exchanged. And that's when it happened.

How Bill ended up with his mouth next to the man's ankle is both a mystery and entirely beside the point. What isn't beside the point is the fact that he decided to bite his opponent. This, from the man who'd warned me a thousand times that as such things went, a human bite was about as nasty as they got. Here he was with his teeth sunk in another man's calf.

"What the hell?" the drunk screamed. "What are you doing to me? Lord, have mercy."

From the concentration on Bill's face you could tell that he had bitten down hard, and it seemed that the louder the perp screamed the harder he bit. The perp rolled and kicked to dislodge Ghetto Man, and, successfully shaking him loose, he rose and fled through the door, the shiny white and pink dentures still firmly attached to his leg.

"My teef!" Bill hollered. "Stop that nigger. He got my teef!"

And so you see: What choice did I have, after all. Handing my hero his now-broken dentures, retrieved from the alley behind the restaurant, and seeing him there with those broken teeth; seeing him filthy, reeking, confused: What choice did I have?

"I run him off," Bill had mumbled.

I'd been too disgusted to respond. And I was determined to not see him humiliated again. The next morning I'd made the call that started the process that led him to this barstool.

"I did stop him," he reminded me again. He took another pull on his Seven-and-Seven. "I did run him off."

"That you did," I concurred.

He dismissed my acknowledgment with another harrumph, and again I wondered what was better: a well-past-his-prime old man messing in things well beyond his powers, or a well-past-his-prime old man wasting his days on *Days* and cheap booze.

"You didn't have to," he mumbled, and I knew that it shamed him to say so; knew because this was the first time he'd said the words out loud to me.

But it had gotten late, and I was way behind schedule and knew there was nothing I could say that would change any of it. And even if there were . . .

"I just wanted to say . . ." I started to say, but he waved his hand to shut me off.

He wouldn't hear any of it, whatever it was. My "thank you" was as meaningless to him as were those of all the people over all the years whose lives he had made better in some way. It's the humility of superheroes—thank them for what? For doing their job? For doing the right thing? Who would expect less? That's how these people think.

"What you staring at, boy?" he asked me before I realized I'd been doing so.

Busted in my attempt to drink in as much of this man as I could, I suppressed saying "you." This was not a sentimental man—I'd known that for half my life—and my eye twitched as I felt the trashy to-sir-with-love good-bye I'd long entertained fade away like a bad pop song on the ancient jukebox.

I chugged the water, stood, gathered the car keys in my fist, signaling my leave-taking as broadly as those actors on the TV and with just as obvious a purpose. Last chance, I thought. Last time I'll see him in this life. That ancient plaid jacket of his caught my eye. Lined with some sort of fleecy material that explodes out into a collar, it was way too much outerwear for this time of year.

"How long you had this old thing?" I asked him.

He chuckled—his warm chuckle. "Longer than you been alive, I imagine." For a moment there his eyes were young again, and I saw in them the little boy who had to become a man way, way too early.

A person has choices then, doesn't he: He turns on the world and pays it back for all it's taken. Or he makes a myth of it all, and the deranged dealer who broke down the wrong door becomes Roscoe the BlingMaster, and the stolen piece he uses to shoot your loved ones becomes a Disintegro-ray.

For a moment—for just a moment—I considered reviving our long-shared fancy: He used to relish my yelling things such as "Floor it, Ghetto Man!" or "When will these criminals ever learn? There's no hiding from justice!" But all that had passed. The neighborhood watch folks (aka Superhero Central) long ago lost his number and here we were in the lives we had now: me, the computer geek, following his intellectual wife off to her next step up the academic ladder, him, another of millions of retirees, lonely and at loose ends.

"You could come with me," I offered. I mumbled it, really, afraid to further affront his dignity. And I couldn't place his propulsive laugh as being either mocking or ironic.

"Oregon: That'll be your territory," he told me.

And that would be that, I figured. I made for the door, for real this time. I did not look back and I did not linger any longer. I walked straight out of that joint and straight into the new adventures ahead. I was optimistic even, even as I crossed the threshold and heard behind those final words, my ultimate punishment, his final curse: Son, you go on out there and do good, you hear.

ACKNOWLEDGMENTS

This book required the patience, generosity, and enthusiasm of a number of people. First among this group are our contributors—they may very well have chosen to participate for the good of mankind, because they sure as hell didn't do it for the money. We obviously couldn't have done it without them.

It's possible that this book could have existed without the marvelous illustrations of Christopher Burnham, but it would have been about half as cool. Thank you, Chris, and we're sorry you didn't get to draw the mechanical attack birds—how about for the sequel?

Our editor, Wylie O'Sullivan, never used mechanical attack birds on us, and we appreciate that. Furthermore, her enthusiasm for this book, and her vision for it, was invaluable.

We were grateful to have had our own Perry White and *Daily Planet* in the form of Ted Genoways and *Virginia Quarterly Review*, in which a trilogy of these stories first appeared. Thank you, Ted.

Not to be forgotten are our agents, Jennifer Bent and Amy Williams. You both rock. (They did use mechanical attack birds during some of the early negotiations, on our behalf, and that was totally cool.)

Finally, we have to express our eternal gratitude to Kelly Braffet and Amy Knox Brown. They save us every day.

ABOUT THE AUTHORS

Tom Bissell's favorite superhero has always been Nightcrawler. He is the author of *Chasing the Sea*, a travel narrative; *Speak, Commentary*, a work of satire he wrote with Jeff Alexander; *God Lives in St. Petersburg*, a story collection; and *The Father of All Things*, a hybrid work of history and memoir. His work has won the Rome Prize, is often anthologized, and has appeared in six languages. Currently he lives in Tallinn, Estonia. "Meeting the Avenger" makes sport of several paragraphs of Tom Junod's July 2007 profile of Angelina Jolie, which was published in *Esquire*. He apologizes to Mr. Junod, whose work he otherwise admires, for any perceived slight.

Kelly Braffet is the author of two novels, *Josie and Jack* (Houghton-Mifflin/ Mariner Books, 2005) and *Last Seen Leaving* (Houghton-Mifflin, 2006). She is a graduate of Sarah Lawrence College and Columbia University. She currently lives in New York State with her husband, the tall and embarrassingly talented writer Owen King, as well as two and a half black cats. Kelly is Cat Woman.

Will Clarke is the author of *Lord Vishnu's Love Handles* (2005) and *The Worthy* (2006)—both were selected as the *New York Times* Editors' Choice in 2006. Clarke was also named "The Hot Pop Prophet" by *Rolling Stone* magazine as part of their annual "Hot List." His favorite superhero is Kitty Pryde because of her role in "The Days of Future Past" X-Men circa 1980.

Elizabeth Crane is the author of three collections of short stories, *When the Messenger Is Hot, All This Heavenly Glory*, and *You Must Be This Happy to Enter*. Her work has also been featured in publications including *Other Voices, fivechapters, Ecotone, Nerve, Washington Square, New York Stories, Sycamore Review, Mississippi Review, Florida Review, Eclipse, Bridge, Sonora Review*, the *Chicago Reader*, and the *Believer*, and several anthologies, including *McSweeney's Future Dictionary of America, The Best Underground Fiction, When I Was a Loser*, and *The Show I'll Never Forget*. Her stories have been featured on NPR's *Selected Shorts* and adapted for the stage and screen. In 2003 she received the Chicago Public Library 21st Century Award. Crane teaches creative writing at The School of the Art Institute and The University of Chicago and lives in Chicago with her husband Ben and their dog Percy. Her favorite superhero is The Tick; his sidekick, Arthur, is a close second.

Michael Czyzniejewski grew up in Chicago. He now teaches at Bowling Green State University, where he also serves as editor-in-chief of *Mid-American Review*. *Elephants in Our Bedroom,* his debut collection of stories, is due from Dzanc Books in early 2009. As for his favorite superhero, he writes, "Green Lantern, as in the Hal Jordan *Challenge of the Superfriends* version. Great costume, jaw like a Buick, and he can create anything his mind can concoct. But my favorite color is green, so it might also be that simple."

Richard Dooling's second novel, *White Man's Grave,* was a finalist for the 1994 National Book Award. His third novel, *Brain Storm,* and his fourth novel, *Bet Your Life*, were both *New York Times* Notable Books of the Year. His next book is *Rapture for the Geeks: When AI Outsmarts IQ,* and will be published by Crown in September 2008. His favorite superheroes are Radioactive Man and Fallout Boy—"Up and atom!" He lives in Omaha.

Sean Doolittle's award-winning crime novels have been praised by the *New York Times*, the *Wall Street Journal*, and such masters of contemporary crime fiction as Dennis Lehane, Michael Connelly, Laura Lippman, and George Pelecanos. His most recent novel is titled *The Cleanup*. His next book, *Safer,* is forthcoming from Bantam Dell in early 2009. Doolittle lives in Omaha, Nebraska, with his wife and kids. Sean writes, "I'm tempted to call Batman my favorite superhero. There was something dark and noirish to The Dark Knight that I seemed to key on even in my relatively bucolic youth. But as a grown-up, I'm forced to hand the honor to The Tick, who I'd like to think is, even now, spreading his buttery justice all over The City. Spoon, big blue guy. Spoon indeed."

Lauren Grodstein is the author of the novel *Reproduction Is the Flaw of Love* and the story collection *The Best of Animals*. Her stories and essays have been widely anthologized. She is a professor of literature and writing at Rutgers University-Camden. Her favorite superhero is Underdog.

Stephanie Harrell has had her fiction published in *Jane, Speak* magazine, and *One Story*. She received her Ph.D. in Creative Writing from Florida State University. She currently lives in San Francisco with her husband and three small children, Jupiter, Justice, and James Geronimo, and is at work on a novel. "Girl Reporter" won the 2005 Fountain Award, given annually to a speculative short story of exceptional literary quality. Her favorite superhero is Superman.

ABOUT THE AUTHORS

David Haynes is an associate professor of English at Southern Methodist University where he directs the creative writing program. He also teaches regularly on the faculty of the Warren Wilson MFA Program for Writers. Several of his short stories have been read and recorded for the National Public Radio series *Selected Shorts*. His most recent published novel is *The Full Matilda*, and his latest novel is currently seeking a good home. He likes all the off-brand, odd-powered members of the Legion of Super-Heroes: Star Boy, Braniac 5, Shrinking Violet.

Cary Holladay is the author of a novel, *Mercury* (Shaye Areheart Books/Crown), and three volumes of short stories, most recently *The Quick-Change Artist: Stories* (Swallow Press/Ohio UP). Her novella, *A Fight in the Doctor's Office*, won the Miami UP novella competition and is forthcoming from Miami UP in 2008. Her awards include an O. Henry Prize and a fellowship from the National Endowment for the Arts. She teaches at the University of Memphis and is married to the writer John Bensko. Her favorite superhero is Mighty Mouse, a cartoon character she used to watch as a child in the sixties. She remembers that he had a wonderful theme song, but try as she may, she can't remember how it went.

Noria Jablonski is the author of the story collection *Human Oddities*. Her stories have appeared in *Swink, Monkeybicycle, KGB Bar Lit,* and elsewhere. She teaches at UC Santa Cruz and was a 2007 Artist in Residence at Headlands Center for the Arts in Sausalito, California. When she was young, she had a series of dreams in which she was a foster child of the Brady Bunch by day, but her true identity was Wonder Woman's daughter.

Graham Joyce has produced eleven adult novels, three young adult novels, and a collection of short stories. His most recent novel is *The Limits of Enchantment* (2005). He won the World Fantasy Award for his novel *The Facts of Life* (2003) and has garnered the British Fantasy Award for Best Novel four times. He has also won the French Grand Prix De L'Imaginaire and the Angus Award for his YA novel *TWOC* (2005). His work has been translated into more than twenty languages. He wrote his first novel after quitting an executive job to live in a shack on a Greek island in 1989 and has been writing professionally ever since. He is a Ph.D. who also teaches creative writing at Nottingham Trent University. Married with two children, he lives in Leicester, United Kingdom. His all-time favorite superhero is Doctor Strange.

Owen King is the author of *We're All in This Together: A Novella and Stories*. His fiction and nonfiction have appeared in *The Bellingham Review, The Boston Globe, One Story, Paste Magazine*, and *Subtropics*, among other publications. He lives in New York with his wife, the novelist Kelly Braffet. In researching the events described in "The Meerkat" he benefited from the kind assistance of Maile Chapman, and the scholarship of Peter Golub, Russian translator and expert in the history of Soviet Nuclear Defense Robots. Thank you, both. As to the matter of his favorite superhero, King writes that after agonizing deliberations, he has settled on Captain Marvel, because "no matter what the situation, it can almost always be improved by simply shouting 'SHAZAM!'"

J. Robert Lennon is the author of five novels and a collection of stories. He lives in Ithaca, New York, and teaches writing at Cornell University. His favorite superhero is Janeane Garofalo's hyperdepressed "The Bowler" from *Mystery Men*. Lennon writes, "The bowling ball with the skull is the perfect literary superhero prop."

John McNally is the author of two novels, *The Book of Ralph* and *America's Report Card*, and a short story collection, *Troublemakers*. His next book, *Ghosts of Chicago*, a collection of short stories, will be published this fall. A native of Chicago, he lives with his wife, Amy, in North Carolina, where he is associate professor of English at Wake Forest University. The first word he ever spoke was "Batman," who has remained, in his darker incarnations, his favorite superhero. John's first creative work, a play written in the fourth grade, featured an overweight superhero who gets stuck inside a phone booth while changing into his costume. He is happy to return to the genre, albeit thirty-four years later.

Jim Shepard is the author of six novels, including most recently *Project X* (Knopf, 2004), and three story collections, including most recently *Like You'd Understand, Anyway* (Knopf, 2007). When asked who his favorite superhero is, he wrote, "Probably Angel from the old X-Men. Flying around with a huge pair of wings: how cool would *that* be?"

George Singleton has published four collections of stories and two novels. Singleton's short stories have appeared in the *Atlantic Monthly*, *Harper's*, *Playboy*, *Zoetrope*, the *Georgia Review*, *Shenandoah*, and elsewhere. He's had his work anthologized in eight editions of *New Stories from the South*, plus a number of other anthologies and textbooks. His next book is *Pep Talks, Warnings, and Rants for the Beginning Fiction Writer*. He lives in Dacusville, South Carolina. His favorite superhero is Droopy Dog. And you know what? Anyone who says Droopy Dog's not a superhero makes him mad.

Scott Snyder, a life-long comic geek, would love to be able to cite someone more obscure, like Animal Man or Dr. Strange, as his favorite superhero, but his number one has always been Spider-Man. Scott's first book, a collection of stories called *Voodoo Heart,* was published in 2007 by the Dial Press. He's currently at work on a novel, also for Dial, to be published in 2009. He teaches at Columbia University and Sarah Lawrence College, and lives on Long Island with his wife, Jeanie, and their infant son, the mutant Jack Presley. Scott and Jeanie wait eagerly to see whether Jack will use his powers for good, or evil.

Jennifer Weiner was born on an army base in Louisiana, grew up in the suburbs of Connecticut, and graduated from Princeton University. She worked for newspapers in central Pennsylvania, Kentucky, and Philadelphia before the publication of her first novel, *Good in Bed,* in 2001. She is the author of four other novels, including *In Her Shoes*, which was made into a major motion picture, and *Certain Girls*, the sequel to *Good in Bed*, as well as the short story collection *The Guy Not Taken.* She lives in Philadelphia with her husband, Adam, who has a superhuman ability to put up with her nonsense, and their daughters Lucy and Phoebe. Her favorite superhero is Aquaman, because she loves to swim, and, as someone who has a small collection of weird and pointless skills, she has always felt a strong affinity for the superhero whose talents were slightly useless on dry land.

Sam Weller is the author of *The Bradbury Chronicles: The Life of Ray Bradbury* (William Morrow, 2005). The book was named by several newspapers, including the *Chicago Tribune* and the *Atlanta Journal-Constitution,* as one of the best nonfiction books of the year. Weller is a host for the Chicago Public Radio program *Hello Beautiful!* and is a full-time professor in the Fiction Writing Department at Columbia College Chicago. He lives in the city with his wife and two daughters. His favorite superheroes are The Fantastic Four.

David Yoo is the author of *Stop Me If You've Heard This One Before* (Hyperion, 2008). His first novel, *Girls for Breakfast* (Delacorte, 2005), was a Book Sense Pick and New York Public Library Books for the Teen Age selection. If David could be any superhero it would definitely be Plastic Man, albeit with the balls of Gleek.

ABOUT THE ILLUSTRATOR

Chris Burnham was born in Connecticut, raised in Pittsburgh, and graduated Summa Cum Laude from The George Washington University. Since then he has designed and illustrated a pile of work for clients both corporate and artistic, animated for cereal commercials and sports stadium Jumbotrons, and drawn a mess of comic books. His most recent effort is *Nixon's Pals,* an original graphic novel he co-created with writer Joe Casey for Image Comics. It's about a parole officer for supervillians and it's awesome. Chris is a company member of The House Theatre of Chicago, a founding member of Ten Ton Studios, and a loving uncle. He stands six foot three inches, weighs around 190, likes Diet Coke better than Pepsi, McDonald's better than Burger King, and Doritos better than life itself. In completing several of these illustrations he was assisted by the ingenious and deadline-slaying pen of one Nathan Fairbairn. His favorite superhero is the Ever-Lovin', Blue-Eyed Thing!

PERMISSIONS